Sally
WORBOYES

Over Bethnal Green

First published in Great Britain in 2000 by Hodder & Stoughton

This edition published in the United Kingdom in 2023 by

Canelo
Unit 9, 5th Floor
Cargo Works, 1–2 Hatfields
London SE1 9PG
United Kingdom

A CIP catalogue record for this book is available from the British Library.

Print ISBN 978 1 80436 348 5
Ebook ISBN 978 1 80436 141 2

Look for more great books at www.canelo.co

Printed and bound in Great Britain by Clays Ltd, Elcograf S.p.A.

I

Over Bethnal Green

Sally Worboyes was born and grew up in Stepney with four brothers and a sister, and she brings some of her own family background to her East End sagas. She now lives in Norfolk with her husband, with whom she has three grown-up children. She has written several plays which have been broadcast on Anglia Television and Radio Four. She also adapted her own play and novel, *WILD HOPS*, as a musical, *The Hop Pickers*.

Also by Sally Worboyes

Keep on Dancing

The East End Sagas

Down Stepney Way
Over Bethnal Green
At the Mile End Gate

Chapter One

On a sunny September morning in 1938 a group of workmen turned up in Bethnal Green Gardens and started to dig trenches. There was such an air of high spirits and so many onlookers that the mood was more comparable to children playing with their spades and buckets at a seaside beach than to preparations for the potential horrors of war. The gravity of the situation soon became clear when just a few days later the fitting and issuing of gas masks began.

–

Cupping her hands round her warm drink in her tiny living room, Jessie Smith, although tired and looking the worse for wear, was at least thankful that her six-month-old son Billy was sleeping soundly after a fretful night of teething trouble. Like most people in Britain, she and her twin sister Hannah, who was on a one-day home leave, were waiting to hear what the Prime Minister, Neville Chamberlain, had to say. In their hearts each of them knew what was coming and the room seemed to have filled with doom and gloom even though in their own way they had been willing the news not to be bad. They had avoided any talk of what might be and fantasised instead about the type of house that Hannah might one day live in should she end up married to the wealthy but boring man who had set his sights on her at Station X.

'The trouble is,' said Hannah, 'there only seem to be two types of men, rich and boring or poor and interesting.'

Jessie found it strange that her twin had not mentioned qualities which she would have named – magnetic, exciting, irresistible. 'What about my Tom? Where does he fit into your ideas about men?'

'A bastard but you can't help loving him?'

Quietly laughing at her sister's honesty, Jessie had to agree. 'Especially when he's been on a drinking binge with 'is dad and brothers.'

'Ah,' said Hannah, all-knowing. 'I remember those nights out. They were always getting up to some kind of no good, sailing on the wrong side of the law. Emmie used to wait for them with a rolling pin. She really did. And she hit them with it too. Across the bottom. She would tell me about it the next day, with a crafty smile on her face. "They pulled it off, love," she would whisper, slipping me a pound note. I hardly knew whether to take it or not.'

Recoiling from Hannah's familiarity towards Tom and his family, Jessie tried to rise above her jealousy. Her sister had, after all, known Tom for years before she herself had even spoken to him. 'He never tells me where he gets the money to drink,' she said. 'He just winks. I don't need to know more.'

'Of course,' said Hannah, laughing. 'Another parcel falls off the back of a lorry at the dock gates and he and his dad and brothers go on the town to celebrate.'

Their diversion from reality ended when from the wireless came a hushed silence broken only by a quiet crackling. The stillness seemed deliberate, as if the BBC was preparing listeners for the worst kind of news. It was 3 September 1939.

With a sickly dread in her stomach, Jessie quietly prayed that the country's biggest fear had not been realised. Head bowed and wishing that Tom, her husband of one year, was there by her side, she listened earnestly to Chamberlain's slow and grave delivery.

I am speaking to you from the Cabinet Room, 10 Downing Street. This morning, the British Ambassador in Berlin handed the German government the final note, stating that unless he heard from them by eleven o'clock, and they were prepared at once to withdraw their troops from Poland, a state of war would exist between us. I have to tell you now that no such undertaking has been received, and that consequently this country is at war with Germany.

Numbed by the announcement, Jessie switched off the wireless. Her mind went back to a dark day in the spring, in April, two weeks before Billy was due. Tom had received his call-up papers ordering him to report to the Tower of London where he would be conscripted into the army. They had been married for just six months at the time and until that morning post had arrived, Jessie believed that nothing could spoil her and Tom's perfect world.

'I can't say I'm all that shocked,' murmured Hannah. 'This war was on the cards.'

'I s'pose so,' replied Jessie, half wishing her twin wasn't there right then and saying such things. It made it too real too soon.

'Life is about to change, Jessie. For all of us. No more thinking the best.'

'I know. I think it hit me really when Tom's call-up papers came in April. I shook like a leaf. Couldn't stop. That poor bloody postman. I feel sorry for 'im now.

3

He was only doing his job but he must've sensed the resentment us wives and mothers felt when he delivered them brown envelopes. Poor sod. You should 'ave seen the look on 'is face.' Jessie covered her face with her hands. She wanted Hannah to go. To explain why would be impossible. She and her twin were very close but for some strange reason she needed to be alone. Wanted to be by herself to think for herself.

'Thank God for Tom's mum next door. Good old Emmie,' she said finally, trying her best. 'I expect she'll be listening in with the other women at work. Three sons to go to war. I don't know what's worse, seeing your husband go off and wondering if you'll ever see 'im again, or watching three sons walk away.'

'Well, aren't you the light at the end of a dark tunnel,' said Hannah, smiling, trying to lift her sister's spirits. 'We Brits have more backbone than that, Jessie. And Emmie's got guts for two strong women. And as for Hitler, let him try to take England. Just let him try.'

'Britain,' said Jessie. 'He won't settle for less.'

'Well then, he's in for a surprise, isn't he?'

'Lets 'ope so.'

'Oh, you can take it from me. If—'

'Hannah, please! I don't want to talk about it.' Jessie's tone was anguished. She glanced across the room at Billy and sighed. 'I don't really want to talk about anything. It's all too much for me.'

'Sorry, Jess. I wasn't thinking.'

With Billy asleep and the wireless switched off, the only sound in the room was the ticking of the clock and the hissing of the fire. Staring into the glowing coals, Jessie glanced at the wedding photograph of her and Tom on the mantel shelf, radiant and in love. Next to it was a group

4

wedding picture showing her mother standing proudly between Jessie and Hannah, and their sister Dolly, with her younger brothers, Stephen, in his Boy Scout uniform, and Alfie in his very first suit. The smile on their mother Rose's face hid the disappointment she had felt. There had been no white satin lace dress for her daughter, no bridesmaids and, worst of all, Jessie had been carrying Tom's child when she went to the altar.

But Jessie had made a beautiful bride and looked radiant in her oyster satin coat with tiny coloured glass buttons and matching skirt, which now hung in the wardrobe upstairs, waiting for another occasion when she might have the chance to wear it.

Jessie couldn't blame her mother for being cheerless at her wedding; she did, after all, have to stand alone to see her daughter married, without her late husband by her side. It had pained Jessie, too, that her dad had not been there on her special day. She knew that her mother had not really taken to Tom and, well-mannered though she was, Rose hadn't been able to hide her feelings. His easy-go-lucky approach to life worried her.

Rose had made her views known to Jessie about her son-in-law's attitude towards the possibility of war. In her opinion, he liked the idea of being paid to train as a soldier, with board and lodging provided, while Jessie received an army pension. Jessie told her mother she was wrong and that once she got to know Tom properly she would realise he had been innocently baiting her. Rose had not been convinced.

Before his conscription in April Tom had given up his job at the docks and taken an offer of freelance work as painter and decorator, which Rose considered reckless of him. The work had been spasmodic and he and Jessie, during those late winter months, had struggled to make ends meet.

Hannah pushed Chamberlain's speech from her mind and went into the kitchen to make them both a cup of tea while Jessie enjoyed the memory of one particular weekend when Tom had been home on leave. Standing by the butler sink, stringing some runner beans, she had been admiring the bluey-pink hydrangea bush in the garden when Tom had crept into the house and sneaked up behind her, giving her the biggest surprise of her life. It was little things like that that kept their love burning. During his periods of leave from the army, they had spent much of the time making love or fussing over their baby, Billy. On that leave Tom had seemed more worried than usual. He'd dropped hints about Jessie being in London with all the French sailors on the lookout for a bit of romance. 'Actually they're called matelots,' she'd said innocently and in fun. It hadn't gone down well. Tom was a jealous man by nature and it was beginning to show. He had related tales he'd heard about the generosity of the French sailors who lavished presents of silk stockings, chocolates and brandy.

'Just don't go leaving our Billy and going out with 'em, that's all,' was his usual parting remark when his leave ended.

'You know,' said Hannah, coming into the room with their tea, 'Tom's very nervous about losing you.' Once again, as had happened before, the twin sisters seemed to have been thinking the same thing at the same time even though they had been in different rooms.

'What makes you say that?'

6

'Well,' said Hannah, sitting down, 'that time when I had a day off and came to see you when Tom was on home leave, he quizzed me on the goings-on around town.'

'Did he now.'

'It's all right. I was quick off the mark. Gave him a look that said don't even think about using me to spy on my own sister. I had, after all, come especially to tell you *my* good news.'

'That you'd been summoned for war work.'

'Yes.'

'And are you still chuffed over it, now that you're there?'

'Yep. I love my work. It's such a fantastic place. The hours are long and it's hard work, but I love being there. And you know how I enjoyed working in the library... I don't even miss being around books.'

Jessie's curiosity was piqued. 'Come on then, tell us what goes on there – or where it is at least. Don't be mean. You know I won't say anything.'

'I can't. I'm sworn to secrecy. Tom tried and failed and you know how persistent he can be,' Hannah said, smiling, hoping that would be the end of it.

'Please yourself. I just wondered what your room was like, that's all. I'm not bothered one way or the other.'

'Oh, I can tell you that. It's small but it's mine and the sun streams in through the window which looks out over the grounds. That's why I like it so much. It's heaven compared to that miserable flat over that dusty shop in Bethnal Green.'

'With a tyrant for a mother.' Jessie remembered Gerta, the woman who had made Hannah's childhood a misery.

'*Foster* mother,' Hannah corrected. 'And it's all buried in the past where it should be.'

7

Jessie turned the conversation back to her sister's work. 'What do you do there then? Just tell me that bit. Office work? Filing?'

'I mustn't tell you, Jess! I can't tell you what I do or where I work and live. It's secret stuff to do with the government and it was made clear that my lips must be sealed. I could get into a lot of trouble for even talking this much about it.'

The room went quiet again. Jessie didn't like the sound of it and didn't like her sister having to be away from the area, especially now. 'So now that war's been declared, will you still be able to come back now and then?'

'I hope so.' The tone of Hannah's voice made the message she was giving clear: no more talk of it. So Jessie pushed it from her mind. Very soon Emmie would be home from work and straight in to commiserate over the announcement on the wireless. They had things to discuss, that was for sure. Emmie would want to make plans straightaway, marking out every single air-raid shelter in the borough and advising Jessie to only shop close by those shelters for the sake of safety. After all, she had her grandson to think of as well as her daughter-in-law.

'I wonder how Tom's taking the news,' said Jessie, feeling worse by the minute.

'He's with men, don't forget. Soldiers. Their instincts will be to protect their territory. Knowing Tom, he'll be in a fighting mood.'

Maybe Hannah was right but on his last visit home, just a few weeks previously, Tom had still been adamant that Britain would not go to war. He had never believed that the day would come when the Prime Minister would make the announcement that Jessie had just listened to on the wireless.

'I think,' said Hannah, 'that Tom plays his cards close to his chest. All that talk about war never coming was a cover. He's not daft, Jessie. He knew.'

'Maybe.' It was becoming clear to Jessie that her twin sister knew Tom better than she did. And there was no denying that Tom knew Hannah better than all of them. But that was understandable. Jessie had only discovered the existence of her twin a year ago and Hannah had been a close friend of Tom since early schooldays. And now Jessie hardly saw anything of Hannah since she'd been posted to Buckinghamshire. What with her sister's absence and Tom having been stationed at Thetford, Jessie wanted to get out of the house sometimes and bring some fun into her life. Every other woman she knew, it seemed, was working in a factory preparing for a war and going out with friends in the evenings for a lively time. If she was honest with herself, she would have had to admit that she did sometimes feel envious. Jealous of her twin Hannah and jealous of her other sister, lively, carefree Dolly. Her own life seemed dull and lonely by comparison to theirs, even if she did have the beautiful son she adored.

'I'm going to have to go now, Jess,' said Hannah, checking the time. 'I don't want to miss my train.'

'No, you don't want to do that,' Jessie said with a touch of bitterness. They hugged and Hannah promised to come and see Jessie as soon as she could.

'It'll work out, Jess, you'll see. This time next year we'll be looking back with relief and smiling.'

Once Hannah had gone back to the centre at Bletchley Park, where enemy codes were deciphered and where Hannah's adoptive father, Jack Blake, had also been stationed months before her, as a code breaker, Jessie felt very much alone in her two-up, two-down in Bethnal Green. It was true that she regularly saw her in-laws who lived in the same street, and her own mother, Rose, twice a week, and sometimes her younger brother Stephen stayed overnight, but for all of that nothing filled the empty gap she felt. She missed Tom's strong arms holding her close in bed and she missed the times when she and her twin sister had sat and chatted for hours on end about everything and nothing.

Jessie's other sister Dolly, true to form, had been having a whale of a time and making the most of the pre-wartime spirit. She was always going out on dates and was very popular with the Dutch marines whose ships sometimes docked in London. The East End, it seemed, was as popular as the West End when it came to night life, the pubs and taverns full of laughter, cheerful music, and song.

On the way to the bus stop to see Tom off on his last home leave, Jessie had been mortified when he said he had thoughts of not going back. The conversation immediately changed into an argument with her telling him not to dare to do anything stupid. She told him to stick it out like the rest of the conscripts and that was when he revealed his true worry to her. He asked if she'd been seeing her old boyfriend while he was away, Max Cohen, whom she had courted for three years before meeting Tom.

The unexpected question had thrown her. Of course she hadn't been seeing Max but more importantly, why had Tom even asked? She had been faithful, unlike some other married women, and hadn't even gone out for one evening, and there he had stood, accusing her. She had refused to answer him at first, which had caused him to be even more testy. She wouldn't deny it and that, in Tom's eyes, made her look guilty. When Tom had demanded to know why she wasn't denying it, she had yelled, 'I shouldn't need to!' not caring who heard. 'Of course I haven't seen him! He's in the bloody army as well, isn't he!'

His reply had shaken her. 'No he's not! As if you didn't know! Got out of it and all because he's got two left feet. Did you know he 'ad two left feet, Jess?'

If she had not been so livid with him she would have found his remark funny. She hadn't thought about Max in a while but Tom had obviously been worrying about leaving her in London with the man she had once given herself to and said she would marry living close by. Now with the likelihood of being posted abroad, Tom would be even more anxious as to what she might be getting up to. She hadn't realised until then just how damaging jealousy could be. It had all started with a light joke from Tom but had grown and was still spreading, affecting them both for different reasons.

With Billy in her arms, awake and contented, Jessie went out into the back garden and picked a dahlia for him to play with before letting Harry out of his hutch for a run-around, which would please her son more than anything. He loved the rabbit and chuckled whenever it ran or hopped or deliberately turned its back on them. Able to crawl about now, Billy struggled to get down from Jessie's firm grip but the last thing she was going to do was let him loose in the back yard. 'You'll have to wait, Billy, till you can walk. Then you and Harry can chase each other.' From the expression on his face, she almost believed he understood every word and had a feeling that he'd do his utmost to pull himself up on to his feet when he was in the old playpen a neighbour had recently given her.

Walking around the garden, pointing out different leaves and flowers, Jessie felt as if she was in a strange kind of dream. Here she was with her adorable baby boy, her rabbit frisking around in the afternoon sun, the roses still in bloom and autumn flowers all around, and yet war had been declared. *War.* It didn't seem possible that it could happen in her country.

She recalled the day in April when Tom had been summoned into the army. It came flooding back as clear as if it was happening right then. Jessie had wept when she saw the letter. She was in bed when Tom let himself into the house and she heard him knocking into furniture and singing, badly and out of tune, obviously very drunk.

'You were meant for me... I was meant for you...' he sang. 'Nature patterned you and when she was done... Jess was all the good things rolled into one... You're like a plaintive... melody...' There was a pause, then he sang loudly, 'Jessie – I've had no tea... I... 'm so hungry I could eat – a horse...'

When he found the letter propped on the table, telling him to report to the Tower, he staggered up the stairs, drunk and flabbergasted, as if it had arrived without any warning whatsoever. 'Jess. Jess... they can't do this to me...' he said, hardly able to end a sentence. 'I can't leave you, Jess.'

His performance irritated her. 'Tom, you'd better sober up. An' didn't you once say, you'd fight to the bitter end to keep Hider's hands off Britain?' She tried, to hold in her anger. 'Stop play-actin' and go to bed – in the box room, where you can snore as loud as you like. I need my sleep.'

But Tom had been in no mood to be quietened. 'I wasn't looking forward to going away to fight Hitler, Jess... and I *don't* snore.' He did and he knew it.

'When you're this drunk you do. Where'd the money come from for your night out?' She had no intention of letting him off the hook.

Winking, hoping to soften her, Tom smiled and then hiccupped. 'Perks. Perks of life. A parcel fell off a lorry as it was coming out of the dock gates... and the driver pulled away without realising.' Hunching his shoulders he sported that look of innocence he often used. 'What could I do but pick up that parcel? I've had a few beers, Jess, that's all. I was celebrating with my brother, Stanley. We sold most of the stuff.'

'And the rest?'

'We've, er, we've stored it,' he said, telling what he would call a white lie. 'Round a mate's house.' Play-acting or not, he suddenly looked like a man in the depths of despair as he sat on the edge of their bed. 'Not much to celebrate though, is there? I've got to leave you, Jessie, and I don't wanna do that.' Watching him waving the call-up papers in the air, she knew very well that he was deliberately being melodramatic, 'They can't mean it. I'm not a bloody soldier, I'm a decorator!' He slumped down on to their bedroom chair, a sorry sight. Looking like a frightened child, head lowered, he sobered up and became more serious and more honest. He said haltingly, 'This has really upset me.'

That got Jessie's back up. 'Upset *you!*' she snapped. 'Well, how do you think I felt? I saw those papers and went crying to your mother and *you* went down the pub.'

'Yeah, but... I hadn't seen the letter, *had* I?' he said, trying to get her sympathy. 'I wouldn't 'ave gone out if I *had* seen it, Jess. You know that.'

It all seemed so trivial now, looking back. But Jessie still believed that it was the stress of Tom's antics and his call-up that had brought on her birth pains the very next day, two weeks before her time. For a while, it had been touch and go if she and the baby would live. Thank God it had been all right.

Pushing all of that from her mind, Jessie left Billy in his pushchair, happily watching Harry the rabbit, and went inside to make herself another cup of tea. After all, there was worse to come now. Bloodshed and killing of innocent people, men, women and children, with bombs dropping all over the world. She feared for Tom who underneath it all was a real softie at heart. He had cried his eyes out on the night Billy was born when they had very nearly lost him. It had been a close thing and they were lucky that their baby had an excellent midwife to watch out for him and Jessie. Not only had he arrived early and unexpected but when she finally gave birth, the house had gone dark. The electric meter had run out of coins. Worse still, the umbilical cord was caught round Billy's neck and the midwife had only the light of a torch to work by.

'Never mind, Billy,' Jessie whispered, 'I won't let anything 'appen to you. No. It would 'ave to be over my dead body.' She looked up at the sky. 'Please, dear sweet Jesus, keep me safe so I can take care of my baby.'

–

To Jessie's surprise and joy, Tom was allowed home for an overnight visit the day after war had been declared and before he was posted abroad. When he turned up on the doorstep, she simply couldn't believe it. He was the best sight for sore eyes anyone could wish for and she didn't want to let him out of her sight. They made the most of every minute together, hardly apart, always in the same room, always with Billy – and for the first time since she had known him, Tom helped her in the kitchen, preparing food, washing up, anything so long as he was by her side and touching her. In bed, they made love for most of the night, clinging to each other as if they might never see each other again.

At the breakfast table, Tom looked terrible. His eyes red and his face drawn. 'I don't want to go, Jess,' he said, choked. 'I want to stay here with you and Billy.'

'You can't, Tom, you know that. Try not to think about it.' She was finding it all too much and her voice gave her away. Of course she didn't want him to go but what choice had they?

'Why am I going?' he said, looking like a child about to be abandoned. 'I don't wanna murder people and I don't want a bullet through my 'ead. All I want is to stay back 'ere in Bethnal Green, go to work, and come home to my family. That's not too much to ask, is it?'

'No, but you 'ave to go for the same reason as every other man. If you don't go out there and stop Hitler, he'll take this country and who knows what kind of a life we'll be facing. This is a free country, Tom. Fight to keep it that way. For Billy, if not for us. Think of his future and our grandchildren.'

'I s'pose you're right,' he said, sipping his tea. 'Greedy bastard wants to own and rule the world. Territorial rights. That's what this is all about. The twentieth century and we're still thinking like cavemen.'

Jessie glanced at the clock. 'We'll 'ave to get a move on soon. You don't wanna miss your train back.'

'I won't miss it, Jess, 'cos I've no intention of catching it. I'll go back in a few days' time. Say I 'ad the flu. Doctor'll give me a sick note. He's all right. We 'ad a chat last time I was back when I met 'im in the street. He didn't know it but I was checking up on what his views were.'

Jessie laughed out loud. 'Silly bugger, Tom. Course he knew what you was up to. Don't you think that scores of other men'll be trying it on? There'll be a mile-long queue outside the surgery, you see if I'm wrong.'

'Well, there you are, then,' said Tom, easing a cigarette into the comer of his mouth. 'There's my excuse. I couldn't get an appointment.'

The banter continued until Jessie realised that he really had made up his mind. He wasn't going back that day and relief began to take over from worry. She would have him around for a couple more days and where was the harm in that?

They made the most of their two extra days together. Instead of Tom going down to the pub, Jessie fetched home ale in a jug and she couldn't remember a time when they had been more in love and so close.

But fate had something up its sleeve. The very morning that he had intended going back, there was a knock on the door and it had the same sound to it as what was commonly known as the 'coppers knock' in the East End. Tom was playing with Billy, jumping him up and down on his lap, his uniform ready and waiting on the back of the kitchen door while Jessie was in the kitchen frying bacon and poaching eggs. Coming into the living room, she paled. 'Tom.' Her voice was no more than a whisper. 'Tom, I think it's the police.'

His mood now sombre, Tom slowly nodded, showing that he was thinking the same thing. 'Take Billy. I'll open the door.'

Dressed only in his trousers with braces dangling, Tom faced them. Neither of the two men on the doorstep said a word, they just stared into his face. 'Fair enough,' said Tom. 'I was going back today anyway.' He waved them in and closed the door. 'Fancy a bacon sandwich? I'm just frying breakfast for the wife while she feeds the baby.'

The delicious smell and sound of the sizzling bacon was tantalising and something that no ordinary man could resist and, duties aside, these two were ordinary men.

'Take a seat,' Tom offered. He winked at Jessie and went into the kitchen to take up where she had left off. They would have to do without eggs – the bacon was ready and he didn't want to keep them waiting longer in case they had second thoughts and resisted the sandwich.

'Them bloody barracks,' said Tom cheerfully, coming into the room, 'damp as you like. Thought I was in for pneumonia.' He handed each of them a sandwich. 'Felt all right when I woke up this morning though – apart from a splitting headache. I was gonna send in a sick note but you know what it's like when you're in bed sweating it out. And the doctor was too busy to come out.'

'I'm sure he was,' said one of the men, chuckling. 'You'd be surprised how many of you have gone down with this sudden epidemic which only seems to have affected blokes ready for war. Strange, that.'

Enjoying a short break from work and the unexpected pleasure of hot, crisp bacon between two slabs of baker's bread, the men kept their thoughts to themselves. And when Tom asked if there was time for him to have a quick wash and shave, they shrugged and told him to be quick about it. He left Jessie telling the officers about baby Billy and how she feared he might have caught Tom's heavy cold on top of having just got over a chesty cough. They only half listened to her; they kept one ear on the movements of Tom upstairs.

Ten minutes later one of the men said, 'Sorry, Mrs Smith, but I'll have to ask you to fetch your husband. It's time to go.'

'Tom!' she called up the stairs but deep down she had a sickening sense he was not there. The creaking floorboards from Billy's nursery had been a dead giveaway as far as she was concerned. There was no reason for Tom to go in there unless he had decided to slip out of the upstairs back window.

Her instincts were right. Tom had gone and a neighbour hanging washing on the line had helped him by opening her yard door which led into another neighbour's garden and then to a narrow alleyway. All of this Jessie learned from her neighbour once the military police, furious and red-faced, had gone. The woman was pleased with herself and Jessie had to smile, though she really would have liked to scream.

'It was good of you to help out,' she said, 'but he'll get into more trouble for it. He should have known better.'

Laughing, the woman left Jessie to herself. She and the other neighbours in the street knew Tom Smith quite well and it didn't surprise them one bit that he'd managed to dodge away. To them it was funny but then they didn't have to rely on him to stay put and ensure that the army paid Jessie her pension to feed and clothe herself and Billy.

Tom made his own way to Thetford, unescorted. Once again, he somehow managed to talk his way out of trouble. He wrote to Jessie, telling her that being on the run from the army and dodging the red caps was not only stimulating but easy. His casual joking about it worried her. To him this was no more than a prank; to Jessie it spelled trouble.

–

Soon after war with Germany was declared, air raid sirens were heard all around Britain but thankfully it was a false alarm – a false alarm, but a grim reminder that during this war ordinary people, young and old, would be a target. But Britain was prepared this time, unlike during the First World War. Prepared and as ready as they could be to face the ordeal ahead.

Gas masks were issued to adults and children and trenches had been dug in readiness. Important buildings were sandbagged and public air-raid shelters, built earlier that summer, were ready and waiting. Air-raid wardens had been Well trained and knew what to do when the bombs began to fall. Auxiliary firemen, too, had been drilled and tested and knew how to tackle a growing fire as well as how to extinguish an incendiary bomb with a stirrup pump. The stamp of active war was present everywhere and the atmosphere, strangely enough, was not of depression but camaraderie as people of differing class and religion were drawn together by the threat they all faced.

Before the month of September was out, communities began to break up as women and children were evacuated and men went off to fight for king and country. Over a million Britons were evacuated from the cities but Jessie had no intention of leaving the East End and neither did her family nor several of her neighbours. They, like many others, chose to stay at home and rely on the government's offer of protection to every household in the big cities – an Anderson shelter, to be erected in the garden. The corrugated iron hut was to be sunk halfway into the ground and covered with earth and sandbags as a means of shelter from the bombing.

It was a strange time for everyone. Women took their responsibilities seriously and were strong, in the face of having to begin new lives without their men and keep their heads above water and hold their families together. It wasn't really until January 1940, when the government issued millions of ration books, that the grim reality of what was to come truly hit home.

Four ounces of butter and four ounces of bacon or uncooked ham a week, with just twelve ounces of sugar per adult, was a joke as far as Jessie's mother-in-law, Emmie, was concerned. She was known for her cooking abilities and she did not want to let the side down. With just herself and Charlie at home to feed, she had volunteered to prepare meals for five old folk in her turning, who would find it impossible to fend for themselves under the circumstances. She wasted no time in rooting out extra provisions via the black market. Her husband, Charlie, too old to be called up, had joined the million other men who had signed up with the Local Defence Volunteers, which proved to be an excellent grapevine as to where those extra provisions might be found or swapped.

Jessie's mother, Rose, continued to run her cobbler shop with her youngest son, Stephen. Stephen's love for the stage had led him to join a local drama group; he found his vocation early in life and his sexual preferences. His mother's inner worry over the years that there might be something different about her son was becoming a reality. Stephen was destined to remain a bachelor boy. Jessie's other brother, the rebellious Alfie who was just seventeen, had secured work in the metal foundry, hoping this would release him from having to defend his king and country should the war drag on. Alfie had other fights to fight when fledgling mobsters crossed the territorial line of his gang's patch in Stepney where he now lived by himself in two rooms above an Italian cafe.

As for Jessie, she worried about her sometimes irresponsible husband and was kept on her toes by her lively baby. The happy family life that she had been looking forward to was now overtaken by the war and the restrictions it brought, including the blackout. Even the tiniest hint of light from the edge of a window at night prompted an angry shout of 'Put that light out!' And, beneath the blackout curtains, like every other household, the windows were heavily taped to prevent flying glass, and so by day as well as by night there was a constant reminder of the country being at war.

But Jessie took the war in good heart and like others began to grow food in every part of her garden. It was the same all over the country. Allotments, gardens, back yards, even window boxes were now being used solely to grow vegetables or fruit.

There were other changes too. Trees, kerbs and lamp posts had been marked with white to help in the blackout and women were doing the work of men in factories, shipyards and railway sheds. Ironically, the war was doing far more for the women's movement than the Suffragettes had managed in earlier years.

Jessie's sister Dolly had applied for a job as a bus conductor, which she loved, it being more sociable than any other occupation she could find. Petrol rationing had been introduced with a severity that forced many people to take their cars off the roads and use public transport. Men from all walks of life now came into Dolly's happy orbit and she was always full of it when visiting her sister and nephew, baby Billy.

While Dolly chatted about the latest and most handsome sailor she'd met, Jessie hid her envy. To her, it seemed an age since she had enjoyed an evening out. To walk arm in arm with one of the tall blond Dutch sailors Dolly spoke of was a dream that often comforted Jessie when she was feeling at her lowest.

'I don't know why you don't come out with us, Jess,' said Dolly, carefully repainting her fingernails. 'Mum would come and sit with Billy, you know she would. You can't stay in for ever.'

'It won't be for ever, Dolly,' said Jessie. 'The war'll be over soon and my Tom'll be back where he belongs.' She strapped her son into his highchair and went into the kitchen. 'Watch him for me, Doll. He's worked out how to undo the buckle on his straps. It's spam sandwich with a bit of mustard for lunch.'

'That'll do me.' Dolly cupped Billy's double chin and kissed his smiling face, finding some of his dribble. 'Erghh, you messy little sod!'

'What's he done now?' called Jessie, pleased to have him off her hands for five minutes.

'Messed up my lipstick!' Undoing his buckle, Dolly lifted her nephew out of his highchair to squeals of laughter. 'He weighs a blooming ton, Jessie! What you been feeding him on?' She tickled Billy under the arm and chuckled with him. 'Little fat sod, ain't yer?' she said, cuddling him. 'Handsome devil. Got your dad's lovely green eyes and your mum's blonde hair. Them little girls are gonna love you.'

Billy babbled on, talking in his own language. 'Gibberish,' said Dolly, laughing at him, 'that's all you can do. Talk a load of gibberish.'

'Juish,' said Billy, demanding more attention. 'Dirsty.' Dolly pushed her face closer to his. '*Juice* not juish. And *thirsty* not dirsty. Billy try. *Thirsty*. Go on then… *th-th-th-thirsty!*'

'Dirsty!' The fourteen-month-old laughed out loud and clapped his podgy hands together. 'Juish!'

'You little tyke. *You* know. Yes you *do*. *You* know 'ow to say it.' She tickled him again. 'I can't wait to get one of these little bundles of trouble, Jess.'

Coming into the sitting room, Jessie sighed. 'You, a mother? Tied down to the kitchen sink?'

'I'm talking about later on once the war's over and I'm ready to settle down. Have you heard from Tom this week?'

'A postcard came this morning. He's getting on all right with the French now. His landlady's come round at last.'

'Blooming cheek they've got, them frogs. I wouldn't mind, our men are out there in France for their bloody benefit, you'd think they'd be grateful.'

'Anyway, he seems all right.' Jessie took Billy from her for his afternoon nap. 'I hope he's behaving himself with all them mademoiselles, that's all.'

'That's doubtful,' said Dolly, biting into her sandwich.

'Oh, thanks! What a ray of sunshine you are,' said Jessie, taking Billy upstairs.

'Trouble with you, Jess, is that you go through life thinking nothing'll change! It's about time you livened up a bit. Come dancing with me and my mates tonight. You won't look back!'

'I'm a married woman, Dolly,' said Jessie, coming back into the room.

'So? Loads of married women whose men have gone to war go out. You can't sit in all the blooming time. Silly cow.'

Jessie dropped into an armchair, fed up. 'I don't sit in *all* the time. Once we've finished this bit of lunch I've got every intention of going out for a walk. You can wheel Billy in the pushchair for me.'

Dolly sipped her tea. 'A nice trip over the park, I s'pose.'

'Yep. And then on to visit Mum and Stephen. It's better than sitting in all day.'

'Yeah, I grant you that. It is better than that. Tch. I don't know. You're getting old before you've stopped being young.'

'And you're getting on my nerves. Be quiet for five minutes.'

That said, Jessie and Dolly sat in silence. Dolly wondered what she would wear to go out that evening and Jessie wondered whether she should hang the washing on the line or dry it by the fire. It was a crisp, bright January day but it could change to cloud and rain within minutes. 'Did you catch the weather forecast today?' she asked, miles away.

'No, funnily enough I missed it, Jess.' The last thing Dolly thought to do was listen to a weather forecast. 'If it rains we'll put our umbrella up. If it don't, we won't. It's risky but sod it, let's live dangerously on our walk, eh?'

Amused by her sister's sense of humour, Jessie snapped out of her mood. A couple of minutes later she went upstairs to brush her hair and put on some lipstick and powder. Staring at her reflection in the dressing-table mirror, she could see that Dolly had a point. She *had* turned into a dowdy housewife.

Wrapped up against the cold air, hats pulled down over their ears, with Dolly pushing the pram and Jessie by her side, they enjoyed the early January sunshine as they strolled along the Mile End Road to take Billy to visit his grandmother Rose. Turning into Whitehorse Road, they heard someone give a wolf whistle. Glancing over her shoulder to see if the admirer was worth a smile, Dolly was amused to see that it was Max, dressed smartly in a suit and unbuttoned dark overcoat.

'Well, well, well,' said Dolly, loving it, 'look who's come out of the woodwork.'

'Who?' said Jessie. 'One of your old flames?' She kept her eyes firmly fixed in front. She didn't want to be tarred with the same brush as her wayward sister. 'Or one of your new boyfriends?'

'No,' said Dolly, cockier than ever, 'one of yours.' Max reached their side and tipped his hat. He had eyes only for Jessie. 'Mind if I walk with you?' he said, showing his row of perfect white teeth.

'Max, it's you!' Jessie, without thinking, kissed him on the cheek. She was pleased to see him and didn't mind who saw. 'Tom said you'd managed to stay in civvi street. Lucky devil.'

'It wasn't good luck, Jessie, it was bad luck. Wouldn't have me because... apparently... my feet wouldn't be up to all that marching.' He turned away from those blue eyes of Jessie's, which he had once adored, and paid attention to

Billy who was sitting up, enjoying a Farley's rusk biscuit. 'He's a mixture of both of you, Jess,' he said, his regret showing.

'Right, well, if you'll excuse me and my nephew,' grinned Dolly, 'we'll be on our way.' Grabbing the handle of the pram again, Dolly strode off, wiggling her buttocks for Max's benefit. 'I'll see you at Mum's, Jessie!' she called back over her shoulder.

'She's a gem,' said Max with a smile. 'Come on, Jess,' he laid a hand on her arm, 'I've got masses to tell you and I want to hear how you've been coping.'

'I'm not sure, Max… you know what people are like. If Tom should get to hear—'

'That you walked along the street with me in broad daylight? Come on, Jessie, this isn't like you. What's happened to your self-confidence?'

'I don't know about that… but yeah, it's not as if it's nighttime, is it?'

'No. But then again, that didn't bother us much once upon a time. So long as we were alone.'

'Don't, Max. Don't stir up all the memories. I'm married now and a mother as well.' She couldn't believe how shy and embarrassed she now felt in his company. 'Not that anyone would take me for anything else but a married woman. Dolly reminded me today how dowdy I was looking.' Jessie would be the first to admit that she was begging for a compliment. Max was right, her self-esteem was on the low side.

'Trust Dolly,' he said, quietly laughing. He remembered Jessie's exuberant, loud-mouthed sister well. 'She never was one for being tactful.'

'So you do think I look drab then?'

He squeezed her arm and an old familiar feeling swept through her. Nothing physical, just a nice friendly feeling. 'You look lovely, Jessie. Although your hair could do with styling. You should go and see the barber again.'

She laughed to be reminded of when she had once had her hair chopped off. Chatting about old times, they soon arrived at Joe Lyons, their previous regular meeting place. 'How's your mum and dad?' she asked, slipping on to a chair at their favoured table by the window.

'More relaxed than they were. At least the war's stopped all the other troubles. They had another brick through their shop window, you know. Blackshirts. I know what I'd like to do if I came face to face with one.' Max looked murderous thinking of the racist attacks his family had suffered.

'Tom and his brother Johnnie walked out, you know, as soon as they realised—'

'That Mosley was likely to be interned?' Max cut in.

'No, it was before all that. They didn't know—'

'Jessie, please. Don't start making excuses for them. They were Blackshirts no matter what. I'll never forgive them. Never. No Jew would.'

Thankful when the waitress arrived with tea and cakes, Jessie took the opportunity to steer the subject back to Max's family. She hadn't heard from Mrs Cohen since she'd married and in a strange way Jessie had missed her. Only once or twice had Mrs Cohen been to visit her mother at the cobbler shop, next door to the Cohens' delicatessen. Having discussed Max's mother and father, Jessie took the bit between her teeth and mentioned Moira, his sister, the one who had been responsible for them breaking off their engagement.

'Moira's fine,' said Max soberly.

'But?'

'But she's been told she'll never have children and it's devastated her.' Max looked serious. 'She and Nathan will adopt children but not until the war's over.'

Breaking off a piece of her fruit bread and popping it into her mouth, Jessie shrugged. 'Let's hope they don't adopt someone's twin.'

Max looked bemused by her off-the-cuff remark. 'What makes you say that?'

'You mean you haven't heard?'

'Heard what, Jessie?' He leaned back in his chair and listened intently as she related the incredible story. Her parents, Rose and Robert, had been young newlyweds just after the First World War and very poor, unable to feed and clothe one baby, let alone two. Rose's half-brother Jack Blake and his German wife Gerta had pleaded to adopt one of the twins since Gerta could not herself have children. It had been a well-kept secret and had it not been for Tom introducing the twin girls much later in life, neither Hannah nor Jessie would have known anything about each other. Hannah would have continued to live in Bethnal Green with her adopted mother, Gerta, who had turned out to be a tyrant – a cold, uncaring woman and a strong supporter of the Blackshirts. Hider was Gerta's hero and Mosley her heartthrob. Since the day the girls had discovered they were twins they had become closer than very best friends. Closer than ordinary sisters. Ending her story, Jessie said, 'I always knew something was wrong. I thought I was losing my mind at times. Missing someone who didn't exist. That I *thought* didn't exist. And then, wham bang, it's out in the open.'

'You've lost me, Jess…' He chuckled. 'My loss, not yours. But there we are – you chose Tom.'

'Max, please. Don't.'

'I can't help it. We would have been married by now. I would have married you, Jess. I *should* have married you.'

'No. Billy wasn't your baby.'

'That wouldn't have mattered. It doesn't matter now even.'

'Maybe not but what *does* matter is that I love Tom. I love him and I'll wait for him.' She sipped her tea and looked at him over the cup, 'You're not shocked then at my having a twin sister?'

'I *am* shocked. You've shocked me. You've really shocked me, Jessie.'

'I know,' she said, enjoying the thrill of shaking the one person she thought was unshakable. 'Mum's been more relaxed since it came out. She's been wonderful, Max. She bought most of the things for the baby – the pram, pillows, blankets…'

'Jessie,' said Max, a faraway look in his eyes, 'I can't believe you've got a twin.'

'You will once you meet her. She's more attractive than me.'

'I don't know what to say.'

'I know what you mean. It came as a shock to me as well.'

'*Your* twin. I can't, wait to meet her.'

'Well, once she's back for good, I'll introduce you.'

'Back? You mean she went off again?'

'War work. For the government. Can't talk about it though.'

'Why not?'

'Because I haven't got a clue what she does. I suppose you've heard about our Alfie?'

'Alfie,' Max chuckled. 'He surprised us all, didn't he? Who would have thought that little wayward sod would have turned out to be so independent and quick off the mark.'

This attitude from Max surprised her. 'What are you talking about?'

'Well, he's employed, at the ammunition factory, he's got himself a nice little flat and he's involved in good work – selling tickets for charity in Mile End. He even helped by selling dance tickets in aid of the Boys' Jewish Club. Made two pounds for us, Jessie.'

Yes, thought Jessie, two pounds for your club and four pounds for Alfie, more like. 'Oh, good. He is keeping up the good work then.' There seemed little point in spoiling her brother's good if false reputation. Maybe he would grow into it.

'Speaking of which, I should be off soon, Jess,' said Max, checking his watch. 'I'm due at the under-eighteens' boxing dub. I've joined the board.' Pausing for a few seconds, he looked into her face, 'Can we do this again? Or maybe go to the pictures instead?'

'I don't know, Max. Let me have a think about it.'

'Of course. Listen, I've just got to pop next door to the tobacconist.' He stood up and Jessie felt sure he'd grown taller. 'Wait here for me. I'll be two minutes,' and he rushed out of the tearooms.

'Did you want some more tea?' The waitress's voice drifted through Jessie's thoughts.

'No thanks. I'm just waiting for my friend to come back from the shop next door and then we'll be off.'

The girl broke into a smile and looked relieved. 'I thought he'd walked out on yer.'

'No… and he's just a friend. An old mate. Not a boyfriend. I'm already married. He's gone to buy some cigarettes.' At that moment, Max returned, carrying a large box of chocolates which brought a different expression to the waitress's face. Jessie saw it as a smile of condemnation. She wondered if she and Max had looked like lovers sitting there, talking together as if the time in between seeing each other had never passed.

'These are for you, Jess,' said Max, offering her the pretty floral box of chocolates. 'A treat.'

'Max, I can't take those.' Jessie was aghast.

'Why not?'

'Well, my mother for a start. I'm just going round there, don't forget. She'll think we're up to something.'

'Don't be silly,' he said, pushing them into her hands. 'I don't know what things are coming to if I can't buy an old flame a small gift.'

'Small? It must have been the biggest box in the shop.'

'Maybe. Anyway, take them to your mother's and tell her they're for you, her and Dolly, if that makes you feel better.'

'It does, Max. Thanks.' Jessie stood up to leave with him and was embarrassed when he took her arm. She could feel the eyes of the young waitress on her and felt guilt creeping in again. She imagined Tom looking in on the scene – he would be angry and jealous, hurt and scared. Frightened that he might be losing his wife.

'Thanks for the tea, and the chocolates. I'll see you… some time. When Tom's back on leave, maybe We could go for a drink together. In a foursome?'

'Maybe,' he said, tipping his hat. 'See you around.'

'Max, don't go.' Embarrassed, she smiled and shrugged. 'Well, not with that look on your face anyway.'

'What look?'

'Doom and gloom.'

Relaxing into his usual easy-going manner, he smiled. 'Jessie, listen. If anything should happen… I mean if you need me, well, you know where I am.'

'Thanks. I'll remember that.' Exchanging a look that required no spoken word, they turned and walked away from one another.

Chapter Two

On 26 May 1940, the evacuation of British soldiers from French soil began and continued for nine long days under heavy attack. The enemy torpedoes bombarded the Royal Navy warships while from the black smoky sky great clouds of German bombers attacked continuously the thick mass of defeated men on the beaches and in the sea. The sea soon became a blanket of dead bodies being washed back towards the place from where they had almost escaped. For those alive in that icy-cold sea it was nigh on impossible to swim through the thick layer of corpses. Nearly all of the rescue boats had been hit and ships torpedoed. On the beaches thousands waited to be rescued and the wounded screamed in pain as they prayed for the hospital ships to arrive. The German army had swept its way through northern France killing, maiming and forcing thousands of soldiers back to Dunkirk.

On the night of 3 June, the final evacuation was conducted under unceasing fire from German machine guns, while men covered the injured and traumatised with their own bodies. It was a living nightmare, like walking through a human slaughterhouse on a scorching day. As for the French soldiers, they, too, suffered appallingly. On one occasion hundreds were mown down in one sweep, within sight of British soldiers. It was shocking. When they went to see if there were any survivors, they found that not one had pulled through.

Eventually, between three and four hundred thousand British and French troops eventually made it to British soil, in what Sir Winston Churchill described as a miracle of deliverance'. And indeed it was. The withdrawal from France was, without doubt, a military disaster but it was also a miraculous achievement. Throughout those nine days of hell there was a continuous line across the Channel as fishing trawlers, yachts, motor cruisers, lifeboats, paddle steamers – every possible type of vessel – ferried the exhausted and injured soldiers to safety. Those who were not butchered or rescued were taken to the German camps. Tom was one of the more fortunate ones. He survived Dunkirk with a wound to his leg. His state of mind, however, would take longer to heal.

On home leave from Scotland where he and many other wounded were convalescing, he could not get the horrors out of his mind and as much as Jessie wanted to, she couldn't bring herself to ask him to tell her no more. Thin, pale and drawn, with dark shadows trader his eyes, Tom looked half the man he had been. His leg had received a bullet in the knee. It was healing but he was not yet able to walk without the aid of crutches. To top it all, his brother Johnnie, who before the war had been on a path to success with his hard work and determination, had been killed on the beaches at Dunkirk. Amidst the thousands of men there battling against defeat, Tom had been just yards away from his brother when he had been shot. Luckily he hadn't witnessed it.

Standing in the doorway of their living room, Jessie felt her heart go out to her husband as he sat slumped in an armchair staring into the fireplace where no fire burned.

It was mid-June and the air was hot and humid. Knowing he was, once again, reliving the horror, she walked slowly across to him and laid a hand on his shoulder.

'You've got to push it from your mind, Tom' She spoke gently.

'I know.' He continued to stare at the same spot.

'Why don't you go down the pub with your...' She hesitated. Johnnie had been the brother who Tom drank with. 'With your mates,' she went on. 'Some must be home on leave as well.' She waited, hoping he would say something. He didn't.

'Well then?' she said, stroking his hair.

'No.'

'What about your dad? I bet he could do with your company. Poor sod. They took it really bad when the telegram came. Really bad. The only words your dad spoke for days was, "Killed in action."'

'I know.'

'They might need you to tell them... something... anything. Anything about the time before it happened. Knowing Johnnie, he must have kept the men going... kept their spirits up.'

'Johnnie was massacred. His pals around him were massacred. Before that they were like the rest of us, shit scared for every minute of the day. We 'ardly dared close our eyes in case those bastards crept up. Vultures... coming to pick off the bones.'

Flinching, Jessie tried again. 'But what about before Dunkirk? You must have had some good times. Johnnie must have had lots of friends...'

'We were at war, Jessie. Johnnie had lovers and enemies like most of the men. You daren't have friends out there.

Friends get killed. French lovers and German enemies – that's what was on offer.'

'I hope you didn't have any lovers,' said Jessie, trying to sound light-hearted.

'No.' Slowly turning and raising his head, he looked at her, a blank, empty look. 'I had you to dream about.'

'Good. 'Cos I've heard all about those lovely French ladies.'

'They were all right. Still are. Good company. Nice voices. They all seemed to have nice voices. Sang every night down the clubs, the way we do down the pub. Better singing though. Better songs – lively and frill of fun one minute and then slow and gutting the next.'

'Oh, so you could understand the words then?'

'Didn't need to. The tunes and expressions said it all. I could understand some French though. Which is just as well. We're all gonna be going back.'

'Course you won't. Churchill wouldn't have that. Not after what happened. Talk sense. You won't be going back.'

'Yes I will, Jess. Face facts.'

Sitting on the settee, her knees almost touching Tom's, she reached out and took his hand. 'Tom, listen, I know you've been through it but—'

He put up a hand to stop her. 'You *don't* know. You had to *be* there to know what it was like. To watch men you'd been fighting alongside who couldn't swim trying to get out to those boats…' Resting his head back he stared up at the ceiling, blocking out that particular agonising memory.

'We made fires on the beach. Cooked our meals on it. Cook anything. In it went. Into the big pot. Cans of this, cans of that. Cook did well by us. He made it tasty. Poor bastard. They shot his head clean off. We still ate the stew though, once we got it out. We were starving. Had to eat the stew. He'd have been bloody annoyed if we'd chucked it away.' Weighed down by the memory of it, Tom slowly shook his head, his eyes staring up at the ceiling, talking more to himself than to Jessie, his voice low and quiet. 'His head fell into the stew pot. I still can't believe it 'appened. And we still scoffed it He was an ugly man as well.'

Jessie was shocked but Tom broke into a strange smile as he stared out at nothing. 'I s'pose it's funny now, now that we're out of hell and back here. Yeah, if it wasn't tragic it would be funny. Still, Cook didn't know anything about it, did he? One of the blokes said he was grinning up at him from the soup. As it happens, Cook did 'ave a sense of humour. He would have loved it. I can just hear him. "Go on then, you greedy bastards, eat it now."'

Jessie remembered something one of her dad's friends had once said – a stand-up comic. He said, if there's a tragedy and you can turn it around and make it funny, you've got talent. 'What on earth did they tell his family, Tom?'

'Killed in action.' Tom went quiet again. 'That's all anyone needs to know. That's all they ever say. Killed in action. Could have been me. *You* could 'ave got that telegram. Still might.' He'd slipped into his other world where Jessie could hardly reach him.

'I was lucky.' He spoke in a monotone. 'I could swim. Bullet wound or not. I swam for my life. Got to a little boat which took us to a big ship. Stark naked. We had to chuck everything away. Keep it light Light? I don't know how the boat didn't sink with us lot on there. Bloody miracle. Hundreds of us, maybe thousands, all swimming out to them little boats.' He began to cry again.

Easing herself out of the armchair, Jessie quietly left the room. To see the man she loved crying was more than she could bear and she knew him well enough to know he would rather cry alone. Emmie had told her, 'Let my son keen if he needs to. You come in here to me and let him cry and keen until he shifts some of it from his chest.'

Tom was sobbing next door while baby Billy was happy and laughing on his grandmother's lap. Emmie was grabbing a little bit of happiness with her grandson while her husband, Charlie, turned Tom's thick grey woollen socks which were on the fender and steaming by the fire. Washing his son's bits and pieces made him feel less worthless. Charlie had fought in the First World War and knew something of what his sons had gone through. To his mind, gutted though he was, his son Johnnie was better off dead. Had they managed to bring him home and remove the bullet from his skull, he would, to Charlie's mind, have been a fraction of the man he once was.

Thinking of his youngest son, Charlie prayed to God that his Stanley had managed to get through without injuries and had not been captured. The word was that he'd gone into hiding before the retreat to the beaches of Dunkirk. That he'd shacked up with a young widow whose husband had been killed and who was hiding him in her small farmhouse on the outskirts of a remote French village, deep in the countryside.

'I think I might pop round and see old Lady Leigh later on.' Charlie squeezed the moisture out of the toe of Tom's sock. 'See how she is.'

'No you won't, Charlie. She can't tell you more than we already know. Johnnie's dead and that's all there is to it.' Emmie's matter-of-fact tone gave nothing away. She, too, had wanted to attend one of Mrs Leigh's seances but had thought better of it. Now that one of her sons had departed, she'd stopped believing in the afterlife and palm-reading. As far as she was concerned, if anyone could break through the barrier from the afterworld into hers, Johnnie would be the one to do it. But there had been no motherly instinct that his spirit was ever present and no feeling of a tragedy on the day he'd been killed.

'I wasn't thinking of Johnnie,' he said. 'I fancy she might be able to tell us where our Stanley is…' Covering his twisted face with his hands, Charlie just managed to get the words out 'I can't take it, Emmie, I just can't take it. I don't know what he might be going through. What if he's laying injured somewhere and dying a slow death. What if he's in a prisoner of war camp. What if—'

'That's enough! Stop it, Charlie. We've got to be strong for Jessie and Tom and… our little grandson.' Emmie leaned over and put a comforting hand on his arm.

'I know, I know,' he said, his voice breaking. 'It's just…' He pulled his big white handkerchief from his pocket and wiped his eyes. 'Who would 'ave thought it? Who would 'ave thought that things would come to this? Two of our boys lost to us. Our boys, Em, our little ragamuffins. They grow up and then they get blown up. Anyone tells me there's a reason and there is a God, so help me I'll—'

Emmie decided she had to be strong. 'Johnnie caught a bullet to the head and wouldn't 'ave known anything about it. And as for Stanley, he'll be all right, wherever he is. My Stanley's sharper than all three of our sons, Charlie. He knew. He knew to get out and he was quick to get under silk covers.'

'Yeah,' smiled Charlie, still weeping, 'under the covers with a French girl. Little sod.' The rat-a-tat on their window told them that Tom was at the door. 'Thank

Christ Tom's all right. On props or not, he'll come through this bloody war.' He went and opened the street door to Tom.

'Course he will. And for that we have to count our blessings. Then our Stanley'll turn up out of the blue carrying a baby in each arm. That's the fight at the end of our tunnel.' Emmie lifted baby Billy into the air and chuckled with him. 'And you're our ray of sunshine, ain't yer? Our bundle of joy. Keep us all going, you will. Keep our peckers up.'

'Fancy a stroll, Mum? In about an hour or so?' Tom eased himself down on to a chair, resting his crutches next to him. 'See me off at Stepney Green. You an' all, Dad. Might as well 'ave what's left of my family there to wave fare ye well.'

'Course we'll come. Be company for Jessie.'

'I'm not so sure, son,' said Charlie. 'Won't Jess want you to 'erself?'

'Probably, but once I've gone through that barrier, she'll sink. That's when she'll need your support.' He glanced up at the window to avoid Emmie's eyes which showed the heartache she was covering. 'Anyway, I want my mum and dad to see me off as well. Trouble is, I don't know if I'll get another home leave before I'm fit to go back and fight.'

'Best not to bank on it then, son,' said Emmie. 'Get your convalescence over with and make the most of your time in Scotland in that hospital. And don't go back until you're more than fit. Bugger what anyone else says. We'll all see each other when we see each other and leave the rest to God.'

Tom shot her a look to kill. God. He didn't think so. Once upon a time he had been open to the idea of there being an almighty but not any more. Not after what he'd seen. 'So you'll both walk up the station with us then?'

'Try and stop us, son,' smiled Charlie, 'try and stop us.'

'And you will keep an eye out for Jessie while I'm away?'

'What kind of an eye?' said Emmie.

'You know.'

'No, son, I don't. You tell me.' Emmie had a very clear idea as to what her son meant but he was going to have to say it. Admit that he didn't trust her. As far as she was concerned, Tom had dropped too many hints already.

'Make sure she's all right and that.' He avoided her accusing eyes.

'And what?'

'Oh, for Christ's sake, Mother! You know what I mean, Make sure she don't go gallivanting with her mates – taking drinks from sailors or anyone else looking for a good night out. She's a good-looking woman. I don't wanna lose her.' He cast his eyes down, feeling very sorry for himself.

'Oh, right. So you think she might lower her standards to yours, do you?'

'What's that supposed to mean?' Still he wouldn't meet her eye.

Emmie put the sleeping Billy into his pushchair which was parked in one corner of her living room. 'Same old story,' she said. 'It's all right for men but not for women.'

Shaking his head and smiling, Tom said, 'What? You think I was playing around in France, do you?'

'I'm talking about Scotland and them lovely nurses up there who, bless their hearts, are doing their best to make our soldiers feel as if they're at home. I'm talking about a nurse called Bridget.' There was a silence as Emmie waited for his excuse.

'Where's the letter?' he said, detaching himself from the guilt she was about to lay on him. Bridget must have written to him after all, and his mother intercepted it.

'I burned it. But not before reading it three times, if not four. Seems that she knows you quite well, son. She pleaded for you not to go AWOL. She said you'd easily get an extension for sick leave once she puts in her report as to how your knee's not healing as well as it might. She signed with love and kisses.'

'You 'ad no right to open my private post.'

'You 'ad no right to give my address to the girl. All's fair in love and war – that's what they say, isn't it?'

'War's hardly fair, Mother.'

'No, Tom, and neither is love, but there we are. It takes a strong character to come to terms with that. The girl spells trouble. You've not been home five minutes and she writes to you.' Emmie slowly shook her head.

'I hope you're not thinking of telling Jessie.' Tom kept up the deliberately indifferent tone.

'I hope you're gonna tell the Scot that you're well and truly married with a child to think of.'

'She knows that already. We're mates, that's all. She looks after me. After what I've been through I need *someone* to show a bit of compassion.'

'I'm sure you do, and I'm certain there'll always be someone around to show you more than that. It's nurses for the men and sailors for the lonely wives left at home. There you go. What's good for the goose is good for the gander.'

'All right. You've made your point.' Reaching for his crutches, Tom pointed one at her. 'You encourage Jessie to go out with her old boyfriend and I won't ever talk to you again.' He pulled himself up and glared at her. 'I can't help it if the nurse's got a crush on me. And she's not a silly cow, before you say it. She's a lovely girl with a tender heart. But lovely or not, I love Jessie. I'm not interested in another woman's body.'

Throwing her head back and laughing, Emmie waved him away. 'Poppycock. Bad leg or not, you've been getting your Scot's porridge oats. I'm no fool. I can read between the lines – not that she didn't want me to.'

'You can be bloody crude at times, Mother,' he said, making his way towards the street door.

'Tom!' Emmie waited for him to turn and face her. 'I don't expect you to turn down an offer here and there, be it in France or back here. The "live for today" sentiment is ripe everywhere over this bloody war so it's bound to affect you as well. Just don't be bloody stupid, that's all I'm saying. Don't listen to any talk of devotion.'

'Give over, woman. Tch. Things you come out with. Jessie's the only one for me. You just make sure she don't go seeing Max. If he turns up at our door, tell 'im to sling 'is hook.' Tom left, closing the door quietly behind him.

Gazing at the closed door, Emmie wondered about her son's behaviour while away from home. He had always been weak when it came to a pretty face. She looked across to Billy, now sound asleep, and remembered her own mother's saying, what will be will be, Emmie, what will be will be. Going on for seventy and having lost one son to the war and another to a French woman, Emmie felt that there was a force far greater than hers at work. Slipping into her sad mood again, she looked at her sleeping grandson for comfort but still found herself shedding a tear.

Meanwhile, next door, Tom was holding on to Jessie as if he might never see her again and he was trembling. Whether it was from shock of all he had seen and been through or because Emmie had made him feel deeply ashamed of himself was hard to say. 'I don't want to go back to Scotland, Jess,' he said. 'I don't want to go back to France to kill or be killed. I just want to stay here with you and be with my family.'

Easing him down on to the settee, Jessie hugged him as Tom held her tightly. 'Tom, I think this is shock coming out. Why don't I get your mum to fetch the doctor?'

'No. I don't need a doctor, I need my family. I don't want to go back. I want to stop here with you and our Billy.'

'Of course you do but you'll need a certificate from the doctor.'

'No. I've got to go back.' His mood had changed within seconds from alarm to passivity, almost as if he needed to hear Jessie say that he should stay. Relaxing his grip on her, he said, 'I'll be all right. A big cup of weak tea is what I need. That's what the nurse always says anyway. It seems to work.'

'Well, that's easily remedied. So, what about your mum and dad? They coming with us to the station?'

'I think so, yeah.' He looked up at her, unsure. 'You won't mind, will you?'

'Course I won't mind, daft. I'll see you soon enough, Tom. You'll get another sick leave before you join the ranks, I'll bet.'

'I hope so, Jess, I hope so.' They held each other tightly and tried not to think of the days of separation to come.

Chapter Three

As things turned out, Tom didn't get another sick leave before going back to war because on 23 August that same year, 1940, the blitz on London began. Although the Royal Air Force had increased their stock of Hurricanes and Spitfires, they could not compete in numbers with the German Luftwaffe, especially since so many British fighter planes had been lost in France and in covering the disastrous withdrawal from Dunkirk.

Even though much damage and suffering was inflicted on the buildings and people of London, Manchester, Liverpool and other British towns and villages, the Luftwaffe's concentration on cities rather than airfields enabled the RAF to train more pilots and build up essential stocks of aircraft.

The air raids on London and especially the East End caused even more families to evacuate to country villages throughout England. Jessie and Tom's family, however, like many others, were holding firm to their belief that it was safer to be at home where there were adequate air-raid shelters and where they could keep a keen eye on each other's welfare, terrifying though it was with bombs dropping from the sky and the loud wailing noise of the sirens giving warning of their arrival.

Through it all, young women, such as Jessie's sister Dolly and her girlfriends, were making the best of bad times and enjoying life to the full, taking turns at each other's houses playing the gramophone, singing noisily, dancing and enjoying the brandy and suchlike which had been given them by sailors on leave. Their way of handling the nightmare was to get too tipsy to worry about the bombs dropping around them. The next morning, after a good session, the girls would return to work at various offices and factories, often to find empty chairs and benches where workmates had sat, alive and well, before the bombing the night before.

Jessie wondered if perhaps her disapproval of her sister and her friends was misplaced. They were, after all, managing to make the most of a dire situation. 'Maybe I will come out with you one night, Doll,' she said thoughtfully one evening, 'to one of your friend's houses for a bit of a knees-up.'

'I should think so. Sitting in the blooming dark all the time,' sniffed Dolly, full of herself.

'I *don't* sit the dark. Once them blackout curtains are drawn, my lights go on.'

A wayward smile swept across Dolly's face. 'We 'ave such a laugh with them Dutch sailors. And I'll tell you something else you should think about as well. Get yourself a little job. Come and do part-time where I work, at my factory. I did the right thing leaving the buses. Used to kill my poor old feet. We could do with some more hands in the canteen, as it 'appens. Tom's mum would look after Billy, you know she would. Or his dad, come to that.'

'I might,' said Jessie, thinking about it and not for the first time. 'It sounds as if you 'ave as much fun there as you do when you go out at night.'

'I do.' Leaning forward, sipping her drink, Dolly winked at her sister. 'I push my tea trolley down and around them long lines of benches, handing out cups of tea and coffee and having a lovely chat, spreading the gossip as I go from one floor to the other. I make the factory buzz with news, Jess. They can't wait for me to come round.'

'Well, I s'pose someone's got to light up their life. Can't be much joy working in an ammunitions factory.'

'Don't you believe it. The girls are on a bonus system, don't forget. Busy, busy, busy, making sure that plenty of bullets and guns go out. They're doing their bit for the war effort and I'm doing mine as well. A lovely cup of tea and bit of a giggle is just what they need.' Dolly finished her own cup of tea. 'And then, after a good day's work—'

'A good time's had by all,' said Jessie, who had heard, more than once, how the girls from work would meet up in the evenings, dressed to kill with make-up on and hair brushed out, eyebrows plucked, cheeks rouged, lips painted bright red, and their legs covered with suntan lotion and lines drawn down the backs with an eyebrow pencil to portray stocking seams. Then they would go out in a happy group, arm in arm, talking ten to the dozen and cracking jokes, ready for a good night out on the tiles, while Jessie sat at home wondering if she would be running with Billy to the air-raid shelter that night.

'Tom wouldn't blame you for coming out now and then, Jess, surely?'

Miles away, Jessie answered blandly, 'I wouldn't bet on it.'

Sensing her sister's melancholy mood, Dolly went quiet. Jessie was thinking about Tom and what he might be going through out there in France. He had been sent back to war as a Royal Engineer. The War Office had sent out a circular to commands in the United Kingdom asking for volunteers for special service of an undefined and hazardous nature. It was the words 'Courage, physical endurance, initiative and resource, activity, marksmanship, self-reliance, and an aggressive spirit towards the war' which had sparked Tom's enthusiasm and caused him to sign up. Once he'd got over the shock of Dunkirk, he was filled with a passion for revenge.

'I do worry about Tom, you know,' said Jessie quietly. 'I don't believe that leg would 'ave healed up by now. Not enough to go back out there and—'

'Don't be daft,' said Dolly, cutting in. 'They wouldn't have let him go back if that was the case.' Standing up and brushing herself down, Dolly slipped into her bossy mode. 'Come on. Let's go and get some fresh air. It's lovely and sunny out there.' She looked at Billy fast asleep in his pushchair. 'We'll take the sprat to see his granny. Mum was only saying this morning how she'd love to see more of him. He is her only grandchild, Jess.'

'She'll be at the shop, Dolly, and Saturdays are always busy, you know that. She'll only feel bad if she can't give us the time of day, especially—'

'Oh, shut up. It's Mum you're talking about, not some blooming stranger. Go and brush your sodding hair and let's be off.' With that, Dolly opened the front door and carefully eased the pushchair through it and outside into the street and the sunshine. 'Fetch a clean bottle and we can boil some milk in the back room of the shop.'

'Aye, aye, captain,' chaffed Jessie, not sorry to be told what to do. 'I'll just have a quick wash and brush-up. Pop next door and tell Emmie where we re going and that we'll be back in an hour or so. You know what a worry-guts she is.'

Once Jessie had washed her face and given her hair a good brushing, she put on some make-up and had to admit that the time it took and the difference it made was worth it. On the way to their mother's cobbler shop, the girls speculated as to what their sister, Hannah, might be doing right then. She gave away nothing in her letters. It was difficult to imagine what secret government work was like, especially when Hannah's letters stayed resolutely off the subject and talked about the weather instead. The conversation turned to their younger brothers, Alfie and Stephen. In Dolly's opinion, Alfie, although wayward, was probably the sharpest of them all. 'You've gotta admit, Jess, 'e's quick off the mark. And 'e's got a wit on 'im, that's for sure.'

'He may be bright but there's other qualities just as important. He would never 'ave made a Boy Scout like Stephen. Maybe, once this war's over,' said Jessie with a touch of hope in her voice, 'Alfie'll use his brain for more honest work and make something of 'imself. And maybe, when that time comes, our Stephen will be a proper qualified actor. Performing up west.'

'We'll see,' said Dolly, 'only don't expect Stephen to get married, Jess, will yer, 'cos as sure as God made little green apples, that ain't gonna 'appen.'

'I don't expect anything of any of us, Doll. What's the point? Anyway, we all know that Stephen's a born bachelor. I think we've all realised that. And we don't love him any the less for it.'

'Mum too?' said Dolly carefully, wondering if Jessie realised what she had been inferring.

'Mum?' said Jessie, raising one eyebrow and smiling. 'She's not daft. If you ask me, she clocked it years ago. I think Dad did as well. Anyway, he'll be all right. He'll be our famous brother one day, you'll see.'

The girls made their way to Rose's shop and were greeted with a welcoming smile and hug from both their mother and Mrs Cohen from the delicatessen next door. Enjoying the sunshine, the women had been having a natter outside.

'Jessie, sweetheart, I haven't seen you in such a while!' Ginny Cohen turned to Rose. 'She looks wonderful, Rose! Look at her. And Dolly too! They look so good together,' she said, her face full of expression. 'Their father would be so proud, God rest his soul. What would we do without them? Our children. Blessed? I should say we are.'

'Hello, Mrs Cohen,' said Jessie. 'How's Mr Cohen?'

'Don't ask. He drives me mad with his worrying over this and over that. Listen,' she flicked her hand at the open doorway of her delicatessen, 'go and say hello to that son of mine. He'll be happy to see you.' Her smile expressed her heartfelt feelings. She had wanted Max and Jessie to be married and had been disappointed when the engagement was broken.

'Max is in your shop?'

'Going through the books, darling. Didn't I always say he would make a wonderful accountant? That boy can turn figures around and make it look as if we're on poor street. Not that we're rich, you understand.'

By now Rose had Billy out of the pushchair and in her arms, smothering him with kisses. 'Leave them alone, Ginny. Let me have my daughters for five minutes at least, before you sneak them off me.'

'You go in, Doll, and put the kettle on. I'll just go and say hello to Max,' said Jessie, disappearing into the Cohens' shop and leaving Max's mother to gaze after her.

'It gets you here, doesn't it?' said Ginny, patting her heart. 'I don't think they stopped loving each other. They should have been married. But who can argue with God? He has a lot to answer for but who can argue with Him?'

Amused by her melodramatic ways, Dolly started to laugh. 'How's your old man, Ginny?'

'Leo? Ha. No different. He still grunts exhausted while I'm chopping the bloody logs. Lazy? Don't start me off. Leave me be. I've got work to do. I'll see you later, Rose.' She turned to a waiting customer and began her usual sales talk. Today she was trying to persuade people that powdered eggs were good for them and that was the reason she was selling them at a special price to her regulars.

Peeping through the small window which looked from the delicatessen into the small back room where Max was working at a kitchen table covered with books and receipts, Jessie felt her heart lurch. Tapping on the window, she grinned as he looked up at her.

Taken by surprise, he was quick off his chair and opened the door, smiling shyly at her. 'You're a sight for sore eyes,' he said, rubbing his own. 'You wouldn't believe the way my parents run this business. A thousand bits of paper which they call receipts.' Same old Max, thought Jessie. Same old lovable Max who still managed to cover his true feelings. He was glad to see her but had to try and hide it. 'I don't suppose you fancy coming to the cafe for a bite to eat? I was just about to go when you arrived. I'm starving.'

'You've taken the words out of my mouth, Max. Not that I came to drag you away from important work…'

'Work can wait. Come on.' He took Jessie's arm and led her outside as easy as if they were still a courting couple. 'We'll go to that new Italian coffee shop down the Highway, give him a bit of support. No one goes near the place since the war started. And I know what that feels like. I suppose your mother's got the baby.'

'Yep. Billy's in safe hands.'

'Good.'

'So the books must wait now? Now that Jessie's arrived?' said Ginny who was known for her natural nagging ways. 'His snout gets a whiff of Jessie's scent and away he goes. He's been eating custard with a fork since the day you married, Jessie, did you know that?'

Directing Jessie away from his mother, even Max had to smile. 'Go and brush your best tooth, woman,' he said, knowing that would bring a peal of laughter from his father who was serving a customer. Taking Jessie's hand, Max told her to run. Enjoying the fun of it, Jessie gripped his hand and together they ran off like a couple of teenagers.

'You see how he takes after his father. Please God my son's brain won't slip down to his feet too. At least he doesn't have his father's legs. You can't trust a man with short legs.' Ginny was enjoying herself, amusing the group of customers waiting, performing as if she were on stage. Considering there was a war on, the mood was light-hearted – until the sound of the air-raid siren filled the streets.

'Oh my God, not again,' were the only words uttered by an ageing woman who looked too tired to run to one of the purpose-built brick shelters. 'Let it come. Let it blow me to smithereens. I've had enough.' The others weren't listening. The Broadway was filled with people running in all directions, some heading for their homes and their own Anderson shelter, others making for public refuge buildings, terrified that all the shelters might be filled before they got there. Screams and shouting as mothers called for their children, telling them to run with them and to keep up, filled the streets.

'Jessie! Jessie, come back!' screeched Dolly. 'Don't leave us!' For all her forthright ways, Dolly lost all confidence when there was an air attack. 'Jessie!' Grabbing Dolly's arm, with Billy clinging on to her, Rose ordered her daughter down into the cellar of the shop. It had an electric light and camp beds and tinned food. 'Leave her!' said Rose sharply. 'They'll go to the nearest shelter. Billy's safe with us. There's enough time for all of us to get to safety.' Rose was calm and collected, remembering an old saying, keep your head while those about you are losing theirs.

'What if she comes back and we've bolted the door?' Dolly was trembling from head to toe. 'We didn't bring our gas masks!'

'We won't need them!'

'What if she can't get in and a bomb drops? What if—'

'Come inside!' yelled Rose. 'Now!'

As if in a trance, Dolly did as ordered and followed Cobbler George and his apprentice down into the cellar. Still outside on the pavement and holding on tight to her grandson, Rose stepped towards the woman who was too weary or too traumatised to move. Gently taking her arm she invited her down into the basement, quietly giving words of comfort as they went. Billy, overawed by it all, was not only babbling but smiling too. To him this was some kind of a game.

Caught up in the rush of people coming and going in all directions, Jessie and Max had had no choice but to go down into one of the public shelters. Max held her close as they sat in a quiet corner where they huddled together. Everybody was hoping that the air-raid warden would soon come and give them the all clear, but after three hours he had not arrived and the horror of what might be happening above was deep in the minds of the people.

'They warned that there might be an unrelenting attack on the way,' murmured Jessie. 'I think this is it, Max. I think this is it.'

Squeezing her arm, and drawing her closer, Max kissed Jessie's forehead and told her to try not to worry and that the attack would soon be over. 'I know you're worried sick about Billy, Jess, but you know he'll be safe with your mother in her basement. They're better off there than in here. Look at them, Jess. Women, the old folk and the young, some crying and some silent and terrified. It only wants one of them to start a panic. Just one to start screaming for fresh air.' He wrapped both arms round her and leaned back, doing his best to make her feel snug and comfortable. 'Try and get some sleep.'

She nestled up to him, breathing in the old familiar scent of him, and closed her eyes. 'I won't be able to sleep, Max. How can anyone sleep knowing that Stepney might be blown to bits by the time we go up from here?'

'Not sleep, doze. It'll help the time go by and stop you worrying… everything will be the same when we go up.'

'I'll doze if you will,' said Jessie, trying to lighten their mood.

'I intend to, Jess. After all, this may be the only chance I'll get of sleeping with you.'

Smiling at his cheek, she laid her head on his chest and slipped into a very light sleep, leaving Max with every intention of staying awake. Every second, with his Jessie so close to him like this, he would relish. If he could turn back the clock to the day they broke off their engagement, he would. At the time he'd believed that they would get back together after a few weeks apart but he hadn't bargained on her meeting Tom.

The several hours of waiting in a stuffy atmosphere filled with sweaty bodies and frightened children should have dragged, but not for Max. It seemed no time at all until the sound of the handbell from above could be heard and the voice of the warden calling, 'All clear! All clear! Fresh tea being served outside! All clear!'

'Where am I?' murmured Jessie, her voice husky and frightened. 'What's happening?'

'It's all right, Jess. It's over. The air raid's over. We can go.'

'Max?' She peered into his face, not properly awake.

'That's right. It's me. But don't worry, nothing happened – not with all of this lot around us,' he said, smiling at her.

Rubbing her eyes, Jessie remembered and sat bolt upright. 'Billy! My baby, Max! My baby!'

'He's with your mother and sister. They'll have taken care of him, you know that.'

'And Stephen. What about Stephen? He wasn't with us. What's happened to Stephen?'

'He's probably at home and in your mother's Anderson shelter, fast asleep. No doubt she's got beds and bedding enough for all of you in there.'

'We've got to go.' Jessie straightened up and looked around her. 'How did we all manage to fit in here, never mind fall asleep?'

'People always manage when there's a crisis. Thank God. Come on.' He stood up and offered a hand. 'Dawn will have broken so you'd best cover your eyes from the light of the sun when we emerge from here.'

Arriving at their parents' shops, Jessie and Max found their mothers outside, peering at the crowds of people who had emerged from shelters and were making their way home, silent and shocked. Shops and houses, buildings and factories dotted along the Broadway were alight. 'Jubilee Buildings have gone!' howled one old woman. 'They bombed Jubilee Buildings! I've just heard! Did anyone else hear that? Is it true?' The poor woman was beside herself. 'Where am I to go? What am I to do?'

Normally someone would have comforted her, but her cry mingled with others who had heard from the wardens which streets had been hit. People were running to their homes, praying they would have been the luckier ones. It was a pitiful sight. Horror, panic and dread everywhere.

'Jessie!' Rose called to her daughter, crying with relief and shock. 'Thank God you're safe!' Falling into her mother's outstretched arms, Jessie began to cry and then tremble. She managed to ask if everyone was all right. Hugging and patting her daughter, Rose repeated herself over and over. 'They're safe, we're all safe… Billy slept through most of it.' Then, thanking Max for taking care of Jessie, Rose took her inside the shop and Jessie glanced back over her shoulder to see that Max was wrapped in Ginny's arms and his father was kissing his face, thanking God for not taking his beloved son.

–

Later, with Dolly by her side, Jessie wheeled Billy in the pushchair through the streets, passing people as they gazed at their burning homes, crying. The fire brigade worked fast, hosing the flames and the bells of fire engines and ambulances rang all about, alerting shocked people to get out of the roads and make way for them. Neither of the girls spoke. Dolly was wondering what she would find when she arrived home and Jessie was scared for Stephen and Alfie. 'What if the boys weren't at home, Doll? What if they couldn't get down a shelter in time?'

'Are you kidding? Alfie would 'ave pushed his way in somewhere and someone would have pulled our Stephen into safety. You know the reaction he gets from people with that little-boy-lost face of his. They'll be all right,' she said, unconvinced by her own words.

It wasn't until they approached a turning which led to Jessie's street that the girls realised just how bad things were in Bethnal Green. The Luftwaffe had had a field day and the East End of London had been its main target on this particular raid. Some of the terraced houses along the way and frighteningly close to where Jessie lived were either burning or flattened, with bits of furniture lying everywhere.

'God, Dolly,' said Jessie at last, 'I hope Emmie and Charlie are safe. You know what they're like, they won't leave their little house for anything. They hide in the cupboard under the stairs and 'ope for the best.'

'I didn't know that. Silly sods. A cupboard's not gonna help 'em if the roof caves in, is it?'

Turning the comer into Grant Street, the girls stopped and stared at the devastation, at Jessie's neighbours, at the piles of smoking rubble where houses once stood. A neighbour whose house had not received a direct hit but whose windows and doors had been blown out by the impact was running from the scene in a shocked state. Finding Jessie amidst all the others, she laid a hand on her arm. 'They think they're still in there, Jess. We tried to get them to come with us to Bethnal Green tube' shelter but they wouldn't. They wouldn't even go down the road to the big Anderson in old man Lipka's stables. You know how stubborn Emmie and Charlie can be.'

Jessie was too shocked to answer. From where she stood she could see that her own house, and the houses on either side, had received a direct hit. The fire brigade had put out the flames but the roof on Tom and Jessie's house had caved in and part of the front of the house had gone. There were bricks and rubble everywhere and Jessie could see right through into the shambles of her front room.

'Oh, Jess,' wailed Dolly, 'look at your lovely home.' Finding it all too much, she began to cry, which started Billy off. 'Come on, Jess, we'll go home. Mum'll fix you up.'

'No. You take Billy for me. I've got to sort everything out. Sweep up and that. Pick up the furniture and fix it.' Jessie spoke in a monosyllabic voice. 'I'll put a sheet up the front or some polythene in case it rains. Then I'll tidy up and... tidy up and...' She looked at the space where her front door had been. 'I wonder if the stairs are still there. How am I gonna get up to the bedrooms to clear up if there's no staircase?'

'Don't, Jess,' said Dolly, trying her best to be mature. 'Don't fall apart on me. You're the strong one. Come on—'

The sudden shouts of joy as both Emmie and Charlie were brought out from their house by the firemen stopped Dolly in her tracks.

'Trust them,' said Jessie, relieved. 'Trust them to defy the odds against survival. Look at the pair of 'em, covered in dust and still smiling.'

'Jess,' said Dolly, 'Charlie's cradling a baby.' And so he was.

It turned out that a young mother, who lived in cheap rented rooms just four doors along, had dumped her baby into Charlie's arms. She had her hands full coping with her landlord's deaf aunt. Waking the slow-witted aunt was a strict order from her landlord. If she did not carry out the task, she would be evicted. But the young mother had found it impossible to see to the old aunt and collect all she needed for herself and her baby before getting them both to safety. And all of this had to be done to the terrifying sound of the air-raid siren. She had got the cantankerous old woman up, dressed and out of the house, and then gone back for the things she would need for herself and her baby. In her haste she forgot the pram, so she handed her baby to Charlie and rushed back for it. It was a fatal mistake.

'They found her covered in rubble and clinging on to the handle of baby Sarah's pram. Poor cow. The lot of us were crying when they carried her away. So young. What a waste. Dreadful.'

The neighbours' words drifted across Jessie's head. She didn't want to think about dead people or orphaned babies. She didn't want to think of what might have been if Dolly hadn't persuaded her out of the house.

'What do you want to do, Jess? Come back to Mum's with me or stop here while I look after Billy?'

'I don't know what's for the best, Dolly. Is it safer for me and Billy to stop here with Emmie and Charlie or go home to Mum's? I don't know. I could sleep upstairs in my bedroom with. Billy by my side if the staircase *is* still there...'

Realising that her sister was in shock, Dolly took on the role of supervisor. 'Come on. Charlie and Emmie have gone back inside with the Red Cross. Once they've been checked over and given a cup of tea, they'll bounce back. You know what they're like. You can come back later and stop with them while the authorities sort out your place.'

Allowing Dolly to take over, Jessie lifted Billy from his pushchair and pacified him. 'I'll make him a bottle up in Emmie's first.'

'Good idea.'

'I think I'd rather stop with Emmie and Charlie tonight. That way I can sweep up. I could get my place in order and—'

'No. Leave it. We'll come back first thing in the morning and do it together. Look at you, you've 'ardly 'ad any sleep all night, I'll bet. You can sleep at Emmie's tomorrow night after we've got all your furniture out of there and in storage.'

'Whatever you say, Dolly, whatever you say.'

–

The next morning, after snatching a couple of hours' sleep at Rose's house, Jessie, pushing Billy in the pushchair, made her way to Emmie's. As she turned into her street, the full weight of the tragedy hit home and she began to cry. Her lovely home had been ruined.

Emmie and Charlie did what they could to raise her spirits, saying that the borough would compensate and the front of the house could easily be put right. She smiled faintly at them and nodded but in her heart she knew that things were worse than that. The roof had caved in, so her bedrooms would be full of rubble and the furniture smashed. The sight of Billy's cot crushed under debris was something she didn't want to see.

'You'll be all right, cock,' said Charlie, sipping a glass of beer. 'We'll soon 'ave your place tickety-boo. Our windows are gonna be put in order today and they're sending a bloke round first thing this morning to put on a new front door. I'll 'ave a word in 'is ear to crack on with your place as soon as poss. Don't you fret, gal, we'll sort you out.' He sniffed, gazed out, then shook his head. 'They wouldn't let us adopt that little baby girl, you know. We saved 'er life, taking 'er in our little cupboard under the stairs. But they wouldn't let us keep 'er. Cruel bastards. We'd 'ave given 'er all the love we can't give our boys any more, wouldn't we, Em?'

'Don't talk rot, Charlie! Keep a six-month-old baby at our age? Silly sod,' Emmie scoffed.

'You're as young as you feel, woman. An' I don't feel me age. No way. I'll be sixty-eight this year, Jess. Bet you didn't know that. People take me for fifty-five. Most people. Well, some. Old Mrs Kent down Cobble Alley does anyway.' Charlie was fine. Charlie had been at the whisky bottle before Emmie had even got out of her bed.

'I know what I'd like to do to that poor girl's landlord,' said Emmie, preoccupied. 'Poor little cow.'

'He had her waiting hand and foot on that old aunt of his, running errands come rain or snow, and for what? For a couple of dingy rooms at low rent. If Tom was back home he'd sort the rotter out.'

'The old aunt is an eccentric, Jess. Did you know that?' grinned Charlie. 'Worth a fortune, by all accounts, but won't spend a penny of it on 'erself – or anyone else, come to that. And her nephew the landlord is her only living relative. And *that*, Emmie, is why he got young Mary to run round after 'er, so he could stay in her good books but do fuck all for 'er 'imself. Lovely looking woman and no more than nineteen, if that. Her 'usband's in for a shock, all right. What a life, eh? Out there fighting for his country and his wife gets killed while he's doing it. *Bloody* war!'

'Anyway, enough of that, Charlie,' Emmie said, firmly. 'We're s'posed to be cheering our Jessie up, not putting 'er down. Our Jessie and Billy's the ones we've gotta think about now, eh, Jess? Have you thought what your next step'll be?'

'Not much to think about, is there, Em? My house has been bombed. There's no roof, holes in the walls and my furniture's in bits. It was second-hand but it was lovely and in good condition.'

'It won't *all* be ruined, love, and you will be compensated, in time,' said Emmie, choked.

'I don't care any more. I don't want to know. All I want, really, is to run away from it all. As far away as possible. Take Billy with me.'

'Now then, now then,' said Charlie in a fatherly fashion. 'We can't have that kind of talk. If Tom was here—'

'But he's not here, is he! I've got to think for myself. I can't write to him and he can't write to me so I've got to work it out. And it don't take much working out, does it? I'll just have to take our Billy and evacuate to the country. A nice quiet village where we'll be safe.' Charlie shook his head, a measured expression on his face. 'No need to go that far, Jess. Our grandson's a Londoner and London's where he should be. You can move into the spare room.'

Jessie shook her head. Suddenly she didn't think she could bear to stay in London, where bombs fell and inno-cent people were killed. 'No. Thanks all the same but no,

Charlie. My mind's made up. I'm going. I'll go round to the People's Palace and report what's happened to my home. According to what I've read and heard, they'll come round and pack everything into crates and boxes. It happened to one of Max's friends. Her 'ouse went the same way as mine and they came up trumps. They went to the 'ouse and collected everything and delivered it to a relative where she's staying.'

'Yeah, and took the best bits for themselves, no doubt,' said Charlie, unconvinced.

'No. Not according to Max. There wasn't a thing missing. Not one thing. And they'd wrapped all the bits up. Not a teaspoon or cup missing. She expected a few disappearances but no, not one thing was missing.'

'Well,' said Emmie, 'it sounds as if your mind's made up, Jess,'

'Yeah, Em, it is. Mum and Granny Ingrid are thinking of doin' the same. Maybe we'll end up in the same village, who knows?' Jessie thumbed her wedding ring. 'Don't worry, I'll write straightaway and let you know where I am so we can keep in touch and you can tell Tom when he comes back on leave. If he comes home on leave.'

'So,' said Charlie warily, 'Max. He's thinking of evacuating to this village as well, is he?'

The pointed remark riled Jessie but she loved Charlie and understood how he felt. 'Of course not. He's needed here. He's a good Home Guard, you know.'

'Pity he's not out there being a good soldier. Still, I suppose if he's a *pacifist*—'

'He's not a pacifist, Charlie. He was gutted when the army turned him down. He can't help his feet, can he?'

'Feet?'

'Yeah. He's got two left feet.'

Charlie leaned back in his chair and peered at her. 'He's what?'

'You heard,' said Emmie, stifling her laughter. 'Now leave it be.'

'Two left feet?'

'Yes! Now shut up and go and pour us another cup of tea!'

Thankful for an excuse to leave the room, Charlie went into the scullery and his strangled laughter could be heard loud and clear. Smiling, Jessie sucked on her bottom lip. 'I suppose it is funny. Poor sod.'

'It is, Jess. I'm sorry, love, I know you was once engaged to 'im but... the thought of seeing a pair of left feet...' Emmie's cheeks flushed and her eyes sparkled before she burst with laughter, 'Oh dear,' she said, wiping her eyes.

'You will come and visit me, won't you, Em? When I get evacuated? I'll need you and Charlie to brighten me. You and your sense of humour.' Jessie treasured her mother-in-law's warmth.

'You can bank on it, love. We'll be there. Just don't expect us to sleep on a straw bed, will you? Make sure there's a spare mattress around, eh?'

'Course I will, Emmie. That'll be in the forefront of my mind when I'm looking for lodgings.'

'Yeah...' said Emmie, leaning back and allowing her imagination to run riot. 'Get yourself into a nice little cottage or farmhouse with roses all round the front porch.'

Charlie came back into the room and sat in his favourite armchair. 'You wouldn't listen, would you?' he said. 'I said we should 'ave used our savings to bugger off to New Zealand but oh no, you 'ad to go and 'ave us all buying a bloody two-up, two-down. I said there'd be a war. I said the East End would be the first hit. I said—'

'Oh, shut up,' said Emmie, a touch guilty. He was right but now was not the time to say so. 'You'll be smiling once the war's over. A man of property – it's what you always dreamed of, once, when you had a bit more gusto.'

'Didn't do our Johnnie much good, did it? There stands his little house and where's he? Six foot under. Who's gonna repair his blown windows? Answer me that.'

'The state, of course. All these houses'll be repaired and painted up better than they was before the bomb dropped. Anyway, what good would the money in the bank be to Johnnie now? You answer *me* that. At least he's left a legacy for his nephew. We'll look after that place and let it out till our Billy's old enough to want his own place.'

'Dream on, Emmie. Dream on.' Charlie's mood was gloomy. 'Jessie's got the right idea. We should all bloody well emigrate to the countryside.'

'*Evacuate,*' said Emmie. 'The word is *evacuate,* Charlie.'

'I couldn't care less what the fucking word is. Just get me out of London. All I want is peace and calm, slow-witted carrot crunchers. That'll do me. Fix it for us, would you, Jess?'

'Leave her be. She's got enough to think about,' said Emmie, hating the thought of leaving the East End, even with the dangers.

'I'll check it out. It might be too quiet for you, Charlie. Too quiet and boring for all of us.'

Jessie made her way back to her mother's. All she wanted right then was to cuddle Billy. Cuddle her baby and thank God that they had both survived another air raid.

During her walk back to the house she'd grown up in, the aftermath of the raid was evident all around her. She passed several houses that had also had a direct hit from a bomb and families were going over the smouldering rubble, looking for their belongings and for their loved ones buried under the debris. Jessie felt as if she was drifting through someone's nightmare – it all seemed so unreal. And no one was talking. Children and the very old were coughing, spluttering and shedding tears but there was hardly any other sound. Shock had created an awesome hush.

Jessie thought back to when she was huddled in a corner of the shelter, in the warm and comforting arms of Max, and before she could stop herself she was turning left instead of right and making her way along the Broadway back to Max. She wasn't even considering an excuse. All she wanted was to feel his arms round her again, his warm body close to hers, taking away the grief. He still was, it would seem, her very best friend who understood better than anyone the way she felt. Yes, that's what Max was, her good friend and her comforter. And for that she loved him. Yes, thought Jessie, I do love Max. I always have and always will. Not in the same way as I love Tom. That's different.

Remembering all the times they had enjoyed together before they broke off their engagement, Jessie found that she was standing outside his mother's shop before she realised. She looked from the open doorway to the shoe mender's, which was padlocked. Rose had stayed home. Gazing at the boots crammed in a heap in the window and still in her unreal world, Jessie sensed Max there before she saw him. Turning slowly, she looked into his sad brown eyes and she saw more than sorrow at what had happened all around them – she saw love. Max still loved her.

'Jess.' Max could hardly speak he was so choked. 'Jess, I...'

'I know,' she said. 'I know.'

He gently took her hand, lifted it to his mouth, and lightly kissed her. 'Don't shut me out, that's all I ask. I won't make demands, I won't pester you, I won't even say how I feel, but please, please, don't shut me out.'

Smiling at his daft ways, she opened her arms to him. How long they stood locked together, drawing comfort, Jessie couldn't say, but she didn't want those moments to end because once again that feeling of warmth filled her. In his arms she felt safe. Safe and secure. 'I just wanted to come back,' she said. 'I wanted to see you.'

'That's what I wanted and it's enough. That's all I want, Jess. Just come and say hello to me now and again.'

'I will.' She slowly drew away from him and nodded, then to stop herself from crying again, she smiled and winked at him. 'Be there,' she said, 'just be there when I do come back.'

Chapter Four

Elmshill, a sleepy village in the heart of Norfolk, seemed to Jessie exactly the place to hide away during the turmoil of war. And while she was packing those of her and Billy's clothes which had survived the blast, the villagers in the small hamlet were preparing to receive evacuees who were to arrive that day, Jessie and Billy included. The entire village was in a state of fervour. It was the most exciting thing to happen for years.

The small, winding lane leading to the village hall was sprinkled with small groups, official attendants and unofficial helpers, sightseers and gossips who could hardly contain their excitement about the forthcoming event. The retired colonel and village bore, Geoffrey Maitland, was having one of the best days of his life, striding from one group to another, repeating his drawn-out anecdotes, nose to the sky.

'I should think they *were* smiling – behind his *back*,' jibed Cyril the lay preacher.

'Laughing, more like. Silly old bugger,' said one of the elders, Alice Davey, a woman who knew far more about the ways of people than the colonel.

Mrs Hilldrop, who ran the post office, turned to the rotund woman who had been born and bred in the village and was looking forward to her sixtieth birthday. 'What you say then, Alice? You going to pick and choose who you'll be heving?'

'That I shall, my dear. That I shall. I'm too old in the *tooth* to be told what I must do. I'll see for myself, my dear, that I *shall*.'

And so it went on, each of the villagers taking their stance as to the way they would deal with the incomers. And once the village hall key holder arrived to unlock, the women filed in, carrying bunches of flowers and clean, starched tablecloths. They had no intention of having the London folk saying they couldn't put on a good show and a good tea. Cakes were baking in ovens in cottages, while in the big houses sandwiches were being made up and wrapped in waxed paper.

The village, like others surrounding it, was a safe haven and one could forgive the locals for sometimes overlooking the fact that some towns in Britain were in the grip of war. Nevertheless, they were in their own way preparing themselves for an attack. The Home Guard took its role very seriously and the presence of the ARP was a reminder that some parts of Britain were under heavy attack. Wardens had been appointed and there had already been a series of lectures on gas, in the market town of Diss, six miles away, though the talks were not taken too seriously. After all, as one man said, 'I doubt they'll go to the trouble of sending a fleet over to drench a tiny village like Elmshill with gas.'

'What you say then, Alice?' said Mrs Hilldrop as she filled the big kettles in the village hall kitchen. 'Will those London kiddies be smelly and running with fleas?' Shaking her head worriedly, she struck a match and lit the Calor gas stove. 'You hear such things…'

'We'll jest hev to wait and see, my dear,' returned Alice as she straightened a gleaming white tablecloth over one of the trestle tables. 'We mustn't go putting them down before they get here. I dare say they'll be hot and bothered when they do arrive. I don't remember an August as hot as this one, that I don't.'

'I wouldn't put anyone down, Alice, you know that, but it's what they're saying at the Women's Institute. That toffee-nosed Mrs Linton who run the drapery at Blackgrave say they shouldn't be allowed. She say they'll contaminate the rest of our young 'uns if not the *entire* village.'

'Well, I don't know about that.' Alice's tone was an indication that this line of conversation should stop right there. The woman had no time for gossips and wasn't going to propagate anyone's drivel.

'Oh ah, we got company then?' said Mrs Hilldrop, tipping her head sideways. 'You look who's arrived.'

Glancing over her shoulder, Alice rolled her eyes. It was the colonel's wife from the Hall. Dressed in her smart red and grey suit with hat to match, she looked rather out of place. A determined clap of her hands brought them all to attention. 'Good afternoon, ladies! May I say how wonderful it is to see you all *doing your bit*! Now I know how busy you all are and how much work there is to be done so I shan't keep you! But before I come around and check my list as to which of you have surplus rooms which might not yet be allocated to our friends from London, I just want to say a *very* big thank you to each and every one of you! Well done!' With a false smile to turn any stomach, the colonel's wife kept her expression fixed as she made her way from one lady to the next, checking her list and ticking off where necessary.

'It's no wonder they call her face-ache. How long she gonna keep up that daft grin? Who the hell does she think she is? She en't got no reason to thank *us*. What we do we do out of our *own* free will. That we do,' Alice said.

'She thinks she's the ruddy queen's *cousin*, that one. I can't take to the woman, Alice, that I *can't*. She rile me so. I jest hope she don't come poking around *me* with her lists. I said I would take two and that I *shall*. Two little uns or one and its mother. I've only got that *one* spare room out the back. I shan't pack them in like they were carrots in a ruddy crate, that I *shan't*.'

'You mustn't let her get to you, my dear. Take no heed. Just you nod and then do what you want when they *do* get here. I shall. I shall take who I think I can get on with and to hell with anyone who say different.'

'She won't say much to you, Alice. She know you're top of the tree in this village. How long she and the old bore of a husband bin here then? Two year, if *that*. If I had my—' A sudden clapping of the hands by the colonel's wife stopped her mid-sentence.

'If I may have your attention, ladies! No long speeches, I promise!'

Alice rolled her eyes but remained silent, waiting, as did the others. The village hall had gone quiet again.

'As you know, we are expecting our guests to arrive some time late this afternoon. They will be arriving by bus and we'll see mothers accompanying their children; the blind, cripples and expectant women. Older children without escorts will also be on board, good management at the London end provided!'

'Sounds to me as if half are coming for a holiday and the other half to *die*!' Mrs Hilldrop remarked loudly to laughter.

'Now then, ladies…' Clasping her hands and locking her fingers, the colonel's wife waited for the laughter to die.

'Sound like we should hev been knitting matinee jackets as well as darning socks, *ladies*! What you say?' More laughter.

'Don't you nor the colonel fret yourselves, Mrs Maitland. We'll sort things out when the time come. You don't want to go worrying over us. We know what we're a doin'. That we do.'

'I have no doubts about that whatsoever, Mrs Davey. I just wanted to reaffirm—'

'That's settled then,' said Alice. 'We know what we're about. Now why don't you stop for a nice cup of tea? We'll find you a nice china cup in that cupboard. And you might like a biscuit as well. You are welcome in here, my dear, whenever you feel like coming in. The hall is for *everyone* who live in the village and some who don't.'

'Thank you. You're very kind.' The colonel's wife looked at her wristwatch. 'Goodness. Is that the time? Well, I must be on my way, ladies. Good luck and very well done!'

'Thank the Lord in heaven she's *gone*,' said Alice. 'Ruddy woman. She's brought us all down now.'

'Don't be so daft, Alice. Course she en't.'

'All that talk about blind people and cripples. We en't equipped to help people like *that*. You can't step sideways in the dark without falling in a ditch or a dike, good eyesight or not. What *must* they be thinking?'

'Well, I don't know about all of *that*. But I do know there are that many rumours goin' round, rumours that we can't choose who we take in. Cyril say some of them'll be the wives of convicts. I said he shouldn't be so *daft*, but

I doubt he was far wrong. I shan't worry over it We'll jest hev to see what arrives on that bus. That's all we can do. Although I might say I am wearing this headscarf to be on the safe side.'

Alice rubbed her aching leg and looked around the hall for a chair. 'Well, I shan't let them interfere, that I shan't. Between you and me, I had a lovely letter from the mother I'm taking in and her bed's already made up. A young mother and her baby. Her husband's a soldier out there fighting.' Pulling a chair out from under a trestle table, she sat down. 'I liked the sound of that young woman. Mrs Smith. Mrs Jessie Smith.'

'I'll go to hell – *Smith!* Well, if that en't a rum thing. We got more Smiths in this village than anywhere else I know. You don't think she's got *family* here then, Alice?'

'No, she en't got family here. I wrote a letter and asked. No, she's a London girl. And a very nice young lady by my recognising. Her baby's called Billy and he's sixteen months old.'

'Well, he en't no more a baby than I'm an old woman. I should think he'll be walking b'now. You've taken on something there, Alice gal, that you hev!'

Just after five o'clock the busload of London mothers and assorted children, from babies in arms to five-year-olds, approached the village church where the official helpers were waiting. Flagging down the bus driver, the colonel's wife gave him instructions to make his way down Church Lane to the village hall. Tired from his journey and fed up with the sound of crying babies, complaining mothers and excited children, he simply nodded and continued on his way. From where Jessie was sitting she had a clear view of the colonel who stood upright behind his wife as if he were on guard. She couldn't help smiling.

She also couldn't help noticing the good-looking young man who stood beside the colonel and who, on her reckoning, was probably in his early thirties. This was Rupert Maitland, the colonel's son. Jessie could see that he was suppressing a smile. Catching Jessie's eye, Rupert glanced at his father and rolled his eyes. Jessie smiled back, understanding that the young man was mocking his father's military bearing. It was odd yet comforting to share this private Joke with a stranger. Especially through the window of a crowded bus.

It took two hours for registration and billeting papers to be handed out. The women were hot and tired from the journey and their children were demanding and very noisy. Those minors who had arrived without parents, looked drawn and frightened. The village hall was packed with arrivals and helpers and stopping a crisis from becoming a drama seemed unlikely. But in their own unhurried way the villagers sorted everyone out and by seven thirty the evacuees had been marshalled into small groups and taken off in cars, carts, trailers and tractors and anything else which had wheels which could take them to their temporary homes. By then, everyone was drained from the long and exhausting day, including Jessie who was carrying the sleeping Billy in her arms, while Jack, Alice Davey's 56-year-old brother, walked ahead, carrying her bags and suitcase.

'My cottage is no palace,' said Alice, walking beside Jessie, 'but there's a welcome mat at my door and I shouldn't like it if you didn't make yourself at *home*.'

'All I want is a bed, Mrs Davey,' murmured Jessie, too tired to make polite conversation. 'Billy can sleep with me. We won't be any trouble.'

'Don't you go worrying about that. There's one for you and one for the child. His is no more than a cot bed but it has a good clean flock mattress so he'll sleep like a log. I've put a rubber sheet between.'

'It's so quiet here,' said Jessie after a few minutes of silence walking down the leafy lane.

'Oh ah?' smiled Alice. 'Well, I should think it would seem quiet after London. I dare say you'll find the dawn chorus somewhat noisy, mind. They make a racket, that I *will* say.'

Jessie was relaxing by the second. 'Waking up to the sound of birds instead of air-raid sirens. It's like another world. Paradise.'

Alice nodded thoughtfully and went quiet again.

Just five minutes away from her cottage, she had to think of the right way of telling this young lady that it wasn't exactly paradise. After all, Londoners were used to electricity and running water – hot water, never mind cold. It was all very well during the summer months but the bitter winter brought its fair share of problems. And her first impression was that Jessie Smith was used to home comforts, and from the look of her hands she had not had to cope with drudgery. Yes, thought Alice, I should think the child is more used to working in an office than out in the fields.

'Our ways are a lot different from town folk,' said Alice as they approached the small gate leading through the front garden which was ablaze with colour, all kinds of flowers and shrubs. 'We still pull our water from the well but sweeter tasting you couldn't hope for. And we use oil lamps to see by and bake in a Dutch oven.'

'Sounds wonderful – except I don't 'ave a due what a Dutch oven is' said Jessie.

'Oh ah? Well, I s'pose you might say it's the fore-runner to the kitchen range. Much more room in the oven though. At Christmas time I get a duck and a joint of pork in there, as well as spuds and parsnips. And it do taste different, you know. You can't get the same flavour with them there new ovens, thet you *can't*. You'll see. And my little lavvi out the back is cleaned every day. It's got a brick floor and a good piece of lino, wall to wall. My brother Jack laid that just this summer so it's practically brand new.'

Following Jack up the garden path to the front door, Jessie noticed that he walked with a limp which looked comical from behind since his baggy trousers held by braces were an inch too short. 'It's just you and your brother then?' she asked.

'Oh yes.' There was a definite tone to Alice's voice which suggested that that was the way she preferred it. Her husband, thought Jessie, must have led her a life and either left of his own fee will or been kicked out. No doubt she would hear about it in the fullness of time.

Going into the house and directly into the living room, Jessie was reminded of her own two-up, two-down, except that all the rooms in this cottage were heavily beamed and even though it had been a hot day, a fire was smouldering in the open brick fireplace. Above the fire, hanging on an iron chain, was a black kettle and on an iron stand next to the fire grate sat a light blue enamel teapot, chipped here and there.

Set around the inglenook fireplace was a well-worn but clean, rose-patterned three-piece suite. Several pieces of furniture, fight and dark wood, were crammed against the available wall space, and ornaments which had been handed down or won at the fairground bedecked every surface and shelf. The window was small so the room, to Jessie, seemed a little on the dark side, though shafts of light from the evening sun streamed in. It was clean and homely.

'I expect you'd like a decent cup of tea,' said Jack. 'They fancy they make good tea down at the village hall. Tea? Tastes more like cat's—'

'That'll be enough of that, Jack, thank you very much,' snapped Alice, making it clear who was the boss in this house. 'We've got company now so you mind your *tongue.*' She turned to Jessie and rolled her eyes. 'You mustn't mind my brother, he sometime forget his *manners.*'

'A cup of tea would be lovely,' said Jessie, 'but if I could take Billy to our room—'

'Of course you must!' exclaimed Alice, embarrassed that she might have appeared ignorant as to how things were done. 'Just you follow me up. Jack, you fetch the young lady's suitcase after us.'

'It's Jessie.'

'Of course it is. You fetch Jessie's things up then, Jack.'

'I heard you the *first* time, woman!'

Leading the way, Alice told Jessie to mind her head when they reached the top of the narrow, winding staircase, 'There's a beam which sits an inch too low for my liking. Many a lodger has cracked his head on it.'

Thankful that she missed the beam by a good few inches without having to bend, Jessie wondered about the lodgers and who else might have slept in the room she was to occupy. Upstairs there was a slight smell which worried her. If it was damp in the height of summer, what might it be like on a harsh winter's night? Once she was in the room, she realised the reason for the smell. The window was closed and on inspection she could see that it hadn't been opened in a very long time, if ever. The latch and catch seemed to have welded together over the years. The room was hot and stuffy.

'If you want we can get Lenny from Three Wells cottage to come and see to that handle. Jack's been saying he'll do something with it for as far back as I can *remember*. Jack by name and lazy Jack by nature.'

Dropping Jessie's suitcase down with a deliberate thump, Jack asked his sister if there were any more instructions for her manservant or could he take a five-minute break.

'Take no notice,' said Alice quietly. 'He's in a snit 'cos he's been up all *day*.'

'Oh, right,' said Jessie, bemused. 'So you're a night worker then, Jack.'

'No, I flippin' well en't! Nights are for bats and owls. But what with this leg, I hev to have a couple of hours on me back during daylight, as well my sister do know.'

'Night worker,' joshed Alice. 'He en't done an honest *day's* work in years.' Turning to Jessie, she said, 'Now, does this room fit the bill? If it don't, then you say so. This is a humble home and I'm not too proud to say so. Clean and humble. But should you want to move on from here to one of the big houses, I shan't be *offended*. Up at the rectory they have got a bigger room which would suit someone like yourself and baby. You wouldn't hev no worry at the rector's wife turning you away. *No.* She'd be *more'n* happy to hev you, that I *do* know.'

Her speech, given in a high-pitched yet sincere voice was enough to wake Billy, who had been enjoying a doze. Opening his eyes to the round face and bright red cheeks of Jack, his cap pulled down over his piercing blue eyes, proved too much. Billy's bottom lip curled and he began to cry.

'I should think he want a *drink*, poor little soul.' Alice placed one finger in the palm of his hand and sporting a sudden smile to match hers, he gripped it. 'Auntie Alice make some milk and honey, *shall* she? Shall she, *then*?'

Snuggling into his mother, Billy nodded and smiled, shyly.

'Do he hev a bottle, Jessie?'

'Yes.' She nodded at her carrier bag. 'There's a clean one in there.'

'Just the job. I shan't be no more than *ten* minutes. Jack, go and make some fresh tea while I pop down to Mrs Reeder before she finish milking. Couldn't be better *timing*, Jessie.'

Suspicion of what her landlady meant swept through Jessie's mind. Surely not, she thought. 'You mean the milk's coming straight from a cow?'

'Well, it don't come from nowhere else, my dear,' said Alice, 'and the temperature'll be just right for this cherub. Oh, yes it will,' she said, talking into Billy's face again and bringing out his smile.

'You mean you won't be boiling it first?'

'Oh, I shouldn't think we'd want to do that. Don't want to scald his mouth.'

'It's just that I usually boil it and then let it cool… ours doesn't come from a cow, it comes from a bottle.'

'Well then, you *should* boil it first if it's been through all of that palaver. Straight from the cow there's no need for all that.'

In for a penny, in for a pound, thought Jessie, shrugging. 'Fair enough. I'm in the country now, so…'

'You won't be sorry for it. You can trust me on that.' Going downstairs, Alice called back over her shoulder, 'And once you've made a pot of *tea*, Jack, you hang your overalls to *air and* collect my washing from the line and fetch in the sheets off the *hedgerow*. They'll be dry be now!'

'Perhaps you can see why I hev a rest during the day – to get away from *her*.' Chuckling, Jack went downstairs, sideways, exaggerating his difficulty and wincing in pain now and then. 'It's an old *war* wound!' he called back. 'I fought in the fourteen-eighteen war!'

Jessie looked around her. The room was heavily beamed and between the beams it had been painted, at one time, grey-blue. The curtains were patterned with yellow flowers on a beige background and the floorboards were bare except for a large, brightly coloured rag mat. From the window Jessie could see the back garden which was full of fruit trees and vegetables. From every bit of earth a vegetable or fruit bush grew. There were no flowers in the back garden and yet it looked lovely. At the far end of the garden there was a small brick building which she guessed to be the lavvi, as Alice Davey had called it. The setting sun was creating streaks of pink against the blue and orange sky. 'I am in heaven,' she whispered, happier than she had been in a long time.

Examining the window catch, she felt sure that with a good dose of oil she would soon free it and once the air blew into the room it would be perfect, except for the walls and ceiling which she would emulsion white if her landlady agreed. She sat Billy on his bed which was just a few inches from hers and winked at him. 'This is it, Billy. This is to be our home for a while. No more bangs and no more sounds of screaming neighbours rushing around. No more air-raid sirens. Just the sound of birds and cows mooing.' Billy clapped his hands as if he understood everything she said. Maybe he did.

Later, once dusk had fallen and curtains and blackout blinds drawn (old sheets dyed black and cut to size) and her boy was asleep, Jessie sat with Alice and Jack by the fire and could see why it was lit. In this house with its thick walls, once the sun was down, the place cooled.

'Well,' said Jack suddenly, pulling himself up from his armchair, 'I'd best go and see how Josh got on at the market. Bit of luck he might hev a lame duck for Sunday dinner.'

'Well, he en't had one for the past twenty years or so, Jack, 'as he?' Alice turned to Jessie and gave her an all-knowing look. 'He say the same thing every time he go to the pub and he go to the pub every ruddy night.'

'You can come if you wish, Jessie,' said Jack. 'Meet a neighbour or two. I expect young Rupert'll be in there tonight, eyeing up the goods.'

'What she want to go down the pub with you for? Daft old bugger. You and your bloomin' cronies goin' on about the old days. And don't you go saying things like that about young Rupert. He's a decent fella, that he *is*.'

'He's a ruddy colonel's son! And you can't tell me that the colonel en't hed his share of rustling in the hay. Dirty old bugger. Can't keep his eyes down when it comes to a pretty face.'

'I think I saw him from the bus,' said Jessie, enjoying Jack's gossiping. 'And I might 'ave seen his son as well. Rupert. Funny sort of name. Perhaps that's why you can read him like a book, Jack.'

'I *can't* blooming well read. No need. I've got my hearing and I can listen in at my neighbour's wireless whenever it take my fancy.'

'He's a good-looking chap, I'll say that for 'im. But there, we shouldn't be talking like this. Jessie being a married woman an' all.'

'Anyway, thanks for the offer, Jack, but I wouldn't leave Billy. I never left him to go out when I was in London, never mind in a strange place. I wouldn't be able to relax.'

'Course'n she wouldn't. Daft? Teh. And don't be late or I shall bolt the door! That I shall. Make no mistake! And don't forget your torch!' Alice called after her brother.

The slamming of the street door was his reply.

Alice leaned forward, smiling, and whispered, 'I say that every time he go out. It riles him, you see.' She leaned back in her old chair. 'Well, he rile me enough. Old bugger.'

'Have you always lived together, you and Jack?' Jessie felt as if she was on a different planet. As if she'd stepped sideways in time rather than back. She hadn't expected country people living in a remote Norfolk village to be so wily and quick-witted. Maybe they couldn't all read as well as town people but they were as sharp as a razor and treated everyone as if they were family. Jessie had only been here a few hours and yet she felt as if she'd known them for years. And from what she'd seen at the packed village hall, these people had a dry sense of humour which reminded her of the Jews in London. Especially Max's parents.

'No.' Alice's expression changed instantly. 'No, I haven't always lived with my brother,' She pursed her lips and shook her head, fixing her eyes on the floor, 'No. When Mother died and Jack was left here by himself, to be truthful I think that's when I made up my mind. That's when I left my husband. He hadn't been good to me. No. He was carrying on, you see. With a cousin of mine. And

I didn't like that. No. So I came back here to look after Jack. Mother left the house to the both of us, you see. My other two brothers weren't too happy about that but there we are. They've got homes and wives so they're all right. And kiddies. I never had children. It never happened.'

'Well,' said Jessie, 'this is a lovely cottage and you own it so…'

'Good will out?'

'Something like that.'

'Ah. You could be right. Now then, what about a cup of cocoa? Would you like that before we turn in?'

'No thanks. I don't think I'll need anything to help me sleep tonight. I'm all in.' She looked directly into the woman's face. 'You've been really kind to me and Billy.'

'Oh ah? Well, I can't say as I've done much. Why you haven't been here for more'n a few hours.'

'Well, I appreciate everything. And I'm not the type to sit on my backside all day or walk around with Billy in my arms. You let me know what's to be done and I'll knuckle down. I get an army pension so I can pay my way.'

Pulling herself up from her armchair, Alice quietly chuckled. 'Well, ain't that a rum thing. I've got myself the *pick* of the busload. I knew we'd get on when I read your letter. Now if you wake in the night and find the black a bit worrying, you light a candle. I've left one by your bed and you'll find a box of matches in the little drawer of the chamber cupboard.'

'I don't think I'll wake up and Billy goes through the night so—'

'Well, it'll only be the dawn chorus or my brother Jack, rolling in after eleven, that might disturb your sleep. I've told him to go quietly. But to tell the truth, he is a very quiet man. I just like to nag him a bit. Keep him on his toes. Well, goodnight, my dear. Don't worry about the oil lamp. Jack will see to that.'

'Right,' said Jessie, stretching and yawning, 'I'll go up then. I can't wait to sink into that feather bed. G'night, Mrs Davey.'

'Good night, my dear. Sleep tight. No bed bugs – no bites.'

–

The following morning, Jessie woke to the noise of Alice's goose and gander in the garden and Billy babbling in the small bed next to hers. He sounded for all the world as if he was having a conversation. Turning over to check him, she saw the reason for his good mood. A tiny mouse was sitting at the foot of his bed. Even the rodents were friendly.

With her candle wick dressing gown on she carried her son downstairs and took him with her to the outside lavatory where she met Alice in the garden picking runner beans. 'Morning, my dear,' she said, a song in her voice. 'Here, let me hold the child while you do what you *have* to.'

'Thanks,' said Jessie, passing him over, relieved to see that Billy remembered the woman and went to her, not with a smile but a look of curiosity. 'I slept like a log, Alice. The bed's lovely.'

'Oh well, that is good. We can't have you tossing and turning. Come into the kitchen when you've done and we'll have a drop of *tea*!'

Standing in the early morning sunshine, Jessie watched as her hostess waddled to the back door of the cottage making small talk with Billy. Checking her surroundings, she wondered what there might be to this village life other than perfection. After finding her own house bombed, she was ready for anything.

After all, the country was at war and remote village or not, it was part of Britain.

Surprised at how fresh the lavvi smelled when there was no chain to flush, she had nothing but admiration for her landlady. Under the polished wooden seat with lid was a chemical toilet which was emptied regularly and hanging on a nail on the whitewashed brick wall was a huge bunch of dried lavender and brown parcel paper cut into squares.

'It's almost as – if we're in peacetime up here,' smiled Jessie as she went into the kitchen to wash her hands.

'Oh ah?'

'Back in London we're reminded constantly. Day and night. I wonder what the others are making of your village.'

'Well,' said Alice, shaking cooking apples into her sink ready for peeling, 'you'll soon find out. Down at the village hall. Did I tell you the district nurse wants to examine each and every one of you?'

'No.' Jessie didn't much like the sound of that. 'Infectious illnesses, you see. Spread like wildfire in a small community. I expect there'll be a few heads that need attention. But there, paraffin wash and a good comb through'll soon see to that.'

'Best to be safe than sorry... I s'pose,' said Jessie, embarrassed at the thought of what they might find.

'And do you know they want us to boil *every* drop of water for the incomers? Never heard the like. If it don't hurt us it won't hurt *you*, is what I say. We never had no trouble from the water we pull out of our well, that we *haven't.*'

'So I'm expected down at the village hall then? With Billy?'

'They want to see each and every *one* of you.'

Jessie was glad of the excuse to find out for herself whether water from the well would be safe for Billy without boiling. And it would be good to see some of the people she had made friends with on the way up from London, on the bus. 'What time are we expected?'

'Ten o'clock.' Alice glanced through the kitchen window up at the sky, at the sun. 'I should say it must be somewhere around eight o'clock be now.'

Jessie checked her watch. 'It's five minutes past,' she said, mystified. 'How could you tell from looking at the sky?'

'From the sun, my dear. At noon it will be just over our horse chestnut tree.'

Before she left for the hall, Jessie learned how the post was delivered. Bob the postman came round once a day with his post horn, and went along the lanes blowing to let the people know he was coming. If he had a letter or parcel he would stand at the gate and give two long blows and a short one and wait for someone to appear for their post. He also carried postage stamps and should there be a letter for posting he would take it. Alice said that there weren't that many letters delivered in the village since quite a few people couldn't read or write.

She told Jessie about the lavender man who came with his cart to empty the lavvi buckets and bins regular as clockwork and took it away to the sewage pit, a couple of miles out from nowhere. 'We give our excrement and he give us lavender,' Alice said, matter-of-factly.

Pushing Billy in his pushchair, Jessie, for the first time since she had arrived, thought about London and her family. She would write and tell them about the village of Elmshill and the fields upon fields of golden wheat which were heavily sprinkled with bright red poppies. She knew her mother would love it here. The haystacks, the fen, the thatched cottages and pretty gardens. And the quiet; most important of all, the peace and quiet.

Turning out of the lane and into Church Hill she could see the village hall and the Londoners she'd travelled with the previous day. The children were chasing around, some laughing, some not. The women were chatting in small groups and the old folk had been given chairs from the village hall. They had also been given a cup of tea and a biscuit. The hospitality seemed endless.

Drawing closer, Jessie could see that standing by a trestle table covered with a white sheet was the district nurse with two helpers in white overalls, combing through the heads of children as they leaned forward, watching to see if anything live dropped from their hair on to the sheet. A shout of joy from one hardened eleven-year-old boy brought the others from their game of chase to look. Yes, this one had fleas – and for this he was a hero? As another and another flea dropped from his head on to the white sheet, a cheer went up and even the nurse and helpers couldn't help smiling. They had expected tears and shame.

'Amazing, isn't it, the mind of a child.'

Turning to see who the voice belonged to, Jessie looked into the face of thirty-year-old Rupert Maitland, the colonel's son. 'That's just what I was thinking. Who would have thought they'd *want* to have fleas?'

'They'll soon change their minds once Nitty Nora gets stuck in. What's your name?'

She liked his friendly but forthright manner. 'Jessie Smith. What's yours?'

'Rupert. Rupert Maitland.' He held out his hand to shake Jessie's. 'Welcome to Elmshill.'

'Thanks. I think I'm going to like it here.' She was referring to the place and not to him, as well he knew, but quick off the mark he gave her a saucy, questioning smile.

'I'm going to like you living here too. It's a small village and one gets a little tired of seeing the same faces all year round. Once you've settled in and heard from the gossips that I'm not a womaniser, maybe you'd like to come out for a drink with me. The local's not a bad place, as pubs go.'

'Well…' Jessie hardly knew whether to smile or be offended. 'You're not slow in coming forward, are you?'

'Not when my interest is piqued, I'm not. What did you think of old Alice and Jack then?' Rupert smiled, and she gave in and grinned back.

'I think they're lovely people.'

'And your room?'

'More than pleased.' She tried to lose the smile on her face but his was somehow contagious. 'How did you know I was staying at Rose Cottage?'

'Ah, that's for me to know and you to find out. Ask Alice.'

'Ask Alice what?'

'Whatever comes into that pretty head. She'll vouch for my integrity.' He tipped his cap and winked at her. 'If you'll excuse me, I have duties to carry out. It would appear that the cold water tap has gone dry.'

'You're a plumber?' Jessie couldn't quite believe it.

'At times.' He backed away in a theatrical manner. 'I also drive a tractor, read aloud in church – from the Bible – cover for the barman at the White Horse, and when I get *offers* I act. Sometimes professionally but, alas, mostly amateur dramatics. The former brings jam to my bread and the latter joy to the heart. Would that it were a perfect world.' With that, Rupert Maitland smiled that mischievous smile and strolled towards the village hall, half turning his head to look back at her before he went in.

Feeling as if she had just been struck by a bolt of lightning, Jessie took a long, deep breath and murmured, 'You can stop that right now, Jessie Smith, you can stop that right now.'

'What a bleeding lark, eh!' Hilda Brown, whom Jessie had sat next to on the bus, cut through her daydreaming. 'Bloody kids! Talk about put you to shame. Little sod. I didn't know he was running alive, I swear it. He's always scratching his sodding 'ead but I never thought he had fleas. Now look at *her*,' she pointed to her curly blonde four-year-old, 'she's doing it now.' The child received a gentle slap to the head. '*Stop it!*'

'I've got 'em as well, ain't I?' said little Molly, not wanting to be left out of it. 'One flew on my 'ead this morning when Tommy was jumping up and down on our bed!'

'Keep your bloody voice down!' Hilda slowly shook her head. 'She can't have fleas – look at that hair. Clean as a whistle and shining like a pin. Fleas. Tch.'

'Well, you know what they say,' said Jessie, amused by it all. 'They like clean hair.'

'NEXT!' came the authoritarian voice of the nurse in charge. 'Three more children, please! Three more! Boys or girls, it doesn't matter which!'

Never had children disappeared so quickly. They scattered in seconds, running for all they were worth and hiding. Hilda had little Molly by the arm as she struggled to free herself. 'Come on. Let's get it over with.' She dragged her daughter closer to the waiting Nitty Noras and before long there was a queue of women battling with their young and slapping them when needs be.

Jessie decided her best plan of action was to go back to Rose Cottage and check both her and Billy's hair herself. She had seen a nit comb in Alice's small bathroom cupboard and no doubt she would have some paraffin wash too. As far as their health was concerned, both were well and would be a lot healthier in present surroundings than they had been in London. As she turned her pushchair round ready to make her escape, a wheel came off, rolled along the lane and disappeared under the much bigger wheel of a tractor. Billy shrieked with laughter in his lopsided pram.

'What's your billet like then? Ours is awful.' Jessie spun round to face a sixteen-year-old girl chewing gum who had escorted her two younger brothers on the bus. 'Gave us rabbit bleeding pie for our dinner last night. Urggghh. Poor little things. You see 'em all over the place hopping and skipping about. And they put 'em in pies. Disgusting. Call this a bleeding 'oliday? I don't think so. No shops, nuffink. And what about fish and chips? And the pictures? There ain't nuffink 'ere. Sod all. A chip van comes round once a week, so someone said. One a blooming week!'

'So you won't be staying-then?' said Jessie. The farm hand driving the tractor leapt down from the cab and examined the smashed wheel, which he retrieved from under his machine.

'Oh yeah, I'll stop for a while. Gotta give 'em a chance, ain't yer? Farmers sons look all right. Well, two of 'em anyway. I told 'em over the dinner table that I wasn't *officially* an evacuee on account of my age. I said I was only there to settle in my brothers.' She drew a packet of cigarettes from the pocket of her slacks and spat out her gum. 'He was all right, as it 'appens. Big broad shoulders... really tanned. Blue eyes an' all. I like blue eyes.' She lit a cigarette and leaned on the trunk of an oak tree. 'So what's it like where you are? Bleeding toilet's smell, don't they? Everything smells. Urggghh... the kitchen – yuk! They let the bleeding ducks come in. Shit all over the place.' Someone else caught the girl's eye. 'Oil Lily! Over 'ere! How'd you get on?'

'It's all right, mate! Not bad at all!' called back the young ginger-headed woman. 'Got a bleedin' sheet on the bed, ain't I! Only time I've seen a sheet on a bed is over a corpse! Handsome, it is. Bleeding lovely! I've got the kids in a little room wiv me but I don't care. Bert ain't 'ere after me fanny so why worry, eh?'

Walking away from the peals of dirty laughter and towards the tractor, Jessie thanked her lucky stars for Alice and Jack and Rose Cottage. As far as she could tell, no other billets had been allocated for the incomers down their quiet lane.

'I don't think there's much we can do about this,' said the farm hand. 'I'm blowed if I saw it coming.' He stood gazing at the wrecked wheel, scratching his head, as if he was waiting for something to happen by magic.

'I shouldn't worry.' Rupert Maitland's gentle but firm voice washed over her. 'Someone will have a pushchair in their shed, you can depend on it.'

Turning to face him, Jessie smiled. 'I think I'm gonna need one. The number eight bus won't be pulling up on the hour, will it?'

'Hardly. Can I be of any assistance?'

'Well, could you do something with my old pushchair? The rubbish dump?'

'I think I can manage that. Anything else?'

'I don't think so, thanks. I'll, er, I'll make a start… back to the cottage.'

'Can the little fellow walk?'

'Oh yeah, but half a mile an hour.' She lifted Billy out of the lopsided pushchair. 'He's not that heavy. I'll carry him.'

'I can't give you a lift?'

'I'll be fine, thanks.' Jessie felt herself blush and hated it. 'Bye.'

Enjoying the sun on her face and chatting away to Billy, Jessie headed for their new home and was surprised to see that on the gate of another cottage on the way along the lane, her name was sprawled in capital letters with a note beneath it which read: 'It's listening time at a quarter to eleven if you should want to come in and hear the news bulletin on the wireless. Alice.'

She had always thought the East End and her mother's street in particular to be neighbourly but this was something else. She, an unknown and from London, was invited into a stranger's home at *listening time*? Deciding against it, Jessie continued on her way. She didn't want to think about the war. Over the past year, she'd sat listening intently to every news bulletin but the thought of a wireless with its knobs, dials, crackling and bad news wasn't something she relished right now. Her mind switched to that fateful day in September when the announcement came that the country was at war with Germany and she felt herself shiver. Not quite over the shock of what had happened to her house and home, Jessie, without warning, began to cry. There was no noise, no wailing, no sobs, just warm tears rolling down her face and neck.

When she reached Rose Cottage she realised that Billy had fallen asleep. The country air was having an effect on him too. Going round the back of the house as instructed by Alice, she found the back door unlocked as promised. That was something else she was going to have to get used to. The front door was hardly ever used and the back was always open in the summer, and when it was closed, it was never locked.

Inside the kitchen on an elm high-backed chair she found Jack, fast asleep with his legs resting on a footstool. Trying her best not to disturb him, she crept through and took Billy upstairs to lie him on the cot bed where he would be more comfortable. On her way in through the back garden she had been struck by the idea of picking some vegetables and making a veggie hotpot as a surprise for her landlady.

Tiptoeing back into the kitchen, she found that Jack was up and about. 'I'm jest about to brew up, my dear. Would you like a cup of tea?' He walked across the room to the sink, limping heavier than he had before. 'I weren't asleep, jest resting my leg.'

'Oh, I realised that,' said Jessie, certain, if his low snoring had been anything to go by, that he was fibbing. She managed to cover her smile though. Lazy Jack is what Alice had called her brother and he was living up to his name.

'Do you think Mrs Davey would mind if I picked some vegetables and threw something together for our dinner tonight?'

'Throw something together,' he said, considering the question. 'I can't say as I know...'

'Cook something. A vegetable stew or hotpot.'

'Ah!' His face broke into a beaming smile. 'I see what you mean. Well, I should think she would be *pleased*?'

'Well, I wasn't sure I—'

'And if you like, you could use up some of that ham off the bone in the larder?'

She was going to have to get used to Jack's voice inflection. Every statement sounded like a question and she wasn't sure how to answer. 'Well, if you think so.'

'I shouldn't dare say it otherwise,' he said. 'You hev to *know* how to read my sister. She don't understand my leg though. She get *riled* if I doze in that chair. I shouldn't like her to think I *was* dozing.'

'Well,' said Jessie, looking through the window to the back garden and covering a smile, 'I can see carrot tops, parsnips, runner beans, marrow—'

'And every other damned vegetable, I should think. If there's a seed ablowing, she'll set it, that she will.'

An hour later, while Jessie used the garden fork to prise out some carrots and Billy toddled about in the garden, Jack lay in a homemade hammock which hung between two old apple trees. Beside him, on a footstool, was a portable pie wireless which he'd picked tip dirt cheap at the Diss market a year or so back. It wasn't the news on but soft music which, as he had explained to Jessie, helped soothe the pain in his leg. It also helped him sleep, thought Jessie. Jack was snoring again, grateful that this young woman from London had lightened his duties. Alice had left him strict instructions to lift some vegetables for tea and weed between the rows of runner beans. The weeding could wait until the morrow.

–

The evacuees, less a few who had returned to London, settled themselves into the country way, more or less, and the locals accepted them, more or less. There were air bases not that many miles away and some of the women found their way there for a night out now and then and some of the airmen found their way back to the village and the wooded fens where courting took place. A blind eye was turned by all, especially since the local ladies were also enjoying the men's company. Jessie had not the slightest desire to join in their fun and games but she did very much enjoy the one evening she spent with Rupert Maitland.

She had expected him to talk mostly about himself but she was wrong, and she found him interesting company. Here was a man who seemed to have everything. So what was the catch? Nothing came to light during the evening in the pub or when they strolled back to the cottage together under a silvery moon. By the time they reached Alice's house, they knew quite a lot about each other. She had even told him about having been once engaged to Max and he had listened. Of course other things came into their conversation – the time before the war, the Blackshirts, her long-lost twin sister. In fact, Jessie had done most of the talking and he the listening. And when they reached the garden gate, after telling her that he'd really enjoyed the evening, he simply lifted her hand and kissed it before saying goodnight.

Soon, thought Jessie, she would find something about Elmshill that she didn't like but she couldn't for the life of her imagine what it might be. For all its peace and quiet, the village was always aware of the war. Telegrams would arrive, telling of men killed in action. Unlike in London, where just the local neighbours rallied round, here all the inhabitants and some from other villages closed ranks around the bereaved and gave everything they could by way of support and comfort.

And as the nights drew in, the ARP wardens took their role very seriously, proper blacking-out being the main bee in their bonnets. Black paper and drawing pins were now something of a rarity in all the local shops and post offices. Even the towns of Diss, Bury St Edmunds and Thetford had run out.

The rule of no torches alight at night caused some dispute and as Jack had said, more than once, 'It's a rum thing when you can't see the fellow you're talking to.' He was referring to his walks home from the pub late at night. Lighting a torch was forbidden but many were lit nonetheless. The streets and lanes in small villages throughout Norfolk weren't lit in any case so locals had less trouble finding their way through the black when there was no moon than the incomers. To Jessie the familiar sound of the wardens calling out, 'Dull that light, please!' or 'Put out that light, please!' brought back memories of London. She was kept up to date on the news by way of post from both her mother and Emmie. Occasionally a card would come from Dolly who was still enjoying the fun side of wartime.

The rows over lights which could or could not be spotted from a German aircraft dominated the conversation in pubs and village halls, between the old men and farm hands enjoying their beer and those involved in the WI enjoying their tea. At least it made a change from domestic and farming chat. Summer fête time had arrived and preparations began for the produce show with everyone doing their bit to make this fête the best in the area. It seemed to Jessie that the country was not much different from the city when it came to competing. Showing off was more like it. They all wanted to impress their London guests with the quality of the produce and cake stalls. The fête was the highlight of the year for most of the hamlets, large or small, boisterous or sleepy.

The beer for the occasion was brewed in big coppers in kitchens in most villages. The men brewed night and day, a month before the fête. Had it not been for his leg, Jack would have taken his turn. Farmers would go to the brewing kitchen and collect the beer in barrels and take it away in a cart. No one minded taking their turn at brewing; there was always someone coming or going and the company was lively. This year was to have been the turn of Alice and her cottage but Jack had stood firm against it. Too many eyes would have seen him in his true light, idle and overweight from loafing and not from the fat of the land. Jessie was disappointed; it sounded fun and she would have loved to have been part of it.

'Of course, had I hev known that you and little Billy would be coming to live with us, I should have got Jack to carve both your names on our prize marrow,' said Alice, admiring her prize entry for the competition soon to take place. 'Wouldn't that have been something? Four of our names on one vegetable. I don't think I've seen that in the past. No.'

'I think it's a smashing idea and I know that Dad would have done the same if we'd thought of it. He loved his garden.' Thinking of her dad for some strange reason reminded her of Rupert Maitland. Jessie laid her knitting on her lap. 'Alice, what do you know about Rupert Maitland?' Having been at the cottage for well over a month, Jessie felt comfortable and settled, completely at ease with Alice and Jack and able to raise the subject of Rupert.

A throaty chuckle from Alice said it all. 'Well, look you here, my dear, he *do* set some women's hearts racing, I will say that, and he do enjoy the attention. But he en't nothing like that snooty mother and father of his.' She straightened, looked thoughtful and then said, 'What do I know about him? *Well*... he was betrothed to a *lovely* girl from Woolpit. Ooh, she was a darling. I don't think anyone had a bad word to say about her. He thought the world of Rosie Brown. Loved her to death. Or should I say loved her *until* death. Poor child.'

'What happened?' asked Jessie. Rupert hadn't mentioned this.

Alice shuddered and pursed her lips. 'Oh dear. I still can't believe it, Jessie, that I can't. No more than twenty-two years old and from a good Baptist family. But then, you know, I recall her mother saying to me one day, "Alice, my child is like an angel and too good for the world." Those were her words. Maybe she was right.'

'Was she ill for a long time?'

'I should say not. She was the picture of health and sang like a bird. No. Young Rosie wasn't a sick child.'

Jessie was quiet while Alice collected herself. Finally the time of remembrance was over and Alice said, 'I don't believe she knew anything about it. Never suffered. She slipped on the very floor she had just polished for her mother. At the top of the stairs. All the way to the bottom she went and there she lay. Lifeless. No. She couldn't hev known much about it.'

'It must have been a terrible shock. For everyone. Her poor mother.'

'And father. Oh, he did take it bad.' Snapping herself out of her dark mood, Alice raised her voice by an octave or two. 'But there. Rupert's got himself together again. I admire him for that. Two years it's taken the chap. Two long years.'

'He seems so nice...'

'That he is, my dear. A very kind man if you know what I *mean*. He threw himself into his work soon after. He's an actor, you know. Never looked at another woman though. Not since Rosie. I shouldn't want anyone else to come along and break his *heart*.'

Picking up on the gentle hint, Jessie smiled inwardly. 'I can't see that happening, Alice. He won't go falling for an evacuee and from what you tell me, he's not interested in anyone else around here. I expect he'll find the right one — one day.'

'Oh, I'm sure he will. Trouble is, he's a catch, right enough. And rich with it. Well, his family's very wealthy, put it that way. They own a fair bit of property around and about. They say they're from blue blood but I'm not so sure about that. The gentry, yes. But royal blood? No. I shouldn't say so.' Plunging her watering can into the rain barrel, she changed the subject. 'So your dad was a keen gardener then?'

'Very. He would have appreciated being here. His dream was to move out of London one day.'

'Never mind. God works in mysterious ways.' Alice sniffed and paused before saying, 'Your father passed away a young man then, Jessie?'

Jessie nodded. 'I was only sixteen. I loved my dad. We were really close. It was an accident. He was a crane driver down the docks and was ordered to take a heavier load than was good for the crane. He knew it as well but had no choice but to do what they wanted. The engine strained under the weight and caught fire, before it plunged into the River Thames – taking Dad with it. He was drowned.'

'Oh, my dear child, I am sorry to hear that.' Alice dropped down on a garden chair. 'What a shock that must have been, and there I was going on about Rosie Brown. I can be a silly old woman at times. But that's the trouble, isn't it? None of us knows what other people have been through if we've not lived cheek by jowl. Even then, no one knows what happens behind closed doors. That they don't.'

Pushing a hand through her hair, Jessie inhaled slowly, composing herself. She didn't want to think about sad things. 'Mum would like to come and visit, if that's all right. Just for the day. She would catch a train to Diss station and I thought I could get the bus and meet her. We could spend most of the day in Diss so we wouldn't impose too much. If she could just come and see how lovely it is here…'

'Course she must come. And if you're happy to have her sleep in your bed with you then I shan't be sorry. To tell you the truth, Jessie, I should like to meet her. That I would.'

'Well, I know she wants to meet you. I told her that you'd been like a second mother to me and how good you are with Billy. It took a lot off her mind knowing that. She's got enough on her plate with my two younger brothers and sister, Dolly. At least me and my twin sister are not giving 'er anything to worry over.'

'Twin?' beamed Alice. 'Well, I'll go to hell. I didn't know you were a twin. Two of you. Well, wasn't that nice for your mother.'

'Yes and no but I'll tell you about that another time. She's had a hard life in one way and a good one in another.'

'Well, you jes let me know when she want to come and I'll get Jack to arrange for someone to collect her. Collect her from the station in a proper fashion. In a motor car.'

—

Jessie was surprised how easily she got into the swing of country living. Before she knew it she was picking the summer fruit which would store well and cooking up for bottling whatever wouldn't. Alice had another brick shed on her small allotment at the back of her neighbour's garden, where there was shelf upon shelf of jars of every size. On this small piece of land, where more vegetables grew, there was also a penned area for Percy, the family pig, who was in actual fact female and almost ready to deliver her piglets. Perfect timing for the summer fête, Jessie thought, but she was wrong. Fattened pork was the order of the day, for taste as much as economy. Juicy pork fat and light crispy crackling meant more to Alice and Jack than the meat itself. Neighbours also enjoyed the treat; in return for all their kitchen scraps they would receive a modest piece of Alice's salted pork at Christmas.

So, with her work in the garden, feeding Percy with scraps and helping out inside the house, Jessie felt as if she was pulling her weight. As for Billy, he was loving every day and his cheeks were growing rosier too. Alice was an old-fashioned cook who didn't skimp when it came to feeding. On the other hand, she didn't believe in vanity spending. Buying clothes to keep up with the latest fashion was something which mystified her. If shoes, boots or clothes weathered well she saw no reason on earth to cast them aside for something new. She preferred to have some money put by ready for an emergency and for a respectable funeral for both herself and Jack. She was hardly a wealthy woman but her income from new-laid eggs, pork, chickens and ducks at Christmas kept her moderate accounts even. From her dozen hens she could expect at least two thousand eggs a year and from Percy, who obliged twice a year, nine piglets in all, which, after fattening up, Alice would sell off, keeping one for herself from each litter. This kept them in pork over the year – fresh pork kept cool down in the well, salted, smoked, and pickled pork, and of course, bacon for boiling and frying. She also brought off six chickens and six ducks on average a year for selling and for her own table. She worked hard and she worked long hours but enjoyed it and she had learned long ago that she needed less sleep than her brother seemed to.

She was awake most mornings at 5 a.m., and ready at 5.30 to feed her fowl and animals and collect the chickens' eggs from all over her garden and allotment, ready to sell to villagers who came along especially for them. Then every morning she would go to Mrs Reeder at Fen Farm and help with the butter making. In return for this, Alice would receive butter and milk. And she would cook the season's fruit ready for preserving; pickle other produce; dry whatever herb or vegetable would keep. This morning, while Jessie slept soundly, Alice was up and picking wild mushrooms, which were plentiful, not only on arable land but along the wide grassy verges of the lane in which she lived. The puffball, a huge round mushroom, which was cut into several large slices and fried like steak, was the most sought after and you had to be up before the early birds. This, together with smoked tomato and fried bacon and egg, was what Jessie would be served for her breakfast this morning. The other, ordinary mushrooms would go into making chutney.

On her return, while she was enjoying a pot of tea to herself in the; still of early morning, Alice heard Jessie in the bedroom above call out in her sleep. Listening intently she then heard her softly weeping. She was missing home, which was more than understandable.

The planned visit by Rose had not happened. Somehow, difficulties and duties kept delaying her in London although she always promised she'd be up soon. No doubt Jessie was missing her family. The war and the evacuation plan had split wives from husbands and torn families apart. Jessie, like millions of others, had had the central pivot of her life removed – that satisfying feeling of being responsible for a loved one. Apart from that, she was living in someone else's home and using someone else's kitchen, and she did not have a bathroom and had to make do with a jug of hot water and china washing bowl in her room.

It neither upset nor surprised Alice to hear those tears. To her way of thinking, they were overdue.

Jessie had been overwhelmed with her new life and now that she had settled, she had space to let other emotions flow. The next sentiment might well be discontentment. After all, having to pull water from a well when she'd never actually seen one in her life must have come as a bit of a jolt – although she never let on.

Jessie came downstairs to the smell and sound of sizzling bacon and mushroom. She crept up behind Alice and hugged her. She then whispered in her ear, 'Thanks for everything.'

'It's been a pleasure, my dear. I've enjoyed it as much as you have. I shall go on enjoying it too, providing you're contented.' Allowing a few seconds to pass, she added, 'I take it you are contented?'

'Course I am. I was feeling a bit low last night, that's all.'

'I shan't ask why. You've had more than your fair share of grief, what with your house being blasted like that.'

'Funnily enough,' said Jessie, drawing up a chair, 'it wasn't that. Maybe I should feel worse about it but all I can think of when that day comes flooding back is thank God that none of my family were killed. I s'pose that's selfish. Hundreds of other poor devils had their light put out in seconds. And thousands of relatives are grieving for them.'

'Oh. Well, I expect it'll be that you're missing your family.'

'I do miss them but to tell you the honest truth, Alice, I had a terrible nightmare. About Rupert Maitland. I dreamt that I was falling down a slope – not stairs – a steep hill which was familiar but not, if that makes sense. I was partly tumbling down, my legs going so fast they left the ground, and then I was flying through the air and heading for a big rock. Then I was lying looking up at the sky and Rupert was kneeling beside me, crying. It was the sound of his crying that did it; He was sobbing. Breaking his heart. Calling me Rosie. Begging me not to leave him.' She quickly collected herself. 'But I'm all right now. Maybe the postman will bring a letter for me today. I've got a strange feeling that something's in the air.'

'Well yes, but don't go thinking too much on it, Jessie. You don't want to get your hopes up. But then there's always a train to take you back, should you want to make a visit home seeing as your mother can't come. You've been a good little worker and you've paid your way. I would be happy to help you out with the fare should you need it. I do get a government grant for having you here. Fair's fair.'

Touched by Alice's generosity, Jessie found herself smiling. 'That's a lovely thing to say but Mum would send money if I was short. I wouldn't be surprised if a postal order doesn't arrive soon. I told her in my letters that I don't need much up here but I know what she's like.'

'Well, she must be worried. That's her grandson up there don't *forget*!'

The sound of Billy shaking the rungs of his cot bed made them both laugh. 'I reckon he smelt that bacon, don't you?'

'Well, he's going to have to make do with boiled egg and *soldiers*,' said Alice. 'This treat is for you, Jack and *myself*. We've got a busy morning ahead of us, Jack included. They need every hand at the village hall today. It's the same this time every year before the fête. The old place gets a *clean*. Windows, walls, floor, *the lot*. And that floor do take some time. It's oak, you know. *Solid* oak. First we give it a good scrub and rinse, and when it's dry, we get back on our hands and knees and work together to give it a good waxing. Oh, but it *do* look beautiful when it's done. The colour come *right* out.'

'You know,' said Jessie, 'before I came up here, I believed some of the rumours going on back home, but now I'm not so sure, unless you really are the exception, Alice.'

'Oh ah? What sort of rumours?'

'That evacuees were treated like beggars demanding charity. Abused. Ill treated. Damp rooms. Enough food to fill a mouse. That kind of thing.'

'Well… I expect there's a bit of all of that goin' on here, there and so on. I wouldn't like to speculate on it, mind. Not with people who live in the same village as myself. No, I shouldn't do that. But I hev heard some stories going around, I will say *that*. I dare say there's *some* truth in some of the tales.'

'Well, from what I've seen of the kids up here, they're not doing bad. Time of their life for some of them. I don't know about those who came without their mothers…' An image of what might be happening inside some of the houses came into Jessie's mind. 'I feel guilty now. I've been so wrapped up in myself and Billy and how lucky we are, I've not given a thought to those poor kids…'

Alice assured Jessie that it would be very easy to find out where they had been billeted and if she wanted, she could take Billy for walks in the big old-fashioned pushchair that Jack had gone out early that morning and borrowed from a neighbour who no longer had need of it. Yes, thought Alice, they can visit the various courtesy houses and cottages sprinkled throughout the village. 'Anyhow, Jessie,' she said, 'you'll be seeing some of them today, I dare say. Once school's finished. They'll be down the village hall, I expect, seeing what we're all up to.'

Jack came into the room. He stretched and yawned. 'I didn't get a wink of sleep last night.'

'Is that right?' said Alice. 'Well then, how come I heard you snoring on and off the night long? Thick wall or not.'

'Bacon? En't my birthday, is it?' said Jack, changing the subject.

'No. It's a day for sweat and tears. If you don't sweat, you'll be in tears. I put you down for scything the nettles around the village hall. You'll need a good breakfast inside you.'

'I en't doing no such thing. I promised Willy Foulger some of my time today. He want me to grease that old tractor of his. I shan't go back on it.'

'You can grease it tomorrow and that's an end to it No weeding, no breakfast – nor lunch nor tea nor supper. Please y'self.'

Sitting down at the table, Jack never said another word. His sulky silences were something Alice was well vised to and enjoyed. It usually meant that she'd won a round and got the lazy sod to work. Or at least think about work. Out of her eyesight, she didn't have a clue, although she could imagine him leaning on his garden tool more than he used it.

The conversation turned to the parachutist who had landed in a neighbouring village and the panic it created until someone remembered that a practice had been scheduled for that day. Then they discussed the local Red Cross workers running first aid points, and how the evacuees and villagers were wheedling anything they could from them in the way of supplies which would be sold on afterwards.

'I thought I might join the sewing circle,' said Jessie, thinking she should do more towards the war effort.

'The make do and mend brigade,' smiled Alice, who gossip more than they sew. 'You'd be better suited to knitting for the evacuees in the garden. Those women who—' She was stopped short by a rapping on the door which had some urgency to it. Quick to open it, Alice was surprised to see the busiest busybody in the village on her threshold. The short, thin, bespectacled Mrs Brown had been in such a hurry to arrive with the news that she could hardly speak, her breath was so short.

'All the way…' she said, stopping to draw air, 'from Scotland. Travelling for… two days… if not more. And him a cripple. A cripple struggling on a pair of crutches so worn they hardly keep him upright.'

'What you rambling on about now, Mrs Brown? Cripple? What the hell hev I got to do with a cripple from – where was it you say? Scotland?'

'In full uniform.' The woman had to stop to catch her breath. Shaking her head, she gestured that they should give her a moment and she would give first-hand news of what she herself had seen. 'And on his way here. Tall, good-looking chap…'

'Tom? Surely not. He's in France.' An icy feeling swept through Jessie.

'I didn't catch the name in the post office but he's come looking for his wife and his baby boy.'

'It is him! It's Tom! I know it!' Wasting not a second, Jessie was out the door and running along the lane. Running as if she was a girl again. Running towards that familiar figure coming towards her. 'Tom! Tom, it's you!'

'Jessie!' Laying his crutches on the grass verge, Tom stood there, hands on hips and then arms outstretched, until she fell into them.

Crying and laughing, she wrapped her arms round his neck and kissed him. 'I thought you were abroad. I can't believe it's you. I can't believe it. I just can't believe it.' The two of them were oblivious of anything or anyone else. Had they seen the group of children who had been creeping along the hedgerows, following the soldier from war, still they wouldn't have stopped kissing and clinging to each other. Nothing in the world would have made any difference. Jessie and Tom were together again.

Strolling back towards the cottage they laughed at the catcalls and jibes from the children while Jessie reeled off all the reasons why they should consider moving to the country once the war was over. 'Mum said that our house would be put to rights at the expense of the government. I'm sure we'd get enough from that to buy something out here.'

'One thing at a time, Jess, one thing at a time. Where would I find work, for a kick off?'

Jessie ignored that and explained breathlessly how the quality of life and clean air would be good for Billy and how much he loved to be around animals. 'He's putting on weight as well.'

Pushing open the gate for her, Tom gripped her arm. 'Jess, I've found two rooms for you in a little terraced house, in Matlock Street, not far from your mum's. It's clean and spacious and the landlady's as good as gold.'

Jessie stopped in her tracks. 'London? You want me and Billy to go back to London?'

'They've given me a month's leave, Jess, to make sure the leg heals properly. It turned septic, you know. If I'm lucky I might be able to swing it and not go back abroad at all. It'll be easier for me to get from Scotland to London at weekends. It's like going to the bloody outback of Australia finding your way to Norfolk.'

'Scotland? They sent you back to Scotland? Why?'

'Because my leg 'adn't healed properly. Why do you think? Anyway, they're not so rushed up there. I'm having physio and—'

'I'm not stupid, Tom. You've put on the agony to get leave. You don't need physiotherapy.' She eased her arm away. 'Something else pulling you to Scotland, is there?'

'What's that supposed to mean?'

'Someone else. One of them nurses, for instance?' Giving him a sharp glance, Jessie thought for a moment that an expression of guilt swept across his face as he smiled back at her.

'Don't be silly,' he said.

Alice appeared in the front doorway holding Billy arid smiling, overjoyed that Jessie's husband had turned up out of the blue. 'Look whose *daddy's* come to see him then. You going to say hello to your *daddy*? Are you then?' But to Billy, Tom was only vaguely familiar. Instead of holding out his arms to Tom, he turned away and nestled into the familiar warmth of Alice.

That night, in bed, after Tom had persuaded her she was the only woman for him and they spent two hours making passionate love Jessie felt sure that Tom would drop the idea of her leaving. Especially after an evening of laughter with Alice and Jack, drinking the last of the previous year's cider over bacon and onion pudding. But she was wrong. He was still doing his utmost to persuade her to go back with him to London.

'But I really do like it here, Tom, and it's much, healthier for Billy,' she said.

'Yeah, I can see that, Jess,' was his measured response, 'but what about the winter? This cottage'll be cold and damp. You can't tell me that's healthy.'

'But I'll wrap up warm and you know I'll make sure Billy'll be well wrapped up.'

'You can't wrap up against damp. It seeps in. And just imagine yourself 'aving to pull water from a well in the freezing cold. Alice and Jack are lovely people. Generous. But they're getting on. What if they go down with flu? What then? You'll be expected to pull your weight.' He put out his cigarette and turned on his side to face her. 'It won't always be sunny like this.'

And so the conversation went on until Jessie was too tired to argue any more. Too tired and too in love with Tom to spoil the visit. Before closing her eyes, she agreed to go back with him to London the next day. The upheaval and saying goodbye to new friends would test her, but Tom was, after all, her husband and she had been brought up to abide by the marriage vows – to love, cherish and obey.

Drifting into sleep, she couldn't stop the nagging feeling which still haunted her. When she had greeted Tom in the lane, she'd thought she defected a faint smell of perfume which had been washed away when he'd shaved before bed.

Once all the sad partings were over and they were on their way to meet one of Alice's neighbours, a farm hand, who was going that day to Diss and the animal market for his master and would give them a ride in the truck to the station, Jessie focused her mind on London and going back home to her family. Her stay had been cut short but at least she had experienced rural living and liked it. Maybe one day she and Tom would move out to the country and start a new life.

When they arrived at the church, the meeting place, Jessie saw Rupert in the churchyard speaking to one of the grave diggers and remembered that there had been the death of a ninety-year-old woman in the village. Shy at first to go and say goodbye, she took a deep breath and excused herself, knowing that Tom would be keeping a keen eye on her and on the handsome Rupert.

'I don't know if you've heard,' she said, 'but—'

'Yes,' he shrugged and smiled affectionately at her, 'I did hear. Mrs Brown was first with the news, of course, and she made sure the village knows. Good luck, Jessie, and take care. Drop me a line should you find yourself in need of some good old country air. There'll always be someone who'll collect you from the station.'

'Thanks. I'll remember that. If I do write, I'll send it via Alice, shall I?'

'Yes. You do that.' He glanced over at Tom and then with one look conveyed the message to Jessie that she should go. The truck was pulling up.

Resisting the urge to peck him on the cheek, she turned away and went over to Tom. Without looking back, she sat in the back seat with Billy on her lap. On the way to the station she wondered if maybe she'd met Rupert in another life. What other explanation could there otherwise be for the feeling they had both had of getting on as if they'd known each other for years. But then she also had an intuitive feeling that she would see him again one day and how could that be? They were from different worlds.

Chapter Five

The nagging doubt in the pit of Jessie's stomach when she was packing her things had not gone away as she'd hoped and as the train approached Bethnal Green main line station she felt sick inside. The same questions were going through her mind, over and over – had she made a mistake? Should she have been stronger and stayed where she was?

Alice had been staggered by the announcement at the breakfast table and Jack wounded. Each of them had asked if they had done something wrong or had not lived up to Tom's expectations. Telling them that her short stay there had been better than she had ever expected, Jessie did in the end convince them that her leaving was for the sake of her husband and for her baby Billy, whom she felt should be in London, closer to Tom's family and her own. She said, although not entirely convinced herself, that Billy should see more of his dad since the opportunity had presented itself. She didn't want to leave this idyllic way of life for London with its threat of danger and death, she told them, but she couldn't let Tom down; he had already suffered enough, having lost one brother to the war and with another on the missing–presumed–dead list.

All of this had been said with conviction but inside Jessie had not felt right about leaving, which in turn had made her feel guilty. She should have jumped at the chance to be back on home ground and able to see Tom more regularly, until the day he was summoned back to fight abroad.

Looking out of the window she was choked to see how many freshly bombed sites there were, which brought flooding back the scene of that terrible day when her own house had been hit. Maybe she had been selfish in wanting to stay away from it all – a coward even. After all, millions of Londoners were there doing their bit for the war effort. Once again she found herself thinking about her twin sister, Hannah. She was missing her badly and sometimes, for a fleeting moment now and then, she had felt as if she couldn't sense her any more. As time had gone on since their first meeting after the long separation of almost two decades, an especially close feeling had grown between them, each of them sometimes knowing how the other felt even when they were apart. She wished then that Hannah would come home and spur her on, telling her she had done the right thing in leaving Elmshill.

'Penny for 'em, Jess,' said Tom, stroking Billy's hair to gently wake him.

'I was thinking about Hannah. Wondering how she is.'

'I expect your mum will 'ave heard,' he said offhandedly. He had other things on his mind – settling Jessie and Billy into their new home. 'I s'pose once you've seen the rooms you'll want to go straight round *there*. To be with your family.'

Warmed by the thought of it, she had to agree. Of course she wanted to see her mother and Dolly and her brothers. Although, if asked, she would be lying if she said she had missed them. Her life in the village had been far from lonely and had kept her mind off home. 'I don't think I want to live for ever in London, Tom,' she said.

114

'What's that got to do with going and seeing your mum? She's not written to say she wants to get out as well, has she?' Tom looked suspicious. He loved his home and had no intention of leaving.

'No. Come on. We'd best collect all my stuff. I'm sure I've come back with more than I went with.' She stood up and steadied herself as the train slowed to a stop. 'Have we got far to walk?'

'Nope. A bus ride and you're there.'

'So it's on the main road then?'

'Two minutes' walk away. Think you can manage that?'

'I should think so. I walked nearly a mile every day in Elmshill – to the village shop or into the next village where the swings outside the village hall were safer than the old swing rope by ours.'

On the platform Jessie strapped Billy into his pushchair. Tom picked up her suitcase and strode towards the exit while Jessie followed behind with Billy, carrying various shopping bags filled with provisions from both Alice and Jack. Tom's crutches had been left behind at Diss station where he'd left them leaning on a wall, forgotten. Apart from a very slight limp, she couldn't see much wrong with his leg now. And from his attitude when she mentioned the village that last time, after talking about it on and off during the journey, she knew that he was jealous of her having been happy without him – never mind what *he* might have been up to in Scotland.

They arrived in Matlock Street in Stepney. Tom stopped outside a terraced house with a freshly painted yellow door, remembered his bad leg and then continued on with a limp. Jessie was disappointed that the well-kept house where he had paused was not where she would be lodging. However, the door on which Tom finally knocked was in good shape and scrupulously clean – the doorstep was almost too white to walk on. Looking around her, Jessie was filled with apprehension. This street, as yet, had not suffered any war damage. Not one broken window-pane. It felt like the calm before the storm.

'The park's not far,' said Tom, peering at the upstairs window.

'I know.' Had he forgotten that she'd been born and bred in this area?

When the door opened, Jessie sighed with relief. Inside, the passage was clean and there was a smell of lavender polish as well as bleach. 'Oh, what a gorgeous baby!' cried Mrs Catlin. 'And don't he look like you, Tom!' She looked from Billy to Jessie and gave her the biggest smile she'd ever seen. 'Don't you look well! Must be all that fresh air!'

'Yeah,' said Tom. 'Sunshine, countryside and roses. She'll 'ave to get used to the old streets of London again now though.'

Determined to get a word in, Jessie said, 'Anyone'd think I'd been away for months.'

'I know. Men are funny creatures, aren't they?'

'Come on in, dear. You'll wear the pavement out.' Mrs Catlin looked down at Billy. 'I hope you're a good boy. I only give sweets to good boys.' As if he understood every word, Billy grinned up at her and babbled as if he was answering.

Jessie tipped the front of the pushchair to go over the front step but was stopped by Mrs Catlin. 'Oh no, dear. Hot through the house. No. Best we get things right from the beginning. Lift him out, fold the pushchair and carry it through. You'll soon get used to it I did. With all three of mine. Course, they've all grown up and gone away now and doing very nicely, thank you. So my house rules didn't do them no harm, did they?'

'Here,' said Tom, lifting Billy out. 'You fold it and—'

'Where should I leave it, Mrs Catlin?' said Jessie, worried. 'Our rooms are at the top of the house, aren't they? I can't carry Billy and the pushchair down every time I want to take him out. Especially not when I'm fetching in shopping as well.' She was tempted to repeat the bit about getting things right from the beginning.

A look of concern clouded the landlady's face as she pinched her lips together and considered. 'Mmm. I hadn't thought of that.' She rubbed her neck and let out a disappointed sigh. 'I've not had tenants with a baby before. I should have thought about all the paraphernalia that goes with babies before I gave in to Tom...'

Jessie kept her mouth shut for fear of tipping things the wrong way. She glanced at Tom and waited, her temper rising.

'Oh, come on, Eileen! One little pushchair folded up? She can keep it in the cupboard under the stairs, surely?' Tom put his free arm round Mrs Catlin and squeezed her wide, squashy body. 'Tell you what, me and you'll go to the pictures tonight. How's that?'

An instant smile flashed across the woman's face and her eyes lit up. 'He's a sod. Gets all the women round his little finger. It's them green eyes, that's what it is. All right. Put it under the stairs.'

Bemused by the little scenario, Jessie imagined Tom getting out of taking the woman to the pictures. He would get out of it, she had no doubts on that, but Eileen Catlin had been more than flattered by the offer. Jessie hoped she would be there when he turned things around so that they could go to see a film and leave the landlady looking after Billy. That was the way Tom worked.

Joking and bantering, Tom and Eileen went ahead, leaving Jessie to follow them through the long narrow passageway with all her baggage. She couldn't help wondering about Tom's life before she met him. He had told her on the train that Eileen had been like a mum to him when he was fifteen and courting her daughter, Marsha, and that she had always wanted Tom for a son-in-law and had believed that he and Marsha would get back together one day and tie the knot.

They had split up after a silly fourteen-month court-ship, had been Tom's way of putting it. Jessie hadn't really thought much about it on the train when he was explaining things. After all, Marsha would be no threat. She was out of the way, living in Stratford, happily married with two babies. But now, Jessie felt as if she was an interloper; Eileen somehow made her feel as if she had only just entered Tom's world. What's more, she had a nagging feeling that the woman was doing it on purpose.

'Here,' said Tom, 'you take Billy upstairs and see how nice Eileen's made your two rooms.'

'That's right. And I'll put the kettle on. You can have a cup of tea with me, down here,' Eileen said, a charitable tone to her voice. 'Not that I encourage that sort of thing normally; I value my privacy. Always have done.'

Tugging at Tom's sleeve, Jessie motioned for him to go with her to the top of the house. She wanted a private word. He went only as far as the passage and, keeping his voice to a whisper, he said, 'What's up with you, Jessie? You could try being a bit more friendly.'

'This don't feel right, Tom,' she whispered back. 'I don't think I'll get on with her.'

'Don't be daft, course you will. She's a diamond. Anyway, you won't 'ave to get on with her. She's got her rules. Never mixes with tenants.'

She never mixes with tenants? The words rolled through Jessie's mind as she envisaged herself upstairs on her own and Tom downstairs with his feet under the table.

'Go on up,' he said, grinning at her. 'You'll love it. Trust me, Jess.' He winked at her and carried the folded pushchair along the passage.

With Billy in one arm and a shopping bag filled with his clothes in another, Jessie climbed the stairs and couldn't help feeling she was making a big mistake. Part of her wanted to turn back and get out of this place. The closer she got to seeing where she was to live, the stronger the feeling of doom and gloom. She didn't expect to love it, as Tom had promised. To simply like it would be fine. But there was something wrong. A kind of atmosphere which couldn't be explained. It wasn't of something bad having happened but more of a feeling of things to come. An inner voice, small though it was, was telling her not to stay.

Pausing before she took the final short flight of stairs, she felt Billy tense before he wrapped his plump arms tight round her neck. Had he felt it too? 'It's all right, darling, we won't be here for long. Just for a little while... and tomorrow we'll go and see Grandma Em and Granddad.' She took another step up, feeling worse by the second. 'Then we'll go and see Nanny Rose and Aunt Dolly. Soon we'll be back in our own little house next to Granddad. We'll be back with all our friends and our family, won't we?'

Her reassuring voice seemed to relax Billy. He laid his head on her shoulder and the love and tenderness between them washed away the fear. But even then she knew that this silent, perfectly kept house would never feel, to her, like home.

Everything at the top of the house was clean and in its place but there was a clinical feeling, more so even than downstairs where Mrs Catlin lived. It had felt warmer on the second floor where another tenant lived and Jessie couldn't help wondering why and who the tenant was. Jessie's two rooms were small. There was a double bed in one, big enough, for the time being, for herself, Tom and their baby. There was no cot for Billy and no single bed. Never mind, thought Jessie, we can pick one up in a second-hand shop, cheap.

'It's not a castle, darling, but it'll do for now.' She tickled Billy under die chin but he showed no sign of a smile. He simply looked fazed by the whole thing.

On the landing was a cooker, a sink and a larder, again, everything was small but usable and clean. Hearing a burst of laughter coming from below, Jessie decided to join Tom and her new landlady. If she could start as she meant to go on, being with Tom when he was with Eileen Catlin, she would feel better about having left Elmshill, Alice immediately came to mind and then Jack and sadness swept over her. She found herself picturing Rupert Maitland but pushed him from her mind. The handsome and rich never stayed lonely for long and he, she reasoned, would soon find someone he felt comfortable with.

'What do you think then, Jess?' said Tom, looking very much at home with his legs very much under the light oak breakfast table. He looked pleased with himself. 'I told you, didn't I? I said you'd like it.'

'She'll be all right, won't you, dear? By tomorrow, with Tom out of the way in Scotland, you'll be able to settle yourself in.' Mrs Gatlin was sitting opposite Tom, holding a cup of tea.

'Tomorrow?' Jessie was surprised at how soon Tom was to depart. She'd expected at least a week.

'Yeah,' said Tom, cautiously. 'Didn't I say I only 'ad a couple of days' leave? I'm sure I told you, Jess. Your memory's going.'

Eileen seemed amused by that and told him not to be so cruel to his wife. 'Losing her memory at her age would be a tragedy,' she said. 'Mind you, I'd soon call the doctor in, if she forgot to pay the rent.' Again, Tom and Eileen laughed at her sense of humour which Jessie did not find amusing.

'You never said a word about leaving so soon, Tom, but then again, I never asked. I just presumed you were back for a while. I thought that's why you wanted me to come to London. So we could be together.' She began to feel her anger bubbling up. Why had Tom made her leave the safety and peace of Elmshill if he was just going to abandon her and Billy to the tender mercies of Eileen Catlin and the Luftwaffe?

'Oh dear,' said Eileen, 'you don't know him as well as I do, by the sound of things. Tom never told lies, he just didn't always tell the truth,' she said, chuckling.

'So why *did* you uproot me and Billy?'

'So that I can see you when I'm back on leave.' He turned to Eileen. 'She don't believe that I won't be sent abroad straightaway. I keep telling 'er though. Ten weeks, the specialist reckons, before my knees are strong enough for me to go back. They're pretty easygoing in Scotland. I'll be home once a week for a couple of days, you see if I'm not.'

'I'd best go and warm some milk for Billy.' Jessie had heard enough. More than enough.

'Do it in Eileen's kitchen. She won't mind, will you?'

'Well… just this once, since Tom's here and it's your first day. You'll find a little saucepan in there. I take it you've got your own milk?'

'Course she has,' said Tom. 'We're not spongers, you should know that. How's your wayward daughter these days, Eileen? Still as saucy as ever?'

'No. She's mellowed now that she's got responsibilities. You wouldn't recognise her, Tom. Lost some of that weight she put on after you packed her in but—'

'I never packed her in. It was by mutual agreement. So what's he like? Her old man? Not too ugly?' Watching the two of them joking and laughing as if she wasn't even in the room wasn't easy for Jessie to take. It seemed as if the Tom she once knew had changed. She couldn't put her finger on what it was but from the time he arrived in Elmshill she had felt as if they were a bit like strangers even when they made love in bed. During the brief time he was at Alice's cottage, he showed mood changes. When he was quiet he just sat, gazing at nothing, or looking at a newspaper but not reading. There had been no conversation between them and yet there was so much to talk about. She had tried, touched on various things that would normally have sparked some conversation, but a soft grunt and then silence was all she got. Was it possible that in such a short time they had grown apart?

'I'll warm the milk upstairs,' she murmured. Either they weren't listening or hadn't heard, for there was no response. Eileen carried on her conversation as if she and Tom were the only ones there.

'Now what did surprise me, Tom, was the way my daughter took to motherhood. Like a duck to water. Mind you, she does dump them on me at times, so her and her friends can go out. I don't mind, though. Who can blame 'em? What with all the men away at war. What can you expect?'

'She's a lovely looking girl, Eileen. Her old man might lose 'er to some handsome foreigner. You should keep your eye on her.' He glanced at Jessie.

'Us blokes rely on their mothers to watch their wives.'

'No. Live and let live, is what I say. Who knows what tomorrow has in store?' said Eileen, missing the point of his remark.

Leaving them to it, Jessie took Billy back upstairs. As far as she could tell, the wool had been pulled over her eyes. Tom, for reasons she couldn't quite fathom, had plucked her from a place where she was safe and happy and bedded her in a place which suited him but not her. A place perhaps where someone could keep an eye on her. And was Mrs Catlin letting her rent the rooms because of old ties and not because she had liked the sound of her and Billy?

Mrs Catlin and Tom were on first-name terms and that was fine but Jessie had a feeling that she would be expected to be less intimate and that suited her well enough. She had her own family and friends and if things didn't work out she could always move into the attic rooms in her mother's house. To be back in the fold was like a fight at the end of the dark tunnel in which she now found herself. She was tired from the journey, of course she was, but still she couldn't quite believe that things would look better in the morning, after a good night's sleep.

In bed, Tom made the same passionate love to her as he'd made in that lovely beamed room of hers in Norfolk, which had been wonderful and which she had put down to absence having made the heart grow even fonder. But now, as she lay between the sheets and he smothered her body in kisses, fervent and hot-blooded, she felt nothing. She couldn't help herself wondering if she was no more to him than any other attractive woman that he had made love to in the past – or present, come to that He seemed to be in a passionate world of his own and not once did he say he loved her, or mention her name the way he used to. As she lay there beneath him, without passion or feeling, he came inside her, grunting and sweating and enjoying himself. And he hadn't even noticed that she had felt nothing.

As she lay beside him in the dark, her tears soaking the pillow while he slipped into a contented sleep, she realised that the Tom she knew and loved so much had changed. War had changed him. But she would be patient. Once it was over, she would get the old Tom back. The man who once put her feelings before everyone else's. Not the man who had, earlier on, not even been aware that he had shut her out totally when in the company of an old girlfriend's mother. Without doubt he had put Eileen Catlin before her. A stranger before Jessie. Jessie whom he had once loved to death and protected. Jessie whom he had once vowed he would die for rather than see her unhappy.

Turning on to her side, she looked at little Billy fast asleep on the makeshift bed of two armchairs pushed together. She sent him loving thoughts. 'For you, darling, for you I'll make everything work. For better or worse, I'll still love your daddy.'

The next morning brought sunshine streaming through the light curtains and a lighter feeling within Jessie. A touch of excitement even. She wasn't looking forward to seeing Tom off but she was looking forward to seeing her family again. It was 7 a.m, and both Billy and Tom were sound asleep. From downstairs she could hear the distant sound of movement and music coming from the wireless.

Turning in the bed and half asleep, Tom was mumbling, asking what time it was.

'Time to get up,' said Jessie, swinging her legs out of the bed before he could wrap a clammy arm round her and begin another round of lovemaking. 'I'm going downstairs to fetch some hot water so we can wash and be out early.'

'Out where?' mumbled Tom.

'To Mum's. She'll want to see you before you go back.'

'No she won't. Stop dreaming.' He turned his back to her and settled down to sleep. 'You go if you want but leave Billy here. You might not be bothered about spending the last couple of hours with me before I go but—'

'*Couple* of hours?'

'Yeah. I'm catching the mid-morning train.'

'Oh. Right. Well, thanks very much. You drag me back down to London and then sod off.'

'Teh. Leave off, Jessie. You're turning into an old woman. A nagging old woman.'

'And whose fault's that?' She pulled on her housecoat. 'If you'd taken precautions like any other decent bloke would have, I might still be a single girl enjoying my youth!' With that she stormed out of the room. It had been bad enough when her sister threw remarks like that at her but at least Dolly had no part in the blame as to *why* she didn't go out in the evenings.

Arriving in the kitchen she found Eileen at the sink, washing her lace curtains. Washing and humming to music on the wireless.

'Where do I get my water from, Mrs Gatlin?' Jessie asked, her voice still tinged with anger.

Startled, the woman clasped her heart, leaving a wet handprint on her grey crepe blouse. 'Oh! You frightened the life out of me!' She dropped on to a kitchen chair. 'I can't have that. I can't have you creeping about like Jesus. Call out in future, dear, please, from a flight up. That way I'll know you're coming down. Not that I expect you to come down, you understand. Into my living quarters, that is. Now, what was you saying?'

'Where's the water tap?'

Eileen looked puzzled and she narrowed her eyes at Jessie as if she was a halfwit. 'In the back yard, dear.'

'Back yard? What about in the winter? When it's freezing out there?'

'You put on your coat and hat. The pipe hardly ever freezes. I make sure of that. Mr Catlin, God rest his soul, always insisted we lagged the pipes thoroughly. I can only ever once remember it freezing up. That must 'ave been… oh, now let me see…'

'So I'll need a bucket?' Jessie tried not to snap.

'Yes, dear, you will. A big bucket, mind, and only three-quarters filled. We don't want it tipping out and on to the stairs, do we?'

Jessie said that she would use the jug from the wash-basin in her room for the time being but that didn't go down well either. 'I bleached that jug inside and out very thoroughly. I shouldn't think you'd want to drink water that comes out of that. No. That's for washing your body and hair and bathing the baby. You don't want to have to keep running down the public baths just to have a wash. Once a week for a bath is more than enough. I'm not keen on public baths myself. No, you'll have to get a bucket from Mr Budgen's shop. We can't have you trundling up and down wearing out the lino with jugs of water all day long.'

'So what do you suggest then? For now?'

'Fill your kettle from the tap outside. Then go down Petticoat Lane to Mr Budgen's shop and buy whatever you need. You'll need more than a bucket, I dare say; once you've thought things through, which I expect you'll do now, over a cup of tea.'

Jessie had got as far as the bottom stair when Eileen called out to her. 'You'll want to be thinking about your washing too. What with napkins and one thing and another. I don't allow tenants to hang washing on the line. I don't like a long line in my garden and the one that's there I use myself, every day. You'll have to use the baths to do your boil–up and washing.' Gritting her teeth, Jessie climbed the stairs to the top of the house. She was glad her rooms were as far away from her landlady as possible but worried at the thought of having to go up and down those stairs with Billy in her arms every time she wanted to go out. And she would be going out. As often as possible. She didn't cherish the thought of spending time at the top of the house with just Billy for company. She'd had enough of loneliness since the day Tom had been summoned to the army.

–

It seemed wrong to Jessie that she should have to knock on her mother's door and not use a key. This was her childhood home. Most of her memories were of this house. Expecting Rose to answer the door, she was surprised to see her German grandmother, and Ingrid was equally surprised to see Jessie, Tom and their baby. At first they simply gazed at each other in silence. A silence which was soon broken. 'Am I seeing things?' Ingrid looked from her granddaughter to her great-grandson in the pushchair.

'No,' said Jessie, holding back her emotions. 'I've come back to London – to stay.'

'I moved her back,' said Tom, grinning like a Cheshire cat. 'She was turning into a soppy country yokel. Wasn't having none of that. My son a carrot cruncher?'

Breaking into a smile, Ingrid waved them in. 'It doesn't surprise me. You always seem to get what you want, Tom.' A candid look passed between the two of them. Ingrid had taken to Tom from the first time she saw him and he had taken to her.

'The house is quiet,' said Jessie, easing the pushchair through the passage and parking it. 'Where is everyone?'

'You expected a hero's welcome when no one knew you were coming? Your mother, Stephen and Dolly are at the hospital visiting that wayward brother of yours.'

'Alfie?'

'That's not what I call him. He is nursing a broken leg and a few bruises. Apart from that he is no less the high-spirited lad you left behind for your mother to worry over. It was not a bomb which caused the damage. I would not like to speculate on what happened. Your mother believes he fell over during a panic rush to the Underground after an air-raid warning.' She raised an eyebrow. 'At least she says she believes him. Would you like tea or coffee?'

'Tea,' said Tom, 'and strong.'

'One for each cup and one for the pot,' Ingrid said, reciting her daughter Rose's instructions. 'Although if my memory serves me, you prefer two for the pot, Tom.'

'That's right. Stand your spoon up in it.'

'An expression I have yet to fathom,' said Ingrid, going downstairs to the kitchen.

Following her, Tom and Jessie shared a smile. This woman changed for no one. War or not, she remained calm, composed and smelling of lavender. Her clothes, always the same colour, grey and snow-white, except for special occasions when she would wear a pretty silk neck scarf. Ingrid had a small drawer frill of them in various colours. The white cotton blouse with Peter Pan collar and a touch of lace was as fresh as the day it was made. Ingrid was a fine seamstress.

'So,' said Tom, leaning back in a chair, legs outstretched, 'you've moved in at last?'

'I was needed here. I have sublet my flat. At the present time, two young mothers each with a baby are staying there. And before you ask if I trust them to take care of my home, I can tell you they are German and from a good background. In these times we Germans must stick together. We are not the most popular people, as you can imagine.'

'I hadn't thought about that,' said Jessie. 'Has it been difficult?'

'I am used to such things.' She poured boiling water into the teapot. 'I keep myself to myself and smile when the time is right. It was a bit of a shock for your mother's neighbours to learn that I was a Kraut. But they see no harm in an old lady who has lived practically all of her life in this country. Your brother Alfie is a different matter.

He has his reputation to think of, as no doubt he will tell you. He refused to let his friends come to the house in case they discover his German grandmother.'

'Come to the house? You mean that Alfie's moved back in?'

'Yes. For his own reasons, naturally. But your mother prefers to believe he was missing his family. Ha!' A humorous expression crossed her face. 'For all of that, I like the scoundrel. But please, never repeat that. It would ruin our relationship.' Ingrid leaned over and studied Billy's features. 'He looks more like Tom than he does you, Jessie. What a pity.' Billy smiled back at her and looked for all the world as if he understood what she was saying. His gurgling and big smile showed he approved. Even he, as young as he was, had taken to the silver-haired lady in grey.

While Billy enjoyed his time sitting on a thick rug on the kitchen floor, munching on a biscuit, Ingrid filled Jessie in on the latest bombing in the area, on rationing and how Rose was coping. Dolly, as expected, was still making the most of things, which amused Ingrid. Tom began to get edgy about the time. He didn't want to miss his train.

'When are you expecting Jessie's mum back, Ingrid?' said Tom at last.

She glanced at the clock on the shelf. 'In about an hour, maybe less.'

'Oh, right…'

'Why? Is there a fire somewhere?'

'I don't want to be late back. In fact, I was warned not to be. They think I might do a runner. Tch. As if.'

'Maybe we should leave now then, Tom. Do you mind keeping an eye on Billy, Gran, while I walk him to the stop?'

'No, I don't mind. Good luck, Tom. God be with you.' Ingrid nodded a polite farewell to him.

'That don't sound fair, Jess,' said Tom. 'You should be 'ere when your mum comes in. What's the difference anyway if you see me to the doorstep or the main road. It won't be easy wherever it is. And you shouldn't leave Billy so soon. Poor sod won't know what's up.'

Jessie simply nodded. There seemed little point in pursuing it. Tom, for whatever reason, couldn't wait to get away from her. All that he had said made sense but it just wasn't like him. Normally she was the sensible and practical one, not him. One of them had changed. Or maybe they had both changed. She pondered on it for a few minutes before giving him a proper answer but he was in first, saying that it would only be a week before he was back again.

'But your crutches, Tom. Won't it look a bit odd, you going back without 'em?'

'I'll get the porter to phone from the station. Say someone pinched 'em off the train. They'll come and fetch me from the station… and I'll ask for a wheelchair back to my bed.'

'Maybe you are the one who should have been an actor and not young Stephen,' said Ingrid, a more serious tone to her voice. 'Do you like the hospital?'

'You couldn't help but like it, Ingrid, after what I've been through and what I witnessed at Dunkirk. It was hardly a holiday with a hotel thrown in.' He looked at Jessie and winked. 'So that's settled then. You can walk me to the corner of the turning. Don't take your eyes off him, Ingrid. She won't be more than ten minutes.'

'I can be trusted, my friend. So long as your plan suits my granddaughter. Jessie? Are you content to see him to the corner or would you prefer to go all the way with him to the station by bus?'

'The corner suits me,' she said, hiding her disappointment and anger. As far as she was concerned right then, Tom could do what he liked. He would in any case. She had other things to look forward to. Seeing her mother, sister and brothers again. And as Tom had said, he would soon be back. Maybe on his next visit they would have time to be alone together to talk, the way they used to.

Watching him walk away from her without looking back, Jessie felt choked. Something had happened. Tom was different and try as he might he couldn't pull the wool over her eyes. That loving feeling that used to ooze from him had gone and she couldn't help wondering if something was going on between him and the nurse in Scotland. She promised herself that she would confront him on his next home leave. Meanwhile, she would have to live with the awful feeling of betrayal.

'No tears?' said Ingrid on Jessie's return. 'I thought you might be bawling your eyes out, as Dolly would say.'

'No. I'll save that for later when I'm in bed.'

'And where is your bed to be?' Ingrid sounded a touch concerned.

'Tom found me a couple of rooms not far from here. A ten-minute walk, that's all, so I'll be able to come and go.'

'You don't sound too thrilled over the rooms.'

'They're fine. Very clean. Are the tenants still in the attic rooms?' Jessie hoped not.

'No. But I am. Myself and my brother's daughter and two children. But should you want to come back, I'm sure we could make other arrangements. It wouldn't be a problem.'

'Don't be silly,' said Jessie, suddenly feeling desperately disappointed. She hadn't realised how much she had been hoping the rooms might be vacant. 'The landlady's an old friend of Tom's and, well, I'll be all right.'

'Well, that's good. Yes. Although I'm sure that once Emmie knows you're back she'll want you and her grandson to stop with her. She has a spare room. She'll soon get over it.'

'Over what?' Jessie's eyes narrowed as she wondered what had been going on while she'd been away.

'Your leaving. She feels you could have stayed. Here with your family or there with her. Billy is her only grandson. You must try and understand how she felt.'

'I suppose you're right. I'll wait till Mum gets back, spend a bit of time with her and then go and see Emmie and Charlie. Have they heard from Stanley yet?'

'No.' Ingrid slowly shook her head. 'A woman gives birth to three sons and watches them grow from boy to man and then stands by helpless as she loses them one by one. Her firstborn killed before he has had a glimpse of the prime of life. Her third and the baby missing, presumed dead. And Tom, probably her favourite son, he comes home on leave from Scotland and doesn't even bother to go and visit her.' She looked Jessie in the eye. 'Can you blame her for sometimes not wanting to get up in the mornings?'

Guilty that she had been thinking only of herself, Jessie made up her mind there and then to take Billy to see his other grandmother first. 'Tell Mum that I'll be back in a couple of hours. I'm going round there right now.'

'Good. I'm pleased to see that this wretched war has not changed you. You know, Jessie, life is like a game of Patience. You think you will never sort out the cards and then all of a sudden it all fits into place. Not always and not for everyone but mostly with time it does. So stop worrying over Tom. If he does have a sweetheart up there in Scotland, he will soon see the error of his ways.'

'How did you know I was worried about that?' Jessie was startled. Once again Ingrid had caught her by surprise. Was she a mind-reader?

'Because you are my granddaughter. Because I hear Rose and Emmie talk and so I know what worries they have. Be strong, Jessie, and don't be afraid to fight. You can win.' Then with a wave of her hand, Ingrid ended the conversation and gave Jessie a firm message that she should leave.

Pushing Billy in his pram, Jessie made her way to Bethnal Green and Grant Street, something she would much rather have done with Tom at her side. She didn't want to see her house the way it was and according to what she'd gleaned from Tom and a letter from his mother to him, the house had only been boarded up and nothing else. At least the furniture was in safekeeping, stored in a disused warehouse along with other people's things. The Red Cross had seen to that.

The look of surprise and pleasure on Charlie's face when he opened the door to Jessie was the best tonic she could have hoped for. Especially since the house next door, hers and Tom's, looked a sorry place. The damaged roof was protected by tarpaulin and the entire front of the house was boarded.

'Well, if it ain't an angel in disguise!' said Charlie, happy and laughing. 'Wait till she sees you!' He clicked his tongue and nodded her in. 'Emmie! We've got visitors!'

Once Emmie appeared it was one big round of mixed emotions and they all ended up crying and laughing, except for Billy, who once again was simply watching the fiasco. Slightly puzzled, Emmie tried to hide her hurt that Tom hadn't called round and instead treated Jessie like a queen, asking for all the news about her time in Norfolk while laying out a delicious lunch. Afterwards, Jessie headed back to Stepney where Rose was eager to welcome her daughter. Stephen had also been delighted to see his big sister, dancing her round the kitchen with excitement.

Returning to her digs after seeing everyone again was a bit of a let down. When Mrs Catlin opened the door to her, the first thing she said was that she couldn't possibly keep running to the door every five minutes and that Jessie should remember her key. Jessie hadn't actually been given one yet but didn't think it the right time to say so. Her landlady was not the chirpy, happy character she had been when Tom was in the house. Jessie wished then that she had taken up Emmie's offer to walk back with her.

She went inside, carrying Billy in one arm and a bag of treats in the other, a large slab of homemade Madeira cake from her mother, together with a jar of plum jam and marmalade that Ingrid had made. From Emmie she had a meatless pie and three tins of condensed milk. From Charlie there was Welfare orange juice, cod liver oil and malt – compliments of the Welfare clinic. If there was anything going, Charlie was there. From Stephen there had been a bundle of well-worn comics for Billy to tear up, his favourite occupation. Rose had also given her the usual groceries, a packet of tea, some sugar lumps, a packet of tea fingers and Scots porridge oats. With her own ration book she had purchased from the Jewish corner shop a loaf of bread and four ounces of butter. She also bought herself five Woodbines and a book of matches. The cigarettes would be put away for when she might need a puff. She had tried smoking for the first time when Tom was home late one night and hadn't, as she'd expected, felt in the least bit sick after her first draw.

After she had brewed herself a cup of tea and put Billy down with his bottle propped on a small pillow, she put up her feet and closed her eyes. It was seven in the evening and she was exhausted. Billy hadn't even finished his milk before he was dead to the world.

It was a quiet tapping on the door which roused her from her dream of being back in Alice's cottage. It was the lady from the room below. 'Hello, kid,' she said. 'I thought I'd come and introduce myself. If your baby's asleep you can come down and 'ave a little drop of sherry with me. I keep a bottle by. I'm Edna, by the way. Edna Redman.'

'How d'you do,' Jessie said politely. 'I'm Jessie Smith.'

'Charmed, I'm sure. Always delighted to make the acquaintance of a neighbour,' Edna said in a joke hoity-toity voice and beamed.

Jessie took an instant liking to her. Her bleached blonde-ginger hair gave her a sunny appearance. Her eyebrows had been completely shaved and pencilled back into a thin arched shape, and her bright blue eyes stood out beneath black mascara lashes, topped by blue eye shadow. She was wearing a bright orange and green frilly blouse which should have looked cheap and gaudy, but on her it didn't. Everything about Edna, right down to the fluffy pink slippers and black tight skirt, went together in a peculiar kind of way. None of her bits matched, especially not the red earrings, and yet she made a lively picture to brighten any dull day. What she would look like outside in the blazing sunshine was anyone's guess.

'You'll be able to 'ear if your little one wakes up. You keep your door open and I'll do the same. That old bat downstairs won't allow smoking in the house so I stand by a window and blow it out there.'

All of this was said in a supposedly quiet voice. Jessie hope that Mrs Catlin was not within earshot. She waited until she was inside Edna's room before she said anything. 'This is a big room. Lovely and light.'

'Yeah, but it's all I've got. There's no space to put anything down. It's what you might call a bedsit-cum-kitchen. Couldn't swing a bleeding cat in it. Not that the old bag lets me keep my cat. Cow. I ain't forgot that nor will I neither. Sit yourself down. You don't 'ave to stand on ceremony for me. I might look like a queen but I'm a simple boy at heart.'

I might look like a queen hut I'm a simple hoy at heart? Jessie lowered herself on to the sofa, taking in what Edna had said. 'She's a strange woman, Mrs Catlin. I can't quite fathom her,' she murmured, flummoxed.

'Don't bleeding well try, love. The woman's not right in the 'ead. If they put bleach and soap powder on rationing, it'll be a blessing. She'll be carted off to Balmy Park to wander aimless with the rest of the crackpots. Here. Taste that. Best sherry, that is.' Edna handed Jessie a crystal glass filled to the brim with the reddish gold liquid. 'It's not rubbish so sip it and make it last.'

'How long 'ave you lodged here?' asked Jessie, feeling as if she'd found a neighbour to brighten her day. She couldn't help smiling at Edna and her mannerisms.

'Long enough. Well, Jessie love, bottoms up! Here's to you and me getting on and turning a blind eye should either of us fetch a fella back. I'll cover for you and you cover for me. We'll run rings round that silly cow down there.'

'Cheers,' said Jessie, chuckling. 'Though I don't know about me and fellas. I'm married.'

Edna smacked her lips. 'Oooh, just what the doctor ordered. So, Jessie love, you must 'ave guessed by now that I'm not all I look to be...' She crossed her legs and posed as if for a photograph. 'Not that you would 'ave guessed if I 'adn't dropped all the clues. I just wanted you to know from the beginning. I can't be bothered with that sodding pretence lark. I'm a bloke in a frock and very much like a lot of religious men who wear frocks as well. Although I won't name names.' She sipped her drink and waited.

'Does Mrs Catlin know?'

'Course she does. Pretends not to though. I pay my rent regular and abide by all 'er sodding rules. Well, I 'ave to, don't I? She's got me by the short and wotsits. Any sign of a manly visitor and she'd be up the bloody station. Or would she? I'm not so sure. She does all right out of the black market. I know people. I get around, if you see what I mean. So, no, I don't ever let a *suited* man step over my threshold, if you get my drift.'

Jessie burst out laughing. 'You mean they all wear frocks and wigs when they come to see you?'

'Good girl. You've got it. It all came out of necessity but do you know what, they pay more because of it. Think it's my speciality.' She pushed her long painted fingernail under her lacquered ginger hair and scratched. 'I tell you, there are more men who like to wear women's clothes than the papers'd like to print. Take no one at face value, love. No one.' She lifted the bottle of sherry and in a theatrical manner asked if madam would like another tipple.

'Go on then,' said Jessie, laughing at her, 'but not too much. I've got a baby to look after.'

'Course you 'ave.' She filled her glass to the rim. 'And if we can get one thing straight right now. Queers do not go in for little boys – perverts do, and I 'ave nothing to do with that lot. So you don't have to watch and worry when I'm playing with 'im upstairs.'

'I wouldn't. You look like a woman and you walk like one so—'

'Ah, that's a lovely thing to say. Ta. I wouldn't mind – does anyone ever imagine a woman messing about with little boys? Course they don't. If they 'ad their heads screwed on they'd realise we're just the same.' She wrinkled her face. 'Makes my stomach turn thinking about it. Anyway, enough of that. That's out of the way. Now Fanny Adams downstairs. Don't slam doors. Never, never hang your washing on her precious bloody clothesline and don't try and be nice to 'er. Wait. That's all you 'ave to do. Just wait. Let 'er think you're not bothered about her and she'll be better for it. Make the silly cow work at getting *you* to take to 'er. I'm not saying you should be unsociable but don't crawl up her arse. Believe me, it don't work. She's a nutcase – leave it at that. What brings you to this house anyway?'

'Mine was bombed,' said Jessie, surprised that she could say it without emotion. In Edna's company you couldn't feel miserable.

'Ah rotten luck. And your old man's gone back to war. Good-looking bloke like that. Oh yeah, I clocked 'im from my window. A real man. Can't beat 'em. Never mind. You'll be all right now. Here in this sterilised shit hole. Now sit back and listen to this. I'm on at the Blue Star in the West End tonight. I'm gonna try my jokes out on you.'

Jessie was laughing before Edna had even started. She was the funniest person she'd ever met. Funny without trying and without having to utter one word. Every movement was affected. Yes, Edna Redman was a natural for the stage. Thank God for people like her, thought Jessie, and thank God she's staying in the same house as me.

–

It didn't take Jessie more than a couple of days to knuckle down to a new routine in her not-so-convenient rooms at the top of the house. Taking the advice of her new friend downstairs, she never once hung her washing out to dry in Mrs Catlin's garden, she had fixed a fairly ingenious line across and round the landing which was known as the kitchen and dining area. At least that way she could open her windows to let plenty of air through and turn on the gas cooker for heat on a damp day. Going forever up and down the stairs to fetch and carry water was not easy. She had always to make sure that Billy was safe in the makeshift playpen which she created by using the two armchairs in the corner of her room. The pieces of furniture were heavy and awkward to manoeuvre but they were feather-cushioned and comfortable. Billy slept very well on them when they doubled up for his bed.

The air-raid siren had gone off a few times and a public shelter not far from the street was where Jessie took refuge. Edna, on the other hand, had stood firm in her belief that she was safer in the cupboard under Mrs Catlin's staircase and that, whether her landlady liked it or not, was where she went. The Anderson shelter in the back garden was so filled with furniture and tinned food that there was only space for one single camp bed and that was exclusively for Eileen Catlin.

Ironically, the street, even though it was closer to the docks, an obvious enemy target, received far less bomb damage than there had been in Bethnal Green. Jessie was surprised how Londoners had adapted to the prospect of bombs falling in and around the city, which was becoming a nightly occurrence. She often thought back to Elmshill and the neighbouring villages but she had stopped hankering for that good and healthy life. She was, after all, a Londoner, born and bred, and felt at home with the East End people all around her. The buzz in the air and the feeling of camaraderie more than made up for the risk.

Comfortable at leaving Billy with Edna who had become his second mother and was loving every minute of it, she had managed to get out with Dolly and her friends and gone dancing with Dutch and French sailors whose ships had docked close by. Most, if not all, of them expected sex at the end of a good evening and several got it. But not from Jessie. All she wanted after a few drinks and an enjoyable night was her bed, with Billy sleeping close by. And Edna's reward for child-minding was to share a glass of something with Jessie and hear a step-by-step account of what had happened on each evening out. Sometimes the pair of them laughed and talked into the wee hours.

Edna had learned all there was to know of Jessie's family and the complicated history. She was looking forward to the day when she would meet all of them. Especially Dolly whom Edna had already taken to even though she'd never seen her.

'Your mother sounds a bit on the posh side for an East Ender, love, but I s'pose we've all got our cross to bear,' she commented. Stephen had been to visit a few times and it had not taken more than one run-in with him for Edna to see where he was heading. 'Leave the poor little sod be,' had been her advice. 'He'll fall in soon enough and when he does, you make damn sure you're there to give all your support. Poor little beggar'll need it.'

It was three weeks after Jessie had moved in, and when she'd gone downstairs to pay her rent, that Jessie and Mrs Catlin fell out. Her landlady had told her not to put washing on the landing at the top to dry. Her words stung Jessie.

'It stinks up there,' Mrs Catlin complained. 'What with that and you dragging that pushchair through my passage every day. I shouldn't have let you have them rooms. Tom should 'ave known better than to persuade me. He knows how I feel about tenants with babies. And you don't clean them stairs properly. Twice a week wash with all the comings and goings? That's not enough. And don't think I can't hear you and that strange tart laughing right through the night. Lord above knows what you get up to. And why Tom hasn't been back yet I don't know. It's as if he's dumped his family and run.'

'What do you want me to do, Mrs Catlin?' said Jessie, ignoring all of that. 'I've got to have water and I can't do much about the stairs. And as for where I hang my laundry, don't you think that *I* would prefer to see my son's napkins hanging on a clothesline, Out in the fresh air! And Edna is not a tart. She brings light and fun into this stony cold home! You should try talking to her! It might bring a smile to your miserable face!'

Furious at hearing some home truths, Mrs Catlin lost no time in telling Jessie to pack her things and get out. There and then. The truth of the matter was that she had already promised the rooms to a professional couple with no children who worked in the city in the government offices. She had deliberately heckled Jessie and won.

'I knew I shouldn't 'ave been taken in by your old man. He always did 'ave the gift of the gab. Coming round 'ere and wheedling his way back into my good books. Thank Christ my daughter never did marry the waster! Bad leg? Pull the other one. There's nothing wrong with 'im. He's a lazy shirker. Won't go back out there and fight for his country! He's no more than a yellow belly. A coward!'

The loud stinging slap to Mrs Catlin's face seemed to come out of nowhere. Jessie hadn't thought of hitting the woman. She hadn't thought about anything. The word 'coward' was still ringing through her brain. Startled and thrown off balance, her landlady fell backwards against the passage wall and slipped on the rug covering the polished lino. As she fell, her sprawling arm hit a large vase, sending it and the slim round table beneath flying.

The sound of broken glass brought Edna to the top of the stairs and as she stared down at the unconscious body of Mrs Catlin, she murmured, 'Oh my God, love, what have you done?'

'She's not moving, Edna. Why isn't she moving? I only slapped her face. She slipped on the rug. Why isn't she moving!' Jessie felt hysteria rising in her.

'Don't bloody panic, love,' was Edna's calm and deeply worried reply as she came down the stairs, 'The old cow's too stubborn to peg out.' Edna felt for a pulse and then looked up to heaven. 'Thank you, Lord. God bless yer cotton socks.'

'I smacked her round the face, that's all I did.' Jessie was too frightened to cry.

'No, you never. You bloody never.'

'She told me I 'ad to leave. She called Tom a coward. A yellow belly.'

'Yeah, and I know why. A right pair of toffs were 'ere yesterday asking for rooms. Go and pack your suitcases, love. And be quick about it.'

'Look at the colour of her face. I don't think she's breathing. All I did was slap her face, honest to God. I smacked her round the face, that's all,' Jessie insisted, beginning to tremble.

Edna stood up straight and pointed a finger right into Jessie's face. 'You never smacked her in the face. I *did*. That's what I'll tell her when she comes round. I'll say she was screaming the odds and I did it for her own good. Now get upstairs and pack before she comes round.'

'I can't go just like that. Where am I supposed to go?'

Edna felt Mrs Catlin's pulse again to double check. There wasn't one but Jessie didn't have to know that. 'She'll be all right but she'll sue you for damages, love.'

'But I only—'

'Go upstairs and pack, you silly cow! She would 'ave 'ad you out within the hour in any case. Move yourself! She'll 'ave you in court before you can blink an eye and they'll take your Billy away from you. Move yourself, you dozy cow.'

Gripping the stair rail and backing up the stairs, her eyes on the strange, lifeless body of her landlady, Jessie was shaking all over. 'She will be all right, won't she, Edna?'

'She'll be fine. Her sort always come up smelling of roses.'

Once Jessie was out of sight and up in her own rooms packing her things, Edna sat on the stairs and contemplated her next move. Her first thoughts had been to drag the body out of the passage and out of sight. She didn't want Jessie to see her when she came back down or for sure she would realise that this was a dead landlady on the floor. Lifting her head gently from where blood was oozing out and on to the floor, she felt for a heartbeat. Nothing. She lifted an eyelid and all was confirmed. If Jessie followed her natural instincts she would want to tell the police all that had happened. A slap round the face would not be readily accepted and she could see her friend standing in the dock facing a murder charge. The thought of Jessie hanging from a noose made Edna go cold.

Going into Mrs Catlin's living room she looked around for a cushion to place under the woman's head and a rug to cover her. She would leave her in that position and tell Jessie that she had come round, had a sip of water, and was suffering from mild concussion and that she was best left where she was until Jessie had gone and Edna had found some smelling salts.

The next step was to go upstairs and help Jessie throw her bits and pieces into carrier bags and get her away as soon as possible. Affecting a calm, untroubled manner, Edna went into her friend's tiny bedroom where she was throwing her clothes into a suitcase. 'I wouldn't go to your mother's if I were you, love. Once the old bat's come round she'll only make trouble for you. I've got a few quid tucked away. I should make your way back to that lovely little village in Norfolk if I were you.'

'I can't take your money, Edna,' said Jessie. 'You never know when you'll need it. I'll be all right. I won't go back home. I'll move on. We'll be all right. I might even go to Scotland to Tom.'

Edna couldn't let her do that. She was nearly forty years old and the wiser for it. From what she had heard and seen of Tom, she didn't trust him an inch. 'Bloody Scotland. Do me a favour, girl. All that damp and cold weather. Lot of good that'll do Billy. It rains all summer from what I've heard, never mind that winter's on its way. You can't go there.' The conversation continued and all the while Billy slept through it. Opening the last drawer she had to clear, Jessie broke into tears. 'I can't believe this is happening.' She sat on the edge-of her bed. 'Pinch me, Edna. Pinch me and wake me up.'

'Oh, shut up, you silly cow. Worse things 'appen at sea. Worse things 'appen round the bloody corner. My favourite pub was hit last week and my favourite barman blown to smithereens.' She looked around her. 'Anything else?'

'Just my soap and toothbrush and stuff.'

'Where?'

'Outside by the little sink.'

'Outside! You brushed your bloody teeth out in the back yard?'

'No. Outside my door. On the landing by the wash-basin. There's a small cupboard there as well with other things in it.' Jessie ran a hand through her hair. 'This is silly. I'm not running away.'

'Course you're not. You're leaving peacefully just like your landlady asked. Those toffs she saw yesterday are ready to come in so your story, should you ever be asked, will ring true.'

'She won't send the police after me, Edna. All I did was slap her face. She slipped on her own stupid polished floor.'

'Oh, well, you never know with her type. She 'as to 'ave the upper hand, and once she comes round, she'll wanna get back at you. Best you're as far from the old cow as possible.'

'I don't know where to go,' said Jessie, bewildered. 'I can't go back to the village, just like that. And I daren't go home to Mum – not looking like this.'

Edna gave her the once over and had to agree. 'You look like someone's old clothes-horse. Stand up straight and brush your bleeding 'air.'

Jessie flopped down on to the bed. 'What's 'appening to me? What's going on? I feel as if I'm losing my grip...'

'You are, love,' said Edna, trying to lighten things. 'Listen. I've had a thought. It's hop-picking time. Get yourself down to Kent. My brother's down there with 'is family. Go to Paddock Wood. Whitby's Farm. They 'ave smashing huts. Brick-built with a window that opens and a little fireplace in the corner. The air'll do you good. Go there. You won't 'ave to find my brother, he'll find you. Johnnie's his name. His wife's a smasher. Eve. Johnnie and Eve. Everyone'll know 'em.'

Unable to think as fast as Edna, Jessie sat on a small chair and covered her face. 'Maybe I should go to Mum's. What do I know about hop-picking? I've only been the once. When I was a kid I went with a family down our street, as company for their daughter, my school friend...'

'Once is enough. You don't need a bloody certificate to know how to pick an 'op. Besides, you don't wanna be in London once the coppers get wind of this.'

Working quickly before Jessie could change her mind, Edna had her outside with Billy in the pushchair, a suitcase perched on the hood, one carrier bag hooked on a wing nut and another two in Jessie's free hand. Opening the button on the pocket of Jessie's blouse, Edna tucked ten one-pound notes inside. 'You can pay me that back when the war's over.' She kissed her friend on the cheek and gave her a gentle shove. 'Don't worry, love. We'll meet again.' Turning away before she broke into tears, Edna went inside the house and shut the door.

Once inside she removed the rug and cushion from Mrs Cadin's body and put it back where she had found it Then she sat on the stairs, thinking. 'You silly cow,' she murmured, gazing at the lifeless body. 'Why couldn't you aye bin a bit more compassionate? This would never 'ave 'appened. What good did it do yet, eh? What bloody good did it do yer?'

She sat for a while longer until she felt sure Jessie was out of earshot. Then she took a deep breath, steeled herself and went into acting mode. Screaming as if she'd just that second found her landlady on the floor, she ran from the house into the street, crying for help and yelling that poor Mrs Catlin had had an accident. Doors soon opened and the neighbours came out, more from curiosity than worry. This woman was not popular, to say the least. She had been the cause of several rows in the street and was known as a troublemaker and too house-proud for her own good.

The ambulance arrived and Edna gave her account of how the woman had been polishing the passage ready to impress the new tenants who were to take the top rooms. A professional couple that Mrs Catlin had not stopped bragging about. She said that Jessie Smith had left: some fifteen minutes before the accident and was on her way to

Kent – hop-picking. Other than that, there was nobody else in the house. She reeled off her story and remembered her lines. She had to make it sound believable for the police when they appeared to talk to her and the neighbours. She wouldn't get one word out of place. Not one.

When they carried out Mrs Catlin on the stretcher, a red blanket covering the whole of her, Edna felt a wave of sadness. Old cow or not, she didn't deserve to have her life cut short. Edna looked down at the rug on the floor and the polished lino and shook her head. 'It's a bleedin' wonder we 'aven't all slipped and cracked our skulls.'

–

When she arrived at London Bridge station, Jessie could hardly remember the long walk there. Her mind had been so full of what she would do if there were no huts vacant on the farm that she hadn't given a thought as to her alternatives. Why was she going to Kent? Why should she run away? Her own mother would take her in, surely? But then she remembered what Edna had said: 'You don't wanna be in London once the coppers get wind of this. Your old man's on the run, don't forget. They'll be down on you like a ton of bricks, girl.'

She smiled at little Billy, who was happy in his own innocent world, making himself very sticky with the toffee apple she'd bought on the way into the station. Waiting on the platform for her train, she found she wasn't the only one making her way to the hop fields of Kent. A woman sat on a platform bench surrounded by three scruffy children and a homemade cart which contained her belongings – cardboard boxes filled with pots and pans, bedding, clothes, Wellington boots, a couple of chairs and a small table. Jessie's heart sank as she realised that she had nothing but her clothes.

'What's up, love? This bloody war made you a widow an' all?'

'No.' Jessie smiled weakly back at her. 'I just thought I'd get out of London and go hop-picking but I never thought that, well, that I would need so much stuff.' She nodded towards the woman's belongings.

'Oh, I've got more than I would normally take, love. My 'ouse is in no fit state to live in. Once picking's over and the fields are bare, I'm 'oping the welfare will 'ave arranged for me and my kids to stay on as evacuees. Plenty of families are doing that, you know. Better to 'ave two or three little huts than live in with a family. I couldn't be doing with that.' The woman looked Jessie up and down, taking in her meagre possessions and strained face. 'Poor cow,' said her expression. 'Never mind, girl, I expect the Red Cross'll help you out. They're very good like that. What farm you going to?'

'One in Paddock Wood.'

'Oh well, you shouldn't 'ave much trouble there. Very good Salvation Army around that way. They'll show you 'ow to go about things. I should make that your first stop. That or the Red Cross. Have you been hop-picking before, love?'

'When I was little. I went with a friend's family. I liked it. I thought the air would do my baby good.' Billy, his face sticky and adorable had fallen asleep again.

'He's a right little love. He'll be looked after. It's a sweet life down 'opping. Dipping into the River Medway by day and sitting around the camp fires by night having a singsong. Hard work though, picking hops from morning till late afternoon; dragging them bloody bundles of twigs to your fireplace from the big pile round some big old tree and then cooking the family meal. Still, you've only yourself and the little fellow to fend for.'

'If it doesn't work out we can always come back.'

'Oh, I shouldn't say that in front of the farmer. He won't give you a hut if he thinks you're just there for a short 'oliday.'

Jessie was having second thoughts. 'Maybe I should turn round now and go back.'

'No, you don't wanna do that. Get yourself out of London while all this is going on. I'm late going 'opping as it 'appens. I should 'ave bin settled in be now. But I wanted to make sure they boarded my place up properly. Thank Gawd it wasn't as bad as I though it was gonna be. Windows blown out and front door blown off. They'll 'ave that fixed for me by the time I come 'ome. They're good like that. Paid me and my kids' fare to Kent,' she said, filled with admiration for state welfare. 'That's one good thing I s'pose about bloody wartime. We all help each other out. We 'ave to be thankful for small mercies.'

The shrill sound of a station master's whistle pierced the air. The train that Jessie was to board was ready and waiting. 'Right then,' she said. 'In for a penny...'

The woman flapped a hand and smiled. 'You'll be all right. Come on. I'll help you on with that pushchair. You look like a bloody refugee with them bags and that suitcase. Gawd knows how you made it to the station. Someone give you a lift, did they?'

'No. I walked. It was a bit of a trek but I stopped at a cafe on the way for a cup of tea and some toast. I'm all in, to tell you the truth.'

Once she was settled on the train, Jessie sat back and watched from the window as she left London behind once again. Her thoughts turned to Edna. Had it not been for her, Jessie dreaded to think what might have happened once Mrs Catlin came round. Edna was right, the woman would have turned nasty. May have even called the police for spite and the whole turning would have known about it in minutes and it would have been exaggerated out of all proportion. A slap round the face, that's all it had been, to stop Mrs Gatlin from going on like a machine gun, insulting and putting her down. She herself had slipped on that rug on that polished floor more than once and had mentioned it to Mrs Catlin but her response had been a smug grin and an aside which suggested that she should be used to polished floors.

Good bloody job, thought Jessie, Good job I did slap her silly face. She didn't blame herself for the fall; she hadn't meant it to happen. Had Edna not convinced her that she would look after Mrs Catlin until she was properly over the fall, she wouldn't have gone – gone without paying that week's rent. But she would send it on once she was properly on her feet. She didn't want to be in that woman's debt.

Closing her eyes, Jessie drifted into a light sleep and dreamt of Edna. Edna in a man's suit instead of a frock. Edna with short cropped hair instead of brassy ginger curls. Stirring at the sound of a passing cattle train, Jessie found the memory of her dream made her smile. She had never met a transvestite before and was surprised at how easy it had been to think of Edna as a woman. She promised herself to buy a couple of postcards as soon as she got off the train. One for Edna and one for her family, explaining where she was. She thought about her twin, Hannah, and where she might be.

When the train finally pulled in at Paddock Wood, Billy was wide awake and her companion was talking to her as if they had known each other for years.

'Lucky for you that Whitby's Farm's only a walk away, down a long winding lane,' the woman said. 'I've gotta catch a bus. If you can call it a bus. Green instead of red and no "up the top".' Pointing Jessie in the right direction, the woman wished her luck and promised she would borrow a bike and pedal the four-mile stretch to see how she was making out. Then she went on her way, leaving Jessie with a warm feeling, even though she knew it was unlikely that she would ever see her travelling chum again. That was the way of East End people. Promises weren't false but hopeful. Once she was back in the fold of her own family and friends, the woman would hardly have the time to go visiting. But the gesture had been made and had her feeling in a better mood than when she started out from her rooms in Mrs Catlin's clinical house.

–

When Jessie entered Whitby's Farm, and the common where the hop-pickers were living in rows of huts, she did so on the back of a tractor-trailer driven by a South Londoner, Barry, who was there for the season not just as a hop-picker, but a farm labourer too. Jessie took to him straightaway. Shorter than the average man and more rounded, he had a smile to put anyone at ease. His face was open and honest and his blue eyes had a twinkle.

When Barry had pulled up and offered her a lift, Jessie had felt that if she didn't stop for a rest her legs might well buckle under her. The shock of sudden eviction from her temporary home where she had just begun to settle down had really hit her once she was walking alone down a strange lane. She hadn't realised at first that she was crying until the tears were cold on her neck. By now it was early evening and the sun was going down and she was not only tired but hungry and that winding lane had turned out to be a mile and a half long and uphill most of the way. Her luggage had seemed heavier and her bags more awkward and Billy was understandably fretful. She had been regretting her impulsive decision to come to Kent and wishing she was back in London at her mother's house when Barry had rescued her from what seemed like a nightmare.

The noise of the tractor made it difficult to have a proper conversation but Barry concluded that Jessie was a young and inexperienced mother who was very much in need of help. In his wisdom he decided to deliver her directly outside the hut of his own mother Nelly Lisbon, who was in her sixties and had been hop-picking on Whitby's Farm every year since she was a young newlywed. Nelly would find Jessie an empty hut and settle things with the farmer. She would scrape together linen and blankets from her own trunk as well as cajoling more from other pickers. She would let Jessie borrow her spare oil lamp and see her fed, be it a chunk of bread without butter and soup without meat. And God help anyone if they poked their noses in. Nelly loved helping out; she was a good woman with a heart of gold who couldn't stand by and see a wrong not being put right. And as far as she was concerned, no one could do it better than she did.

By the time Barry had turned off his engine outside his mother's hut, Nelly and some other pickers were gathering to see who he'd brought with him. By now, Billy was crying and Jessie was close to collapse.

'Someone looks as if they could do with a bleeding good sleep,' said Nelly, introducing herself.

'My friend advised me to come here… for the country air,' said Jessie, climbing down from the trailer. 'I'm to ask for Johnnie and Eve.'

'Oh, right. They're over in the black tin 'uts. Nice family but too many of 'em. I know someone who can 'elp you out though. With a little hut, that is.' Those few words were like music to Jessie's ears. She should have known she could trust Edna to point her in the right direction. Having gone into the unknown, she had been, to say the least, anxious about what she might have let herself in for. Her worries were slipping away by the minute.

Jessie sat inside Nelly's wallpapered hut sipping hot tea in a white enamel mug, while a contented Billy sat on her lap, sucking on a bottle of watered-down Welfare orange juice.

A family who had secured a spare brick hut for weekend visitors, offered Jessie the use of it. By ten o'clock that night, it had been rigged out with a straw bed, a chair, oil lamp and a little table. Clean sheets and pillowcases and towels had also arrived from somewhere. There was a glow from the oil lamp which was hanging from a broom handle, and it warmed the cockles of Jessie's heart, as Nelly would say.

Later she sat around the camp fire talking and listening to Nelly, Barry, and Edna's family, feeling very much at ease and in the company of trusted friends. Billy was sound asleep on his bed of straw in the hut.

The fact that Edna was a transvestite didn't come into the conversation. Not that it was a secret to be kept in the dark, it was simply taken as natural. Edna was Edna and they loved her. The only difference was that Jessie referred to her friend as 'she' while the family and friends spoke of Edna as 'he'. They weren't ashamed of his leaning but proud. Proud that he was a born entertainer with a great sense of humour and a lovely singing voice. A man, they said, who would, one day, be famous.

'Well, you lot,' said Nelly, finally. 'I like your company but I don't like the hours you keep. I'm turning in. And don't you go crying in your bed tonight, Jessie. You're down 'oppin' now and we like to look on the bright side, war or no sodding war. Gawd help us if we didn't. First thing tomorrow we'll see the farmer fixes you up with an 'opping bin. You'll be able to earn a few bob to buy what you're gonna be needing. What we can't get together between us, you can buy in Tonbridge. There's a smashing little second-hand shop there, set up specially for us pickers. My Barry'll take you in 'is track tomorrow. If you're skint, there's a decent pawnbroker there as well. You can pawn your wedding ring and your other bits of jewellery and get it back out again at the end of hop-picking.' She chuckled at the look of horror on Jessie's face. 'Well, it's either that or we'll 'ave to nick some stuff for yer.'

'I'm all right. I've got some money.' She gazed down at her wedding ring. 'I couldn't...'

'If you bleeding well 'ad to, you would. We all do it from time to time. The pawnbroker's the poor man's bank. Well, g'night, all, and don't make too much bleeding racket out 'ere.' With that, Nelly went into her hut and closed the door behind her.

'Take no notice of Mother,' said Barry. 'She's got an 'eart of gold really. Just don't always think before she gives her orders.'

Jessie thanked her lucky stars that she did have some money with her. Hopefully it would be enough. The other hop-pickers, from what she had seen, had fitted out their huts as if they were country cottages, with bits of makeshift furniture covered with coloured fabric or painted light green and cream. And from small windows or open doors a lovely glow from oil lamps came out of the huts.

The next day in Tonbridge she and Barry popped into the Bull pub and while they were enjoying a glass of cider each, Barry reeled off from the list which Nelly had written all the things Jessie would need: pots, pans, oil stove, oil lamp, knives, forks, cups, saucers, plates and spoons. A large enamel water jug, a bucket, broom and cleaning materials. A bread bin, teapot and kettle.

'I can see what your mum meant now. Maybe I will run out of money.'

'Depends how much you've got, Jessie. None of these things are dear to buy.' Barry was talking to her as if they'd known each other a lifetime. 'They have seconds as well. Chipped enamel, that sort of thing.' With Billy on her lap, she and Barry chatted on for nearly an hour, Jessie doing most of the talking, filling him in on her life story. 'But what about you, Barry?' she eventually said. 'Your mum said you was jilted at the altar. Is that right?'

'No. Bloody woman. She gets everything wrong.'

'Well, what then?'

'We were engaged for too long. Ten years. My girl-friend wanted us to buy a little back-to-back house before we tied the knot. By the time we'd saved up enough for a deposit and that – and slept there a few times while we was getting it ready – the sparkle had gone. I think she started to see someone else but, to be honest, I didn't really care.

So the wedding was cancelled a month before it was due. Everything 'ad been ordered and paid for.'

'That's sad, Barry. You know the old saying, eat your ice cream before it melts in the sun.'

'I s'pose so. We did it on a shoestring,' he said, remembering. 'Her mother made the bridesmaids' dresses and the wedding dress was gonna be hired. But there was things we'd paid for that we couldn't take back. We'd been buying the beer gradually over months. We 'ad a bloody good party on it though. Mine's a big family. Best party ever.'

'That must 'ave helped.'

'It did, I'll tell yer. I was ready for something like that. My girlfriend nagged me silly for the ten years I was courting 'er so I wasn't broken up by it. And then something much worse 'appened and put everything into perspective. My dad died.'

Those three words hit home. Jessie couldn't bring herself to tell him that she had been through the same thing. 'What happened to your little house?'

'Her family clubbed together and took over the payments. She still lives there. Married with four kids and looks worn out. But that's not why I live with Mum. We get on well. Always 'ave done. Look out for each other, if you know what I mean.'

'And no one special came along after that?'

'Oh, yeah. I've courted some lovely girls. But marriage? No thanks. Love 'em till they up and go, that's my motto.' Barry stood up and stretched. 'Come on, we've got shopping to do. I could've picked six bushels of hops by now.'

As Barry pushed back his chair ready to go, Jessie reached out her hand and covered his, and looked straight into his open face. 'Thanks. Thanks for everything. I really appreciate what you and your mum are doing for me.'

Shy at the sudden closeness, he simply shrugged and said it was all right. But he knew what she meant and wanted to say more but couldn't quite find the right words. It doesn't often happen that complete strangers, coming together in unusual circumstances, become soul mates. This wasn't a romantic relationship, it was a natural union of two ordinary, like-minded people.

Chapter Six

Surprising herself, Jessie found that settling into a completely different way of life down on the hop farm was not only easy but enjoyable. She wrote a letter home to her family telling them where she was. She also sent a note to Tom telling him that his old and trusted landlady friend had ordered her out and that Edna, the tenant in the room below, had come to her rescue, suggesting she go to this farm where her relatives would look after her. Her message was short and to the point. She ended by saying that she was happy where she was and although she wished she had not left Elmshill in Norfolk, this was better than rooms in Mrs Catlin's house in Stepney.

Sealing the envelope, Jessie found her appetite for breakfast was evoked by the smell of sizzling bacon coming from outside. Unlatching her hut door quietly so as not to wake Billy, she unhooked her coat from the hut door and went outside to see Nelly Lisbon sitting by the fire, turning bacon in the hot pan. Her son Barry was up too, splitting small logs of wood for the fire.

'Fancy a nice bacon sandwich, Jess?' Nelly asked cheerily.

Taking the old kitchen chair from outside her hut to the fire, Jessie sat down and looked into her new friend's face. 'I don't know what to say. You fed me yesterday and you've done more than anyone could expect already and now you're offering to give me breakfast.'

'That's 'cos today I want you to wash up the frying pan and plates afterwards,' she chuckled, 'and that's not as easy as it sounds. You've gotta queue up at the one and only water tap and then wash greasy things under freezin' cold water.'

'No I 'aven't. I've got a primus stove now. I'll boil a kettle of water and wash up in the little blue enamel bowl I bought yesterday.'

Nelly laughed out loud. 'No kidding you then, is there? Do you want marge on your bread or 'ot bacon fat from the pan?'

'Bacon fat from the pan.'

'So,' said Nelly, lifting crispy bacon on to a slice of bread. 'I'll be the cook and you be the bottle-washer then. How's that suit yer? It's carrot and onion pudding for dinner.'

'Suits me fine.'

'And apple dumplin' for afters. No custard though. You'll 'ave to imagine you've got custard – or tinned cream. Soddin' war. Can't get everything on the black market. Not down 'ere anyway. Still, the apples are free and so's next Sunday's roast.'

'Roast?' said Jessie, impressed.

'Yeah. Roast chicken. Courtesy of the farmer over the bridge.' Again Nelly's contagious laughter rang out 'Rabbit stew tomorrow. Cold the next day. And soup the next. If you don't like rabbit, go and make friends with the gypsies. They eat baked 'edge'og. You can 'ave that instead.'

'I love rabbit, thanks,' said Jessie, laughing.

'You'll be sick of the sight of it if Mother's gonna supply your dinners,' said. Barry. 'It's all she ever does. Rabbit, rabbit, rabbit.'

'Only when I'm dahn 'ere! 'Cos it's free. So's the chicken, come to that.' She had missed his joke but Jessie hadn't. She gave Barry a mock scolding look.

Edna's sister-in-law Eve went to the office at the farm and fixed Jessie up with her own bin. She followed Nelly and Barry to the hop fields. This was the part she had been dreading. She didn't believe she would be able to get on with the work but in fact she found that it was much easier than she'd expected.

Sitting on the timber frame of the hessian bin, the mid-morning autumn sun on her face, she felt content, happy even. She was back in the countryside, Billy was happy in the pushchair by her side, being spoilt rotten by all and sundry. There were three mothers with babies on the camp and all three babies were like a magnet to women whose own offspring had become adults but had not yet delivered grandchildren.

Jessie loved the smell of the hops and plucking them, once Nelly had given her a pair of cotton fingerless gloves, was easy. How long it would take her to pick eight bushels she couldn't imagine. When the singing in the fields started up, she joined in and felt happier than she had in a long time. Apart from the outside lavatories, she couldn't find much to complain about and wondered why her mother had turned her nose up at people who went hop-picking. They were no different from her neighbours and as the days went on she began to feel as if she was part of a strong community. The jokes were bawdy but very funny. Women, it seemed, were more relaxed about their crude sense of humour with their men out of the way.

The camaraderie never ceased to amaze Jessie. Even when the weather was against them, the pickers buckled down to getting the hops into the bins and to the kilns, singing louder than ever. 'Hang Out the Washing on the Siegfried Line' was a favourite. Whether it was from sheer tenacity that everyone did their bit to keep up spirits or their need to push from their minds what was happening in London was neither here nor there. The first days of the Blitz had been a terrible trauma and the strong spirit of the people had not at first asserted itself. No one had been ready for it and it took time to get used to being bombed every night. After a night in an air-raid shelter, returning to see family, neighbours and perhaps their own homes in ruins was a painful experience. Now they lived life for the moment.

After nearly a week of living on the farm, Jessie heard from Edna's family that Edna was arriving by train for a brief visit. Jessie couldn't have been happier and couldn't wait to see her friend. But there was another surprise in store. Just after five o'clock on the afternoon before Edna was due to arrive, a baker's van pulled up and Tom climbed out, looking far from pleased. Once he'd tipped the baker for giving him a lift from the station, he followed Jessie into her hut and sat down. She had only just come back from the hop fields with the other women and though she was surprised to see him, she hid it under a friendly welcome.

'I s'pose you thought it was clever,' he said, 'running off without a word.'

'I sent you a postcard,' she said, pouring water from her enamel jug into a kettle. 'Anyway, I didn't run off. I walked. All the way to the station, bags, baby and push-chair. I must 'ave looked a right poor cow.'

'So why'd you do it, Jessie? You never 'ad to do it. You could 'ave gone to your mum's or to mine. Dragging Billy all this bloody way. London not good enough for you now?'

Jessie was ready to give him a piece of her mind but then reality hit home. What was he doing here? Why wasn't he fighting like other men? From the way he had stalked towards her hut, there wasn't much wrong with his leg now. Before she could ask he answered for her.

'All packed and ready to soldier off to Italy with my regiment, then I get your note. Short and to the point. So I thought, fuck it, I'll go AWOL.'

'Don't be like that, Tom. You needn't swear. Anyway, you can't have gone AWOL. There's a war on, you'd be up for desertion. I've heard that they shoot people for that.'

'They shoot people at war as well. I'd sooner die in my own country than out there fighting Mussolini's mob. I've seen what the Italians can do back in the East End. They don't ask questions first.'

'How much leave 'ave you got?' asked Jessie, pouring them each a mug of tea. She tried to conceal her dismay and anxiety at Tom's recklessness. Did he never think of her and Billy?

'Till they find me. And I've no intention of that 'appening.' He stretched his legs and leaned back. 'I'm a fugitive from war.'

'You can't kid me. If it was true, you'd be looking over your shoulder,' Jessie said stoutly. She couldn't help admiring his tanned face. 'Scotland's done you the world of good. Your colour's back and you've put on the weight you lost.'

'Yeah, it's all right up there. Colder than down south but the sun still shines. So what happened between you and Eileen Catlin then?' He sipped his tea and waited.

'She didn't like Billy. Simple as that. She was happy enough to take the rent but would 'ave been happier still if we'd have stayed in our rooms all day and night. We made the place untidy by just being there. I s'pose you heard that she met with an accident?'

'No.' Tom looked puzzled.

'Just before I left. Stupid woman. Slipped on her own polished floor. Maybe she'll learn from it.'

That amused Tom. He quietly laughed at the thought of it. 'She always was too house-proud. She'd 'ave polished me if I'd stood still long enough. Them cakes look nice.'

Convincing herself that he had been kidding her about desertion, Jessie relaxed, pleased to have him for a couple of days. Pleased that he would be sharing her bed that night. He had annoyed her when he moved her from the village to those two rooms but as usual his charm was winning her over. She loved Tom and now that he was here with her the old hurt was slipping away. She wanted to feel his body close to hers and those strong arms holding her tight.

'Edna's coming down tomorrow,' Jessie said, enjoying herself. 'You're gonna love *her*.'

'Who's Edna when she's at 'ome?'

'Mrs Catlin's other tenant. She's got the room on the middle floor. Lovely looking woman. I'll 'ave to keep my eye on you.'

'You reckon?' He paused. 'You're making a few friends then? People I know nothing about.'

'So are you, up there in the Highlands.' She studied his face for guilt.

He just shrugged and said they were all friendly enough up there but not like Londoners. Friendly in a different sort of way.

'I bet,' said Jessie, goading him.

As if he'd only just remembered he'd got a baby son, Tom asked where Billy was.

'Edna's sister's making a fuss of him round her hut. They're spoiling him rotten and he loves it. He loves their parrot as well. Chuckles whenever it talks. They're trying to get it to say "Billy's a lovely boy".'

A smile which Jessie recognised swept across his face. 'So we could shut the door then and have a cuddle on that straw bed?'

'We could, yeah.'

He gazed lovingly into her face. 'But you'd be shy 'cos outside they'd know what we were up to?'

'No. They're not like that. Truth be known, one of them would probably love to shut the door for us.'

'Oh, well then,' he said, getting up off his chair, 'I'll save 'em the trouble.' He quietly closed the door. 'Where'd you get the oil lamp from?' He was impressed. 'Looks really cosy in 'ere, Jess.'

'Home from home,' she said, unlacing her ankle boots.

Tom patted the mattress under the thick cotton floral eiderdown, 'Very cosy. I 'aven't slept on a straw mattress since I came hopping when I was a kid. Didn't think that much of it then.'

'But you do now.'

'Yeah, I do now.' He wrapped his arms round her and held her tight, smelling her hair which had a mixed scent of shampoo and hops. 'I love you, Jess,' he whispered, 'and I've missed you till it hurts. I can't stand us being apart. Come back to London with me, Jess. Come home.'

Aroused and filled with a longing she had not experienced before, Jessie found herself tugging with urgency at his shirt, not caring that the buttons were flying off. She was passionate; she was angry; she was punishing. Seconds later they were on the bed and their lovemaking for the very first time was a mixture of hot-blooded love and hate, all rolled into one. And all to the low sound of pickers singing around their camp fire... 'No one seems to love or understand me... oh what hard luck stories they all hand me. Warm my bed, light my light, I'll be with my love tonight... Blackbird 'bye 'bye...'

Jessie, deeply in love with Tom again, was very happy to be sharing her life with him and Billy and with her new friends. Seeing her husband and son enjoying their time together made her forget the darker side of things. Tom's return to his regiment was never mentioned, never discussed, and Jessie began to believe that maybe he really had deserted. The fact that her army pension would be cancelled if he had was something she shelved. They were together with a roof over their heads and enough to eat. As far as Jessie was concerned, produce from the fields and orchards belonging to the rich farmer was God's gift to the needy. And she was not alone in that thought. The 'live for today' sentiment was strong but so too was the commitment to work. Everyone was up at the crack of dawn and in the fields or in the orchards, earning whatever they could. The old saying was to the fore – make hay while the sun shines.

But Jessie's short burst of happiness soon ended. Just a few days after Tom had arrived and after a very good Sunday lunchtime at the village pub where Edna entertained them all with her humour and her strong voice singing popular wartime songs, a bit of harmless fun turned into a crisis.

On their way back to the camp site and a touch on the boozy side, the hop-pickers, strolling and singing, passed over a bridge where some Italian prisoners-of-war were clearing the river edge with just one British guard watching over them. It was Edna who started off the saucy banter.

'Well, I will say this for you lot, that garlic sausage you shove down your throats goes straight to your bleedin' muscles!' She turned to the other women. 'All brawn and no brains, eh, girls!' Raucous laughter followed. Edna gave the men a true Hitler salute and began to sing, 'Oh, Mr Fuhrer, whatever shall we do? We wanted to stay and fight your war but they dropped us at Waterloo. Mr Mussolini, whatever will you do? Your hero's fucking Hitler... but he's copped his lot on you... Altogether now!'

Shooting out their arms, the others joined her for a second rendition of her ditty, except for Tom. The last thing he wanted was to bring attention to himself. Slipping into the background, he lit a roll-up and watched them, amused by the scene.

'Engleesh whore!' hollered one prisoner-of-war. 'What do you want? You English bastard!'

'Do bloody what?' Edna turned to the others. 'Got a bleedin' nerve, ain't he? Skinny little sod!' She turned back to the Italians who were either spitting at the ground or showing two fingers. 'Right!' Before anyone could stop her, Edna strode down to the river bank while the others watched, laughing, from the bridge.

Jabbing a finger into one of the Italians, she told him where to go and what to do when he got there. The

Italian's face was filled with rage as he pushed his face close to Edna's. Whatever she said next was, for that soldier, too much. He gave her a back-hander, right across the face. Seeing Edna humiliated like that was too much for Jessie. The few ciders she'd drunk gave her courage she might not usually have had and she stormed down the muddy slope to fight. The rest of the women and a couple of old boys followed her.

The bemused soldier on guard duty looked on and did not interfere. He happened to glance up and saw Tom. He wondered why he wasn't in there too – wondered why he was there at all. A sudden scream from one of the prisoners-of-war caught his attention. Jessie was biting his hand. The fighting got worse, the women showing what they could do and the enemy showing they couldn't care less whether it was men or women they were slapping around and kicking. They were getting as good as they were giving, which angered them even more. British women were almost a match for Italian men!

The shrill sound of the guard's whistle and the arrival of another soldier stopped the rumpus and within seconds the men were back to their work and the women back on the bridge, wounded but not down. They were euphoric. The adrenaline was pumping. Continuing on their way back to their huts, they sang loudly, 'Hitler has only got one ball…'

The next morning, the military police arrived on the common, asking questions and looking for a woman with glaring blue eyes and long blonde hair. The Italian who had been bitten by a wild woman was in hospital and had had to have stitches. The woman, whoever she was, was wanted for questioning. Of course nobody knew what they were talking about or who they could possibly mean.

Word was got to Jessie's hut in a flash and her blonde hair was brushed up into a French pleat and she was ordered by Edna to take off her red cardigan and put on a pale blue one. She was then given someone's knitting and told to sit outside her hut with Billy in the pram next to her, looking as demure as she could. The guard who had been on duty was with the military police, and he had told them about Tom, and that he had been seen walking away from the bridge with the woman they were looking for.

After their futile investigations, the MPs left, not unduly bothered, but the guard felt differently. He resented the fact that while he was away from his family, a younger man was free to enjoy himself with a very sexy and attractive woman.

'Tom'll 'ave to move on, Jessie,' said Edna, once things had quietened down. 'That bloody guard must 'ave seen 'im and welshed. He can't stop 'ere now.'

Jessie shrugged, disappointed. 'I might 'ave known it was all too good to last. I'll have to go back with him. Back to London. Back to all the bombing.'

'Don't be a silly cow! He goes back. You stop down 'ere.'

'No. I'll go with Tom.' It was plain that she had made up her mind. This worried Edna. Now she would have to tell Jessie what awaited her if she did go back. She had been putting it off from the moment she arrived. And she had arrived for one reason and one reason only. To find the right time to explain what had really happened to Mrs Gatlin, their landlady.

'Jessie, love, you mustn't go back to London. Not yet. Give it six months.'

Jessie didn't much like the sound of this. 'Why not, Edna?' She wanted a straight answer.

Rolling her eyes to heaven and sighing, Edna took a deep breath. 'When that silly house-proud cow slipped on that rug and bashed her head, she did more damage to 'erself than we thought.' There was a silence while Edna gave her friend time to take it in.

'How much worse?' said Jessie, dreading the answer.

'Well, put it this way. She'll be in 'er element up there in heaven. They only take in good clean people, don't forget. She'll be chief scrub and polisher by now.'

Pressing her hand against her mouth to stop herself from smiling, Jessie couldn't find her voice. She turned her head away to hide her reaction. Edna was telling her that Mrs Catlin had died from her injuries and she was smiling. She was shocked by the news but she couldn't feel anything.

'It's all right, love,' said Edna. 'We all do it at one time or another, grin or laugh when we 'ear bad news. Gawd above knows why.' She scratched the side of her face and waited. Jessie's silence seemed never to end, but Edna had learned to be patient. Waiting for answers after auditions had taught her a lot.

'Are you saying that the police are looking for me?'

'Oh, don't be so daft. Looking for yer, tch. They wanna question you, that's all. You know what they're like. War or not, they still 'ave to follow the formalities. Other than me, you was the last person to see her alive. Lucky cows, ain't we?'

'Do they know about me slapping her round the face?'

'Course they don't.' Edna pointed a finger at her face. 'And I'm telling you now, if you go confessing all, we'll both go to the gallows. I've lied for you so don't you go being honest for me. I said you'd been gone fifteen minutes or so when I heard a bump and a cry. The rest is obvious.'

'But it was my fault, Edna—' Jessie felt a wave of guilt wash over her. Was she a murderer?

'Oh, bollocks. Don't go all drippy on me, for Gawd's sake. Your *fault*! You didn't polish the sodding floor, did yer?'

'Course not,' Jessie said.

'Well then. Giving her a slap round the soddin' face 'ardly amounts to murder. Specially since it was after the old cow insulted you.' Edna's patience had run out. 'Look, I'm sorry, love, I can't be bothered with all this. She's dead and that's an end to it. Decent people are being slaughtered by the minute in this fucking war so don't ask me to mourn over an accident like that.'

'You're right. It wasn't my fault. It was 'er own fault. Accidents happen. But… I will go back to London. You don't 'ave to worry, I won't break down in tears. I'll go to the police station, tell them that we met up down 'ere and… you told me what happened. Then I'll go over the story the way you told it.' Edna wasn't so sure. 'You're too soft, that's the trouble. I can't rely on you to—'

'You can, Edna. I've got my baby to think of. You can trust me. I'd die before risk having Billy taken away from me by the authorities.'

'I bleedin' well 'ope so.' She went quiet and then said, 'Well, we may as well go back together on the train. I can't take this hop-picking lark. Bleeding great big spiders and cobwebs, smelly lavatories…' She shuddered. 'No. I like my running hot water, thank you very much.'

'Well, I like that, I must say,' said Nelly when she heard that Jessie was leaving with Tom. 'We just get used to you and you sod off!'

'I'd stay if I could, Nelly. I love it down 'ere.' She looked at Barry and shrugged. 'Tom can't risk staying now… now that I've drawn the attention of the law.'

'It wasn't you, it was that bleedin' Edna. She started it. There'd not been a cross word between us and the Italian—'

'There 'asn't been any words between us, Mother, that's why,' Barry interjected. 'We've ignored 'em – apart from you shooting dirty looks.'

'Course we ignored 'em! They're nothing but trouble,' Nelly sniffed.

'That's not what you said previously. If my memory serves me right, you felt sorry for the poor sods. Said it wasn't their fault there was a war.' Barry enjoyed goading his mother.

'I bloody never said that. As if I'd say that.'

'You did.'

'No. I *said*, don't start trouble with 'em. Anyway, enough of that. Are you gonna fetch baby Billy to see us once we get back to London?'

Jessie smiled. 'Course I will. But I thought you were staying on – evacuating down here?'

'We are. But the war ain't gonna go on for ever, is it? Talk sense.' She opened a drawer of her kitchen table. 'Here, I've written our address down. Don't lose it.'

Jessie packed her bags and settled Billy in his pushchair on the truck, ready to set off once again. She looked around for Tom and Edna. She finally spotted them sitting at someone's camp fire, enjoying a pint of ale each, and she couldn't help but smile. Edna was wearing khaki slacks and a red blouse and even though she had all of her make-up on and her ginger hair was set as usual, she looked more masculine as she slouched by the fire, talking to the men.

This was the first time Jessie had really thought about her being a man in women's clothing.

'You couldn't do me a favour, could you, Barry?' said Jessie. 'Go and fetch Tom and Edna for me? If I go over there I'll have to do another round of goodbyes to her family and I think we should be getting on our way, don't you?'

He checked his old watch. 'Yep. Leave it to me.' Checking to make sure she hadn't left anything behind, Jessie felt a wave of sadness. Between them, the pickers had made the brick hut cosy for her and Billy. She made a vow that later on in life when things were back to normal, she would come back down to the Kent hop fields again. It didn't suit Edna but it suited her.

'All ready then, Jess?' said Tom, arriving with Edna who was struggling with her large suitcase.

'Brought me best frocks down as well,' she moaned. 'Waste of bleeding time in a dump like this.' Her complaining about the lack of facilities continued until they got to Yalding and the station. Barry helped them to unload their things from the truck and then he shook Tom's hand, gave Jessie and Edna a peck on the cheek and went. He wasn't one for long goodbyes – or short ones, for that matter. He liked Jessie and had got on well with her but as far as he was concerned they would either get in touch and meet up again by mutual choice or go their own ways.

Once they had boarded their train, settled down into their seats, they relaxed. Edna hated long journeys so made it clear that she would sleep for most of the way and to only give her a gentle nudge if she snored. 'Wake me up and I'll bloody strangle you,' were her exact words.

Happy now to be going back to London with Tom, Jessie contentedly slipped her hand into his.

While they had been busy on the platform, sorting themselves out, plainclothes military officers were inside the stationmaster's office. A description of Tom had been sent to London police stations, naming him as a suspected deserter. The information which came back was that this man was canny and had already slipped the net twice. Not wishing to take any chances, they had decided to arrest him on the train, but Tom had privately been expecting that this might be the case and had made certain that they had seats as close to a door as possible. He kept an eye on the platform for men travelling without women who would, in normal circumstances, be in uniform. Sure enough, just before the train began to move, two smart and official-looking gentlemen boarded – two carriages behind theirs.

'Keep your eye on Jessie for me, Edna,' he said, getting up. 'Don't worry, Jess, I'll catch up with you.' He kissed her on the cheek, cupped Billy's chubby face and then winked at Jessie before strolling casually to the door and lighting up a cigarette by the open window. He was waiting for the train to move before he made his escape.

Open-mouthed, Jessie and Edna were speechless. All they could do was watch him get off the train, slam the door shut behind him and disappear over the station wall. It was only a few minutes before the military police came along the aisle, checking both sides as they went. Jessie could feel her cheeks burning bright red as they closed in.

'So I told 'im, cheeky sod, I said, now you listen 'ere, cock,' said Edna in a loud voice, digging Jessie in the ribs to get her attention. 'I said if you don't cough up and pay me double for picking twice as fast as the other la2y sods, I'm off back 'ome. I mean, what we 'ave to put up with. One bleeding tap between the lot of us. No wonder you've gotta take your baby 'ome. It's a miracle we haven't all got the runs. I told 'im where he could stick his soddin' hops.'

Edna's foil worked. The men didn't pause by them for a second and once they'd moved into the next carriage, she sighed with relief, whispering in Jessie's ear, 'I'll kill your old man when I get back 'ome, so 'elp me I will.'

'I can't believe it,' was all Jessie could murmur back.

'No, too bleedin' lovestruck, that's why. I'll say one thing for your Tom, he's as quick as a ferret. Pity he 'asn't put that brain to better use.'

'How did he know?'

'He never knew. He's too streetwise for his own good. Out-thinks all and bloody sundry. You can bet he had a plan C tucked up 'is shirt sleeve as well, just in case plan B never came off. Quicker than bleedin' lightning.' Edna shook her head.

'What am I s'posed to do now?' Jessie was still in shock.

'What you would 'ave done if he hadn't 'ad to leg it. Go to your mother's. She'll be more amenable with 'im not there, from what you've told me. God works in mysterious ways. You're better off without 'im.'

'Don't say that, Edna.'

'Oooh, strike me dead for telling the truth.' She gazed out of the window, leaving Jessie to think for herself.

'What do you think they'll do when they catch him?'

'What do *you* think they'll do?' Edna was acting again, pretending to lose her patience. In truth she felt sorry for Jessie but sympathy wasn't going to help right then. She knew that. Plain talking was what her friend needed.

'Fine him and then send him back to fight?' said Jessie hopefully.

'Chance'd be a fine thing. They'll shove 'im in the glasshouse or prison. And you can forget your army pension while he's on the run or banged up. I hope to God your mother loves you to death. She's gonna 'ave to keep you and Billy for a while, poor cow. You get sod all on ration as it is.'

'He's done it again,' said Jessie, sinking lower by the second. 'Appears out of the blue, takes me away from where I'm contented and then leaves me to get on with it.'

'That's a girl!' said Edna, full of encouragement. 'You're in the real world at last. Life's not a bowl of roses, love. Far from it. You've gotta toughen up a bit, Jess, and you've gotta enjoy life a bit more. Men don't think nothing of loving and leaving yer – I should know.'

Jessie's looked into her friend's lined face. 'Is that what happened to you?'

'Oh, yeah. Me and a million others. Love? I wouldn't give you tuppence for it.' She turned her face away and sent out a clear silent message that she wanted to be alone with her thoughts. And the silence continued for the rest of the journey.

When the train pulled into London, Edna turned to Jessie. 'Let me 'ave your mum's address so I can forward my new one to you,' she said. 'I don't wanna stay in them rooms now. I've found a nice bedsit by Victoria Park. Moving in next month. If I get fed up I can sit on a boat and go round the lake six times.'

'Billy'd love that. Perhaps I could pop round and see you sometime, for a cuppa?'

'You'd bleedin' well better 'ad. Foul or fine weather, I'll take no excuses.'

–

Jessie arrived at her mother's front door in Tanner Street in Stepney feeling tired and low. The same thought had been going through her mind a thousand times. What should she tell her family? How much should she tell them? If she lied or tried to cover up, they would see right through it. If she told the whole truth, Tom would come out in a very bad light. She would just have to let things roll – answer questions as they came.

She was about to knock on the door when the familiar voice of her brother Stephen lifted her spirits.

'Jess! I've got a key – don't knock!' Half walking, half running towards her, Stephen had a broad smile on his face. Falling into his outstretched arms, she had to use all of her willpower not to weaken and burst into tears. She had to be strong. She had to look as if all was well. Now, at fifteen years old, Stephen was at last beginning to fill out. He no longer looked scrawny and he had grown taller too.

'It's good to see you, Jess. I was thinking of catching a train down to Kent. What did you wanna go down there for?'

'For the fresh country air and to feel safe. Billy loved it.'

Pulling away from her, he pushed his face close to his nephew's. 'Who's a little darling then, eh? And who's your favourite uncle? Not that 'orrible Alfie, eh? He's a naughty boy, ain't he? Yes he is. Not like your Uncle Stephen…'

'You don't 'ave to talk like you're a three-year-old, you know,' said Jessie, feeling better by the minute. 'Unlock the door and let's get inside. I'm dying for a cup of tea.'

'Mother's not all that pleased with you,' said Stephen, opening the door. 'Reckons you're turning into a traveller.'

'Give me a horse-drawn caravan and I would. Tom's on the run so why shouldn't I follow in his tracks.'

Stephen spun round and pressed his back against the street door, closing it behind them. 'Jess, he's not?'

'I'm afraid he is, Stephen. Don't say anything though. I'll fill you in later.'

But Stephen being Stephen had to know more there and then. 'Is that why you're back?' he whispered. ''Cos of Tom?'

'Yeah. He came down for a visit, there was a bit of a rumpus on the farm between us lot and the Italian POWs. Tom was spotted by one of the guards.'

'They'll put 'im in the glasshouse, Jess.' He looked really frightened for his brother-in-law whom he had come to love.

'No they won't,' said Jessie. 'He got off the train as they got on. They won't catch 'im. He's too quick.'

'Stephen, is that you?' called Rose from below.

'Yeah! And I've got a surprise for you!'

'Save that for later. Run down to the Eagle and fetch a jug of ale for me, would you? I'm mixing the Christmas puddings!'

'I hope you haven't cut the peel yet! You know that's my job!' Jessie called back. There was a silence and then creaking on the stairs as Rose came quietly up.

'Jessie?' she said, her voice no more than a whisper. 'Jessie, you've come home.'

It was an emotional scene with mother and daughter wrapped in each other's arms and shedding tears.

'Can I stay for a while, Mum?' Jessie asked, comforted by the closeness of her mother.

The question was a plea and this worried Rose. She pulled back and studied her daughters face. 'What's happened?'

'Nothing. I just want to be with my family.' Jessie tried to hold her mother's piercing gaze.

'And Tom?'

'What about Tom?' Jessie said carelessly.

'Don't try and pull the wool over my eyes, Jess. I've had the military police round today. They're looking for him.'

'I'll, er, I'll just go and fetch the ale then,' said Stephen, getting out of the way.

'Fetch the baby down, Jessie, and we'll talk about it.' Rose's expression said she had a load on her mind.

With Billy on her lap in the old family kitchen, Jessie became calm again as she waited for Rose's expression to lighten. It didn't. She looked preoccupied and tense as she set the table with cups and saucers and then filled the kettle. 'So where is Tom?' she finally said, her back to Jessie.

'I don't know, Mum. And that's the truth.'

'I take it you realise just how serious the law sees desertion? Desertion in wartime.'

'Don't say that. Tom's not a deserter. He's not taking it well, that's all. Being away from me and the baby. You can't blame him. At least it proves one thing – he thinks more of us than he does of himself. He faces prison, you know,' she added.

'Prison? I doubt it. Why would they want to fill our jails with our own soldiers?' Rose set the kettle on the stove and sat down. 'No. He'll be shot.'

Jessie went cold. 'Don't be silly. They'll put him in the glasshouse for a week or so to teach him a lesson, then he'll be sent abroad like the rest of our men. Whether he likes it or not.'

'If he was to give himself up straightaway, maybe. But if he stays on the run for much longer they'll judge him a traitor. And I can't say I would blame them,' Rose said sternly.

'Don't be daft. Traitor. Tom's not a traitor,' Jessie said firmly. She believed it. Going AWOL was different to betraying the country.

'No, but he is a deserter. A coward. Why did you leave that village and come back to London?' Rose was trying another avenue of attack.

Jessie decided it would be best not to try and keep anything from her mother. 'Tom came and fetched us. He'd found nice rooms and thought I would be better off being nearer to you and to Emmie.'

Rose got up, filled the pot with boiling water and then poured them both a cup of tea. 'Why did you leave the rooms and go to Kent?'

'Mrs Catlin, the landlady, asked me to leave. She had a couple lined up. She never really liked my being there.' Jessie spoke without feeling. She simply explained herself. 'She's house-proud and didn't want a mother with a baby. The couple don't have any children.'

'Tom should have told her you had a baby and done things properly before fetching you back to Stepney. But then he never thinks things out properly, does he?'

'All he wanted was to get me and Billy back here and they were the only rooms… clean rooms, that were going. I can't see much wrong with that.'

Rose stared at her over the rim of her tea cup. 'Why did you leave Kent?'

Irritated by the questions, Jessie locked her fingers tight, desperate to stay calm and not row with Rose. 'Tom came to visit and I couldn't bear to see him leave without us.'

'Stop telling lies, Jessie. I'll ask you again, why did you leave Kent?'

Ashamed and embarrassed at the way Rose was staring into her face, Jessie hung her head. 'Tom wanted us to stay together. It's what I wanted as well.'

Rose slammed her fist on the table, rattling the china cups and causing tea to spill over. 'I've never heard such tommyrot! How *could* you stay *together* with him on the *run*!'

'I wasn't thinking straight!'

'No! And you weren't thinking of your baby's welfare neither! Sex. Sex and Tom! That's all you were concerned with. It's all the pair of you have ever thought about! You had sex with that man before you'd been courting two months!'

Jessie recoiled as Rose swept the cups off the table with the back of her hand and shot up from her chair. The sound of breaking china startled Billy and he began to howl. 'You've behaved like a whore from the day you met him! He's turned you into a common whore!' Billy's crying as he nestled into Jessie's bosom stopped her from insulting her daughter further. 'He needs a bottle,' she snapped instead. 'The milk pan's on the shelf. Warm him some milk.'

'Can you hold him for me while I do it?' Jessie, too, was crying now.

'No. You're going to have to learn to hold him on your hip while you get his food ready. Other mothers manage – myself included. I've cleaned windows holding one of my babies! You're going to have to learn to do a lot of things from now on. If you think you can stop here and be waited on, you're wrong! You've made your bed, you can go and lie on it. I've had enough of your disgraceful behaviour!'

This was more than Jessie could take. She held Billy tight and stood up. Stood up to her mother. 'You are so innocent? You didn't have to give away a baby because you couldn't afford to feed it?'

'That's enough of that, my girl—'

'Oh yeah. We mustn't mention *that* must we? We mustn't even think about two little one-year-olds, *twins*, being *parted*! Didn't *you* stop to think that we might have missed each other? Pined and cried for one another? We shared the same womb! We shared the same cot! We shared the same pram! We *must* have cried for each other! Didn't *you* ever wonder if *you'd* behaved disgracefully!'

Rose stretched herself to her full height. 'If you weren't holding that child I would slap your face.'

'That child?' said Jessie, quieter. 'That child? Don't you mean Billy? Your grandson?'

Rose turned away. 'I disown the pair of you. Leave this house and don't come back.'

'Don't worry, I'm going. I'll go to Emmie. She'll take us in. She adores her grandson and she thinks better of me than you do.'

'Well, she would, wouldn't she? Tom is her offspring, after all's said and done. You took a load of trouble off her hands. I should think she was grateful more than anything else. Close the street door behind you.' Rose's set shoulders indicated she had nothing more to say.

Jessie felt as if she had been thrown out with the rubbish as she pushed Billy in the pram along Tanner Street, the street where she used to play and laugh. The street where she recognised every crack in the pavement, every doorstep and every tree. The trees, which in spring were heavy with pink and white blossom, were now thick with red, gold and yellow leaves. Autumn had always been her favourite time, when the air was fresh and the smell of smoke from garden bonfires wafted through and around the quiet avenue. She thought of her dad strolling home from work at the docks and smiling, his newspaper rolled in his hand, sweets in his pockets on a Friday for herself, Dolly, Stephen and Alfie. Sweets for them and a small box of dark chocolates for their mother.

Had it not been for the fatal accident at the docks when their much-loved father, trapped in the blazing crane he was driving, plunged into the river and drowned, all of their lives would have been different. Her mother would never have behaved so wickedly towards her. Jessie knew that. The tragedy had hardened her. Rose Warner had not been able to forgive the National Dock Management, who were to blame. The compensation they paid was no compensation. No amount of money could replace the happiness which had been snatched away from her because of greed.

I wish you was here, Dad, thought Jessie, I wish you was here to make everything all right again. The tears on her face felt cold as they trickled down her neck. It's not fair. It shouldn't have all turned out like this. She looked up at the sky as if he might appear, smiling his fatherly smile. But the only ray of light she could see through her tears was the orange-pink setting sun behind purple clouds.

Chapter Seven

In Grant Street, Jessie's eyes were drawn to her house. It still had tarpaulin over the roof and the doors and windows were boarded, but two other houses along the road which had suffered less bomb damage than hers were in the process of being restored; one was almost complete. By now it was evening and dark and the tiny cracks of light coming through the gap in Emmie and Charlie's blackout curtain warmed her. She knew there would be a welcome there and that the fire would be burning. Smoke from chimneys was in the air.

Billy was hungry and cold. Jessie more so. Drained by her travelling and traumatised by her confrontation with her mother, she knocked quietly on the front door of her in-laws' house, desperate to see a welcoming smile. When Emmie opened the door to her, Jessie opened her mouth to say something but a feeling of nausea swept through her body and a million white stars filled her head. She heard Emmie scream out for Charlie before everything went black.

'Oh my good Gawd,' said Charlie, arriving from the back of the house, 'now what?'

'Grab her arms – take her legs,' ordered Emmie.

'What 'appened?' Charlie, as always, was slow to take it in. 'Who did it?'

'No one, Charlie! She passed out! Now grab her arms!'

Struggling, they carried her through and laid her on the settee by the fire. 'She's a dead weight,' said Charlie, flopping down on to the armchair, exhausted. 'Fetch the baby in, Em, while I catch me breath.'

'If she comes to, don't let 'er get up.' With that, Emmie ran back outside and returned with Billy still in the pushchair. She looked from her daughter-in-law to her husband, wondering which of them looked the worse for wear. 'You all right, Charlie?'

'Yeah… I'm all right.' He leaned his head back on a cushion and closed his eyes. 'I can't take this, Em. I'm getting too old for all this.'

Lifting Billy from the pushchair, she did her best to show a smiling face for him. 'Nanny make you a nice bottle, eh?' Hugging him to her bosom, she went into the kitchen.

Jessie began to stir. 'Where am I? Where's my baby? Who's got my baby?'

'It's all right, Jess. Emmie's sorting Billy out. You fainted on our doorstep. Stop where you are for a minute or two then I'll make us all a weak cup of tea.'

Easing herself up, Jessie grabbed a cushion and placed it behind her neck. 'Oh, thank God I'm here. Charlie—'

'Don't talk, gal, just lie back and rest for a minute or two.'

'I've been travelling since this morning. From Kent. I don't think I've had anything to eat or drink. I can't remember having anything…'

'No wonder you dropped. Emmie! Put the kettle on!'

'I have done!' she yelled back. 'Stop where you are and keep Jessie company. I can manage out 'ere!'

'I don't remember walking here, Charlie,' said Jessie, dazed. 'I don't remember walking to Mum's even. All I

187

know is that I've gone from pillar to post… but getting there…'

'Don't worry about it, gal. You'll be all right now. We'll look after you. To tell you the truth, she's bin worried sick over you and Billy. We got your postcard saying you was down hopping and for the life of us we couldn't fathom it. You left the bleeding countryside for London so why did you wanna go back again?'

'It's a long story. Anyway, it don't matter.' Jessie raised her head and looked into Charlie's face. 'Can we stop here for a while, Charlie?'

'Course you can. You and Billy can kip in here. That settee's bloody, comfortable, I'll tell you. And you'll be warm 'cos of the fire.'

'No. I'll stay in the back bedroom. I'll put an oil heater in there. That'll see to the damp. I'm not spoiling Emmie's living room. It wouldn't be fair.'

'You ain't got no choice, Jessie, mate. We've taken in a mother from Bancroft Road. Mrs Birch. Her and her two little 'uns. Their 'ouse was hit last week – worse than yours, Jess. There's no more than a few bits of furniture left. That's all she's got to see from her and her old man's hard work. They had that fruit and veg stall down the market. Tom and Lily. Poor cow widowed and 'omeless in one fucking strike. Bastard war.'

'Charlie! You stop that swearing!' yelled Emmie from the kitchen.

'Words, woman! Words, words, words! That's all they are, Jess. One word instead of a dozen to get the meaning across. That's why I swear. No other reason.'

'I know. I've found myself doing the same thing,' said Jessie, feeling more relaxed.

'Not in front of your mother, I 'ope.'

188

'No. Not in front of my mother.' Jessie managed a faint smile. 'I won't be saying my prayers in front of her neither, Charlie. She's banished me from her life. Billy as well.'

Charlie narrowed his eyes and peered at her, his face full of questions. 'Say that again?'

Pushing her hands through her hair, she told him it didn't matter. She didn't want to go into it. She didn't want to have to explain everything, especially since Tom was at the root of her mother's anger. 'You do know that Tom's on the run, don't you, Charlie?'

Her father-in-law looked away, avoiding her eyes. 'Yeah. On the run from the Germans.'

'Have the military police been round yet looking for 'im?'

'They 'aven't knocked on the door, Jess, but then they wouldn't, would they? Crafty bastards are probably watching the back and front of our 'ouse. Waiting for 'im to come 'ome so they can jump 'im.' Charlie looked scornful at the idea.

The rest of the evening was spent in the sitting room where Billy, having been fed and watered, as Charlie put it, had fallen asleep on a makeshift bed of cushions from the settee laid out on the floor. Feeling much better after her hot meal and ten-minute doze, Jessie gave them a rundown of past events. Emmie was shocked and upset to learn that Rose had thrown out her own daughter and grandchild. She could not believe that her long-standing friend would do such a thing, no matter how bad things looked. Had she barred Tom from her house, that would have been different, even Emmie had to agree he'd been more than irresponsible. But Jessie and baby Billy? Thrown out on to the streets?

Emmie was silent as Charlie and Jessie chatted about her house and how she had to keep on at the borough if she wanted it fixed up straightaway. The other houses which were getting attention were doing so because the tenants or owners had demanded action. During their conversation, Charlie had not stopped fiddling with his various wireless sets. He was waiting for a repeat of the Queen's speech which he had missed.

'If you wake our Billy with those bloody wirelesses, Charlie, I'll chuck the lot out into the back yard, so help me I will.' Emmie turned to Jessie. 'Your mother couldn't 'ave meant it, love. She just couldn't have. I'll walk back round with you tomorrow and we'll—'

'No. I'm not going back. Don't go on about it, Emmie, because my mind's made up. I can't go back.'

'Course she bloody well can't,' said Charlie, one ear to his favourite wireless. 'What if Rose don't let 'er in? How's she gonna feel then? No. You stop 'ere, gal. Wait till your mother comes round and apologises. That's the best way. Then you can make up. Give 'er a bit of time and – 'ello! Here it is… I've tuned in Em. We can turn the others off now.'

'Thank the Lord for that.'

'Right,' said Charlie, snuggling back in his armchair. 'No more yakking. Let's see what the Queen's got to say.'

Emmie and Jessie glanced at each other and raised their eyebrows, but neither said a word. Charlie loved listening to his wirelesses, especially his favourite Pye Universal. More than that, he was an ardent royalist. He had even stood up for the king's brother when he had abdicated from the throne, blaming the American tart who, in his opinion, was after the crown jewels and nothing else.

'So—'

'Shh!' Charlie's finger shot out as a warning and Jessie pursed her lips, trying not to laugh at the lovable man. In silence and not daring to move a muscle, Emmie and Jessie listened along with Charlie.

'Many of you have had to see your family life broken up, your husband going off, your children evacuated to a place of safety. The king and I know what it means to be parted from our children and we sympathise with all of you who have bravely consented…'

'Switch it off, Em,' said Charlie. 'Switch it off.'

Jessie was there in a flash. It was too much for any of them to bear. 'Oh God, I've gone cold at the thought of all the grief.' Slowly shaking her head, Jessie spoke more to herself than to her in-laws. 'Where did all of this come from? For years it was just talk… and then…' She sat down and covered her face.

'My Johnnie…' said Charlie, his face twisted with grief and hate, and tears streaming from his eyes. 'He was a good boy, never did harm to a soul, and what does he get? A bullet through the 'ead. One bullet and my Johnnie's dead. Finished.'

'Try not to think about it, Charlie,' said Jessie, crying into her handkerchief.

'No point in us getting upset,' said Emmie, sobbing.

'I'm… not… upset…' cried Charlie. 'I'm not upset. No. I shan't cry no more over it. No.' He mopped more tears from his face.

'Me neither,' said Emmie, 'me neither. What's done… is done… Eh, Charlie, what's done is done.' She blew her nose and pushed her hand through her hair. 'Our Stanley'll be all right. He's just missing, that's all. He won't be dead.'

He won't be dead… Emmie was wishing the worst away. Those words were too much to bear and the three of them cried their hearts out. Through it all, Billy slept as if the world was at peace.

The following morning at the crack of dawn, wrapped up warm in her winter coat and hat, Emmie crept out of the house without so much as a cup of tea inside her. She hadn't wanted to risk waking Jessie or Billy. As she made her way through the almost silent back streets, she could have been forgiven for believing that this was peace-time and that they were not in the grip of war. Workers who were up and about, market traders, office cleaners and street vendors, went about their business in a sombre mood. There had been no bombing in the East End that night.

On her way to Rose Warner's cobbler shop, Emmie remembered happier times and the day she turned up out of the blue to warn her friend of old that her son Tom and Rose's daughter Jessie had met up and there might be trouble ahead. The trouble, as it turned out, had a happy ending, if happy was the right word. Tom, a childhood friend of Jessie's twin sister, Hannah, had unwittingly opened a can of worms when he had brought the girls together after sixteen years of separation. Rose had wanted Emmie to keep her son away from Jessie and protect the family secret and Emmie, in her own way, had tried. But love had proved to be a stronger force and it had been impossible to keep the lovers apart.

When at last the truth was out, Hannah had been the one to have an adverse reaction. She had been shocked to find that the man she had believed to be her father and whom she adored was actually her uncle, and the cold-hearted Gerta, her so-called mother, was in fact her aunt by marriage. It had been a turbulent time for all of them but in the end the twins' coming together and Jessie marrying her much-loved Tom had proved to be a bridge over deep and troubled water.

Knowing that Rose would be unlocking her shop at 7 a.m. Emmie went into the tearooms along the White-chapel Road to kill a bit of time, keep warm, and enjoy a warm muffin and cup of tea. Inside the small and friendly place, early-morning workers, a policeman, a nurse just off duty and a couple of street walkers were chatting quietly, the topic of conversation being the latest news on how our boys abroad were faring. Pencil drawings covered the walls. Pencil sketches of Hitler drawn by all and sundry. Some were funny, others brought home the cruel streak of a despicable little man with a stupid little moustache.

On a shelf there was a small wireless and from this came the voice of Vera Lynn singing 'We'll Meet Again'. 'And so we will,' murmured Emmie to herself. She was thinking of her friend Rose, with whom she had been as thick as thieves in her younger days before, during, and after the First World War.

Emmie found herself quietly singing along with the others in the cafe – 'And won't you please say hello, to the folks that I know…'

Her mind flew to Stanley, her youngest son, and she raised her voice, sending the message in that song to him. They *would* meet again. She *would see* her son smiling and full of life when he returned in his full uniform carrying his old kit bag. Vera Lynn's song ended and the familiar bleeps announced the time for the news. Emmie didn't want to hear it right then so she sang over the top of the BBC programme producer as he made his opening announcement. The others in the tearoom joined in, until the newscaster was drowned out.

'What's the use of worrying, it never was worthwhile, so… pack up your troubles in your old kit bag and smile, smile, smile…'

Uplifted by the camaraderie, Emmie left smiling and made her way to Rose's shoe menders. The low light coming through the shop window told her that her friend was there, getting ready to open up. Reminding herself that she was not here for a row but to make peace between mother and daughter, she took a deep breath and went inside. 'The old penny's turned up again, Rose,' she said, keeping things light.

'Hello, Emmie. I was expecting you. Not this early but there we are. Would you like a cup of tea?'

'No, ta. I've just had one in Kate's Cafe.'

'I expect you've come to try and persuade me that your Tom's doing the right thing in leaving my daughter and grandson stranded without any money for food,' Rose said shortly.

'No. No, that's not why I'm here.' Emmie had to bite her tongue over that one. Normally she would have stretched to full height and defended her son to the last. 'I wanted to have a chat about Jessie, not Tom. Jessie and Billy.'

'Go on then. Let's get it over with before my shoe mender and apprentice arrive. Get it off your chest but don't expect me to waver. Jessie's nearly twenty-two, she's not a child and, what's more, she's a mother. I'm no longer responsible for her, which is just as well because I've my other three children to worry over.'

'That you have, my dear, and I don't envy you.' Emmie was going to have to play her hand very carefully. Rose had been expecting her that was clear, and she would have rehearsed her answers. Her friend had not changed. 'Mind you, Dolly must be all of nineteen by now and Alfie – what? Seventeen?'

'Yes, and Stephen is fifteen. Not children, Emmie, I grant you, but what with the war and all… If it goes on as predicted and last years not months, my sons will be called up. That's not a prospect that puts me at ease. Young men are being killed by the thousand.'

'Yes, I know. We're short two sons already.' Emmie's mood and tone of voice betrayed her. How could she keep up her buoyancy now?

The shocking news affected Rose. She went quiet and as she turned to face her old friend, her expression broke and she began to cry. 'I didn't know, Em, I'm sorry… I didn't know.'

'Never mind. Maybe our Stanley will walk back in through our front door one day. Who knows? He's missing, presumed dead.'

Choked, Rose pursed her lips. 'And Johnnie?'

'Killed in action. Dunkirk. Perhaps I will have that cup of tea.'

'Of course you must. Come out the back and take the weight off your feet.' Rose glanced at her friend. 'Weight. You've certainly lost some of that, Emmie. And no wonder.' She walked through to the back room, shaking her head.

They were on old terms again but it didn't help Emmie knowing that it was the death of her son which had changed the mood. She and Rose had been the best of friends at one time. Helping each other in times of need both during the First World War and after it. It had been Emmie who had vowed to keep an eye on Hannah and her welfare when Gerta and Jack Blake fostered her as a baby. And watch over her she did, encouraging her sons to treat the girl like a sister. Escaping from the dictatorial cold woman she had believed to be her mother, Hannah had spent most of her leisure time in Emmie's front room.

'I haven't come to preach, Rose.'

'I realise that.' Rose managed a smile. 'We go back a long way. I know you better than most. You're going to try and persuade me, though. If I thought I could stop you, I would. But if I know you, wild horses couldn't hold you back now.'

'I can't help it,' said Emmie, thankful for the chair and the cosy room at the back of the shop. 'Jessie needs a roof over her head and she needs it to be yours.'

The kettle boiled, Rose poured steaming water into the brown teapot. 'She should have thought of that sooner. We're full to overflowing as it is. If she comes back, she and Billy will have to go in with Dolly and a war orphan we've taken in. Her mother was killed when their house was hit and her father's fighting abroad. She's no other relatives to speak of. Would you have me turn her out?'

Emmie slowly shook her head. 'That things should come to this, Rose. How could our government let this happen? They should be the brains of Britain. Who can we rely on if we can't rely on our politicians and peace-makers?'

'Exactly.' Rose joined her friend at the table. 'And that's what's so depressing. Most of the people who come into the shop seem to have given up on the government. I'm not saying their spirit hasn't strengthened because of it. No. If the women could go out there and do their bit, they would. I know what I would like to do with Hitler and his army of murderers.'

'It's what keeps me going when I can't sleep at night I fantasise myself out there as a spy dressed like a housemaid. I've worked the whole thing out.' A smile spread across Emmie's face. 'I know just how long I'll wait before I machine-gun Hider and a room full of his murderous comrades. How I'll pretend to hate the English before-hand and how I'll lie in their beds if they fancy a bit of the other with an old woman...'

Rose found that amusing. 'So you've been taking lessons in German then?'

'No. I'll do it all by sign language. Only need one or two words to express myself. "My darling, I love you" and "Die, you bastards, die". That's when I'll be spraying them with bullets.'

Throwing her head back, Rose burst into laughter and Emmie, too, was unable to contain herself. To hear them no one would have believed the grief they had suffered. 'Oh dear,' said Rose, 'you're a real tonic, Emmie. But there, you always were.'

'Not always. We've had our differences in the past and we're probably going to have one now. Jessie?' Rose avoided her friend's searching eyes. 'Look, Emmie, tell me truthfully. Do you condone your Tom for deserting and leaving Jessie with no roof over her head?'

'Well now, that's not fair. It wasn't Tom who dropped the bomb on their little house, now was it?'

'No. But it's because of his antics that she won't be able to afford to pay for a room while they're fixing up her place. They've stopped his army pay by now, that much I do know. You'd be surprised how many more women who've been into this shop are in the same boat. I can hardly believe that men would do such things but there, Tom's our living proof.'

'Put like that I don't really 'ave an argument, do I?' Emmie felt ashamed that one of her sons was being grouped in with men who wouldn't go out and fight.

'But I don't lay the blame entirely at his feet. Jessie's just as bad. She knows how to handle Tom. She could have got him to go back, but no, she's tarred with the same brush. She wants him with her. I don't blame her for that, but what if all the women behaved as selfishly?' Rose stared at Emmie and waited but her friend was too shamefaced to look back at her.

'No one likes war, Em. No one wants to kill or be killed, but there's nothing we can do about it now.' She sighed heavily. 'I sometimes think that if we mothers – if all women, young and old – had stood up to Chamberlain and refused to be part of a war, maybe we'd be at peace now. We're an island. Britons are not Europeans. We shouldn't have got involved.'

'I don't know any more, Rose, and that's the truth. But were talking about our children, not Chamberlain.'

'We've got to put them right when they're going wrong, Em. Jessie can't just up and leave places of safety at a whim. If you or I shelter and feed her, she'll never get Tom to go back. Why should she when he's safe in England, tucked away somewhere, being cosseted by some bloody pacifist family? And all the while waiting for him to slip back to her for a night of passion.' Rose shook her head. 'No. I won't do it and I wish you wouldn't either. She's got to learn, and so has Tom.'

'I take it that's your final word?'

'Yes, sadly, it is. It's not easy but I know, deep down inside, that it's the right thing to do, for both of them.

She's no fool. She'll soon realise and so will he. Word gets to him, don't you worry. There's a grapevine out there. He probably knows her every move. The umbilical cord was cut a long time ago, Emmie. At birth.'

On her way back home, Emmie thought about all that Rose had said. When she was there with her in that back room, it somehow made sense. But now, outside in the real world of horror all around, she couldn't accept her friend's way of thinking. But that was another matter. The fact was that Jessie would not be welcome if she turned up on Rose's doorstep on a cold winter's night. She would have to persuade her daughter-in-law to get Tom to give himself up. And if her third son going off to possibly meet his maker in some diabolical way didn't kill both her and Charlie off, nothing could. She would have to resign herself to it. And she would have to give Tom a dressing-down when he turned up on her doorstep. For turn up he surely would now that Jessie was helpless.

It hadn't gone the way she had wanted it to with Rose but remembering when she had made a similar visit some four years back when she had warned her that the odds of Jessie and Hannah meeting up were high, she had been treated the same way.

Her mind filled with Hannah, the girl she had practically brought up even though she hadn't lived under her roof. Hannah had become like a daughter to her and now she, too, was away somewhere secret, involved in the bloody war, Emmie wondered if life would ever get back to normal or if this was the beginning of the end. Low in spirit, she turned the key in her front door to the sound of three wirelesses going at once. She went into the front room to find Jessie with Billy on her lap. She looked relaxed as she sat by the coal fire feeding her boy. Jessie smiled at her.

'I've been thinking about Hannah,' she said. 'I'd love to see her. Has she been to visit you since she left for that place?'

'Just the once and for twenty minutes. I've been thinking about her too, Jessie, funnily enough. Maybe it's an omen; eh? Maybe she's writing to us now saying she's coming home on leave?'

'Maybe,' said Jessie. 'Maybe.'

–

At a hidden location, fifty miles outside London, Station X, at Bletchley Park, a large mansion in beautiful grounds, was where Hannah was stationed. She, like hundreds of other women there who had been called upon to work in secret, was amazed at the size and grandeur of the palatial establishment in the countryside. It was Hannah's duty, along with hundreds of other women, to set up machines, type at speed, file and keep records. There were hundreds more women, from varying backgrounds, mostly debutantes who could be relied upon to work alongside and in secret with the brains of Britain: mathematicians, historians, scientists.

Hannah had soon become part of the busy team working in hastily erected purpose-built wooden huts at Station X where some of the country's very best people were operating the British code machines, which had been adapted to imitate Germany's secret and sophisticated code machine, the Enigma. Messages came pouring from it on teleprinter rolls. These were typed into machines by the likes of Hannah and came out as strips of paper containing valuable information. These strips were torn off and glued down on to sheets of paper, like a telegram, which were read by the experts. These were then sent to the linked decoding hut through an adjoining cupboard which resembled a short tunnel. Intelligence then sorted them into letter groups, some of which had words missing and some which didn't make sense at all. The importance of this operation was to see what the Germans were saying to one another. These secret decoded messages were sent off to Whitehall and to commanders on the battle front. The lives of thousands of British men fighting abroad depended on whether they were right or wrong.

At Bletchley people knew far more about what was happening in the war than those who were actually fighting it. They knew when Britain looked to be losing the war and when her armies were being defeated on mainland Europe, when convoys were sunk in the Atlantic and when cities were bombed; they were always the first to know.

In the grand hall of the mansion, the list of missing and killed printed in *The Times* newspaper appeared daily on the noticeboard for everyone to see and to check up on their family and friends. This was how Hannah learned that Johnnie, Tom's brother, had been shot on the beaches at Dunkirk.

On the day she read the news, a young woman of twenty-three was standing beside her, and had also been staring at the list, her face white and stricken. Her brother had been listed as killed. Sensing the girl's grief, Hannah had reached out a hand and squeezed hers, whispering, 'What's your name?'

'Helen,' had been the dull reply, 'Helen Brewster.'

Shattered by their news, they had walked out together through the gardens and grounds, trying to come to terms with their shared heartache. At first neither had said very much but once they started to talk, they did not stop – and they were still talking. They filled each other in on their lives before Bletchley and before the war had started, reeling off their stories as if they had to shift everything. It helped. The sharing made it all more bearable. Hannah had at last found a friend. She hadn't spoken to anyone before about the discovery late in life of her twin sister, Jessie, but with Helen it was different. She found she could easily talk to her about it and her new-found friend listened with real interest. Soon after that first meeting, Hannah moved out of her bedsit in the great house and in with Helen, who had by chance been allocated a self-contained flat in the grounds of the mansion. The flat, which had a small spare bedroom, was part of the old stable block.

Helen worked more closely with the decoders than Hannah, who was in a different hut attending to Bletchley Park's giant card index system. All intelligence messages were catalogued, the smallest detail of which could be of vital importance. Every name, every place, every unit mentioned in the decoded messages was painstakingly filed and cross-referenced. Through this work, Hannah got a glimpse of what was possibly the greatest file of the war.

The long hours of intense and concentrated work was relieved by the social life and dances which took place some evenings. People were so involved in their work that they often worked until midnight and sometimes through to the crack of dawn because they couldn't leave it alone and because it had to be done.

To dress up in evening clothes and float around the floor to a live band was wonderful. The women outnumbered the men, but in good spirit they shared them and when there wasn't a man available they danced with each other. It stood to reason that there would be far more girls there than men during a war. The girls were the work force. And had they not worked as hard as they did, the efforts of the super brains would have been in vain. But being away from the battlefields did have an effect. The men felt it was wrong that their contemporaries were flying over Berlin, being burned alive and shot down while they lived in comparative luxury.

Hannah made sure that she and Helen made the most of what Bletchley Park could offer. They played rounders, tennis, cycled around the grounds, even joined teams playing hide and seek – anything to create light relief and some fun. They worked hard but they were safe. What danger they faced occurred when they went on leave, crossing London in the Blitz. But cross it they did, especially those women from privileged backgrounds who could afford a day off to meet up at Claridges or the Ritz – the debutantes' assembly rooms, as they were sometimes referred to. Helen Brewster was one of that set but more reserved than most of them. She had been to such places but only with her parents and in peacetime. Hannah had tried to persuade her to show her the ropes. Helen had said only that she would think about it.

'Be content, Han,' she told her friend. 'The pilots are in next weekend for the supper dance. There'll be lots of good-looking young men – we'll have a wonderful time and, who knows, we might find a bit of romance. The band was marvellous last time and I can't wait to hear them again.'

'So it's no to the Ritz?' Hannah joked.

'For now.'

'But we will catch a bus to Sloane Square soon, before winter sets in?'

'We'll see,' she said, giving Hannah a promising smile. 'We'll have to catch, the milk train back, mind – at one o'clock in the morning. We can't be caught looking over-dressed for work.'

'The other women do it all of the time. Why shouldn't we?'

'Personally I would rather we went to a nightclub, away from those we work with. The West End or the East End. What do you think?'

'Why can't we do both?'

'We can. What say we go to the East End first? I've never been there and I'll need you to show me round.'

'All right,' said Hannah, 'providing you then take me to Claridges and show me how your lot live.'

'It's a deal.' With arms round each other they strolled around Bletchley lake, giggling at the comical sight of a couple of young lovers sneaking into the maze and behaving like hunted spies. Howard, the wealthy fifty-year-old who had been chasing Hannah, was having an affair with at least two women. It hadn't taken Hannah long to see through him.

'Let's go this coming weekend,' said Hannah suddenly. 'Please, Helen. Come with me to meet my family and my friends. I want to know how Jessie's coping and I want to see my little nephew, Billy. I want to see all of them and I want them to meet you. My best friend.'

There was no more to be said. Helen wanted to see how the other half lived but more than that she wanted to see the place where Hannah was brought up and the school she'd gone to. 'Are there any secrets back there I should know about first?'

Hannah stiffened at the question. 'Well, there is but… I'm not sure if I know you well enough yet to tell you. Know you well enough, that is, to trust that you'll believe I didn't choose the life I once led.'

'Sounds very mysterious,' laughed Helen, sitting down on one of the oak benches around the lake. 'You tell me yours and I'll tell you mine. I have secrets too, you know.'

'Such as?' said Hannah, joining her.

'I once stole a bar of chocolate.'

Hannah went quiet. 'Mine is much worse. Although…' she looked her friend in the face, 'I had no choice.'

'Oh, come on,' said Helen, stop fluffing about. 'What did you do. Murder someone?'

'No.'

Then, taking a calculated risk, Hannah slowly unveiled her dark secret – that she had been a member of Mosley's fascist Blackshirt movement.

–

While Hannah was laying her past before Helen, Jessie, at Emmie's house, was wondering what her future held. 'It's all a bit of a mess really,' she said to Emmie, downcast.

'Maybe not. But what do you want to do, Jessie?' Emmie wished she hadn't let a homeless family move into Johnnie's house. Jessie and Billy could easily have lived there until their place was put right. It would have been perfect, in her opinion. 'Do you want to stay with us for the time being?'

'I don't think so. I've still got a bit of cash left from Edna. She lent me some to go hop-picking. I didn't spend it all so—'

'There can't be many more 'ops left to pick, surely? And everyone's rushing to Kent as evacuees. They won't want babies, they'll want mothers with children old enough to go to school – out of their way. It ain't out of love that folk are taking in families. It's money. Pure and simple. While the men are away, the women need to earn some extra cash.'

Jessie shook her head. 'I'm not going back to Kent. I'm gonna go and see someone about one of those houses in Whitehead Street off Whitechapel. Some of them were boarded up before the war started, ready to be demolished. They're not so bad. Not as bad as the state my place is in. I know someone who knows the landlord. If I can make one of them nice till mine's ready to move back into, that'd suit me fine.'

'Oh well, that makes sense,' said Emmie, relieved. 'I might 'ave known you'd come up with something.'

'I had to, didn't I?' Jessie gave her a knowing smile. 'No luck with Mum?'

Blushing, Emmie waved her hand. 'She'll come round. Annoyed with that bloody son of mine, that's all. Once he's back in with other soldiers, she'll soften up.'

'So you think Tom will give 'imself up, then?'

'Oh God, yes. Once he knows your army pension's been stopped. Course he will.'

'He does know.'

Emmie hadn't been prepared for that. She stared at Jessie. 'You mean he knew when he jumped that train?' Jessie said nothing – her face said it all. 'I don't know what's wrong with him, Emmie. And I know you don't wanna hear this but I've a feeling it's to do with another woman. Up there in Scotland. I think he only comes back to see me and Billy to ease his guilt. I think she's more than 'appy to hide him away, feed him, love 'im.'

Emmie eyed her daughter-in-law with caution. 'What proof 'ave you got?'

'Woman's instinct and... someone else's perfume on him. That and strands of long auburn hair on his shirt.'

Hiding her relief that, unlike herself, Jessie had not found any telltale letters in Tom's pocket, Emmie smiled reassuringly at her. 'I thought you was gonna tell me he'd got someone in the family way for the minute.'

'Oh, thanks. You're a ray of sunshine, I must say.' Jessie went quiet and thoughtful. 'I'd be screaming the odds if that was the case.'

'Well, there you are, then. Look 'ow bad it could 'ave been. A waft of scent and a couple of strands of hair? Someone give 'im a cuddle, that's all.'

'That's more than enough. Men. They make me sick.'

'Can't 'elp themselves. It's not their hearts that lead 'em astray – it's their dicks.'

'You're doing it again, Emmie. You're making excuses for 'im. Tom could easily be in love with another woman. It does happen. He's a rotter not just cos he's dumped me – he keeps me hanging on. Hanging on with no *army* pension!' Jessie couldn't hide her outrage.

'I'll tell you what,' said Charlie, coming into the room. 'If he turns up at that door, I don't care if they hang me for it, I'll fucking kill 'im.' Tom's dad, older, skinnier, sadder, was threatening to kill the only son he had left who was known to be alive and safe.

'Maybe I've got it all wrong,' said Jessie. 'I don't know. I can't tell any more. I'm too tired to think about it. Let's drop it, shall we? Let's give 'im the benefit of the doubt.'

'That's more like the Jessie I know!' said Emmie, pleased that that bit of dirt had been swept nicely under the carpet.

The longer Jessie stayed in that house in that street, the more she wanted to be away from it. She told Emmie that she'd be fine sorting out somewhere to live for herself. From Tom's latest fiasco she had somehow drawn an inner strength which she hadn't realised was there. She would get that little house and for a low rent she would do it up, and for no rent she would do up the others, so that the landlord could let them out in these times of troubles. She would make absolutely certain that she and Billy would be more than all right. And she would depend on no one but herself. No one. Getting help was different. That she would do whenever she could. And right then was as good a time as any.

'Emmie would you do me a great favour?'

'You only 'ave to ask.'

'Will you look after Billy for me today while I go and see the landlord and try and sort something out?'

Charlie cut in. 'She don't 'ave to stop in, Jess. She can go with you. I'll look after my grandson.' He turned to Emmie. 'You'll wanna go, won't you?'

'If she'll let me,' Emmie replied.

'Right,' said Jessie, lighting up. 'I'll need a broom, scrubbing brush and bucket, soda crystals and plenty of clean rags to clean the windows and that.'

'You don't even know if he'll let you take one of the 'ouses!' said Emmie.

'If he won't – and I think he will – I'll break in and nail up the door from the inside.'

Charlie liked the sound of that. 'No need for that. I've got a spare lock and key in my shed. Take that, my drill and my screwdriver. Tell you what, take the fucking lot. My tool box'll fit on to your pushchair. Gawd knows where you got it from, Jess, but it's big enough for two Billys, let alone one. It looks like it's come out of the Ark.'

'Hold your 'orses, Charlie. We don't wanna go—'

'Oh yes we do,' said Jessie. 'Come on, Em, let's get moving!'

–

Leaving Emmie outside the best of the boarded houses in Whitehead Street, Jessie went along to the top of the turning and into Cleveland Way, where Mr Martin the landlord lived. The man didn't bat an eyelid, he just listened to Jessie's business proposition. If she could have the house rent-free she would fix it up and also fix up the two others along the road as a way of paying him. He had nothing to lose. Workmen were hard to get now that the war was on and he had already seen how women could get things done when push came to shove. So it was agreed and they shook hands on it.

Almost running back down the turning, Jessie punched the air. 'I've got the key!' she yelled. 'Emmie, I've got the key!'

Once inside, they went from room to room checking to see how much damage there was. 'It smells damp, Jess, but that's mostly 'cos of the windows being shut, I think. It's not so bad up in the attic room where the windows broken.'

'I didn't even know there was an attic room. That makes three bedrooms!' Jessie couldn't contain her excitement.

'No, silly. It's no more than a box room with a window. But it will do for storing things. We can fetch bits and pieces over from your little 'ouse to keep safe while the builders work on it. As they will do, now that you're back and I'm on to them. As I shall be first thing tomorrow.' She scraped thick, damp dirt with the toe of her boot. 'We'd best get started. I'll light a fire in that grate and pray that the chimney's not too bad. We'll need to heat up a bucket of water.'

By four thirty it was beginning to get dark and all they had was one burned-down candle that was thick with dust. 'I'll pop round Vinestein's shop and buy more candles and more bleach. That lav out there will need plenty to fetch it up.'

When Emmie had gone and Jessie was alone in the house, she flopped down on to the old two-seater she had found under a pile of moth-eaten covers. It was a brown leatherette, worn but very comfortable. A bit of furniture polish and it would be fine. The filthy rugs had been given a good beating and a soak in cold water in the sink, and were now hanging outside on the line in the yard. Curtains had also been taken down and those which could be used folded in a neat pile ready for the laundry rooms. 'Make do and mend' was a favourite saying of Emmie's and now Jessie knew exactly what she meant. The walls, ceilings and paintwork were still dirty but tomorrow was another day.

She had found three oak kitchen chairs which after a good scrub with soda water had come up a treat. A small oak kitchen table had also been scraped and scrubbed clean. Jessie wished she had asked Emmie to buy some beeswax polish so she could finish off this one room – the living room.

The fire was still burning in the grate and they had wire-brushed the black iron surround which brought out a dull shine and revealed the ornate Art Nouveau pattern. The red-tiled surround needed a second wash and a bit of a dry polish too, but that would have to wait until the next day. With her head resting back on the settee, Jessie slipped into a welcome doze.

When Emmie returned with the supplies, Jessie felt better for her sleep. She insisted that Emmie take the settee while she slipped out to get them both some fish and chips. Her mother-in-law did not resist too strongly. She was tired too, and even before Jessie had left the house on her errand, Emmie was quietly snoring. That was good. It meant that once they'd eaten their tea they could get in another couple of hours before they went home. Before they could even think about scrubbing the floors they had to clean the grime from the window frames and sills, not to mention the skirting boards. Luckily it hadn't been a cold autumn day but a sunny one and the open windows were still letting in plenty of air.

The next day it would be the floors in every room and, if there was time, Jessie hoped to start on the garden. It was wildly overgrown and full of leaves but it was very private with all the trees and pretty in its own way. She had a feeling she might be staying in that house for a while, especially once she had placed her furniture in there. On her way back from the chip shop she made a note to go and see the Red Cross and arrange for her things to be delivered to Whitehead Street. A feeling of excitement and hope was creeping back. Things seemed to be working out and the turning felt safe, especially since at the end of the street was the Toby Club and a place of safety for when the sirens went off. The huge cellar rooms were being used as a public air-raid shelter.

Letting herself into the small terraced house, Jessie caught a glimpse of herself in a mirror hanging on the wall. It was so filthy that she hadn't noticed it before. She wiped her coat sleeve across it and was horrified at the sight of herself. She looked dreadful, with a grubby face, strands of hair hanging from beneath her hat and dark under, the eyes. Never mind, Jess, she told herself. Soon you'll be back to your old self. She leaned closer to the mirror and spoke silent words to her reflection: 'You're doing all right, Jess. Don't give up. Don't you ever give up.'

–

Early the next morning there was an exodus out of Emmie's house. Charlie had insisted he went with them to give Billy a walk. Emmie had a shopping bag in each hand with a packed lunch of sardine and tomato sandwiches for all of them. In one flask she had steaming onion soup, cooked the night before, and in the other potato and carrot broth for Billy. Jessie's bags were filled with more cleaning rags, white gumption, soda and a jar of homemade beeswax polish, compliments of Emmie's next door neighbour who kept just about everyone in the street supplied.

'I wonder who got it last night?' said Charlie, peering up at the sky. 'I reckon it was around Old Street. That's where the siren sounded as if it was coming from. That direction. Poor bastards.'

'Try not to think about it, Charlie,' said Emmie, pleased that no bombs had dropped around them.

'Easier said than done,' he murmured.

'Take a leaf out of our Billy's book. Look at the tinker. Happy as a sand boy with that biscuit.'

'So will I be when we get to Whitehead Street. A nice cup of tea and a rusk before I start work on that garden, eh, Jess?'

'Whatever you say, Charlie, whatever you say,' Jessie laughed.

'Dolly can make the tea,' suggested the incorrigible Charlie.

Emmie shot him a look to kill. He caught her scowling at him and sniffed innocently. 'Got a nice dry sunny day again. Not bad for this time of the year. Blooming leaves are a nuisance though. What I need for my back garden—'

'What do you mean, Dolly can make the tea?' said Jessie. 'She don't even know about this yet.'

'Oh, didn't I tell you? Must 'ave forgot. Yeah. She came round yesterday while you and Emmie was out. Yeah. I told 'er all about it. She reckons one of her school chums used to live in Whitehead Street. She's gonna pop in today, in her lunch hour. Not on the buses any more, is she?'

'No, she's not. She works at the ammunition factory. I wish you'd 'ave said something, Charlie. She'll go blabbing to Mum and Granny Ingrid. I wanted to make it nice before they saw it.' Jessie tried to hide her irritation.

'No she won't. I told 'er not to say anything.'

'Well, that's something,' said Emmie, placing her hand on the pram to stop him sailing across the Globe Road without looking out for a cyclist speeding along. 'You know enough to tell *her* not to say anything but you couldn't keep your own mouth shut, could you? Had to tell Dolly.'

Safely across the road, Charlie found an excuse to change the subject. 'They reckon this site's gonna be filled with new cottages and flats. Flats with lifts, and playgrounds, and gardens. Bancroft Estate, that's what I 'eard. If they do go up once this war's over, I wouldn't mind one of 'em. Brand spanking new cottage. Lovely.'

Exchanging glances and hidden smiles, Jessie and Emmie paid no more attention to him. If Dolly turned up, all well and good. If Rose and Ingrid arrived, it wouldn't be the end of the world. They would soon wire in and help turn the place into a little palace. These were the thoughts that ran through Jessie's mind. The hopeful thoughts. But when they arrived in the turning, it was Stephen they saw leaning on the wall waiting for them.

'Stephen!' Jessie lowered her shopping bags to the ground and held out her arms and he came running towards her laughing, as if he hadn't seen her for years. 'I'm so pleased to see you, Stephie,' she said, holding him tight. 'Where's that sister of ours?'

'Dolly will be 'ere later, Jess. Come on. I'll carry your bags for yer.'

She asked if their mother had softened towards her at all. Stephen shook his head as if it didn't matter. 'She'll come round. You know what she's like. Granny went all quiet when she heard. Clever cow. She knows how to make Mum feel bad.'

'And Alfie?'

'Gone to Scotland.'

That stopped Jessie in her tracks. 'You are joking? Tell me you're joking.'

'No. What's funny about it? Alfie goes all over the place. Reckons he had "a little bit of business" to do up there. He's dealing in the black market, Jess, in a big way. Making a bomb as well.'

'Choose your words carefully, Stephen.'

'Oh yeah.' He chuckled at his own pun. 'Mind you, knowing him—'

'Don't! A thief he might be but not that.'

'Well, well, well!' said Charlie, loving the family get-together. 'Looks like we've got an army now. We'll soon 'ave your little place shining like a pin, Jess.'

'Never mind that. Why ain't you working, Stephen?' asked Emmie.

'Woke up with an 'eadache, didn't I? Anyway,' he sniffed, 'I work hard when I'm there, they know that.'

'When you're where, Stephen? I thought you couldn't find work in the theatre?'

'I work on building sites. Bombed houses and that. It's all right. I like it. There's a bloke with a mouth organ an' he plays it in our break. There're women on the site an' all. Everyone gets up and dances the Lambeth Walk and sings. It's good. It was great last Monday when we all 'ad to charge down the air-raid shelter. Turned into a party down there. Four hours it lasted till the-all clear. War's all right… sometimes.'

'And when you came up?'

'The pub under the arches by Balmy Park had gone. So 'ad most of the row of 'ouses. Only one killed, though. Plenty injured but only one dead that time. Much worse two nights before. A block of flats got hit. Peabody Buildings. Everyone that didn't get out got killed.'

Jessie felt her heart sink. Where would it all end? How many East End families would be left without someone

215

having been killed? 'So long as you're all right, eh?' She opened the front door of what was to be her home and they all filed in.

'Cor, Jess, it don't half pong! How many stray cats did you find?' said Stephen.

'None. That's good old-fashioned dirt.'

'Well, you'd better give me a good old-fashioned bucket of water then. And some bleach.'

The morning had no sooner started than finished. Everyone had got stuck in and it was left to Charlie to walk Billy up and down the turning in his pram when he got fretful. By the time Charrington's brewery hooter went at one o'clock, Emmie was unwrapping the sandwiches and had brewed a big pot of tea. With Jessie and Emmie on the settee, Charlie and Stephen sitting on the floor, resting against the living-room wall, they enjoyed their break and made the most of the time filling each other in on the happenings of the past few weeks. Once or twice Tom's name popped up but an awkward silence followed, as if he had died, not deserted. Fifteen minutes after their break there was a knock on the front door. It was Dolly. Dolly and someone else. She had brought along Max, having bumped into him along Whitechapel.

Jessie was pleased to see him and didn't care who saw. But there was nothing untoward about it, they were just a couple of very good friends meeting up again. Coming back into the room, after he had checked that Billy was still asleep and warm in the pushchair in the back garden, Charlie waved a banjo in the air. 'Look what I found in that old shed out there, Jess!'

'I thought that door was stuck for eternity,' she said, hoping he wasn't about to play.

'I gave the locks and hinges a good soak in oil first thing. That did the trick. You should see what's in there. It's packed with stuff. Wasn't you asking for a scrubbing board earlier on, Em? 'Cos there's one of them in there an' all. Every blooming thing under the sun. I could spend a couple of days clearing and sorting that lot. Aladdin's cave, it is.'

'Can you play that thing, Charlie?' Max was still looking bemused by the whole thing. 'We could have a singsong.'

'Can I play it? Listen to 'im. Tch.' He tinkered with the keys like an expert and then with no introduction he began to play 'When I'm Cleaning Windows'. They all joined in and predictably Stephen was on his feet in a flash, tap-dancing and singing. With all thoughts of war and depressing things gone out of the window, the house was suddenly alive with the sound of music, song and dancing. It was the best spontaneous party Jessie could have wished for. This was her housewarming.

By the time Charrington's siren went again, reminding not only the brewery workers that it was time to get back to their chores, Charlie the self-appointed foreman was blowing his little whistle and putting down his newly acquired musical instrument – his present from the shed. 'Come on, you lot! A stitch in time saves nine!' He turned to Emmie. 'That's what you say, ain't it? A stitch in time—'

'Yes, Charlie, that's what I say. Go and do your gardening. I'll be at the top of the house, working my way down, scrubbing them stairs down to clean timber.'

'I've gotta go, Jess,' said Dolly, 'but I'll come back after work if we finish early enough. Otherwise I'll see you in me lunch break tomorrow.' Grinning, she looked from one to the other. 'It's all right this, innit? We can do this every day. I love a little party.'

'As if we didn't know that,' said Jessie, giving her sister a squeeze. 'Say hello to Mum and Gran for me, eh?'

'Course. You coming, Max?'

'Not yet. You go on, though. I'll see you back here tomorrow, at lunch break.'

'Fair enough. Ta-ta, everyone!' With a wave of the hand and a slam of the street door, she was gone and one by one the others left the room to go about their given work. Stephen included, He was on windows.

'Well,' said Jessie to Max, brighter than she had been in a while, 'that was uplifting, wasn't it? I really enjoyed that. Nothing like a singsong to lift the spirits.'

'I know. So you didn't mind my popping in?' Max asked, smiling at her.

'Course not. Come and see us whenever you want. We're old friends, Max. And old friends should keep in touch. This war's taught me that much.'

'Mmm.' Max went quiet. 'I wanted to have a few words with you, Jess,' he said, looking a touch sheepish.

'Oh, don't start getting all serious now. We've 'ad a lovely time. Don't go and spoil it.'

'I'm not going to spoil things. Why would I want to do that? I've got a message for you, that's all. From Tom,'

Jessie's eyes narrowed as she stared at him. 'You've seen 'im?'

'Yes.'

'Where is he?'

'Right now I've no idea. I don't know where he's holing up. We use the same drinking room in Mile End Road.'

'What do you mean, drinking room? What *drinking* room?'

'It's just a room above a shop. What does it matter anyway what it is or where it is? Don't you want the message?'

'I'm not sure.' She went quiet. 'Is he in trouble?'

'No. He has a knack of staying out of trouble. Out of harm's way. He wanted me to tell you that he's well and you're not to worry.'

She could hardly believe her ears. He had left her without any money or home and all he had to say was that she wasn't to worry? 'Well, is he gonna give himself up or what?'

'Of course not. He's become a pacifist.'

'Oh, right,' said Jessie scornfully. 'A pacifist! Well, that would explain it all then, wouldn't it?' She slowly shook her head at Max. 'If you believe that, you'll believe anything. Does your club donate money to pacifists who've gone AWOL?'

'Yes, but not much. Enough to see they don't starve. And one way or another they get a roof over their heads.'

'Everyone hides someone, you mean? There's always a *worm* in the wood.' Jessie was angry and wanted him to know. 'Bloody charities! They're a sodding nuisance! If he'd gone back when he should 'ave, I wouldn't be scrubbing the skin off my fingers! What does he think he's up to!'

'Jessie, it's not like that.'

'Oh really? Since when did *you* know my husband better than me?'

'Tom's not well. I don't mean physically, it's his mind. Ever since Dunkirk and being there when his brother was shot—'

219

'That's what he told you, is it? That he's still in shock?'

'We sat down and talked for over an hour. He's a very sensitive fellow. You can't blame him for not wanting to go back and kill men his own brother's age and younger. You can't blame a man for that, Jessie. Not after what he's been through.'

'Max, millions of young men have had to go back and fight after Dunkirk. Not just British men either. Do you think they went storming for it? Course they didn't! Who the hell in their right minds would want to go to war? This war? This butchering bloody war! But they *have* to go! We *all* have to do our bit to wipe Hitler off the map! The man's evil! *Evil*. And yet he manages to get millions of people behind him. He kills Jews, Max. He has them slaughtered. Remember Austria – it wasn't long ago. What do you think he's done with the Jews? Put them all up in a lovely big hotel? All the thousands of men, women, children, old people?'

'That's enough, Jessie.'

'Is it? Is it, Max? A few angry words from me and it's all too much to bear. Well, what do you think people are going through in Europe as he butchers his way through?' She slapped her chest, hard. 'People just like us. Made of the same flesh and blood. Is that what you want to happen to us, in England, throughout Britain? Is it?'

'You know it isn't.'

'Well then, don't talk to me about men in drinking rooms who don't wanna go out and fight for the freedom of their country and for the lives of millions of women and children over 'ere. Don't tell me those things because I don't want to hear it.'

'Things are not that black and white, Jessie. You know that. Try and calm down. I know you're angry, you've got every right to be. We're all angry. But shouting at each other isn't going to make it go away.'

Jessie had had enough. She slid down the wall, hugged her knees and buried her head, too tired to cry or to think. 'I'm sorry,' was all she could murmur. She felt alone and yet she was surrounded by her family.

'Don't cry, Jess,' whispered Max as he moved as close to her as he could. 'I'm so proud of you. All you ever say or do is right. Always right. My Jessie.' He kissed her long blonde hair. 'My little Jessie.'

'You never alter, Max,' she said, dabbing her eyes. 'You're a good, warm person.'

He stroked her cheek with the touch of a finger. 'So are you. You're lovely. Please God all of this won't crush your spirit.' He wanted to tell her that he still loved her, that he would always love her, that he had never once stopped loving her.

'Is Tom all right?' she asked. 'He's not too miserable, is he?'

Collecting himself, Max slowly shook his head. 'He's not happy with the way things are but he'll feel better knowing his parents are rallying round you.'

'Tell him I'm keeping my chin up and Billy's fine. But Max, please, please promise me you won't tell him where I am. I don't want him coming here and causing me to have to move on again. I can't go through all of that again, I just can't. I like this house. It feels right. I'll make it my home. Small, warm and lived in. Don't let Tom come back and drag me away from it.'

'He won't like it, Jess, but…'

'Promise?'

'Promise.' With his hand on the door handle and ready to leave, he turned back to her. 'I don't know why I'm

221

saying this but… Tom's a good bloke. His heart's in the right place.'

'I know.'

'Jessie, if you're ever out there when the air-raid warning goes, make for the new underground shelter at Bethnal Green. It's to be the new tube station, eventually. It's clean and it's big. I've heard say there are a thousand bunk beds down there and they're planning to set up a canteen as well as a library.' With that, he nodded goodbye and left.

A library. Jessie couldn't help smiling at him. As if anyone could get into a good book while bombs exploded above them. Still the same old Max.

That night, lying in her makeshift bed in Emmie and Charlie's front room, staring into the glowing embers, Jessie imagined herself living in that little house in Whitehead Street. They had all worked really hard that afternoon, right into evening. She had arranged for the chimney sweep to go there early the next morning, and while he was busy, she planned to go to the Red Cross and arrange for her things to be taken out of storage. Emmie was going to lend her a sewing machine which Charlie would wheel round on the pram. Soon she would be in her new home running up curtains of dyed cotton sheets, compliments again of Emmie, who had been busy with her copper boiler. There was rose-red for the sitting room and mid-blue for the two bedrooms. The old nets which had been taken down and soaked for two days were white again and ready to go up. Having found a huge container of emulsion in the shed, Charlie couldn't wait to give all the walls and ceiling a coat of paint.

Warm and comfortable under her silky eiderdown, Jessie closed her eyes, exhausted. Exhausted but looking forward to the next day. And while everyone in that house slept, there was the distant wailing noise of the awesome air-raid siren.

The Great Eastern Stables in Hare Marsh were taking a fire raid. Several horses trapped inside would most likely have to be slaughtered the next day to put them out of their painful misery. The locals could be forgiven for thinking the air raid was the storm after the calm. During the past couple of weeks it had been fairly peaceful in and around the Bethnal Green area. Before then, however, it had been diabolical. Throughout September air raids had continued without a break with high-explosive bombs dropping, two parachute mines and thousands of incendiary bombs falling on Bethnal Green. Familiar buildings everywhere had been hit – Bethnal Green Hospital, the Queen Elizabeth, the Central Library, Columbia Market, the power station, the Hadrian Estate, the Burnham Estate, the Vaughan Estate and the Bethnal Green Estate were all hit and the parish church of St Matthew's and St Paul's Church in Gosset Street were totally destroyed. On the night of 24 September, Columbia Market, which held a very large public shelter, was the scene of a shocking calamity when a fifty-kilogram bomb, by a million to one chance, entered the shelter through a ventilation shaft and caused horrendous casualties to those inside.

Not so long before, a visit from His Majesty the King and the Regional Commissioner had helped lift the spirit of the people. Simply to know that the King was aware of what Bethnal Greeners were going through made a difference to morale. They were not the forgotten borough by any means. Ordinary men and women, boys and girls were taking everything in their stride. Each and every change, shock or new enemy terror was becoming a routine occurrence.

Even the Boy Scouts had come up trumps. When they were first asked to undertake the task of erecting three thousand three-tier bunks in the Bethnal Green tube shelter they were said to have outwardly trembled at the thought of it. But they did it. They worked for months, every evening and often at weekends. They worked in true Boy Scout style, in teams, competing against each other and scoring points. Bethnal Greeners were proud of their Scouts, as were Stepney and Rose Warner, Jessie's mother. Her little Stephen had shot up in his teens and become an active, respected senior Scout.

In the first months of the Blitz, shelters hadn't been properly prepared for overnight sleeping and during the first winter some people had to sleep on the concrete floor of the shelters, on damp ground arid under leaking roofs. Again the Scouts had come to the rescue with all they thought useful from their camping stock. Fortunately conditions did rapidly improve and floors, heating, fighting and bunks were fitted and Canteens opened in the larger public shelters.

All that said, if there was a choice, most Londoners would have preferred to have stayed in their own homes but common sense, plus terror, ruled the way for the majority. Jessie's biggest fear was that in the rush for safety there could so easily be a problem which could have devastating consequences. What if someone were to fall over as crowds of frightened people rushed down into the shelters? What if there was panic? What if a fire started by accident? What if the exits were blocked after a night of raids? What if the people below began to suffocate one by one?

Waking suddenly out of a nightmare, Jessie sat bolt upright and then relaxed. She was in Emmie's front room and all was well. There hadn't been an air-raid siren or a thunderous blast, it was all a dream. Dropping her head back into her soft pillow, she closed her eyes.

The next morning she would hear about the Great Eastern Stables and the horses trapped inside the raging inferno and realise that it had not *all* been a dream.

Chapter Eight

By the time December came round, people were getting into the Christmas spirit regardless of what was happening around them. Jessie had settled into her new home while her own house in Grant Street was still boarded up; the borough workmen were well and truly behind schedule. So many buildings, big and small, had needs greater than hers and, like so many others, she had slipped to the bottom of the priority pile. At least the house was protected against rain coming in through the damaged roof and the boarding had been firmly fixed. Whenever she went to visit Emmie she stopped at her front door and said the same thing, 'Never mind, house, one day we'll all be together again.'

On a particularly cold evening while Jessie sat beside her fire chatting over a mug of cocoa with her friend Edna, other parts of the East End were experiencing a particularly bad raid. This was far enough away for them not to have had to rush to the Toby Club shelter at the bottom of the street. Fires elsewhere were gaining hold and were worse than ever before. Some places were a sea of flames. The wood blocks which surfaced the road were catching fire and burning through almost to the Concrete underneath. Hundreds, possibly thousands of incendiary bombs were falling, as well as high-explosive bombs.

'Jesus Christ,' said Edna. 'I dread to think what it looks like out there. The raid might be nearly over but I wouldn't like to think how many buildings are burning. Please God everyone got to safety this time.'

'I don't know, Ed. Who would 'ave thought, just a few years ago, that we'd be sitting here like this, wondering what the death toll'll be in the morning. Strange really. The way we're all taking it in our stride now.' Jessie shook her head and sipped her cocoa.

'Ain't got much bleeding choice, 'ave we, love? Ha, the press call it East End grit. Salt of the earth we might be but that don't mean to say we'd sooner be like the others, all silk, satin and pearl lustre skin. The rich won't be crouching underground in a bloody railway station, I bet. No, they'll be in the basement rooms of the Ritz, doing the Lambeth soddin' Walk. Still, I know where I'd sooner be.'

'Me as well. Shall we listen to the wireless?'

'Oh, do me a favour, love! It'll either be Vera soddin' Lynn belting out a song or the newscaster giving us some nice cheery news. No. The crackling of this fire'll do me. Put a bit more coal on. Sod it, let's live it up.'

Forever amused by Edna, Jessie reached for the biscuit tin. 'Mum dropped in some of 'er shortbread today. She's beginning to come round at last, after the dreadful row we had.'

Edna snorted. 'I bet it's bleedin' short as well. Short of marge. Soddin' rationing. It's gettin' on my nerves.'

'Plain or cocoa mix. What do you fancy?' Jessie asked with a giggle.

'A big Dutch sailor. Give us a brown one. I'll fancy it's a chocolate biscuit. I could murder a bar of—'

The quiet tapping on the front door stopped Edna's chat. She looked from the door to Jessie. 'Bit late for visitors, love?'

'It's only eight o'clock, Ed.'

'Is it? Jesus Christ. Don't the time fly! Well, go on then, lightning. Open it. See what the fire bomb's blown in.'

To Jessie's amazement and joy, it was Hannah, with her friend Helen. The squeals of delight, the hugging, the jumping about, caused Edna to grimace. It was all a bit too girlie for her. Too carried away for introductions, Jessie let Hannah take over. She stepped forward and offered a hand to Edna. 'Hello. I'm Hannah and this is Helen.'

'Pleased to meet you,' said Edna, unsure if they would get on. Hannah did, after all, speak with a slight inflection, having been brought up by a German woman. '*Posh cows*,' she murmured.

'I'm sorry? I didn't catch that,' said Hannah, guarded.

'You weren't meant to, love, I was mumbling to myself. Pay no attention. It's age creeping on. I wet me knickers as well.'

This brought a short burst of laughter from Helen and a smile from Hannah. 'Salt of—'

'Oh please,' said Edna, dryly, 'don't.'

'This calls for a celebration.' Jessie opened the pine meat safe in the corner of the room and pulled out her prized possession. A bottle of sherry.

'Oooh, you are honoured,' said Edna. 'She's 'ad that 'idden away for I don't know 'ow long.'

'I can't believe you're 'ere, Hannah. I just can't believe it,' Jessie said excitedly as she opened the sherry.

Hannah smiled. 'I did say I would come… in my letter. In one of my letters.'

'Yeah, and I couldn't write back and ask when or tell you to get a move on before we're all blown to smithereens, could I?' Jessie retorted.

'Oh, yes,' said Edna, coming alive. 'She told me about that. It's a bit secret service, *she* said.'

'*She* has a name,' said Hannah, affronted. Jessie looked worriedly at Hannah and Edna. The two seemed to have taken a dislike to each other, she could feel the tense hostility in the air. She wondered if there was a touch of jealousy involved – after all, Edna had got used to having Jessie to herself.

'Oh, pardon me for breathing. So what do the pair of you do then?' There was a deliberate silence as Hannah gave Edna a smug look, which was a mistake.

'You can wipe that expression off your bleedin' face as well. Tell you the truth, I couldn't give a shit what you do. It's *her* I was thinking about. Silly cow's always talking about yer. You being twins, I s'pose she would. Only natural. Anyone with a heart would want to know how their twin's faring. Must 'ave been a *nightmare* for you, Jessie love, not being able to write to your own flesh and blood sister. *Twin* sister.'

'Oh, stop it, you two.' Jessie sighed with exasperation. 'This is a celebration not a cat fight. Go and fetch some glasses out of the scullery, Ed. There're four in the cupboard under the sink.'

'Anything else while I'm up?' said Edna, pulling one of her comical faces. 'I'll scrub the oven if you like. And if you've got a broom I'll stick that up me jacksie and sweep the bleedin' floor as well.'

That was too much for Helen. She burst into laughter. Of course that pleased Edna, always one for an appreciative audience. Looking back over her shoulder, she gave Helen a wink, as she disappeared into the kitchen.

'She is *so funny*?' said Helen. 'I've never met anyone like her before.'

'She is funny. Funny and strange.' Hannah eyed her sister. 'Large bones for a woman.'

'She's a man.' Jessie kept a straight face. She was enjoying herself. 'Shocked?'

'I'm not,' said Helen, still chuckling. 'But it's even more comical now.' She dropped down on to the sofa and doubled up with laughter.

Coming into the room, Edna was in full swing. She knew she was centre stage and was playing it to the limit. 'Come on then, girls, get your fags out. If I know you spies, you'll 'ave plenty of black market tucked in your 'andbags.' She glanced down at the leather hold-all on the floor. 'That's a nice bulge. I 'ope you've got some gin in there, amongst other things.'

'Brandy,' said Hannah, hiding a smile. 'Brandy, chocolates, and cigarettes. Just in case Jessie still smokes.' She was hinting that there was nothing there for Edna.

'She does. And so do I.'

Settling down for a girls' night in, they soon found that the atmosphere relaxed and they chatted nineteen to the dozen. While Hannah caught up with all of Jessie's news, Edna was giving Helen the rundown on her life story. Between the four of them they got through the bottle of sherry and were halfway into a bottle of port. 'Do you know what I fancy?' sad Edna, right out of the blue.

'I wouldn't like to guess,' Helen said.

'You'd probably be right, Helen love, but at this precise moment, it's my stomach that's rumbling. A piping hot saveloy.'

'I wasn't far out then.'

'She's bleedin' well disgusting, you know. That's what I mean. The posher they are, the worse they get. Saveloys and pease pudding. That's what I'm 'aving. Anyone else?'

'Plenty of mustard for me,' said Jessie, taking her purse off the mantel shelf.

'Put that away, soppy cow. Same for you two?' The girls nodded in unison. 'Shall we pay when you get back?' said Helen, not sure of the East End protocol. 'Or would you like me to come with you?'

'Oh, no offence, love, but they're my friends *and* my public out there. I would hate to lose any of 'em. See me walking along with you and they'd swear to God I'd gone straight and peculiar.' Leaving them to fathom her rhetoric, Edna swanned out of the house.

'Jess, is she really a he?' asked Hannah, incredulous.

'She's a man in woman's clothing, with the body of a man but the feelings of a woman,' said Jessie, her eyes sparkling from the drink. 'If that makes sense.'

'Of course it does,' said Helen, impatient with her friend. 'Hannah should know all about that. Remember the club in Soho? Female impersonators?'

'Yes but they were showbiz people. Performers. Singers. Professional singers.'

'So's our Edna,' said Jessie, with a hint of a slur to her voice. 'Our Edna sings in them clubs professionally. Ah, you should see some of 'er frocks, Hannah. Gorgeous. She said I could borrow one. Ha. When and where am I going to wear an evening dress?' Jessie, suddenly aware of her shabby appearance, pushed her fingers through her long, wavy, natural blonde hair. 'Anyway, I wouldn't leave my Billy. Dolly would look after him for me and I trust him with her but, well, I'm content stopping in.'

The girls looked at each other with pity in their eyes. Helen said, 'You could always come to a club with us, you know. We could meet you at, say – oh, I don't know, Piccadilly Circus?'

'That's very nice of you, Helen, but I'm not really the type that goes to nightclubs. But thanks for asking.'

'Rubbish. You're no different from anyone else. You would love it! The mood is fantastic – which is to be expected. Everyone's using the age old excuse – live for today, for who knows what the morrow will bring. Poppycock! The nightlife's buzzing in the West End. Wartime fervour. Long may it last. The fervour, that is, not the war. Do you know, people are still doing the Charleston. You'd think it would have died out by now. It's the Charleston or the Lambeth Walk that are most popular. We have great fun, don't we, Han?'

Hannah had been watching Jessie while Helen was chattering on. She had changed. Not just her appearance but her self-esteem. She lacked the confidence of a beautiful woman, which she still was, unkempt or not. She was smiling all the while but Hannah knew that tears were very close behind. Now wasn't the time to try and boost her. Helen, unwittingly, had just put Jessie down and if she was to try and lift her, her twin would see right through it and feel ten times worse. She would have to steer the conversation elsewhere and with tact.

'I don't suppose I'm allowed to take a peep at my nephew, am I?' she said, with a touch of plea in her voice. 'I promise not to wake him.'

Seeing her sister's motive, Jessie felt their closeness return. Hannah knew exactly how to put her on a pedestal. 'Course you can take a peep. He's worn out. A tank could drive through the place and it wouldn't wake him.' She turned to Helen. 'Do you wanna come up and see my little pride and joy?'

Helen raised a hand. 'Not me. You go ahead. I can't get my head around this baby thing. Sorry, no offence.'

'You haven't got maternal feelings then,' said Jessie, feeling more like an equal again.

'No. I don't know why but I just don't like people until they're adults. It's my loss, I'm sure, but there we are. You must think me odd.'

'Course not. I'll tell you what, Han, let's wait a bit. Sod's law he'll hear us go in and wake up just to prove me wrong. I don't want him down 'ere with us. We don't wanna spoil our only bit of time together, do we?'

Edna arrived with their supper. 'It's like a ghost town out there! And you should see the sky. Bright orange. Looks like that's on fire, never mind the buildings.'

Helen suddenly looked petrified. 'Has everyone gone to the shelters?'

'No, stop panicking. We haven't missed the sirens. You'd 'ave to be stone deaf to do that. No. Everyone's gone over to the west end of Bethnal Green to 'elp out. Street vendor reckons we're all right now. No more raids tonight. Let's 'ope he's right.'

An hour or so later, with everyone watered and fed, the mood in the room was very relaxed. Jessie had offered the girls overnight shelter but they insisted they catch the one o'clock morning milk train back. Edna, with her harmless but well thought out questions, managed to wheedle a bit out of the girls as to what it was like at Bletchley Park. Their tongues were looser than they would have otherwise been because of the alcohol. Hannah told of the social life, the games of rounders they played using a broom handle, the tennis, and best of all the dances held in the great hall. Helen, carried away, leaked top secret information that she had picked up from one of the brains at Station X. Decoded messages from the SS in Germany. Hider was preparing to take Russia and certain German signals revealed that a mass execution and systematic slaughter of Russian Jews was planned. Hundreds were to be shot and hundreds more executed in an indescribable manner and when Churchill saw the decodes he was heard to say of the merciless butchering, 'We are in the presence of a crime without a name.' This shocking story from Helen stunned both Jessie and Edna. Edna was almost speechless. Almost.

'You're not telling us that you've rubbed shoulders with Churchill?'

'No. We only hear that he's been once he's gone,' said Hannah, worried. 'You know we could be shot for passing on this sort of information.'

'It's all right, love. Your secret's safe with me. And you know Jessie well enough to trust her. And to be honest. I've not really taken it in. I don't think I want to.'

'I caught a glimpse of Churchill once. From a window in my rooms. He was just about to get into his ear and leave,' said Helen, proudly. 'Do you know what they say he likens Bletchley Park to? The goose that lays the golden egg but never cackles.'

'Precisely, Helen,' said Hannah, warning her friend to say no more.

'I don't s'pose you're allowed visitors,' said Edna, hope-fully. 'Sounds right down my street, that place. Bletchley Park. Born to the manor, that's me.'

'No, Edna, we're definitely not,' said Hannah. 'And I swear to you that we would be imprisoned *at least* for having told you the name of the place.'

'Ah, look at 'er face, Jess. Pale and worried.' Edna reached out and placed a hand over Hannah's. 'You've got my word, love. Once you've gone, with you will go everything you've told us.'

'We shouldn't have come. We would be in so much trouble.'

Edna sighed and smiled. 'Jessie, get over 'ere. And you, Helen. Come on, move yerselves! We're gonna swear. We're gonna put our hands on top of each other's and we're gonna swear to God that everything said in this room is from this moment wiped out. And what's more, just to make you feel better, we're gonna swear on little Billy's life.'

Without another word, Jessie and Helen moved close to Hannah and followed Edna in all she did, even repeating the final lines after her: 'I swear by Almighty God that all things promised here this night will be kept and abided by till death us do part. Amen.' After a short silence, Edna said, 'Right, that's it. Get up off your knees. I'm gonna make us a fresh pot of tea.'

Filling the kettle, Edna was aware that Hannah was in the doorway, watching her. 'Do you feel better now, love?'

'I do, Edna, yes. You're a very special person who—'

'I know, I know. Bloody Saint, l am.'

Hannah wasn't going to let her wave it off so easily. She very firmly took the kettle from Edna and put it on the draining board beside the sink. She then wrapped her arms round the peculiar friend that Jessie had found, and whispered, 'Thank you. And thank you for all you're doing for my sister. I hope you'll do the same for me one day when this war's over.' Patting her back and smiling, Edna asked what she meant. 'What could an old queen like me do to help someone like you, Hannah? You, who's got a good brain and a lot of common sense?'

'Be my friend too.'

'Ah, take it as done, sweetheart. Take it as done.'

–

Christmas Day was very much a family affair. Everyone, including Hannah and her foster father, Jack, Rose's half-brother, all congregated at Rose's house in Tanner Street. While certain provisions were on ration, other treats, such as fruit for the Christmas puddings and cake, were more readily come by. Christmas Eve was Jessie's birthday but she had pleaded with them not to make a fuss, saying that she would rather celebrate her birthday later on in the year, when the war might be over and everyone back where they belonged. She was thinking about Tom being at home.

In the afternoon, with Emmie and Charlie there, everyone enjoyed playing parlour games organised by Stephen, to the background entertainment of the special festive show on the wireless which included singers such as Bob Hope, Flanagan and Allen and George Formby. When Vera Lynn opened her spot with 'We'll Meet Again', the games stopped and every one of them in the room sang full out. At the end of the song there wasn't a dry eye to be seen. They were all missing Tom, Johnnie and Stanley. As for Rose, who was shedding more tears than anyone, she was thinking about her beloved husband whom she still sorely missed. It seemed inopportune to carry on with game-playing after that emotional scene, so the suggestion of a ten-minute nap all round before teatime was greeted with enthusiasm. After washing Billy's sticky face and hands, Jessie carried him to her old bedroom to find Dolly and Hannah on the twin bed, cuddled up and out for the count.

Emmie and Charlie were content to doze in the armchairs by the fire, while Rose, her mother Ingrid, and the boys dozed on their own beds in their own rooms. Outside, the moon was just beginning to show, as were the stars. The sky, thankfully, was calm and restful and quiet. Peace and good will had at least been shown on this special day. The wireless had been turned down and the low sound of a church choir carol singing was perfect for a light slumber on a Christmas afternoon, by the fire. Charlie seemed to be breathing deeply in time with 'Away In A Manger' but Emmie was too drowsy to be bothered to reach out and thump him.

Until the quiet tapping of the street door knocker an hour later, everyone in the household was sound asleep. It was Emmie who heard it first. 'I'll go...' she mumbled. 'I'll go.'

Half asleep and still slow from the effect of her Christmas drink, she opened the door and had to blink in order to focus properly. A young man was standing there. A young man who looked familiar, handsome in his own way. He was smiling at her; not like old friends might but as someone who wasn't too sure of himself. 'Do I know you, son?' she said.

'We've met a couple of times. My parents have the shop next door to Mrs Warner's shoe menders.' It was Max.

'Ah. Well, come on in then. Is she expecting you? Rose?'

'No.' Max stood awkwardly in the passage. This was the first time he had been here since he and Jessie broke off their engagement, after Tom came on the scene. 'I won't intrude. I wonder if you could tell Jessie I'm here. I just want a few words, that's all.'

'Is that right?' Emmie didn't like the sound of it. 'She's married to my son, don't forget.'

'No, I won't forget,' he said, smiling fondly at her. 'I've, er, I've got a message for her…' His words trailed off as if he wished he'd never opened his mouth.

'A message?' Emmie was quick to wake up. 'From?'

'A friend, that's all. Nothing important. I said I was passing and would knock. That's all.'

'Ah. Right. You go down into the kitchen and I'll find her. Rose would never forgive me if I left you standing in the passage like a tradesman. I expect her old bedroom's up there somewhere…'

'It's the first on the left of the landing.'

'Is it now?' she said, raising an eyebrow.

Going into the kitchen, Max at once felt at home. Not much had changed. The dishes from Christmas dinner were washed, dried and stacked, ready for Dolly to put away. That had always been her chore. He remembered that. He also remembered that she hardly ever did put them away, just left them until Rose or Jessie couldn't stand it any longer.

'Max?' Jessie stood in the doorway. Turning slowly to face her, he felt his heart melt. She looked so lovely having only just woken up. He wanted to go to her, be close, smell her hair and skin. 'Emmie said you had a message for me.'

'Yes.' He lowered his eyes, avoiding those light-blue searching eyes. 'Tom wants to see you, Jessie. He's waiting at the top of your turning.'

'Whitehead Street?' Her voice was still husky from sleep.

'Yes.' He thought about the saying, all fair's in love and war. Love was never fair. Not when it came to himself and Jessie. He had broken a promise. Tom had made him break a promise and tell him where Jessie was living. 'I couldn't not tell him, Jess. He's in a dreadful state. It's not very nice to see a man cry. Especially not someone like Tom. He can't bear Christmas without seeing you and Billy.'

'That's all right,' she said, her mind racing. 'But the others mustn't know. Especially not Mum. And we can't tell Emmie. She'll be out of 'ere like a shot and it'll all come out. What do you think we should do?'

'Say nothing. Go and get Billy and wrap up warm. I'll wait down here. Then we'll go out together. If anyone asks, we're going to have a Christmas drink with my parents. I'll say they asked me to come and see if you would go round.'

'That's good,' said Jessie, thoughtful, 'that's credible. They'd think of me at this time of year, of course they would. But don't wait down 'ere. Wait outside. Best not to tempt providence. Someone's bound to come down and the questions will start. If asked, I'll say you're out there because you're having a smoke.'

'How did you know I'd started smoking?' His familiar chuckle warmed her.

'I didn't.'

'Let's hope I can get past Tom's mother. I think she might have smelt a rat.'

'Well... we meet at last, Max.' Hannah stood in the doorway, smiling. 'Emmie just told me you were here.' She stepped forward and offered her hand. 'I'm Jessie's twin sister, Hannah.' Max looked dumbfounded. 'She has told you about me?' said Hannah.

239

'Of course she has.' There was an awkward silence and to Jessie's amusement, Max was blushing and going shy. Then he broke into a genuine smile. 'I'm sorry… it's just seeing you right out of the blue…' He splayed his hands and sported a look of amazement. 'You look so alike!'

Hannah broke into laughter, which was unusual; Jessie hardly ever saw her laugh out loud. She waited to see who would make the next move. It was Max. 'How long are you home on leave?'

'Three days,' said Hannah.

'Right. Three days. Well, that's better than nothing. Why don't I take you out for a meal before you go back, now that we've met…'

'I would love that,' said Hannah.

'Good. That's good. Shall I come back this evening?'

'I don't see why not. What do you think, Jess? Will it be all right if Max comes round?'

Jessie's reaction to their instant rapport was confusing. She was completely thrown by it. She didn't want them to go out for dinner without her. 'Course it'll be all right. Mum thinks the world of 'im.'

'Well, that's settled then. I'll see you later.' Hannah smiled shyly at him and went back up to her room.

Without saying another word Jessie went about her business of getting Billy's hat and coat on while he was still half asleep.

'That was easy,' she told Max outside. 'You couldn't've arrived at a better time.'

Walking carefully through the back streets, neither of them mentioned Hannah. Their boots crunched on the snow, torches shining ahead of them in the dark. Max put his arm round Jessie and pulled her close. 'I'm not getting fresh, I just don't want you slipping over with Billy,' he said.

'I know, silly.' She squeezed his arm. 'I trust you more than I trust anyone in the world, Max, do you know that?' He didn't answer but walked on in silence, happy, very happy to have his Jessie so close again.

'Is Tom really in a bad way, Max, or just playacting?'

'Of course he's not play-acting. He wants to be with his wife and son, never mind it's Christmas. Whatever he's done, Jessie, he does love you and Billy. It's not his fault that he can't face killing his fellow man, German or otherwise.'

Arriving at the corner of her turning, Max stopped. 'I'll leave you to walk the rest of the way. Tom's probably hiding in the shadows.' He looked at her, smiled bravely and turned away.

'Max!' she called after him. 'Happy Christmas!'

He didn't stop, just carried on walking slowly away with a hand raised to acknowledge her good wishes. With mixed emotions, Jessie made her way along the turning, checking both sides for any sign of Tom. There was none. As she turned the key in her front door; there was a telltale shred of light coming from a tiny gap where the blackout curtain didn't quite meet the window frame. She hadn't left a light on. Money was scarce and to waste electricity would have been sinful. It could only mean one thing. Tom was inside.

'Hello, Jess. Happy Christmas.' He was sitting by the fire she had made up and he had lit. 'Why didn't you fetch Max in? I've brought a little bottle of brandy to celebrate.'

'How did you get in?' Jessie couldn't believe the way they were talking to each other, as if they hadn't been apart for months. 'Did I leave the back door unlocked?'

'I never thought to check. I forced open the window – it didn't take much to do it, Jess. You should get that seen to.'

'Oh, right, I will.' She carefully laid Billy on the settee. He was still sound asleep.

Tom gazed up at her from his armchair. 'See, miracles do 'appen,' he said, smiling his old smile. 'I never thought, not in a million years, that I'd be sitting 'ere in your front room this Christmas night.' He held a hand out to her. 'Come and cuddle up to me, Jess.'

'I don't know about that You didn't exactly leap up when I came in, did you?'

'Nope. Every second counts. I can see you best from where I'm sitting. All I've been waiting for by this fire is to see you in the flesh again. If I get up. I might wake up and find it's all a dream. I don't wanna risk that 'appening.'

'You soft daft sod,' she said, moving towards him. 'Uncross them long legs of yours and straighten them. That armchair's not very roomy.' He did as asked and she lifted the skirt of her frock and straddled him, looking into his eyes. 'Where 'ave you been, you sod?'

'Here, there and everywhere but you've always been with me, Jess. Always, always on my mind.' She kissed him passionately to stop his talking. 'I didn't want it to be like this…' he murmured.

'It won't be once we've got this bit out of the way. Take me, Tom. Now. Don't make love just get inside me.' She was trembling and she was hot. Hot and sweating.

'Jess, Billy…'

'He won't wake up. Tom, *please*. Please, Tom. Please.'

'All right, Jess. All right, darling. I love you, baby. I love you.'

'I know, I know.'

Impatient with him in his loving, gentle mood, she pushed his hand away and simply pulled the leg of her silk knickers to one side and sank down on to his manhood, and the floodgates opened.

Later, much later, as dawn was about to break, Jessie lay in Tom's arms in bed, passion spent, after many times making love. He was sitting up and smoking a cigarette. 'Why can't it be like this always? Why did that *bloody* war 'ave to 'appen? What *right* 'ave those bastards got to make us leave our families back 'ere to be blown to smithereens.'

'There's nothing we can do about it, Tom. We're just pawns on a chess board.'

'I shouldn't 'ave to sneak into my own wife's bedroom, for fuck's sake.' He smoked angrily.

'Don't swear, Tom. Don't let them make you swear.'

'I can't 'elp it. It's like a fire inside, I'm so bloody *angry*. There should 'ave bin a revolution before this kicked off. No ordinary man wanted this. I don't care what nationality. We should 'ave stood up an' been counted. We outnumber government, for Christ's sake. We could 'ave stopped this.'

'No you couldn't. Don't be daft. And *stop cursing*.'

'It makes my blood boil.'

'There'll always be one throughout the ages,' said Jessie, pensive. 'A madman like Hitler who other weaker madmen will follow. It's just bad luck that the insane bastard is in our lifetime. Anyway, that's all it is, life – just one big game of take your chance. We were born at the wrong time, that's all. Let's hope that our Billy'll grow up in a peaceful, wiser world after all of this.'

'You do understand, don't you, Jess? Why I'm a pacifist?'

Try as she might, Jessie couldn't help smiling. 'It's me you're talking to now, Tom. Stop playacting. Pacifist. You don't wanna go back to what you left behind in Dunkirk. And no, for that I don't blame you. But you're gonna have to go back. Go back and fight to make sure Hitler's wiped out. You've got to. All of you. He's evil. I've heard things that'd shock you. If you knew how many thousands of Jews and gypsies he's 'ad murdered, you would go on a one-man trek to get the bastard.'

'Heard what things and from where?' He looked at her curiously, his green eyes glinting.

'Never you mind. It's secret information and it's true. Atrocities are going on abroad and if he conquers Britain, the same thing'll 'appen here. He's Satan. The devil himself.'

'So how is Hannah?' he said, all-knowing.

'She's all right. And I never said it was her who told me. Anyway, enough of that. We're together and we shouldn't be—' A sudden crash at the front door stopped her. 'Oh God, Tom. Surely not.'

'Bastards!' he said, jumping out of the bed and grabbing his clothes. 'It's the military police, I know it. Someone must've told. Deny it, Jessie. Tell 'em it was someone else! Anyone else!' With his clothes and boots under his arms, he was out of the window and jumping down into the back garden. Jessie was left feeling numb. He had told her to blacken her name. To lie and to slander her own good name. And all because he loved her and couldn't bear to be miles away? It didn't add up. This feeling of betrayal, justified or not, was something she could take no more of.

Jessie went downstairs in her dressing gown and opened the door, blank-faced and shocked, to the authorities. The military police did not stay long.

They asked if Tom had been there and Jessie said nothing. She climbed back in bed with the blankets pulled up to her neck and watched as they checked the open window, blew their whistle, and then searched the room. They found one of his cast-off socks, his cigarette pack, a book of matches, his cufflinks on the side table and his empty teacup. Then, refusing to say how they had known Tom was there, they left.

Getting out of bed to see to Billy who was by now frightened and crying, Jessie vowed never to trust Tom again. Walking up and down, comforting her son and trying to get him back off to sleep, she thought about Max and the part he'd played in tonight's fiasco. The part he'd played up front and the one he might have played behind the scenes. Had he gone along with Tom's request simply to have him caught and sent back for disciplinary action? Had this been his feeble way of getting her back? Jessie felt sicker by the minute. The two men in her life may well be the two men who had badly let her down.

The following morning, before she had had her first cup of tea, she had a visitor. Her landlord. He had been questioned by the police and was livid. Most of what he said went above her head but the words which brought her up sharp were the ones which cut deep.

'If I'd have known you were going to hide a rotten deserter I would never have let you take this house. Get your things together and get out! Today!' he shouted, furious.

She pleaded, she begged, she cried, she tried to reason with him, but all in vain. He was in no mood to listen. He wanted her out and he wanted her out that day. 'I can't go just like that,' she said, the tears pouring down her face. 'My furniture—'

'If you can't get it shifted today, leave it. Whoever I let come in will be some poor cow whose home's been blown apart. She can use your things. Now pack your bags and get out. If you're still here tomorrow I'll paint things on the window you'll be ashamed to see.'

Slamming the door behind him, he left Jessie with a terrible thought in her mind. Might it not be better if she and Billy went to sleep for ever, wrapped in each other's arms? Wouldn't it be easier simply to crush a bottle of headache pills and wash them down with warm milk?

One hour later, after crying herself dry, she began to pack her bags once again and go on the road. Where she would go she had no idea. Word would get round and the scandal would soon reach her mother's ears. She would not be welcome there. And she couldn't face Emmie or Charlie. She didn't want to hear them making sad, pathetic excuses for their son who brought constant shame to them. Max came to mind. Good old faithful Max. If he had an inkling of what she was going through, he would be there like a shot. But she couldn't face him either. All she wanted right then was to go where nobody knew her, where she could simply fade into the background with others who were in a similar position, women like her whose homes had been bombed out. Women who knew it all too well to bother asking questions. The last thing she wanted was to have to face Max's sister, Moira. Smug and snobbish, Moira had never wanted Max to marry Jessie. She looked down on anyone who wasn't of her own class or of the Jewish faith. No, Jessie would not give her the satisfaction.

Washing her naked body by the sink before she dressed to leave, Jessie felt physically sick. She felt as if she had been used. Used like a whore. The worst of it was that she had so enjoyed their lovemaking. It had been full of love and passion – for her, at least. She wondered if she really knew Tom at all. He had slept with the nurse in Scotland, she knew that now. She didn't need concrete evidence. She just knew it. But perhaps there were others too. He was leading a life that was completely detached from hers. Anger started to creep in. She had been a fool. She hadn't really taken stock. Now she would have to pay for her naivete and pay heavily. With just a few shillings in her purse and on Boxing Day, she would once again take to the streets like a refugee, a vagrant. But vagrant or not, she had her pride. She would find her self respect again. The old Jessie would come through, war or not!

But this couldn't have been a worse time for Jessie to be homeless. The crisis of homelessness was steadily worsening in London and especially in the East End. Most of those made homeless by the bombings were having to stay with friends or relations, which was better than having nowhere to live but didn't offer a real solution to the growing problem. Some families who had been bombed out were staying in Anderson shelters, sleeping six to a purpose-made bed, nose to toe. Public baths had in some areas been taken over by the authorities for people in need and although shelterers made good use of the facilities and returned clean to their makeshift Anderson home, there wasn't much that could be done about the smell of men's sweaty boots and socks which could be unbearable in small, unaired, damp shelters. Then of course there was the snoring.

The next best thing that Jessie and others could hope for were the council rest centres, but the great mass of people having to sleep in them meant that conditions were becoming intolerable. There was no doubt that rehousing was at the top of the welfare emergency list, but the LCC were incapable of meeting the new challenges. In the first few months of the Blitz, the councils in London had rehoused only just over seven thousand of the two hundred and fifty thousand homeless in the capital.

There was a glut of empty houses in London, privately owned, and while the councils did have the power to requisition and use them as billets for homeless families, they didn't seem to be using this power, despite the dire problems. In some cases, billeting officers were known to be connected to the local estate agents, who looked after their own business interests to such an extent that not many, if any, of their properties were requisitioned.

In Bethnal Green and Stepney, the worst hit areas, the borough council was in chaos, with inadequate billeting and rehousing departments. The crisis was becoming so deep that the Ministry of Health had organised, through local councils, the transfer of several thousand East Enders into empty houses in well-to-do western and north-western boroughs like Paddington, Hampstead, Finchley and Westminster.

Going into the People's Palace, Jessie was shocked by the queues of depressed families there in need of shelter, clothes, household goods and money. She had to queue up for a cup of milk for Billy and hot tea for herself and it was nearly an hour before she was sitting on the floor next to the pram sipping her drink, surrounded by dozens of women in the same situation.

'What a life, eh?' said a mother breast-feeding her baby. 'I've bin 'ere for nigh on two hours and spent most of that time queuing up to be told I've got to keep on coming back. Can you believe it? And the forms we're given to fill in. Endless, pointless questions.'

Looking around her, Jessie felt sorry for mothers, young and old, who through no fault of their own had been reduced to begging the authorities for help. The misery showed in their faces. 'I don't think I can queue for that long,' she murmured, more to herself than the woman sitting next to her. 'I'm hungry now. Starving, in fact.'

'It's come to something. Boxing Day. The day we usually eat all the lovely cold turkey and cheese and pickles. You should 'ave seen the Christmas dinner they dished out at the paupers' cafe. I 'ad to queue up round the comer for a ticket for over an hour as well. Still, they're doing their best, I s'pose. The Women's Voluntary Service is all right and the Salvation Army. They run mobile canteens, bless 'em. You can always be sure of a cup of tea and a bun off the Sally Army.'

'What do you do for food normally?' asked Jessie, building up her own picture of what was to come.

'Queue up round the comer, next door to the Bancroft library, at the RO. They give you lunch tickets or tickets to get bread and that' The woman rubbed her tired eyes. 'Still, they've started work on my place. Reckon it'll take a month to make the roof safe again. That'll do me. My own roof over my 'ead, that's all I want. What road you from, love?'

'Grant Street.'

'Oh God. That took a blow, didn't it? Never mind, it'll come out right in the end. I was thinking of doing what my cousin's done – move into one of the better-off boroughs – Paddington or Westminster. She got 'erself billeted to a nice big room in Finchley. Then managed to get a bit of work clearing rubble from the pavements and that. Landed on 'er feet, that one.'

'Where did she have to go for that? The Borough?' Jessie could see a light at the end of the tunnel.

'Probably should 'ave done. But it's not her way of doing things. She caught the free bus and presented herself with her two little uns at Finchley town hall and they sorted 'er out within the hour. I might do that, I don't know. Trouble is, I don't think I'd like it much. Finchley... it's not friendly like Bethnal Green or Stepney, is it? I've only bin to visit my cousin the once. It's too clean and clinical for me. Too posh, if you know what I mean. Better the devil you know.' Jessie kept her thoughts to herself. Clean, clinical and posh sounded fine by her. It was food for thought. But right then she needed food in her belly. She would go along to the Great Mission Hall in Whitechapel where the Salvation Army ran their voluntary canteen. Where she would stay that night was something she would face when the time came.

'Are you stopping with relatives then?' asked Jessie, teasing a bit more information out of the woman. 'Or 'ave you found somewhere else to go?'

'Yeah, I've found somewhere for me and baby to sleep at night. I could have gone to my in-laws but, no, that wouldn't 'ave worked out. I catch the council bus to the Majestic picture palace in Woodford. It's not all that safe but better than some places. I sleep on one of the seats and lay baby along two of 'em. I only catnap really but it's all right. It's dry. If the sirens go off we don't have far to go – down a flight of steps into the cellar. Sometimes

I go to St Stephen's Church in Walthamstow. But there's nothing there but straw on the floor for beds. Refugees, that's what we are. It's one life for the rich and one for the poor. Not that I was poor before this war. My husband's a carpenter by trade. Now he's God knows where – fighting or shot dead. Who knows, eh? Who knows?'

Jessie had heard and seen enough. Wishing the woman good luck, she left the packed and busy building to make her way along to the Mission Hall to get some food inside herself and Billy. After that, she thought she might go to one of the other places that the woman had mentioned. Try her luck in Westminster perhaps.

Easing Billy's pushchair through the slush which had, just the night before, been fresh white snow, she felt better for having been to the People's Palace and seen what the majority of people were going through. She didn't feel so alone now. Thousands of others were as badly off, if not worse, than she was. And the woman had been right in her assessment of East End people. They were friendly and even though things were getting worse in all their home lives, their privacy becoming public, still there was a strong spirit of community and solidarity. Those hundreds of people dragging themselves in and out of the People's Palace seeking help and refuge were no different to her.

They had suffered too. If they could swallow their pride and ask for charity, so could she. And if other women could make a new life *and* get work clearing bomb-damaged streets, so could she.

Walking with a new determination, Jessie chatted to Billy, telling him they were going on an adventure once they had had something nice and hot to eat. Billy was happy enough in the pushchair, stamping his feet and chatting to a stray dog, a brown and white mongrel, who had joined them at some point and looked set to stay with them. Nodding and smiling back at complete strangers as she made her way along Whitechapel, Jessie was startled when her name was shouted at top voice.

'Jessie! Jessie, wait! Jessie!'

It was Max. Slowly turning, she watched as he tried to run towards her, slipping and sliding on the slush and small patches of black ice. Her face broke into a smile – he looked like Charlie Chaplin in one of his funnier films. Suddenly his feet slipped from beneath him and he landed with a severe bump on his arse. Jessie, like other women around her, shrieked with laughter. They were all laughing at Max who sat on the ground, his legs spread-eagled, a bewildered and puzzled look on his face as if he couldn't understand how he could possibly have slipped out of control.

'Well,' said an attractive redhead, still laughing, '*that* is what I call falling for a woman!' She then went to his aid followed by others who wanted to be part of the fun.

'She must be special,' said a bubbly blonde, winking at Jessie, ''cos you're an 'andsome fella. I'd nurse your bruises any time.'

Enjoying the flirtations, Max thanked them all with a hug here and a kiss there and they loved it. After all, their men were away from home and had been for a while. In good spirits, the females left him to Jessie. 'Are you all right?' she asked, feeling guilty for thinking that he could ever have welshed on Tom. Now she saw him, she knew it was impossible.

'You see…' he said, putting on a brave face, 'it's my two left feet. Now you know why the army wouldn't take me.'

'Come on. Come and treat me and Billy to a hot meat pie and a drink.'

Walking alongside her, with one hand on the push-chair, he asked if Tom was back at the house. His question was innocent enough but in a different mood she might have read something into it. 'I don't know where he is, Max. The military police crashed in at dawn and he skimmed the drainpipe. They knew he'd been there, though. He'd left bits and bobs everywhere.' She refrained from telling him that she had been thrown out. She didn't want him to start arranging things for her. Not now that she had decided to leave the East End. 'To tell you the truth, Max, I did wonder if you'd set Tom up.'

He stopped in his tracks. 'Jessie! I can't believe you would think such a thing.'

'I know, and I'm sorry. Everything piled on top of me, Max. I was confused. Of course you wouldn't do a thing like that. I soon came to my senses. How did your date with Hannah go?'

'It wasn't a date, Jessie,' he said, embarrassed, 'but it went very well. We went out that evening and spent all of the next day together. I took her up west to see the Christmas lights. We had a lovely time.'

'That's good.' Jessie felt her heart sink. 'You'll be seeing 'er again then?'

'Yes, On her next leave. It's really strange,' he added, his face lighting up again. 'She looks so much like you.'

'She's prettier, Max. I know that. Anyway, I'm really pleased that you've—'

'Jessie, listen. There's something I've got to tell you.' His expression changed yet again, to one of deep sadness.

'What, Max? What's 'appened?'

'Jessie…' his voice was quiet and grave, 'I've just heard from my mother that your grandma was taken ill on Christmas night. Did you know?'

'She what?' Jessie couldn't believe it. Ingrid had been as healthy as anyone else when she left to meet up with Tom. 'Are you sure, Max?'

'Yes. She's in the London Chest Hospital at Victoria Park.'

Continuing on their way, Jessie was quiet and Max left her to her thoughts. Hating herself for it, she knew she was going to have to delay going to see Ingrid. She had to get away from the area and try and make a life for herself. 'I'll go and see her later on today,' she said, lying to Max for the first time ever. He took her hand, and found them a warm cafe where he bought them all a filling meal.

That evening, Jessie and Billy went into a hostel for the homeless in Aldgate where she spent the worst night of her life. She had to share a room with three other women and two children and have Billy in a single camp bed with her. A bucket of warm water was placed outside each room early the next morning and from that Jessie was allowed to draw a small jug of water to fill her small enamel bowl for washing both herself and Billy.

The sheet she had been given for the camp bed had been clean but the thick rough blankets smelt damp and of cigarette smoke. She had lain awake for most of the night for fear of mice or rats climbing into the bed. That there were fleas and bugs crawling in the bedclothes, she had no doubt. But fleas and bedbugs could be got rid of. When she had actually dozed, the dream still on her mind when she woke was of Max and Hannah having a white wedding. This she pushed from her mind, scolding herself for being possessive about a man she no longer had any claims on.

First thing the next morning she left the hostel and made her way to the baths where she asked for a dose of something to kill off anything live that might have been on her. Lying in the tub with Billy sitting between her legs, she didn't mind the strong smell of disinfectant. She welcomed it, in fact, and was more than happy to let her long hair soak in hot water before washing it with the small complimentary wedge of carbolic soap.

Feeling better for her good soaking and having got through her tiredness, she began her journey to Westminster, a place which she had never set eyes on. She was a touch disappointed when she arrived. There were some very grand houses but there were also some back streets not dissimilar to Bethnal Green or Stepney. After stopping off at a small cafe for toast and tea, she made her way to the town hall. It was a very different scene from the one she had experienced at the People's Palace. It was no more grand, less in fact, but there weren't so many people there and within twenty minutes she had been given an address where she would be able to stay, bed and breakfast only, for free.

At first she had trouble finding the street but an ARP warden soon pointed out the way and from there it was easy. The street was long and tree-lined • but the houses which once would have been homes to the middle classes were fairly rundown.

Heavy hearted, she pulled on the bell and her worst fears were confirmed when a dishevelled woman answered the door, looking tired and depressed. Jessie started to explain why she was there but the woman had heard it all before. She gestured for her to go in and nodded towards a door in the hallway. 'The lady of the house is in there. Don't let her put you down.'

Whispering to Billy to be a good boy, Jessie tapped on the door and waited. The lady who answered was tall and thin and had an air of elegance about her.

But the clothes she wore, although of very good taste, were dated and a touch worn. There was no doubt in Jessie's mind that this woman had enjoyed a privileged lifestyle at one time. Without saying a word, she looked Jessie up and down and then glanced at Billy. 'Have you come from the town hall?'

'Yes,' Why the woman intimidated her she couldn't say, but she felt like something the cat had dragged in from the streets. 'We won't be any trouble and my son sleeps right through the night.'

'Are you used to sharing a room with strangers?' She spoke in a dead voice, her face expressionless.

'No. I'm used to my own house which my husband bought when we were first married.' She felt herself bristle. 'It was hit during a night raid and won't be fixed for a few months. I don't want to share a room with anyone. I'd rather be cramped in a box room than share.'

The woman showed a glimmer of respect. 'You can have the attic room. You'll share the small bathroom with four others. That's the best I can do. There's nowhere for you to cook and I don't allow food to be brought into the house. You must use the mobile canteens set up especially for people like you. They tell me the food is quite good. I don't like people to use the house during the day but there is a very good park with adequate benches not so far away – and a library, and a museum. Breakfast of porridge and toast is served in the basement at eight thirty. There are rules listed on every door so you can't miss them. If anyone breaks the rules, they're asked to leave. Bed linen is changed once a fortnight and a clean towel is provided once a week. I don't allow any wireless playing or any visitors at any time. I keep a quiet house.'

Whether she was meant to be put off by this woman's speech, Jessie had no idea and she cared less. All that she had said sounded like heaven. Jessie liked the quiet too. She had no intention of starting a social life and she wouldn't want to stay cooped up in her room all day. She would only be there, after all, until her own house was ready for her to go back into. 'That sounds fine,' she said. 'Thank you.'

'You may leave the pushchair at the back of the hall, under the staircase.' The woman handed her a key and left her to it. Whether she had softened slightly, Jessie couldn't tell, but she felt sure that her expression had become a touch less austere and guarded.

January didn't prove as difficult to get through as Jessie had imagined. The strange setting and the lack of cheap shops in Westminster didn't matter because she had no money and was relying on charity. The local Catholic church hall was a godsend; she could go there each day and be sure of a meal of sorts and Billy had other children to play with. With just three months to go before his second birthday, he had well and truly found his feet and was looking more and more like his dad. That he had character nobody could deny. His smile and his charm drew other toddlers to him and because of this, Jessie always had other mothers to chat to. At first she felt like a fish out of water, but once she had found her way into the kitchen at the rear of the church she slipped easily into her new way of life.

Until she helped out the back, all the work was left to the nuns who already had enough on their plates. Jessie hadn't realised just how hard they worked until she got talking to one of them while washing up. If they had five hours sleep at night they considered themselves lucky. When they weren't at the church hall being charitable they were visiting the poor who were, for one reason or another, housebound. They also fitted hospital visits into their busy schedule. It was during a floor-mopping session that Jessie asked the Mother Superior if she thought it a good idea to work out a rota system, involving the women, in the kitchen.

Praising Jessie for coming up with something that they really should have thought of before then, she left her to call a meeting and see if she was right in her thinking that a good majority of the women would appreciate the involvement. No time was lost in putting up a hand-written note and on the very day it went on the notice-board, Jessie was approached by both women she had not met before and those who she had already got to know. Ideas were being thrown at her as if she was already in the driving seat. One woman who came from a long line of rag and bone tradesmen said that she would rather not be in the kitchen but would happily head a team of women who might take care of clothing. This idea, to all of the women, was the best of the lot. As they sat in a circle, throwing in ideas, the church hall suddenly had a different atmosphere – one of excitement and new beginnings.

'We're in just the right area an' all,' said Gloria, a twenty-two-year-old mother of three. 'Posh frocks or what? I'll push the bleeding wheelbarrow round the streets, no trouble.' She cupped her mouth and hollered, 'Any old clothing!' A round of applause, laughter and calls from the others followed.

'Bring out your tat! Your jumpers, your skirts, your old felt hat!'

'Your worn-down boots your old-fashioned suits!'

'We lost our lot in the East End Blitz, we'll take hand-me-down clothes and a bit of glitz!'

'And we promise to keep well away from your ruddy Ritz!' yelled one of the nuns, carried away. This was followed by total silence and then a roar of laughter filled the hall.

—

That evening, as Jessie sat in her quiet room carefully writing a note to be pinned on to the board the next day, she was puzzled to hear a rat-a-tat-tat on her door. No one had knocked before. Another of the house rules was that tenants were not to visit each other's rooms. Expecting there to be something wrong, she opened the door to find her landlady standing there, with the faint hint of a smile on her face. A few seconds passed as they looked at each other, waiting for the other to speak.

'Is something wrong?' asked Jessie cautiously.

'No. Not at all. I just thought that, well…' She looked over Jessie's shoulder. 'Is your little boy asleep?'

'Yes,' said Jessie, suspicious of her reasons for being there. Surely she wasn't going to be ousted again. She felt her hackles rise. 'I'm sorry I can't offer you a cup of tea or coffee…'

'Oh… no… I wouldn't expect you—'

'My flask only holds three cups and there's only enough left for my first hot drink of the day. *Warm* drink.'

'Yes… I was thinking about that only yesterday. It must be difficult.' Another awkward silence.

'Mrs Bertram, is something the matter?' Jessie was finding it all a bit frustrating. She wasn't used to this kind of thing. She was used to people getting to the point.

'No. No, there's nothing wrong. Apart from this wretched war, of course.'

'Ah, right. So? What can I do for you?'

The woman looked embarrassed, awkward. 'I don't want to wake your son. Should I be whispering? I don't know about these things, you see.'

Jessie found herself smiling. 'My son's slept through an air raid, in a shelter, with hundreds of other people. I don't think us talking will disturb him.'

'Hundreds of people? Goodness! I hadn't realised the shelters held so many. I just go down into the basement, you see. And there's an Anderson big enough in the garden for my guests. It's been quiet since you've been here, of course, so... there we are. Well now, I expect you're wondering why I'm here. Out of bounds, so to speak.'

More impatient by the second, Jessie locked her fingers and managed a polite smile. 'Well, I've got some work to do, for the nuns down at—'

'Which is exactly why I'm here. One of the nuns called in, as they do, for a collection, and she asked about you.'

'Did she now?'

'Oh no, please! Don't take it the wrong way. She wasn't checking up or anything like that. No, she simply, well, she was praising your good name and really just mentioned in passing that one of my ladies had brought new hope to the cause. That was all.'

'Oh. That was nice of 'er. I'm sorry if I was a bit short. I thought you might have come up to turn me out.'

'Goodness, no. Why would I want to do that?'

'Well, I've got a two-year-old... the pushchair...'

'No, on the contrary. I was taken with you right from the beginning...' Her words trailed off, she had obviously embarrassed herself. 'I do get all sorts of people knocking here, you know.' She looked across at Billy sleeping like an angel. 'I was wondering if you'd like a glass of sherry. But I don't know. Are you allowed to leave a child asleep? Alone, I mean?'

'Well, I wouldn't normally but there's hardly anything in this room for him to hurt himself on, is there? A bed, a chair, a chest of drawers and a cupboard.'

'Oh well…' A smile spread across Mrs Bertram's face. 'If you'd like to then?'

'Why not? I'll leave the door open and listen out for 'im.'

Walking into the drawing room was like walking into another world for Jessie. It was beautiful. Persian rugs, heavy, lined, silk curtains, luxurious armchairs and antique furniture everywhere. 'This is lovely,' she said, 'really lovely. I've never seen such a high ceiling.'

'I know. I hope it's warm enough in here.'

'There is a nip in the air but the sherry'll soon warm the blood. Is it all right for me to sit by the fire?'

'Of course. How rude of me. Please, do sit down. Now, dry, medium or sweet?'

'Medium.' Sinking into the big feather-cushioned armchair and gazing into the flames of the fire, Jessie was reminded of her grandmother's flat close to Victoria Park. Ingrid's two armchairs were similar although half the size. Guilty feelings swept through her. She hadn't been in touch with any of her family or friends. She had wanted to take some time away from everything and everyone. She wondered if her gran had recovered properly from whatever it was that had caused her to be taken into hospital on Christmas night.

'A penny for them?' said Mrs Bertram, offering Jessie her glass of sherry before sitting in the other armchair.

'Oh… I was just thinking about my family. I haven't seen them since Christmas.'

'That doesn't sound such a long time ago. Five weeks? Do you have brothers and sisters?'

'I should say so. Two brothers, younger, a sister, younger, and another sister, my twin. Then there's Mum and Gran. Dad was killed in an accident at the docks, just over four years ago, not so long after my grandfather died and Mum inherited his business – a cobbler shop in Whitechapel.' Not wishing to be questioned further, Jessie turned the tables on her hostess. 'What about your family? Do they live close by?'

'I don't… have… any family.' She shrugged as if the question had never been asked before. 'I was an only child. Both my parents are dead. My mother was an only child, and my father's family are in India. I've no idea where or who they might be.'

Jessie glanced at her left hand for a wedding ring. There was one, thick gold, next to a cluster of diamonds. 'You didn't have any children?'

'No. I wanted a daughter… I was four years married when my husband left me for his secretary. They married and had children and now live in Canada, where, his family business first took root. I understand they're very successful in every way.' Jessie suddenly felt extremely sorry for this woman. 'That's a very sad story and I—'

'Oh, it's all right really. Time heals, as they say. He was very generous – still is. Twenty-three years on and I still miss him. Daft, isn't it? You're probably wondering why I never remarried. I loved him, you see. I loved him deeply. As he once loved me. I was terribly hurt. Couldn't really believe he wouldn't come to his senses and return. I couldn't risk that sort of thing happening again. And time goes by, you know… and you get used to your own company.'

'No…' Jessie swallowed against the lump in her throat. 'No, that's not good enough. Being used to your own company's no compensation.' She could feel her anger rising to the surface as her eyes filled. Why a complete stranger should make her feel so, emotional she had no idea, but she really was very angry.

'Twenty-three years. *Why?*' She looked into the woman's face, eye to eye. 'Why didn't you do something? Look at yourself. You're beautiful! You've got money. You've got a lovely home. You should have been sharing it with someone you love and with children you wanted! You should have loved *again*!'

Mrs Bertram looked flabbergasted. Shocked. 'Should I?' she whispered. 'Should I have? But… I believed there's only the one person in life. That you only ever really love one person.'

'Codswallop!'

Her trembling hand to her mouth, Jessie's landlady began to laugh quietly. 'Oh dear… you do say what you mean, don't you? Goodness.'

The two women looked at each other and knew that this could be the beginning of an honest friendship, brought about by extraordinary circumstances. In normal everyday life, their paths would not have crossed and if they had, they would most likely have passed each other by. 'You'd best get used to the idea that your new life could start tomorrow morning. Come to the church hall with me. You don't 'ave to do anything. You don't 'ave to make any promises. Just come, stay, watch, and listen.

See how hard the nuns work. Then tell me you were right to shut yourself away in this ivory tower, mooning over someone who's probably wiped you from his mind.'

Jessie's words were hard but they came from the heart. And if truth be told, she was giving vent to some of her own feelings. Maybe she and Mrs Bertram had something in common. Maybe Tom had found his other life, on the run, more exciting than the one he could share with her once the war was over. The thought didn't make her sad. She had turned a corner when he left her to face the music. She didn't know any more if she loved him or not.

'Thanks for the sherry,' she said, rising. 'I'd best go up now. I've got that notice to write out.'

'Wouldn't it be better if each of the women had a leaflet to take away with them? So they could read it properly and have time to think about it in private?'

'Of course it would, but I've only got one pair of hands.'

'I didn't tell you what my husband's family business was, did I?'

'Should you 'ave done?'

'Machines,' Mrs Bertram said, smiling. 'Office machines. You know the sort of thing. Typewriters, printing machines…'

'So?'

'Would you like to see what's stored in the basement?'

'Mrs Bertram, are you saying what I think you're saying?'

'Please, call me Joyce. Do you want to try out the typewriters now or in the morning? Or maybe you would rather set up the printing machine.'

Unable to contain herself, Jessie quietly laughed. 'Is there a light in the basement?'

'Oh yes – and blackout curtains. So we shouldn't attract any attention from the sky if the Germans decide to hit Westminster tonight. All we need to know are the names of anyone who might be able to type.'

'You're looking at one now.'

'Ah. I should have guessed. You went to evening classes?'

'Pitman's College.'

'Who better.' Joyce Bertram was certainly impressed with this girl from the East End.

'And I worked in the offices of a cosmetic factory from when I left school at fifteen until I married. I haven't worked a Gestetner but I used to have to type the skins and take them to the printing room. I've seen how it works. I don't s'pose you've got the special ink as well?'

'I've no idea what's in those cardboard boxes down there. It's a very big cellar and very full. I should think it'd take weeks to go through everything. It's as my husband left it when he left me.'

'Well, we'd best get started then. No time like the present. I'll check Billy and keep on checking 'im every ten minutes or so.' As she reached the door she turned.

'I don't s'pose you've got something I could put across the bedroom doorway in case he does get out of bed.'

'You mean a gate?'

'Something that'd serve as one, yeah.'

'What about that?' She pointed to a tall, wide, black iron mesh and brass fire guard. 'We could stand it against the doorway and then shove a heavy chair against it.'

'Perfect. Is there anything you *don't* 'ave, Joyce?' Jessie laughed.

Joyce went quiet and swallowed the lump in her throat. 'Friends?'

'I shouldn't worry about that. I think you'll find things'll be a bit different from now on. Not because of me, not because of what you're gonna do for the war effort, but because of you. And I think you know what I mean.'

Jessie had no idea that cellars under houses were as spacious as the one she now stood in. Not just one room, but several, archway after archway, and shelves stacked with files, bulging boxes piled high on the floor, typewriters and odd bits of furniture everywhere. Then of course there was the wine and port cellar. In one corner there was a very comfortable single bed with a small table beside it. As she sat on the edge of it, she glanced up at Joyce Bertram and raised an eyebrow.

'I know what you're thinking, Jessie. That there should be many more beds down here and my tenants shouldn't have been sheltering in the Anderson.'

'Those places are damp, you know, and not very spacious.'

'I'm sure. I haven't actually looked inside...'

'Well, maybe you should.'

'Never mind. It's never too late to change things.' Embarrassed, Joyce turned to the old printing machine in the comer. 'Golly, that looks ancient, doesn't it? It must be all of thirty years old.'

Smiling, Jessie went across to it and ran a finger along the top. 'This takes me back. The one in the soap factory was just as old. And that worked. It was typical of that factory. If it goes, don't chuck it out.'

'The thing is,' said Joyce, 'what on earth do we do with all of this stuff if we're to make space for an office and shelter?'

'Sell it. What we can't sell we'll give to the rag and bone man. He'll be in 'is element down 'ere.' She winked at her new friend. 'Out with the old and in with the new, eh?'

'Yes, I think so. We'll need a team of workers…'

'Oh, don't worry. Those women at the church hall don't like feeling useless. This is exactly what they've been waiting for. A bloody miracle!'

Four weeks later, after an army of women had descended upon Joyce Bertram's cellar, space had been created for a small print area, a sewing space complete with two treadle sewing machines, and a long trestle type table which served as the typing desk. On here stood three old-fashioned but serviceable black typewriters. Once boxes upon boxes of outmoded office equipment had been taken away and hundreds of old ledgers had been thrown out, there was shelf space galore for the other boxes which contained good stationery, envelopes of all sizes, adhesive labels, parcel tags, date stamps, adding machine, pens, pencils and just about everything an office could possibly require. A guillotine in the corner had proved to be one of the most useful items. The company name on the stationery had been sliced off, leaving thousands of sheets of clean white paper for use as handouts.

The atmosphere during the big clear-out and sorting time had been terrific, the girls forever excited by something else which had surfaced. There was even an old gramophone which was immediately oiled and used. Music was always being played in the cellar. 'Music while you work' was at first intended as an incentive to keep the girls coming back. But as it turned out neither Jessie nor Joyce need have worried. The project was proving to be a massive success and kept morale sky high. The sound of group singing coming up from the basement would be a joy in peacetime, never mind during a war.

The sewing side of the little enterprise was proving an even bigger success. Once the leaflets had been delivered around Westminster, the sacks of clothing came flooding in. Clothes for women, clothes for children. The menswear, shirts and trousers, ties and belts, were dutifully passed on to the Red Cross. The buzz in Joyce's basement when the girls were pulling out clothes, especially evening frocks, confirmed all that Jessie had said. Joyce Bertram's life had turned around and so too had her priorities and philosophy of life. People were what mattered. All people from all walks of life. Some of the women were more rough and ready than others but they added colour and some of them were very funny without realising it. Even the swearing no longer bothered Joyce. She could see that it was to them just a way of expressing themselves, and she herself had, under her breath, used a common swearword more than once when someone had got on her nerves.

Of course, with the mothers busy in the basement, sewing, typing and printing, there were children to be taken care of. Another room in the house, known previously as the library, had been taken over as a nursery, with mothers watching over them on a rota system. The nuns, always in pairs, dropped into the house perhaps more than was necessary, because they, too, were enjoying the new venture which had come out of an idle conversation in the kitchen of the church hall and was now known as TWW – The Westminster Women.

During this time, Jessie had not once written home to any of her friends. If asked, she couldn't easily have been able to explain why. It was almost as if she dared not. As if it would be tempting providence for them to know where she was. She always read the newspapers, checking which streets in Bethnal Green and Stepney had been hit during a raid, and it was a case of so far so good where her family were concerned.

It was during one of the tea breaks in the library, when the women had stopped whatever work they were doing and come up from the basement for twenty minutes, that Jessie was reminded of the time when her house had been hit.

'There just wasn't anywhere to go for a good cheap meal,' one of the women was relating, 'or to wash ourselves or our, clothes.' The woman, in her late thirties, was already going grey and her face showed that she had suffered. She was the mother of three small children. 'We camped out in a brick street shelter. We hadn't 'ad a proper meal for two days, so I went back home to my bombed-out house 'oping to find something in the larder. Ha. I should be so lucky. The larder was a pile of bricks. There was no gas or water or electricity in the 'ouse, but I managed to salvage some bacon and tins of beans out of the little comer shop along our road which 'ad bin hit. Most of the food 'ad gone but they'd missed the bacon. The beans were under a pile of rubble. I only just saw 'em. I only took two tins and left the rest tucked away, so I could go back for more as and when I needed food...

'I made a bonfire in my back yard with some broken wood and I was in the middle of cooking for me and the kids when the landlord came along. He asked about the' rent. I told him to sling 'is hook. I took the cooked bacon down to the brick street shelter for the kids. Our 'ouse was in too bad a state to try and live there again. Pity. It was small but it was 'ome. Our family 'ome. Still, there you go.'

Looking from the woman to Joyce Bertram, Jessie could see that she was moved by the woman's tale. When another started up with her horror story, she half expected their landlady, who had led a privileged life, to quietly slip away. But she was wrong. Joyce leaned forward, engrossed. This was all news to her. Real people that had truly suffered and were still suffering but still managed to smile and sing and pull together, as all the members of TWW had.

No one could deny that this group of women were becoming very close; a sisterhood seemed to be forming. Jessie supposed that it must be because they didn't all live under the same roof that rows never broke out. Not all the members were in at the same time, there were far too many. If they weren't at Joyce Bertram's they were at the church hall or on their rounds, collecting for the cause. Jessie thought about her dad who had once said to her, 'You'll find that in a crisis people don't get carried away with drama.' And he was right. The war was on. It was a crisis. And no one was turning any of it, no matter how bad, into a drama.

Here, in the comfort of Joyce Bertram's spacious house, were women of various ages who had had their homes blown to smithereens, had slept in Underground stations night after night in the East End without washing facilities or sanitation and had had to walk down tunnels which were used as lavatories, creating a stench in which they had to live. In the older Underground tunnels a plague of mosquitoes thrived on the heat and sweating bodies, not to mention the rodents. Their lives now were easy by comparison.

The deep shelters had been gruesome and humid but at least they were cut off from the noise of bombings and were safe, so shelterers could at least snatch a few hours' sleep, whereas the less protected surface shelters made sleep impossible. All of this and more tested the London working classes and although the discomfort of it all caused arguments, still their tremendous adaptability to hardship had grown more solid. The strong sense of humour and spirit came to the fore as it had never done in the past. In the tube shelters neighbourliness had flowered. It was no wonder that TWW were in their element now that they had moved temporarily into the safer borough of Westminster, away from the worst hit East End of London.

Another woman told how during the first days of the Blitz she had had to stay in improvised rest centres which also had a dire shortage of sanitation and no facilities for the shell-shocked families who had just lost their homes. The woman wasn't blaming anyone, she was simply relating how no one had truly believed that the capital of London could be so devastated. Ending her tale, she lowered her head and quietly added, 'I lost my daughter. She was only eleven years old. She was buried under the rubble. When they pulled her body out, she was still holding our cat, Molly. Molly was alive but she was so terrified she scarpered, never to be seen again.'

There was a minute of silence. A silence of respect. It was Joyce whose quiet voice drew them back. 'My cat's called Molly.'

'Is she?' said the woman. 'Well then, that must be fate, mustn't it?' She smiled and nodded, her eyes glazed as she remembered. 'Our Molly was a fight gold colour, with white markings. Do you know that cat understood every word I spoke.'

'My Molly's black and white. Sophie's ginger.'

'That's nice. Two for company. That's 'ow it should be. I've never seen 'em.'

'They live in my quarters and have a cat flap out into the garden. They're getting old, mind you. Prefer to laze in front of the fire, on my armchair – until someone pops in. They're not used to visitors. They're out and into the garden like a shot.'

'What about when there's an air raid? Where d'they go then?' She looked genuinely concerned.

'I carry them down with me, to the basement.'

'Course. You've got a ready-made shelter down there. And good luck to you, I say. Not all our houses are built with cellars, more's the pity.'

'They are in Canada. My brother went out there years ago. He writes to me. Tells me all about it. Yeah, they've all got basements out there.'

'When we could do with 'em over 'ere,' said another, smiling at the irony.

'Shall we have some more tea?' said Joyce suddenly.

'An extended tea break?'

'Sounds good to me,' said another. 'We're all gettin' a bit morbid, gals. Come on. Buck up. Put a bit of music on, Joyce. We could do wiv a singsong.'

'We don't need music,' came the soft Irish voice of an older woman. She stood up and began to sing.

Her voice was beautiful…

On Mother Kelly's doorstep,
Down Paradise Row, I'd sit along a' Nelly,
She'd sit along a' Joe.

She'd got a little hole in her frock,
A hole in her shoe, a hole in her sock,
Where her toe peep'd through,
But Nelly was the sweetest down our alley.

She waved a hand, signalling for the others to join in, and they were not slow to pick up the chorus: 'On Mother Kelly's doorstep...'

Before they had a chance to sing another line, the awesome sound of the high-pitched air-raid siren echoed through the streets outside and Joyce panicked, as she always did when the warning came. 'Oh my God. Oh God. Quick, everybody! Quickly! Downstairs. Down. Now. Come on! Come on, come on, *come on!*'

She needn't have worried, the mothers were up from their chairs and rushing out into the back garden to collect their children and usher them down to the cellar. Those without children quickly filled buckets with tap water and carried them downstairs. Others checked the provisions while Joyce collected the enamel buckets with lids, making certain that a bottle of carbolic was inside one of them and a wad of tissue paper in another. Going to the lavatory during a raid was something that each and every one of them, children included, had to do whether the raid lasted twenty minutes or went on for hours.

The sudden change of mood from melancholy to organised panic was something that all of them were used to, except for Joyce. 'Hot-water bottles!' she hollered. 'Were they taken back down?'

'Yes, Joyce!'

'What about the dried food? Powdered milk and eggs?'

'I've got the box!' yelled another. 'Do you want me to take down these tins of peaches from the larder, Joyce?'

'Well, no… oh, yesl l don't care. Take what you think! Tin opener! We'll need—'

'There's one down there!'

And so it went on until each of them was safely in the basement with the door barred and the lights on. 'On to your beds, children. Make space for us to work. We may be down here for a while and so we'll need to prepare dinner!'

'We've 'ad our dinner,' said a grubby, rosy-cheeked, six-year-old lad. 'We 'ad it before we come 'ere – dahn the church 'all.'

'That was lunch,' said Joyce. 'You'll be hungry again later and you'll want—'

'Our tea. We 'ave our tea before we go abed. We never ad lunch, we 'ad dinner, didn't we, Gran?'

'Fuck knows what it's called so long as it's food. Put yer 'ead dahn, Danny-boy, and get some shut-eye. Give us a bit of peace.'

'I ain't tired. It ain't bedtime. Can't 'ear nuffink dahn 'ere. No bombs, nuffink. Who wants to be in a bleedin' cellar? I bet there're rats dahn 'ere. Bet we get trapped in. If the 'ouse gets it, we'll be shitting well trapped, won't we, Gran?'

'Shut your noise, Danny.'

'Can't we clear off, Gran?' he said, scratching his ear. 'Can't we go up the uvver shelter? At the park?' The small boy began to shiver. 'D'yer reckon they've come yet? D'yer reckon this 'ouse 'as got it? Can't 'ear anyfing dahn 'ere. Gran! Gran, I wanna go ome! I want me mum!'

The old woman went to him and he threw his little arms round her waist, burying his face in her bulky clothes. 'There, there, sweetheart, there, there. It'll all be over soon. Be a brave boy for Gran. You're frightening the others. We'll play a game, shall we? We'll play "I Spy".'

Joyce stepped in and stroked little Danny's hair. 'We're safe down here. Much safer than most places.' Wiping his eyes with the cuff of his sleeve, he looked up at her. 'Where's your cats?' A silence which could be cut with a knife filled the basement. 'They was in the garden but run in their little door when the siren went off.'

Without saying a word, Joyce spun round and made for the door. Jessie was after her in a flash and grabbed her arm. 'Joyce, don't.'

Glaring at Jessie, she pulled her arm free. 'Don't tell me what to do!'

'They'll be all right, Joyce. Nine lives?'

'I'm going to get them.'

'No.' She grabbed her arm again and held it tight. 'No.'

'I have to. They're all I've got. I love them as if they were my children. Would you leave Billy up there if the tables were turned?'

Jessie's hand slipped to her side. 'Go on then, but if you can't find them—'

'I *will* find them. They'll be looking out for me.' Not wishing to lose another second, she pulled open the heavy door. Rushing off, she left it open.

'Close the door,' said little Danny's gran. 'Shut it.'

'No,' said Jessie. 'I'll wait by it for 'er. She—'

'Close it! Now!'

Jessie turned to face her. 'Why?'

'There's no time.' Pushing Jessie aside, the woman yelled from the open doorway, '*Joyce!*' She waited for a few seconds, listening out, then slammed the door shut and turned to the gaping faces of the rest of them. 'Get under the beds. Hold on to each other.' There was authority in her voice as she gave her orders and without question the others did as they were told. Before Jessie could even think about going up for Joyce, there was a horrendous and almighty explosion which rocked the very foundations of the house and caused everyone to scream out in shocked terror as dust seeped in and a terrible smell similar to burning motor car oil filled the air.

The thunderous sound from above as the house caved in was shocking. Now, in complete darkness, with, no electricity, the children began to cry in terror. Still the walls and ceiling of the basement shook and shuddered and sent chunks of plaster and bits of bricks and untold dirt and dust falling to the ground.

'Are we gonna die, Gran?' came the thin, frightened voice of Danny.

'No. We'll be all right. It'll soon settle and we can light some candles.'

'I'd like to know 'ow we're gonna do that in this pitch black. I'm blowed if I've seen candles dahn 'ere!' said one of the women from a far comer.

'I don't go nowhere without a couple of candles in me apron pocket. Them and a book of matches. Learn a lesson from it,'

'We'll suffocate before the fire brigade get 'ere!' cried another of the shelterers.

'We won't do nothing of the sort!' Gran again. 'There's plenty of air down 'ere, don't you worry. And don't you go scaring the nippers with that kind of talk!' The old and wiser woman waited a few moments to see if there were any others about to panic. There weren't. She had them listening. 'Now then, I'm gonna strike a match and light a candle. Jessie Smith, give me a call. I need to know where you are!'

'Over 'ere.' Jessie's voice was shaky and quiet. She was hugging Billy tightly in the darkness.

'All right, Jessie. Do you know where Joyce put the box of candles?'

'There on a shelf near—'

'Never mind where. I'll fetch the lighted candle to you and we'll light more once we've laid our hands on 'em. Everyone else stay where you are. And keep calm. We've survived one of the worst bombs – that was a high-explosive or my name's not Mabel Hurst! If we can do that, we can do anyfing!'

The silence continued but there were quiet sighs of relief here and there as they settled down again. Striking a match, Mabel lit the candle and peered around for Jessie who held up a hand. Slowly manoeuvring around the others, they met and went through an archway into the storage space to lift down the box of candles. Crumbling plaster was still falling here and there but that Was all.

'How did you know?' whispered Jessie. She was trembling. 'How could you tell?'

'Call it a sixth sense. Now then, be a good girl and hold this lit candle while I set the others on to the saucers Joyce left there for the purpose.'

Obeying the calm and resilient woman, Jessie asked if she thought that Joyce had got it. 'It'd be a miracle if not,' she said, 'but I doubt she'd 'ave wanted it any other way. Like she said, them cats were more like her babies. She 'ad to go after 'em. She won't know nothing about it. It would 'ave bin quick.'

Once they'd lit enough candles to light up the room, Jessie was horrified by what she saw. No one was injured but they all looked like ghosts. Their hair, skin and clothes were covered in dust, soot and dirt and there was a layer of grey powder over their clothes. Their shocked faces stared at her. She would have to be like Mabel. She had to be strong for the sake of the old and the very young, some of whom were starting to cry again.

'Well now,' she said, 'ain't we the lucky ones? Safe and sound down 'ere in Joyce's cellar.'

'Yeah,' came a very quiet voice from somewhere, 'we are. But she's not, is she? Perhaps we could say a little prayer for 'er.'

'She might not be dead!' said little Danny, finding his voice.

'No, but we could still say a prayer… just in case.'

'Yeah,' said another, 'we should anyway. The Lord's Prayer.'

There was a short silence as they prepared themselves and then Mabel led them in the prayer. Each and every one of them joined in. It was the most moving experience Jessie had ever known. Women and children praying with feeling and because they wanted to and not because they were in a church or school assembly.

When they had finished, seventy-year-old Mabel began to make tea and gave instructions for a large jug of orange juice to be made up for the children. Biscuits laid aside for such times in the makeshift larder cupboard were emptied on to plates and handed around.

'Well now,' said Rosie, the Irish woman with the lovely singing voice. 'Wouldn't it be nice if we had a little singing while we wait for our rescuers to dig us out.'

'What d'yer mean? Dig us out? We can go out through the door, can't we?' said little Freddy, wiping juice from his lips. 'Once the bombing's over, we can go.'

'Unlikely, son,' cut in Mabel, preparing them for what had gone on above and the fact that the house was no doubt just another bombed site. 'There'll be rubble piled up outside that door I expect. But they'll dig their way in like they always do.'

'I know what we'll sing,' said Rosie, standing. '"Altogether Now".' Then, in true Gracie Fields style, she began the song, encouraging them all to join in. And they did.

We're all *together now,* all *together now,*
Ready to do, ready to dare,
What do we, what do we, what do we care*!*
We're all *together now,* all *together now,*
Cloudy or fair, what do we care,
What do we, what do we, what do we care*?*
There's a war we have to fight,
It's the war that must be won,
So we've all got to join and get things done*!*
We're all *together now,* all *together now,*
Ready to do, ready to dare,
What do we, what do we, what do we care*!*

A spontaneous cheer went up at the end of the song and it was clear they were in the mood for more. Rosie asked for requests and Mabel said could she sing a solo, one of her favourite songs, 'Side By Side'. In truth it wasn't her favourite but she wanted to keep up the spirit; and this one rather than a melancholy tune seemed appropriate. She also knew that the others would join in, solo or not.

'Is it worth trying the door, Mabel? We don't wanna stay down here—'

'No, best leave it be, Jessie. You'd be surprised 'ow the sight of someone trying to get out causes panic. It only wants one of us to 'ave a fit or, worse still, a heart attack. We would be in trouble then.'

Jessie nodded but her expression spoke volumes – it was wrong not to at least try. After all, somewhere up there was Joyce Bertram who might be in need of comfort and help right at this very moment.

'I know what you're thinking,' said Mabel, her voice almost a whisper, 'but I've been in a situation like this before. You can take it from me, Jessie, the 'ouse 'as been flattened and it's gonna take a lot of digging before they get through to the basement door. The best thing is to feed and wet them and keep their spirits up. We'll raid that wine cellar as soon as we've all lined our stomachs.'

'Get drunk, you mean?'

'That's right. Drink until we can't keep our eyes open. We're in for a long wait so we might as well sleep our way through some of it.'

'So it doesn't look good then?'

'No. I'm not saying we 'aven't got enough provisions to stop us from starving till they get through to us—'

'If they even realise we're down 'ere,' said Jessie, thinking the worst.

'Exactly. So no more talk of Joyce and her cats, eh?' She placed a hand on Jessie's. 'I'm trembling as well, love, but I daren't show it. This could turn into a horror story if we don't keep our heads.' She looked straight into Jessie's face. 'You understand what I'm saying, don't you?'

Taking a deep breath and holding it to stop herself from bursting into tears, Jessie nodded and then slowly exhaled, something the midwife had taught her to do during labour.

'I do. We could be buried alive?'

'No. That could never happen. All I'm saying is put on a cheerful front. The quicker we get them all to accept this place as their temporary home, the better. Once we've fed 'em, we'll get the kids interested in them typewriters and the printing machine. Keep them occupied and their mothers will take care of themselves.'

'It's crazy,' said Jessie. 'One minute we're right on top of things and then, bang…'

'That's right. That's what war's all about. Always 'as been. Let's hope this one'll be the last, eh?'

'Please God.'

Chapter Nine

Jessie couldn't know that while she and Billy were trapped in that cellar, various parts of London had been hit just as badly and not only where she had been born and bred, the East End, which as usual had been hit the hardest Even areas such as Twickenham, which was not normally a target area, had been hit not severely but enough to alert all Londoners that nowhere was safe from the Luftwaffe.

The most serious incident, and one which would have thrown Jessie into further panic had she known about it, was the bombing of the London Chest Hospital, Victoria Park, where her grandmother, Ingrid, had been admitted on Christmas night and re-admitted three weeks before this latest tragedy. The elegant Queen Anne-style red-brick building had suffered badly. Even though the fire service had had five hoses playing on the hospital and the nurses' quarters, it was impossible for them to control the flames. By morning, the top wards had disappeared and entrance was possible only through floods of water and charred timber. Futile attempts were made to move patients, Ingrid being one of them, into the basement, but water had begun to penetrate there and it was vital to evacuate the patients.

Emergency calls had been going all through that night for ambulances to move the patients out of Bethnal Green but it had been one of the worst raids and, once again,

Bethnal Green and Shoreditch had taken a hammering. The casualties were very high and at the end of a desperate attempt from the ARP to get help to the hospital, only two large ambulances were available for the short shuttle from the burning building to a local school, Parmiters, just a hundred yards away, which was to be utilised as a temporary hospital.

There was so much activity and panic all around Bethnal Green that doctors were rushing from one emergency to another. A lady doctor, with a steel helmet on her head, was taken by the ARP controller to Parmiters School where she was to act as resident doctor. But there was no electricity in the school and the windows had been blown to pieces. This meant working by the light of dimmed hurricane lanterns.

All the patients, nearly one hundred of them, were transferred to the school with, miraculously, the loss of only one.

At 3.30 a.m., Jessie lay awake in her bed in the basement, thinking about her family and, in particular, her gran. Then her mind turned to Tom and how distraught he would be if she and Billy did not get out of here alive. Her mind raced from one thing to another; sleep was impossible. Turning in her camp bed yet again, she looked into the face of Mabel who was also awake.

'What's up, love, can't you sleep?' she whispered.

'No. I was thinking about my husband,' Jessie whispered back. 'The morning after he'd been called up. He's a bit of a tealeaf now and then,' she said, waiting to see what the reaction might be.

'Ain't they all, love. From toffs to toerags, everyone gets what they can. What did your Tom nick?'

'A load of raincoats.'

'I 'ope he got away wiv it.'

'Only just. He's a real rogue, I'm telling yer.'

Chuckling at the thought of it, Mabel said, 'Ne' mind. Didn't do no 'arm, did it? Now try and get some sleep, there's a good girl.'

More relaxed, Jessie nodded and turned over, thanking her lucky stars for people like Mabel. She wasn't quite ready for sleep and couldn't help thinking about her family.

Meanwhile Ingrid lay in her bed in a makeshift ward at the school, wondering if she would ever see Jessie again before she passed on. It had, after all, been almost three months since her granddaughter and great-grandson had left without any warning or giving any forwarding address. For all they knew she could have thrown herself and Billy in the River Thames. No one had heard from her and no one knew where she was. All that Max could tell them was that when he had last seen her she told him that the army were in hot pursuit of Tom but she seemed fine.

Ingrid looked up at the pale Irish nurse taking her temperature, with a question in her eyes: why bother? Leave me to die. But the nurse had seen it all and many times. Most of the old people she tended would rather not have to stay around for the duration of this diabolical war. Ingrid was no exception.

'Things will get better now,' she said, smiling warmly. 'The Women's Voluntary Service and lots of other helpers have turned up. There's gallons of tea being brewed. Would you like a cup yourself?'

Ingrid nodded. She was very thirsty but hadn't liked to bother anyone for a glass of water. They had all been tearing about and must themselves be exhausted, was her thinking – and she was right. The doctors and nursing staff worked under considerable strain and difficulty and but for the courage, resource and determination shown by everybody at the chest hospital, the casualties would have been far worse.

Slipping the thermometer from Ingrid's mouth, the young nurse, on reading it, was satisfied. 'You're a resilient lady, that you are. Temperature normal. Well done. You've all been pushed and pulled from one place to another and no complaints. Crying out in discomfort, yes, but no complaints. I love you all, I do.'

'I was thinking about my granddaughter. Now I will see her. It will be in the papers. She'll come to visit. I hope she comes before I die.'

'Oh, now then,' said Patsy, 'you've got a few years to go yet, that you have.'

'I hope not.'

Patsy sat on the edge of Ingrid's bed and stroked the hair from her face, 'Come on. You don't mean that.'

'Yes. I mean it. I hate it. I hate this war.' Try as she might, she couldn't stop the tears. Ingrid, as a rule, never cried. 'Germans are not bad people. They don't want all this killing. It's Adolf Hitler. All of this is not the work of a human being. No. The devil is behind it. If I die, I will be one of the lucky ones. I would like to die in my sleep.'

'And what if the war's over two weeks after? Wouldn't you be angry in heaven?'

'I would. Ha. Just like my granddaughter – a way with words. Tea?'

Quietly laughing at her, Patsy made her way to the next bed to take the next patient's temperature and blood pressure. None of the patients was sleeping. How could they settle down after what they had been through.

'Where the bloody hell 'ave you been?' said the patient in the next bed. 'I'm gasping for a drink.' Just as Patsy was about to tease old Isobelle, who thrived on banter, a nursed rushed in. 'All hands on deck! Front entrance now!'

Patsy ran from the makeshift ward. 'What about my bloody tea!' yelled Isobelle.

'The WVS will fetch it! Stop shouting.'

'Not now, they won't. Something more important than us as 'appened! We're only *old*. What do we matter?'

As far as the carers were concerned, no patient was more important than another, but there were other patients being brought in, just a few, but in critical condition who needed emergency treatment.

A house close by in Approach Road had been partially demolished and was on fire, the six who had been brought to the school were the only survivors and in a very bad way. The other eighteen trapped in the basement had all perished.

'What the bleedin' hell you doin' in a school, Gran!' Dolly, now a voluntary worker, had arrived. Pushing a trolley normally used by school kitchen staff in the children's dining hall, she was making her way to the end of the row where she would start her rounds. She had had a report from Patsy that her gran was in fine fettle but a bit depressed and fatigued, Ingrid gave her a smile and watched her as she reached the end bed, whose occupant was hunched under the bedclothes.

'Come on, Sarah!' said Dolly. 'I ain't daft. I know you're awake. Bleedin' well sit up or I'll go and get Coughing Colin to come in and give that fanny of yours a squeeze.'

'Dirty cow,' mumbled Sarah from under the covers.

'If you don't sit up now I'm not making a special trip back when you do fancy showing yer face. I know you. Make me walk up and down for the fun of it. Get up now or go wivout.'

'Go without. Leave me to die. It's what you all want. No one likes me. All I ever do is watch other people enjoying 'emselves.'

'I doubt it. Not in this bleedin' ward. Now down Whitechapel—'

'Yeah, we know. You tart. Wounded soldiers in the London Hospital. I bet you get through a lot of rubbing-in cream there.'

The other women in the ward, used to Sarah and Dolly's banter, were pulling themselves up into sitting positions, laughing, ready for a show. Both of them were on form.

'So where do you have to rub cream, Dolly?' asked old Sadie in her usual droll way. 'Not on their bums, I hope?'

'No, I won't touch bums. I only do fronts. I start at the neck and massage all the way down to their little toes. I'm not sure if they enjoy it or not, Sadie, 'cos, do you know, they often beg me to stop. I can't fink why, can you?'

'You're a dirty little cow, that's what you are!'

And so the conversation and jokes continued and as usual the older contingent were much ruder than Dolly – in fact, they were the ones who had taught her. Approaching her gran's bed, she quietened down and behaved herself. 'How do you like it then, Granny German? Better than the Ritz, I reckons.'

'Haven't I told you not to call me that?'

'Yeah, lots of times, but I don't take no notice, do I? And you know why. It's not your fault that we're at war so you shouldn't try and 'ide it. They all know you're a bloody Kraut anyway. You haven't 'ad any bangers in your bed, 'ave yer?'

'No. Besides, it's not the German bit I was referring to, it's the title. Just call me Ingrid.'

Dolly handed her a cup of tea, 'I like saying it. Granny. It sounds good.' Before Ingrid could made a retort, Dolly was at the next bed. 'You're looking a bit grey, Sadie.'

'Listen to it! We're all looking a bit grey. What do you expect? We've just escaped having been blown up.'

'Yeah, that's true. Blimey Riley, it must 'ave bin bloomin' frightening.'

'Dolly!' Ingrid called out to her granddaughter.

'Hello?'

'Answer your grandmother with respect. Hello? What is that supposed to mean?'

'What d'yer want, Gran?'

'Why are you speaking in exaggerated Cockney?'

'It's all the rage. All the posh lot are doin' it.' She started to sing and did a little jig around the ward. 'Everybody's doing it, doing it, doing it. Picking their nose and chewing it, chewing it, chewing it.'

This brought a round of laughter which kicked off a round of coughing. These patients were from the chest hospital, after all. But Dolly was enjoying herself and enjoying the attention; their laughter was a tonic. Enjoying herself so much that she didn't notice the arrival of Matron who had come to check up on the patients. 'Miss Warner! Have you quite finished?'

Freezing on the spot, Dolly waited for a good stripping down in front of the patients, who were still laughing and coughing. But Matron's eye had been caught by something far more urgent. One of the patients who had been laughing was having trouble breathing and by the look of her face was in pain. She pushed Dolly out of the way and went over to the bed, to Ingrid, and a very quick once-over had her yelling for Dolly to fetch the doctor from the next floor up where she was seeing to other patients.

Dolly didn't move. She simply stared at the bed, at her gran, who was holding out an arm to her. On her face was an expression that Dolly didn't like. It was a look of desperation. Ingrid wanted Dolly close to her and that was out of character. She walked over and took her hand and the two of them just gazed into each other's eyes. No words were necessary. Her grandmother was saying farewell and she was smiling.

'Don't you leave me, Granny German... don't you leave me...' Dolly whispered.

Ingrid's face relaxed as if the pain had just slipped away, she smiled at Dolly again, and murmured, 'He's here. At the foot of the bed...' Then she closed her eyes, sighed away all the pain that life had delivered her and slipped quietly away.

'Gran?' whispered Dolly. '*Gran?*'

A nurse arrived and instinctively pulled a curtain on wheels across the room to give them privacy. Matron, in a different mood, put an arm round Dolly's shoulders and spoke in a quiet, kind voice. 'We didn't expect her to live this long, Dolly. She had such a strong will. She knew she was dying but she said she was waiting for the right time. Waiting for someone to come and fetch her.'

'Grandfather. She was waiting for my grandfather. He was there. He's still there. They're both here.'

'Can you see them?' whispered Matron. 'Can you really see them, Dolly?'

'Not see, no. But they're here.' She smiled through her tears. 'You came to get 'er after all this time, Willy Gunter.'

Tears were rolling down her cheeks. 'I was her favourite, you know. She saw something of herself in me, she said so.'

'Come on. Come and sit in the office and we'll send one of the volunteers to fetch your mother. She's not far away, is she?'

'No. I'll go. I'll go to the shop and tell her myself.' She turned to Ingrid, kissed her on the cheek, said goodbye and pulled the crisp white sheet up and over her face. 'At least you wasn't blown up by one of your own, Gran. You wouldn't have liked that, would yer?'

When Dolly arrived at the shop she was surprised to see that the shutters were up and couldn't believe that the news had travelled that quickly. Ringing the bell, Dolly felt her stomach turn.

When Rose came to the door, puffy-eyed and red-faced, she beckoned her in without saying a word. She followed her through to the back room and was mystified as to why there were two nuns there. They were, after all, Church of England.

'You'd best sit down, Dolly. I've some bad news,' said Rose, her voice breaking with each word.

'But Mum, I already know.' She looked at the nuns. 'I don't understand. I've only just left Gran and I came straight here. Who told you?'

'What do you mean? Told me what? Has something happened to your gran?'

Dolly's voice seemed to have deserted her, she tried to say that the hospital had been hit but it was as if her throat had dried up. She sat down and wiped perspiration from her forehead and tears from her face. She wanted to ask the nuns again why they were there but she felt sick. 'A glass of water,' she managed to say.

Once she had collected herself, she asked why the nuns were there. She couldn't bring herself to tell her mother that Ingrid was dead. Not until she knew what else had happened. Rose's lips trembled as she said, 'Its Jessie… and Billy.'

'Oh no. No. No it's not. Not that. No. No, Mum. Tell them to go away. Send them away. Don't listen to them. Not our Jessie and Billy. No. No. *Not…*' The nuns looked to Rose to explain but she was covering her face. It was too much. 'What's happened to your gran, Dolly? Tell me.'

'The chest hospital was hit. They got them all out and used a local school to bed them all. Gran was laughing at me messing about. They all were. She started to cough and then… She held out her hand to me. She knew she was going. She said Grandfather was at the foot of the bed. She was smiling.' Dolly pushed her hand through her hair. Her eyes were wide as she screamed, 'What's happened to Jessie?'

'She and several other women and children are trapped in a basement but—'

'No! It can't be. Jessie wasn't living round Victoria Park. We would 'ave known. You've made a mistake. It can't be.'

'Why do you say Victoria Park, child?' asked one of the nuns.

'Approach Road, Victoria Park. Eighteen people were trapped in the basement and died. No one said anything about a little boy. They just said people. They would 'ave said if—'

'Not Victoria Park, child,' said the other nun. 'In Westminster. The rescue team are there now. We believe that those who were down there will have survived. We just felt that Jessie's family would want to be there.'

'It's where she's been living, Dolly,' Rose said. 'She gave my name and address as next of kin. That's how the nuns found us. Do you want to come with me?'

'Of course I do.' Dolly sounded as if she was about to fall asleep. 'Just give me five minutes...'

'There's no rush. You could both come on later. It will be quite a few hours before they clear the debris and get to the cellar. They have to be very careful, you understand. They have found the remains of one body and that's all. The landlady who, for whatever reason, didn't take shelter in the basement.'

'Is it burning?' asked Dolly, unemotional.

'Not any more.'

'How long 'ave they been down there?'

'Well... the house was hit yesterday afternoon around teatime. But, Dolly, you can be sure they wouldn't have gone without food and drink. The cellar is one they use every day as workrooms and shelter when necessary. It's very well-equipped.'

'Is there a lavatory down there?'

'No.'

'A tap?'

'Well, no, but they keep buckets and jugs in readiness.'

'How many people?'

'Well, it's hard to tell but we think... somewhere around twelve, thirteen perhaps.'

'Thirteen? Let's hope not.'

The nun turned to Rose and put a hand on her shoulder. 'I'm so sorry to hear about your mother. This has been a very sad day for you. You have our blessings and we will pray for you.'

'Thank you. I would appreciate that. Especially if you prayed for my daughter and my grandson. My mother's in heaven. God will look after her.' Rose wiped away a tear.

'Not God, Mum. Grandfather,' Dolly said stoutly.

'Please don't get up. We'll see ourselves out.' With that the nuns quietly slipped away.

'How can you talk about God after all this? We were lucky to 'ave escaped last night. You should see the buildings, Mum. The burning buildings and rows of houses that were bombed. Some are still burning. Most are smouldering. How many people were killed last night? And the night before and the night before that?' Dolly looked at Rose, her face full of questions. 'We're losing the war. Hitler won't stop till he's wiped us off the map.'

'It does look that way, Dolly, but we're not alone, don't forget. Other countries are fighting this war with us. We mustn't give up. That's what he wants. He'll keep on and on and on, hoping to crush our spirit. We must never let him do that. Never.'

Before Rose could go to Westminster, there were a couple of visits she and Dolly had to make first. Sending her daughter to Emmie and Charlie with the news about Jessie and Billy, Rose went to the Chapel of Rest where Ingrid's body had been taken, to say goodbye to the mother she had known for such a short time – the first six years of her life and the past four, with a very big gap in between when Rose hadn't known whether her mother was alive or dead. At least the few years they did have together were good ones. It brought her some consolation.

As she stepped off the bus in Hackney, just a short walk from the Chapel of Rest, Rose was shocked by the devastation all around her. A row of houses had been reduced to a pile of bricks and rubble with bits of furniture strewn everywhere. The worst and most telling sight was a red bus which had been gutted and even though the charred bodies had been removed, there were bits of burnt clothing lying around and broken glass everywhere. The area smelt of smoke and smouldering wood.

Rose's mind was filled with memories of England in its heyday and her life when her family were young and her husband Robert alive and full of love for her and their children. Life had been hard but she had learned the most important lesson which would see her through this terrible time and this horrendous war – let yesterday go and step boldly into the future. Her thoughts returned to Jessie and her only grandchild, Billy. They would be all right, she felt safe with that belief and dared not think otherwise. Her elder and wayward son, Alfie, had just the day before been called to serve in the army. Soon he would be going off as a young soldier to do his bit abroad. If he survived, she felt sure it would be the making of him. She hoped that the war would be over before Stephen, her youngest, was old enough to be enlisted. As for Dolly, the light of everyone's life, she would survive to tell the story in years to come. Yes, thought Rose, Dolly was a survivor.

–

'Well, this is a surprise,' said Emmie on seeing Jessie's younger, cheeky sister on her doorstep. 'Fancy you paying us a visit. Come on in.'

'I've got some sad news, Emmie. Mum wanted me to come and tell you straightaway,' said Dolly, following Emmie through the passage. 'It's Granny.'

'Oh dear,' said Emmie, pulling out a chair in the kitchen for her visitor. 'Sit yourself down and I'll put the kettle on.'

'Um, I don't s'pose you've got anything a bit stronger in the house, 'ave yer?'

'A drop of brandy in the medicine box...' said Emmie thoughtfully, 'for emergencies.' She looked at Dolly's face and her red eyes. 'I should think this is one of them times, eh, cock?'

'Yeah,' said Dolly, the other side of her character showing. 'I'm not really coping with all this, to tell the truth. It just seems to go on and on.' Taking Emmie by surprise, the usually carefree girl broke down in tears. 'There's more as well,' she said. 'It's not tragic or that but... well, it might be.' She looked up at Emmie, a desperate look in her eyes. 'God wouldn't be that cruel, would he? Two really bad things at once?'

'And what might the other bad thing be?' said Emmie, tipping a little brandy into two small glasses, fearing the worst.

'It's our Jessie and Billy.'

The room took on a tense silence, with just the soft ticking of the clock in the background. Emmie didn't want to ask questions for fear of the answers. Dolly couldn't bring herself to break the news of them being trapped in a cellar under tons of rubble. Smouldering rubble. Rubble in which one body had already been discovered.

'Well,' said Emmie at last, 'you'd best get it off your chest, love. What's happened?'

Between sips of brandy, Dolly related all that had happened according to the nuns' story. She tried to sound as hopeful as they had. 'Mum thought you might like to come with us to Westminster, to the… to the bombed site. The emergency services are there, 'ave bin all night, by the sound of things.'

'I'll just get my coat,' said Emmie, not wishing to speculate further. 'I've got some letters here for Jess that the postman delivered to me. They've made a start on her place, you know. Reckon it'll be fit to live in, give it two or three weeks.'

'Yeah, until they drop some more bombs.'

'Now then, Dolly, that's not like you. The same spot's never 'it twice, you should know that. I'll leave a note for—' The sound of the street door opening stopped her. 'That'll be 'im now. We're gonna 'ave to tell a white lie, love. Bear with me, there's a good girl. And put a big smile on that pretty face of yours.'

'Hello, Dolly!' grinned Charlie, Woodbine cigarette in the comer of his mouth. 'Ain't you a sight for sore eyes!' He glanced at the two glasses with the telltale brandy. 'Celebrating, are yer, girls?' His voice was still buoyant but there was worried suspicion in his eyes.

'That we are, Charlie,' smiled Emmie, 'that we are! This little darling 'as found out where Jessie and our Billy's been sheltering and we're goin' over there now to tell 'er that she can move back 'ere in a few weeks. Now ain't that something to drink to?'

'Fuck me,' he said, taking off his cap and throwing it up in the air. 'I bloody well knew something good was gonna 'appen today! I'll come wiv yer.'

'No you won't. You stop 'ere and get dinner ready. With a bit of luck I'll be fetching 'em home and you'll be my reason. I'll tell her your heart's breaking with worry over the pair of 'em. That should do the trick. You know she thinks the world of you.'

'Yeah?' He liked that. 'Yeah, you could be right. Gawd love a duck! Our little Billy coming 'ome!' He was over the moon.

'But there is a bit of sad news, mind.'

'Tch. Trust you. Can't let me be 'appy for five minutes. Go on then. What's happened?' He was still smiling. Nothing could bring this man down now. His grandson was coming home.

'Poor old Ingrid's passed away. God bless her soul.'

'Oh, Dolly gal, I am sorry.' He shrugged and splayed his hands. 'But be honest, she wouldn't 'ave liked a long slow death, would she? Be truthful now. She would 'ave been bloody cross if that'd bin the case. Wouldn't she?'

Dolly couldn't help smiling at him. 'Yeah, you're right, Charlie. She wouldn't 'ave liked that. I was there when she went. And to tell the truth, she did look ready for it – relieved even. She reckoned that Grandfather was at the foot of the bed, holding his arms out to 'er.'

'Well then, he was then. She wouldn't lie about that. Old Willy came for 'er, eh? See what I mean, Em? If I go before you, you can rest assured that Charlie'll be at the foot of your bed an' all. Yeah, I won't let you down.'

'Well, there's a thought. You waitin' for me. An' I thought my soul would get a rest.'

'Cheeky cow,' he said, still smiling. 'Our little Billy coming 'ome.' Shaking his head, he went out into the back yard to shed a tear. It wouldn't do for women to see Charlie crying. Oh no.

When Rose, Dolly and Emmie arrived at the scene of the bombing, they realised that things were worse than they had first thought. There was a mountain of rubble not only from the house above the cellar where Jessie and the others were but from the neighbouring house too. The 1,000 kilogram bomb which had hit this Regency row had been intended for a more important building in the area. At least the fire was now out, thanks to the untiring efforts of the fire service, and the door to the underground cellar had been located. Getting to it was not impossible but it was taking longer than the emergency services would have liked. They knew that the lack of fresh air in the basement, plus the dust and heat, would be making conditions below very bad.

Ambulances, the Red Cross and the WVS were on hand as well as the nuns and TWW. Numerous cups of tea were being handed around from the mobile tea hut and the families of those in danger were being comforted. Arriving late on the scene, Rose, felt a little out of place but Dolly soon rallied her and Emmie round, drawing them into conversation with the others. Rose, though, felt more, comfortable with the nuns who had brought her the news. She wanted to know more about her daughter's involvement in TWW.

'It all happened so quickly,' said one of the local women who was with the small group of nuns. 'A leaflet was posted through my letter box requesting spare clothes which could be passed on to women and children who had come into the area after their homes had been bombed. Well, I don't think there's a woman anywhere who couldn't honestly say her wardrobe wasn't a little overstocked, even in these times. We tend not to follow fashion, you see, but buy good quality which will last. Before I knew it, I was signed on as a member of The Westminster Women. It was good for all of us, gave us a feeling of being useful while our men were away.'

'Well,' said Rose, 'I'm pleased that my Jessie found help like that but—'

'Jessie? Jessie Smith?'

'That's right. You know her then?'

'Everyone knows Jessie. She founded the group. She's a lovely girl – strong character. I don't think I've met a woman like her. But who am I to be telling you that?' said the woman, smiling. 'You're her mother. You must know her better than anyone.'

Rose smiled back at her and then slowly turned to watch as one of the workmen manoeuvred a mechanical claw to remove heavy roof timbers from the wreck. She was reminded of her husband, Robert. It seemed ironical that a similar contraption to the crane he used to drive was being used to save the life of his favourite daughter, Jessie, and her son.

'Let's hope I haven't lost her,' said Rose.

'Oh, I'm sure they'll be all right down there. It's a spacious cellar.'

'You've been down there then?' she said, heartened by the woman's optimism.

'Several times. I quite like sewing, you see, and, well, I learned how to use a sewing machine. I'm quite adept at alterations now.'

'It's a sewing room then?'

'It's a lot of things. They type down there, print leaflets, stack and store the leaflets and of course those like Jessie who have a room there use it for shelter when the siren goes. You might not believe it, but there are twenty-one beds down there. Three-tier bunks, all provided by the Borough of Westminster once they realised TWW were playing such an important role locally.'

Keeping her thoughts to herself, Rose couldn't help worrying about the lack of air and if they were all gasping for breath down there.

'You all right, Rose?' said Emmie, joining her.

'I will be. Once that crane—' There was a gasp from the onlookers as the mechanical claw very slowly lifted its heavy load and faltered. In silence they all waited with bated breath as the manoeuvre started again. Carefully and expertly, the driver managed to remove the threatening debris. A round of applause and cheers filled the street.

'It won't be long now,' said Emmie. 'They'll soon 'ave them out.'

'Do you think they'll be all right, Em?' Rose was sick with worry and didn't mind her friend knowing it. She could keep up her brave front for strangers but not for her old friend, Emmie Smith.

'I know they will be. Don't ask me how, I just know.' Emmie waited a few moments before she said, 'I've heard from Tom, by the way.'

'Have you now?'

'Just before he was flown out to North Africa with other Brits.'

'Oh. He's a soldier again then?'

'He is. I think he's learned a very hard lesson. A stretch in the glasshouse and prison. I don't think he'll go on the run again. He was very repentant about giving us all that grief. I've a letter with me for Jessie.'

Rose sighed, relieved. 'Well, that is good news. At least she'll get her army pension again. I'll let you be the one to tell her, when she comes out.'

'I've a bundle of letters for her. Three from Tom, one from a friend called Edna who popped a note in for me, asking me to pass it on. And another from a Mrs Nelly Lisbon who put her address on the back of the envelope. You've got to admit it, Rose, your Jessie does make friends easily.'

'So it would seem. She's highly respected around these parts as well, by the sound of things. I don't know, Emmie. You worry yourself sick over them and all the time they're making a life for themselves. I had visions of her tramping around England, going from one refuge to another. And all the time—'

'Oh my God,' said Emmie, cutting her off. 'Rose, look. They've got to the door. Look at them, all those men, working as if they 'aven't got a second to waste. May God bless and spare them.'

Ten minutes later, two burly men in civilian clothes were easing the door open. Now was the telling time. As the men went in, there was total silence from the crowd. When one came back out and took a deep breath, it seemed as if he could hardly speak for grief. 'No casualties!' he suddenly yelled. There were screams and shouts and crying from the families of those trapped inside.

Then, one by one, the tired, dusty faces appeared and sheltered their eyes from the light as people rushed forward to collect their own.

'Where is she?' cried Rose. 'Where's Jessie?' All composure gone, Rose was shaking and sobbing. 'Where's my daughter?'

Jessie, with Billy in her arms, was the last to come out and was greeted by a cheer from those who knew her. When Jessie caught sight of her mother, her sister and dear Emmie, she threw Billy into the arms of one of the men because her legs were buckling under her. Another of the men caught her before she hit the ground. It didn't matter. She was out and she was alive!

Rose had a real battle with the doctor on site and the nurses who were insisting on all the survivors going to a nearby hospital for a check-up. But once Jessie had come round, all she wanted to do was go home. Go home with Emmie or Rose. Go home to familiar surroundings and a comfortable bed. In the end the authorities agreed and a taxi was hailed by Dolly, who had done most of the arguing. She had just got her sister back and she wasn't going to let her go.

They dropped Emmie off at her house and asked the taxi driver to wait while Jessie took Billy in to his grand-father, Charlie. 'Fuck me,' was his reaction when he saw the state they were both in. 'You look as if you've bin buried alive, gal!' He didn't know how close to the truth he was. Once he'd given Billy a hug and was satisfied that Jessie was back in the East End to stay, he agreed to let her go home with Rose.

'Funny thing 'appened while you've been gone, Em,' he said, scratching his head. 'We 'ad a visitor. A country bloke. Posh, sort of. All right, though. Yeah, nice bloke. He said it was a flying visit while he was in London. Not going to war 'cos he's a farmer. Funny sort of name… What was it now? Blowed if I can remember…'

'Rupert?' said Jessie, too tired to explain if they asked about him.

'That was it, yeah. Fancy calling a bloke Rupert. Anyway, he left you some flowers, Jess, and said they was from… now, what was their names…' He slapped the side of his head as he swayed from side to side. 'My memory's going…'

'Alice and Jack?'

'That was it! Yeah. Anyway, I'm to tell you you've got a job should you ever need it. That Rupert fella needs a live-in housemaid – good money an' all. I asked if he wanted a gardener as well. I thought me and Emmie could—'

Emmie cut in. 'Shut up, Charlie. Housemaid? As if me or Jessie'd want that!'

'Anyway,' said Charlie, ignoring Emmie, 'he don't need a gardener. Pity, that.'

Emmie leaned forward and smelt his breath. 'Brandy?'

'Oh yeah, I forgot about that. He left a bottle of something – it's on the sideboard.' And so it was. Two-thirds full. 'We 'ad a little drink together before he went. Nice bloke. Yeah, all right, he was…'

Jessie, Rose and Dolly left him to Emmie who would no doubt put him to bed, more for peace and quiet than anything else.

Back in the taxi and on their way home, Jessie read Tom's letters.

'So Tom's learned his lesson then?' Rose asked after a while.

Jessie smiled at the thought of it. 'I knew he'd see sense. I bet he didn't think much of being sent out to North Africa, though.'

'Never mind. This war'll soon be over and he'll be back. You can start afresh,' said Rose, which was her way of saying she forgave him and at the same time telling Jessie that she was sorry.

'That's right, and we can get back into our little house and rebuild our lives. Ain't that right, Dolly?' she said, bringing her sister into the conversation. Jessie thought she looked a bit on the lonely side. A bit pensive. Of course she was wrong.

'Good-looking is he? This rich Rupert bloke who needs an 'ousemaid?'

'As it just so 'appens, yeah. Why, you thinking of taking up the offer, Doll?'

'I might, Jess, you never know.'

Privately, Jessie thought otherwise. Her sister would appear a little too on the brash side for the gentleman farmer she had got to know in the short time she was in Elmshill. She brought his tanned smiling face to mind and felt a warm glow inside. It had all been like a fairytale: the rich, tall and handsome stranger, the roses around cottage doorways, the golden landscape. And then, of course, there had been dear old Alice and lazy Jack. So much had happened in such a short space of time. She had gone from the heights of happiness when Billy was born to the depth of despair when her lovely home was bombed.

'They like a rough diamond you know,' murmured Dolly, still pondering on a trip to Elmshill. 'What d'yer reckon, Jess?'

'I reckon you should stop 'ere and keep me company and keep an eye on your nephew.'

'Oh,' said Dolly, 'so you do appreciate me then?'

'Course I do. I need you around me, Doll. I've missed you.' There were tears in Jessie's eyes which brought a lump to Dolly's throat. 'You don't know how much I appreciate having a close family to turn to. It means a lot. A hell of a lot.'

'Course it does, silly cow. I said she'd come to her senses, Mum, didn't I?'

Rose could hardly speak, she was so filled with emotion. 'Never mind all that,' she finally said, 'let's just get ourselves home and count our blessings.'

Yes, thought Jessie, let's do that. Let's count our blessings and face the fixture together, whatever it brings. 'The war can't go on for ever...'

'That's right,' said Rose. 'We thought the first world war would never end, but it did. You never know, this time next year might be an entirely different picture. You just can't tell.'

'No,' said Jessie, smiling, 'we none of us know do we?' And what Jessie didn't know right then, was that she was, once again, in the family way.